DUST ON THE PAW

Robin Jenkins (1912–2005) studied at Glasgow University and worked for the Forestry Commission and in the teaching profession. He travelled widely and worked in Spain, Afghanistan and Borneo before finally settling in his beloved Argyll. His first novel, *So Gaily Sings the Lark*, was published in 1951 and its publication was followed by more than thirty works of fiction, including the acclaimed *The Cone-gatherers* (1955), *Fergus Lamont* (1979) and *Childish Things* (2001). In 2002 he received the Saltire Society's prestigious Andrew Fletcher of Saltoun Award for his outstanding contribution to Scottish life.

ROBIN JENKINS

Dust on
the Paw

Introduced by David Pratt

To Helen and Bryan

First published by Macdonald & Co. (Publishers) Ltd in 1961.
This edition published in Great Britain in 2006
by Polygon, an imprint of Birlinn Ltd

West Newington House
10 Newington Road
Edinburgh
EH9 1QS

9 8 7 6 5 4 3 2 1

www.birlinn.co.uk

ISBN 10: 1 904598 84 6
ISBN 13: 978 1 904598 84 8

British Library Cataloguing-in-Publication Data
A catalogue record for this book is
available on request from the British Library

The publisher acknowledges subsidy from

Scottish
Arts Council

towards the publication of this volume

Typeset by Hewer Text UK Ltd, Edinburgh
Printed and bound by CPD (Wales) Ltd

According to the eleventh-century Persian poet, Firdausi, the powerful ones of the earth were the lion's paw, and the humble the dust on it. In some places it is no different today.

Introduction

AFGHANISTAN has always been a harsh land. It is more than 20 years since I first came to this remote country, crossing on foot from neighbouring Pakistan to report on the conflict taking place between the Afghan guerrillas and the occupying Soviet army.

Since then I have returned many times, a witness to Afghanistan's tortured journey through war and natural disaster – a journey that would leave any nation exhausted. First it was the Soviet withdrawal and the country's descent into bitter factional fighting, then the rise to power of the Taliban, probably the world's most extreme Islamic fundamentalist group. These days the nation is wracked by the war prosecuted by the West to root out this lingering Islamic militant group and the remnants of Osama bin Laden's al-Qaeda.

Somewhere in between all this, two hugely destructive earthquakes added 10,000 to the death toll of over one million Afghans killed by bombs, bullets, shells and mines over the last two decades.

Throughout all this suffering, I have rarely seen an Afghan cry. A truly extraordinary people, they are among the toughest and most resourceful on earth. Fiercely proud, Afghans smile when most others would throw up their hands in despair. They are also a generous people whose hospitality at times can be so overwhelming that the visitor often feels embarrassed.

Perhaps it's not surprising then that the Afghan character, like the rugged uncompromising landscape out of which it is moulded, has always fascinated writers, from novelists and poets like Rudyard Kipling to chroniclers of travel, adventure and political intrigue like Robert Byron and Peter Hopkirk. Afghanistan has provided a marvellous setting and wealth of human characters for literary exploits; it is a place that really is larger than life.

Yet, in part due to the stereotypes created by a colonial mindset, Afghans themselves have too often been portrayed as little more than a band of devious, violent and unscrupulous brigands. 'Trust a Brahmin before a snake, and a snake before an harlot, and an harlot before a

Pathan,' Kimball O'Hara tells Colonel Creighton in Rudyard Kipling's famous novel of life on the North West Frontier, *Kim*, published in 1901.

The Pathans to which 'Kim' refers are the largest of the tribal groups that make up Afghanistan's rich ethnic mix. Others include Tajiks, Uzbeks and Hazaras, each a product of the country's unique position at the crossroads of Asia, which itself has accounted for much of the political instability and given rise to the Afghans' warlike reputation.

Given this literary predilection to portray Afghanistan and its people in such a cardboard cut-out way, it was with some apprehension that I picked up Robin Jenkins' novel, *Dust on the Paw*. It seemed to me unlikely that a writer from a Scottish background could do real justice to the exotic richness and vitality of the Afghan culture and way of life.

It was in 1957 that Jenkins – a Lanarkshire boy, like myself – took a British Council teaching post in Kabul. 'Snow came in through the roof and I taught wearing my overcoat, scarf and bunnet. It was pretty primitive,' Jenkins recalled. Out of his experiences in this city, surrounded by the Hindu Kush mountains, came his tale of Abdul Wahab, an Afghan science teacher, who eagerly awaits the arrival of his British fiancée, Laura Johnstone, whom he met while when he was a student at Manchester University.

Within a short time the couple find themselves the talk of the expatriot community as Miss Johnstone's arrival stirs the attention of the Afghan Royal household and one Prince Naim, who sees her as the seal of approval on an East–West union.

In this almost claustrophobic community, characterised by diplomatic double-dealing, and memsahibs in opera gloves, a story of interracial love set against the backdrop of 1950s Kabul unfolds. With its cross-cultural gossip, scandal, hearsay, and emotional manoeuvring, it's a story worthy of those recounted in the crammed *chaikhanas*, teahouses, of the North West Frontier's 'storytellers' bazaar' where, over endless glasses of sweet green and black tea, Afghan business is done, and the vagaries of life talked about and mulled over.

Somewhere in the background to Jenkins' tale lurks a Cold War prelude to the years ahead, when Russia would ultimately flex its military and political muscle and invade Afghanistan.

For anyone who has spent time living in the closed environs of an international community in a turbulent land, it's Jenkins' portrayal of such a disparate group of people – albeit one in the 1950s – that gives *Dust on the Paw* enduring resonance.

For more than ten years during the Soviet occupation of Afghanistan, the frontier town of Peshawar on the Pakistan side of the Khyber Pass housed just such a community. Like Saigon in Vietnam, Peshawar became the haunt of diplomats, guerrillas, journalists, mercenaries, aid workers and spies. All were there for the war raging across Afghanistan's mountains and plains from Kabul to Kandahar.

Like the International Club in Jenkins' story, Peshawar's American Club was where most of these roaming global misfits hung out. At 'The Club' they would sit at bar stools, covered with dust fresh from their last trip 'inside' (Afghanistan) describing the battle they had been in, might have been in, or wished they had been in.

For those who were part of such a community it was a decade of adventure, but it was also a time of hopeful anticipation for the Afghans we befriended, in an Afghanistan we thought would soon be at peace.

In the end of course the Soviets finally went home, pulling the last of their troops out and crossing the Amu Darya river into neighbouring Tajikistan. As the Russian tanks rumbled into history, this international enclave quickly moved from their frontier post in Peshawar into Kabul itself. While Kabul might have been 'liberated' from the communists, brick by brick it would now slowly be destroyed by rival Afghan militias fighting to control its streets.

The city then was a place far removed from the quaint civilised surroundings Jenkins describes in *Dust on the Paw*. The kind of place where it was possible to sleep under trees 'undisturbed by the wailing, from Indian and Afghan love songs, which went on all day from morning till midnight'.

I remember at that time, in the mid 1990s, during a particularly bad bout of street fighting. iIt was like the Hundred Years War fought with twentieth-century weaponry, as gunmen emerged from mud homes to blast each other with rocket launchers and machine guns. Kabul's canyons of ruins and pancaked buildings turned it into a latter-day Dresden. According to a United Nations report it was one of the most war-damaged cities on earth – and all this was before the arrival of the Taliban.

These days things are little better. Kabul remains a dangerous, strange and contradictory place. Gone are the Taliban's roaming enforcers from the department for the Prevention of Vice and Protection of Virtue. Newly arrived, however, is fortress Kabul, a mushrooming US base. It's almost as if the ancient Bala Hissar castle that sits on the capital's outskirts had been substituted by a new high-tech version in the heart of the city. Instead of mud and stone, the walls are high concrete ramparts padded with protective anti-explosive cladding and razor wire. The watchtowers are manned by nervous US soldiers in wraparound Oakleys and carrying M16s. Alongside bullet-pocked buildings housing refugees sits a Thai restaurant run by a woman who is said to follow the UN around the world's troublespots providing culinary boltholes for its extensive international staff.

These people are today's real-life heirs to Alan Wint, Howard Winfield, Harold Moffatt, Laura Johnstone and the other characters that flit across the pages of this novel.

While this is a Kabul that Robin Jenkins could never have imagined, it is one where the sights, sounds and smells described in *Dust on the Paw* still linger: the houses and buildings 'like so many mud boxes flung down higgledy-piggledy on the hillside; the holy man's tomb, sticks festooned with rags protruding from it like flags of humility'.

The union of East and West so sought after by Prince Naim in Robin Jenkins' story remains elusive in today's Afghanistan. In its contemporary mode the power brokering that seems so considered in his narrative is now a brutal struggle for dominance in this long-suffering land.

'It was his passionate belief that a writer found his material everywhere and near-at-hand,' said writer Brian Morton in a personal appreciation of Jenkins after the novelist's death in 2005.

Jenkins certainly found material in Afghanistan, as he did in Barcelona, Borneo and other locations in which he found himself over the years. One can only imagine what he would have made of Kabul had he been alive to visit Afghanistan today. In one sense, so much has changed, but at the same time there is something enduring and persistent about life in this wonderful country: a place where multiple divisions remain – ethnic, sectarian, rural and urban, educated and uneducated.

Afghanistan remains a deeply conservative country. Robin Jenkins, it's probably fair to say, was a deeply conservative writer. Perhaps for that reason he got beneath its skin as few novelists ever have.

David Pratt, 2006

One

IN HIS pale-blue distempered office Alan Wint, First Secretary and Head of Chancery, sat white-shirted, smoking,
and dreaming in the Asian alpine sunshine of the day when,
silver-haired and knighted, he would preside as His Excellency over some great embassy, in Washington, say, or
Paris, or even Bonn. He would not have called it dreaming,
though he would have conceded it was not quite reality. He
had a secret name for it: purposeful meditation; and he
considered it as useful a preparation for diplomatic advancement as the study of Oriental languages, or the courting of
Whitehall potentates. Certainly it was more delightful and
dignified than those, disturbing neither head nor conscience.

The telephone on his desk rang. Instantly, with a tug to
straighten his tie, he snatched it up, fearing it might be the
Ambassador, reported to be irascible that morning. But no,
it was the voice again, or rather the voices, for there were at
least two; giggling, and gently uttering what he had been
informed by Howard Winfield, the Oriental Secretary,
expert in Persian, were improper proposals. Howard had
supplied him with an appropriate rejoinder, and this he now
spoke severely into the mouthpiece, causing the giggles to
become, if anything, more seductive, so that he actually
found his cheeks turning warmer.

'Extraordinary,' he murmured, as he put down the receiver, knowing it would ring again almost immediately, for
the little bitches were persistent. And extraordinary it surely

was, in a country said to be the third most backward in the world, as far as feminine emancipation was concerned. No woman over the age of puberty was allowed to appear in public without a long flowing gown of silk or cotton that shrouded from crown to toes, with a peephole of lace. The young men among the Afghans, who felt embittered about it, called a woman so enveloped a walking tent or a shuttle-cock.

The telephone rang again. Wint pounced on it and repeated the instruction before the giggles could even get started.

'What the devil's the matter with you, Alan? Have you gone out of your mind?' The voice, loud, was sufficiently masculine and aggressively ambassadorial.

Christ, breathed Wint. 'Yes, sir?' he said, as brightly as he could.

'Did I understand you to tell me just now to go to hell?'

'No, sir. Of course not, sir.' Damn Howard's conceit and juvenile sense of humour; and damn, too, his own so vulnerable trust. No wonder his wife Paula often warned him. A diplomat of all people, she would say, should know instinctively when to doubt. He was almost as trustful, she might add with satirical fondness, as the Reverend Manson Powrie, the minister of the American Church, who would hardly tell the devil himself to go to hell.

The Ambassador, too, was an expert in Persian. He appeared to chuckle. 'That, I assure you, Alan, is what the idiom means. Who's been giving you lessons?'

'I suppose Howard, sir. I thought the expression meant: go away and don't bother me.'

'It does, Alan. But isn't it a strange one to use on the telephone?'

'Perhaps not in the circumstances, sir.'

'What circumstances?'

'You see, sir, I thought it was those girls again.'

'What girls? You don't happen to be referring to our respected clerks, the Misses Winn and Anderson?'

'Of course not, sir.'

'What other girls do you keep about the office?'

'I was intending to mention them to you, sir. I don't of course keep them about the office. No, it's like this, sir. These girls telephone the Embassy, ask for me, are put through, and then, well sir, it appears that what they say are, according to Howard, improper proposals.'

'Improper proposals? Be more explicit.'

'Well, sir, it appears they ask if I would like—'

'Well?'

'Er – to put it bluntly, sir – to have certain relations with them.'

'That's hardly putting it bluntly, Alan. Are you their only victim?'

'I believe so, sir.'

'Why?'

Because, darling, Paula had said, you are the only handsome man in the Embassy.

'I really couldn't say, sir. It's a mystery to me.'

'Are you sure they're Afghans?'

'Oh, I think so, sir. Very young, too; no more than schoolgirls.'

'When did this start?'

'Three days ago, sir.'

'Any suspicions? Sounds as if it might be someone's idea of a practical joke. Couldn't be Americans? It has the flavour of transatlantic humour.'

'Doesn't it, sir? But I think they really are Afghans.' He did have suspicions, though, or rather Paula had. She thought it was the kind of puerile prank, conceived in drunkenness, that Harold Moffatt would stoop to; and he was almost the only one of the foreign community in contact with Afghan women. Besides, was he not always accusing

him, Alan Wint, of having no sense of humour? Too many
people believed that, thought Wint indignantly; including
H.E. himself.

'What does Paula say about it?'

Wint frowned, not quite seeing why H.E. should ask that.
It was extraordinary how, even in the most intelligent
people, the desire to create laughter made for irrelevance.

'She just laughed, sir.' But she had also cried out, so
loyally, that she'd like to smack their dusky little bottoms –
her own so rosy. He smiled, almost forgetting the monocled
presence at the other end of the wire.

'Well, it's your problem, Alan. But do something about it.
After all, this *is* an Embassy, not a co-ed high school in
Massachusetts.'

'Yes, sir.'

'What I rang up about was this morning's bulletin. I've
just seen a copy. It can't go out like that. Whose idea is it to
spell Moslem with a small *m*?'

'Well, sir, Tom Parry takes it down from the radio, but
it's Howard who usually edits it.'

'I thought so. It's Howard I want to talk to then. I don't
care what piece of damned philological sophistry he has to
explain or excuse it, it won't do; it's got to be put right
before the bulletin's issued. After all, this is a Moslem
country. How would we feel if the Afghans in England
spelled Christian with a small *c*?'

Wint smiled; it served Howard jolly well right. The smile
dimmed a little as he realized that the rocket, however high-
powered and explosive, would descend upon the Oriental
Secretary's premature bald spot like a puffball.

'Perhaps it was just a typing error, sir?' he suggested
generously.

'It wasn't. The word occurs four times, and each time with
a small *m*. Either it's deliberate policy, or pure illiteracy. I'll
talk to Howard. I'm not having any of his Ezra Pound tricks

fathered on me. By the way, have you seen Gillie this morning?'

Bob Gillie was the Consul.

'Just for a moment in passing, sir. Any special reason?'

'You'll find out in the next few minutes. He'll be in to see you. I've just sent him a small present.'

Panging with jealousy, Wint still managed a chuckle like a good sport. 'I didn't know it was his birthday, sir.'

'Don't be a fool, Alan,' roared the Ambassador and banged his receiver down.

Before the Ambassador, in his snow-white residence, had the glass out of his eye to give it the calm, silky wipe that always terminated a rebuke to a subordinate preparatory to beginning another, Wint was up, fleeing from his unknown folly, out of his office, and along the corridor to Howard Winfield's.

The Oriental Secretary, young, bespectacled, and relaxed, with bald spot tanned, was seated at his desk reading, by a coincidence, a recently published book of criticism of Pound's poetry. Having the responsibility of ordering for the Embassy library, he ordered thrillers for the rest and esoteric volumes like the present one, which were much more expensive, for himself and anyone else he could convert.

The four hundred copies of the news bulletin, soon to be dispatched by orderlies to the various Embassies, Legations, and Government Departments, as well as to many private addresses in the city, were piled in front of him. Indeed, the fingers of his left hand were playing on them a tune that, in its subtlety and liveliness, was giving him great pleasure though he was composing it himself. Everything he attempted gave him similar pleasure. He had been known to fail, but never to be discomfited. The collar of his dhobi-tortured shirt was frayed, but the neck it adorned was tougher, under its tan, than bronze.

Wint had been going to warn him about the Ambassador's annoyance but changed his mind. 'I say, Howard,' he said instead, annoyed himself. 'Those girls just phoned me again.'

Winfield smiled up, but before he could answer, the telephone rang. Sadistically Wint watched as his colleague, with characteristic delicacy, picked it up, shifted in his chair to achieve a posture of ease and grace, set his brain to work, oiled with the astutest self-interest, and said: 'Winfield speaking,' in that marvellously rich, sure voice that Oxford had nurtured but nature took most credit for. As he listened to the expostulatory crackles, a smile of Napoleonic craft took up position on his big flexible mouth. His ear, big too, with some dried scented soap on its perimeter, showed never a twitch. His foot, encased in native sandal of red leather decorated with gold stars, tapped on the floor, as if to cheerful music. Yet as Wint, himself an unappreciated expert, knew, Winfield danced chacha, samba, rock-and-roll, Duke of Perth, fox trot, and Viennese waltz as if they were all the same dance, to the incredible enjoyment and hilarity of his partners.

'I accept responsibility in toto, sir. No, I do not hide behind that subterfuge; it was considered policy. Well, sir, there is no proper noun from which the word Moslem is derived, as there is for Christian or Buddhist. If Mohammedan had been chosen, then of course there would have been no debate: the capital would undoubtedly have been in order.'

Then, smile unrouted, he listened to what Wint was sure must be a full-scale assault. Of course Howard was an impregnable favourite: he partnered the Ambassador's wife at bridge and, besides having amusing prattle, played well enough for two. Wint, on the other hand, overworked in the office, at bridge squandered tricks, dropped asleep, reneged.

'Granted, sir,' murmured Winfield, with a wink at Wint.

'But, with all due respect, would it really be politic to alter today's issue? I mean, making the alterations would only bring notice to what I now see, thanks to your lucid explanation, sir, might be construed in certain bigoted quarters as a slight. You think nevertheless it should be altered? I shall attend to it forthwith.' His brows went up. 'No, sir, I do not smoke American cigarettes. Of course, the entire staff. I'm very sorry about this. The explanation may be that during my schooldays I acquired a stylistic prejudice against proper adjectives; even today I'm never sure what to do about a word like un-Christian. It could have been because I had a master who spelled his surname with a small letter. Or it might have been the example of Bernard Shaw who left out apostrophes because he thought they gave the page an untidy appearance.'

The engagement over, he set down the telephone and, in subtle parody, with his smile still in good order, coolly removed his spectacles and wiped them. Having two lenses, he succeeded in outdoing the master. Wint's admiration was a little blemished by envy. Without meditation or fancy, Howard would one day be an ambassador; it would help that his father, Sir Timothy, already was one; but there could be no gainsaying he had his own appropriate ability. Better than anyone he knew how the Ambassador abominated Shaw and all his works.

Now he was telephoning again, his voice at its most charming, to Miss Katherine Winn, temperamental clerk and embittered exile in dusty, mud-built, department-store-less, pre-Pankhurstian, malodorous Afghanistan. He was asking her to come along for a minute, quickly, if she could. He did not add, as Wint fatally would have, out of loyalty to his chief, that the Ambassador was behind the urgency. Katherine did not get on well with H.E.'s wife, whose invitation to a dull Embassy function she had refused, on the impertinent grounds that she had a prior engagement, which turned out to be a gramophone and frankfurters party with some girls from the American Embassy.

A minute later Katherine arrived, flushed, peevish, belligerent. 'What is it, Howard?' she demanded. 'I'm fearfully busy. Certain documents have to be ready for a certain place at a certain time.' She managed to put into the adjective the feeling that another adjective, also frequently reiterated, is alone supposed to convey.

Wint frowned, but Winfield was chuckling. 'Katherine, would you be so kind as to take away these ghastly bulletins and distribute them among the staff, with my most sincere regrets and apologies—Hello, Bob'—this to Gillie who, best dressed as usual in white linen suit, white shirt, and mauve tie, had come scowling in, with a sheet of paper in his hand—'and ask them to amend each copy, thus.' As he spoke he altered with his Biro the small *m*'s to bold capitals. 'It shouldn't take long, if everybody buckles to. There should be about fifty copies per person. Here you are, my dear.' He placed the bundle in her hands, as if it was a bouquet of flowers.

'But, Howard,' she squealed, 'this is ridiculous!'

'Now, Katherine,' murmured Wint.

'It is ridiculous,' agreed Winfield.

'And it's not the only thing that is,' barked Gillie.

'It's not just ridiculous,' she cried. 'It's so trivial and unnecessary, like most of the things done here. Who cares whether it's a capital or not? All you're going to do is to stir up a grievance in people who would never have noticed if you'd left well alone.'

Shrewd, thought Wint; it was obvious that for years she'd worked among diplomats. But it was a shrewdness she had no right to exercise there.

'But Katherine,' said Winfield, his voice sad, 'would you help to nip in its bud a career so full of fragrant possibilities?'

'Oh, stuff!' she said, but marched off with the bulletins, muttering something about nothing being fragrant in that country. Her last post had been Rome.

'I'm afraid Katherine's getting a bit much,' commented Wint.

'She hates the bloody place. That's the trouble with her,' said Gillie, in his way called blunt by his friends, coarse and rather vulgar by Wint but to Paula only. 'And I must say,' added the Consul, 'that at this moment I'm not particularly enamoured of it myself. Up to the ears in work, and now this.'

This was evidently the 'present', but it was of such a nature that Wint saw his jealousy had indeed been unwarranted. Fastened with a small gilt safety-pin to a foolscap sheet of official notepaper, with the lion and unicorn waltzing at the top, was an empty cigarette pack. Scrawled under it, like the signature to a death warrant, were these words: 'This object was found this morning in my flower bed.' That was all, nothing else; but it was a great deal. No wonder Gillie's big red obtuse face was growing bigger and redder and more obtuse every minute as he scowled at it. Pride in dress was an excellent quality, Wint had often thought, but unfortunately it so noticeably showed up the lack of other, on the whole more valuable qualities, such as intelligence and suavity.

'Did H.E. send it?' asked Wint.

He put the question in spite of its obviousness, because in any discussion he liked to start from bedrock. That others less conscientious were infuriated, and fumed against him as a canny old woman, was known to but firmly ignored by him.

'Either that,' replied Gillie, lowering his voice, 'or else some poltergeist temporarily residing in his body sent it.'

'What is its significance?' then asked Wint.

'That's what I've been trying to discover for the past ten minutes,' grunted Gillie. He gave the impression he had had a magnifying glass on it.

'American,' commented Winfield. 'Now I see why he asked me if I smoked American cigarettes.'

'No one on the staff does,' said Gillie. 'I've gone over every name.'

'Is it empty?' asked Wint, suddenly appalled at the thought of what it might contain. He had no idea himself, but the possibilities seemed appalling.

'Yes, it's empty.'

'Odd, I must agree.' As soon as it was said, Wint regretted it. Somehow he had supported Gillie's poltergeist theory.

'Hello, hello. Mind if I join the congregation?' It was Bruce Rodgers, the Military Attaché, who came breezily in. To be breezy wasn't really his nature, but it helped to conceal what that nature might be. All his conscious days he had played at that concealment, and had married a woman willing to play at it too. An artifice in the game was his long sandy moustache, so well groomed that it caught and kept diverted inquisitive attention. He had, too, a habit of screwing his right eye tight without actually closing it, when looking at anything carefully. His wife took every opportunity to remark that Bruce had had that habit in his last post; indeed, he had acquired it during the war, when he had been an artillery lieutenant looking at distant explosions through binoculars.

Now he picked up paper and pack, and looked with care. Boyish amusement, or professional solemnity, could be read on his smooth well-shaved face, according to one's estimate of his intelligence. He sniffed it and smelled tobacco. Briskly he asked and dourly was told how it had come into Gillie's possession.

'Some careless fellow chuck it there?' he asked.

'I think it's a kind of concealed intelligence test,' said Winfield.

'Do you?' grunted Gillie. 'I take it it's my intelligence you think's in need of testing.' He glowered at each in turn, but longest at Wint.

Well really, thought Wint, smiling, you are often a bit slow and cumbersome, Bob. After all, that furniture for the big house, ordered from the Ministry of Works, Delhi, months ago, still isn't even on its way. No doubt your letters and telegrams of protest have been logical, coherent, and sufficiently imperative, but still they must have lacked that essential something. Gillie of course was a category B diplomat.

'I meant all our intelligences, Bob,' Winfield was saying. 'The brightest is the one that first discovers the solution.'

'Surely it's simple?' said Wint. 'Bruce is right. H.E. is simply objecting to his flower bed being used as a trash basket.'

'Or as a philanderer's couch,' suggested Winfield.

'Go on,' said Gillie. 'Every suggestion exhaustively considered. One carton, empty, clean, small, doesn't constitute garbage. Philanderers haven't time to smoke.'

Some of the clerks had American girl friends, and Katherine often had Americans to tea, afterwards taking them for a walk through the grounds. But, surely, thought Wint, if there were to be any spooning, or petting, nobody would be so foolish as to do it right under H.E.'s drawing-room windows, in the midst of his antirrhinums? He uttered the thought.

'American seductresses,' said Winfield, 'all seem to have read Freud, in digested versions naturally.'

'Well?' Gillie waited.

'The empty pack, if left by a woman, might signify the empty womb.'

'For God's sake, Howard, be serious.' Gillie turned on Rodgers. 'Bruce, the garden's your pigeon.'

'Hardly that, Bob old man. I mean, you won't find it entered anywhere among my official duties, will you?'

'Granted.' But Gillie grunted it as if he doubted whether he'd find any duties at all entered there, except touring the countryside. This was his constant grievance, his burden so heavy, and the M.A.'s so light that the latter had time to collect and drill his fabulous set of toy soldiers. 'But you do superintend it, all the same. I mean, it's you who decide, let's say, what trees ought to come down.'

Last autumn while the Gillies were on a few days' leave, a big walnut tree in their garden had been cut down, at the Colonel's order. To be fair, he had also ordered one in his own garden to be felled, but his hadn't been the only supplier of shade and privacy. Neither Gillie nor his wife would ever forget or forgive.

'The tree was dangerous, old man,' said the Colonel amiably. 'H.E. himself took a look at it.'

'I've said it before,' said Gillie, 'and I'll say it again. You could have waited until we returned.'

Wint had noticed an orderly hovering outside with a slip of paper in his hand. That meant a visitor had called and was waiting to be interviewed. The slip would have on it his name and business, and the name of the official he wished to see. From Gulahmad's smile Wint himself in this instance was the official.

Glad of the excuse he went out and took the slip.

'Moffatt Sahib,' said Gulahmad.

'Thanks, Gulahmad. I'll go along and fetch him myself.'

He read the slip, expecting and finding that facetiousness so unfortunate in such an able fellow. At the top Moffatt had printed in block capitals CONFIDENTIAL, and, in the small space where the nature of his business should have been briefly and clearly stated, he had written in unnecessarily microscopic letters: 1 Operation Diploma 2. Operation St George.

Wint strode along the corridor to the waiting room, smiling, ready with a vigorous and sincere welcome, for despite his shortcomings Harold Moffatt must not be made to feel alien here, on this patch of British soil in a foreign land – even though he had, incredibly, a Chinese wife met in Indonesia, drove a Volkswagen, tutored the Russian Embassy in English, taught at the University, wrote poetry published in the *New Statesman*, advised Prince Naim, third son of the King, on British affairs, had once founded and now presided over the International Club, and never contradicted a claim, often made on his behalf at various functions and cocktail parties, that he did more for British prestige and influence than the whole Embassy combined.

Two

IN A country where most Western people grew thin, Harold Moffatt was tubby and fat-bottomed. Along with that plumpness, his soft flaxen hair with moustache to match, pink seemingly ingenuous face, and mild voice, all combined to disguise his fiery humaneness and his liability to erupt into reckless enterprises. Though he was prone to facetiousness in Wint's opinion (irony, in his own), he could cause astonishment all around by suddenly displaying a stubborn sense of responsibility that he would as soon relinquish as a bulldog its grip on an enemy's throat. Yet most of the time he was placid and mild-mannered, which his friends attributed to the influence of his small, dainty, sweet-natured, and imperturbable wife.

He was seated in the waiting room under a portrait of Sir Winston Churchill. He looked rather more subdued than Wint had expected, judging from those flippancies upon the slip.

'Good morning, Harold,' he cried, with genuine cordiality. 'You want to see me?'

'I think it should be you, Alan. You can tell me if it isn't.'

Wint laughed. 'All right. Shall we go along to my office and make ourselves comfortable? No trouble, I hope? Personal, I mean.'

'Well,' said Moffatt, grinning, 'what was it Donne said about the tolling of the bell?'

'Nobody ill, I hope?' Yet it could easily be Moffatt's wife Lan, who always struck Wint as being much too fragile for ordinary knockabout existence. Her place was in a museum with other frail, beautiful things. Paula, no Amazon, could make two of her.

'No.' He hadn't expected Wint to understand his allusion, and was again surprised to find himself liking the tall diplomat for his peculiar unawareness, which left him so vulnerable to ridicule but which seemed to Moffatt to have its source, partly at least, in a fog of innocence. Wint was eight years older than himself, yet he often thought of the Head of Chancery as in many ways still a schoolboy, the captain of the school, with a code of honour and duty so absurdly unsuited to the shabby intrigues and expediencies of the adult world as to be quite furiously resented by most of his subordinates, some older than himself, who objected to being rallied like rebellious fags or wilting teammates five minutes from the final whistle.

On his way along the corridor to Wint's office Moffatt was greeted cheerfully three times, once by Howard Winfield, once by Douglas Fairbairn, the archivist, turning small *m*'s into big ones, and once by John Langford the Commercial Attaché, who invited him to his house afterwards for a glass of beer and a chat about the forthcoming production of the drama society. Moffatt declined the invitation, which Wint had listened to with smiling envy. The Head of Chancery also got invitations but somehow never to friendly and witty chats over beer.

In the office he asked Moffatt to take a seat.

'Now, Harold old man,' he said, 'tell me about these two operations, Diploma and St George.'

'Sorry I expressed it in that way,' said Moffatt. 'I forgot, Alan, you would think it lacked dignity.'

'All right, Harold, I do believe in dignity, especially here. After all, dammit, the flag does fly above the Residence. I know it's fashionable to sneer at such things today, but they mean something to me.'

'I'm glad to hear that, Alan, because it means you are the man I want to help me.' He took a sheet of parchment out of his brief case and handed it to Wint.

The latter, as he put it down on the desk in front of him, pushed over a pack of cigarettes. 'By the way, Harold,' he said, lighting a cigarette himself, 'perhaps you can help me in a little matter that's arisen recently. A couple of girls – I think there are two, Afghans from their voices – have taken to ringing me up and, well, making improper proposals. They did it this morning, just half an hour ago. You're more in the heart of things down there in the city than we are up here in our little enclave. I wondered if you'd heard of this sort of thing happening to others.'

Moffatt grinned at that portentousness. 'I have.'

Wint was so relieved he threw back his head and guffawed. 'I knew it,' he cried, 'I knew I couldn't be the only one. Is there any theory as to the culprits?'

'Schoolgirls, I should think.'

'Schoolgirls? Here, in this outpost of medieval prudishness?'

'Yes. At home its equivalent would be scribbling obscenities on lavatory walls. But I suppose they do that here too.'

Wint's daughter Annette was a schoolgirl in England. He looked shocked but incredulous. 'Obscenities? Boys yes, but surely not girls.' Then catching a glimpse in imagination of Annette's small face so often mysterious in its contemporaneousness, he began to gape as confidence sighed out of him. Paula though, in pig-tails, never had; he was certain of that.

'They say girls are worse than boys,' said Moffatt. 'That's a City and Guilds diploma, you'll observe.'

Wint laughed. 'Who say, old man?'

'The caretakers of girls' schools. The diploma was awarded to an Afghan student, Mir Abdul Rahman.'

'So I see. Would you say there's no need to notify the police about this telephoning?'

'You'll have to decide that for yourself, Alan.'

'What would you do?'

'I'd get Abdul to answer them.'

'This fellow?' Wint pointed to the diploma.

'No. My cook. He's got as rich a vocabulary of abuse as an Irish docker. He'd soon tell them where to stuff their improper proposals.'

'But, really, Harold, if they're only schoolgirls!'

Moffatt was growing impatient. 'You mean, you don't think you should be rude to them?'

'Not quite that. Really, doesn't it come back to dignity again?'

'All right, Alan. You tell them, with dignity, to—off. That diploma was awarded after a successful five-year course in Civil Engineering, at Brixton Technical College.'

'Yes, so I see. Who is this Mir Abdul Rahman?'

'I've told you. He's an Afghan, not long back from U.K. He was sent there on a government scholarship.'

'That must have cost them a lot. Pretty commendable.'

'Since he came back he's been working for the Ministry of Mines. His trouble is, and he's by no means the only one, his Ministry won't accept his diploma. They say it isn't as good as a degree.'

'Well, is it?'

'No. But it's a damn sight better than an American degree, or even many an American doctorate.'

'I agree. Lord knows what you can get an American doctorate for. Howard says for collecting the tops of cereal boxes.'

'This diploma represents a lot of hard study.'

'I should think so.'

'And a level of proficiency very high by the standards of this country?'

'Certainly.'

'Well, Mir Abdul Rahman's grievance is that colleagues of his who go off to America or Germany and come back in a couple of years or so with one of these phoney doctorates are immediately raised to a certain rank in their profession and paid accordingly. He has applied to be raised to that rank too, but he's been turned down. He reeled off to me the names of at least six others in the same position, all with U.K. diplomas and certificates whose value isn't recognized here.'

'Interesting, Harold, but why bring it to me, except as an illustration of how a backward country always wants to leap too far ahead? They think if they've got a lot of men addressed as Doctor they're an educated country. A lot of cock, of course, but surely you can sympathize with them. Don't think the Embassy isn't aware of this apparent discrimination. Howard, I'm sure, could add another half dozen to your list.'

'The discrimination isn't just apparent; it's as plain as your nose.'

Wint smiled; if Moffatt had said his ears, it would have been malicious; these were big, bigger even than Howard's, but his nose was normal.

'Even so,' he said. 'There's still nothing we can do about it. It's purely Afghan business.'

Moffatt chewed at his cigarette; it was a danger signal. 'What about that ruddy flag?' he asked.

Wint frowned. 'Afraid I don't follow.'

'I should have thought it was up to us to make sure that where we're still good – and we are still good, in education – everyone should be made know it and respect it. Especially in a country like this one, still uncommitted. We can't lend them millions of dollars or roubles, but we can still make it clear to them that the name British on something means it's good. In the bazaars, you know, British is a synonym for good quality. If they say an article's British they're recommending it, even though you find it was really made in Germany.'

Moffatt's face was red; sweat glistened on his brow. The heat was internal. Only Wint could ever have provoked him into so jingoistic an outburst; and only Wint could have listened to it with such uncynical agreement.

'I couldn't agree more, old man,' said the First Secretary, very warmly, 'and I'm very glad to hear you say it. Far too many British people abroad think it beneath them to say a word in their country's praise.'

'All right, then. What are we going to do about these diplomas?'

'Insist upon their true worth, of course.'

'Good. Will the Ambassador himself take it up with the Minister of Education?'

'I hardly think so. I meant we should insist as individuals. You're doing a good job, and I thank you for it. No, Harold, I'm serious; I do thank you.'

A wild light had come into Moffatt's eyes.

'This is an instance,' went on Wint, 'where the onlooker doesn't see most of the game. You've got to be in this job, right in the heart of it, to appreciate the difficulties, and I grant you, the limitations of professional diplomacy.'

'So as far as the Embassy's concerned I can take this back to Mir Abdul Rahman and tell him it's so much bumph?'

Wint looked hurt. 'I know how you feel, Harold, but you do exaggerate. Be fair. Show a proper sense of proportion. This is really a small matter, rather too small for ambassadorial interference.' His confidence faltered a little as he remembered the cigarette pack found in the flower bed. 'Besides, it's purely an Afghan affair. I suspect it's a dodge on their part to save a little money. They'll be out to recoup some of the cost of his scholarship. Is he a friend of yours, Harold?'

'I never saw him before yesterday when he came to see me at the University.'

'I hope he realized he was running the risk of compromising you with the authorities. They've been known to tear up a contract, you know. What difference is it making to him, in terms of salary, I mean?'

'Two pounds a month.'

'You see, it is a small matter.'

'His present salary is five pounds a month; so to him it's not such a small matter. The Embassy will do nothing, then?'

'There's nothing we can do. I'll put it up for discussion at our next policy meeting, but I'm convinced H.E. will want to let it lie.'

Moffatt grabbed the diploma and thrust it back into his brief case. That light in his eyes was wilder. More percipient friends than Wint would have seen that he was minded to jump up, shout an obscenity from a lavatory wall, and rush away. That he sat still showed the second operation, St George, must be important to him. 'Well, I'm damned if I'm going to let it lie.'

'So long as you do nothing rash.'

'You'll have heard of Mrs Mohebzada?'

Startled by the transition, Wint reflected suspiciously; he knew how people so often tried to get their own back at him, even when all the harm he'd done was to tell them the truth. 'Can't say I have. You know we seldom get an opportunity to meet Afghan women. I take it she is Afghan?'

'She is, though she was born in Ealing, has blue eyes and fair hair.'

'Yes, I remember her now. She's the little English girl who married an Afghan, about a year and a half ago, just before I arrived. She's not connected with Operation St George, I hope?'

'She's living in my house, or was when I left this morning.'

'I see.' But clearly Wint did not. Moffatt's was one of the most hospitable houses in Kabul. Representatives of at least thirty nationalities visited there, including Afghans who, in their own capital, were more elusive even than Russians. That he should have received this fellow countrywoman as his overnight guest was hardly remarkable.

'She's run away from her husband.'

'Has she, indeed?' Still Wint saw no reason for much concern. All over the world women were running away from husbands, or husbands from wives, especially in the most civilized countries. Afghanistan with reluctance admitted herself to be backward industrially, but claimed with some justification to have been civilized long before Britain. She had cinemas, though none suitable for Europeans; a theatre where in crude adaptations of Molière or Shakespeare boys took the parts of women; buses, presented by the Russians; macadamed main streets, also the result of astute Russian benevolence; electricity and automatic telephones, thanks to the energy and enterprise of Germans; and two daily newspapers, published by the government. Why then should she not also have runaway wives and shattered marriages? It would probably astonish everyone, Wint had often mused, to learn what went on under those shaddries and behind those high compound walls.

'And from her child, too.'

Ah, that was different. That was not merely symptomatic of civilization in malaise: it represented a tragic failure of humanity. Wint had two children, Annette and Paul, snug at school, but snugger still in his own and Paula's affection. The Moffatts so far had none, though they had been married for five years. Were they afraid that their little slant-eyed half-castes would be received unkindly by a world itself so impure and mongrel?

'And she's threatened to kill herself rather than go back to him.'

Now Wint perceived through the veil of his thoughts that a human being – familiar, bristling, and crimson with passion – was across his desk talking to him about another human being – female, British in origin and outlook, in distress about her child and husband. He could not quite see Moffatt as St George, nor any Afghan as a dragon, nor Mrs Mohebzada (whom he remembered as a rather unintelligent girl who had worked in a shoe shop and no doubt had been enticed away with lies of riches and luxury) as an innocent maiden to be liberated. Still, the situation was of more consequence than small or capital *m*'s, or cigarette packs in flower beds, or walnut trees chopped down.

'And she means it.'

Then, in the midst of his compassion, it struck Wint with the impact of a camel's hoof that in this case, too, there could be no interference.

'You'll have to persuade her to go back, Harold.'

Moffatt's pugnacious jaw dropped. 'Did you hear what I said? She'll kill herself rather than go back.'

'Distraught women say that often enough, Harold. The point is, she comes under Afghan jurisdiction; we've got no responsibility for her at all. I'm not saying we don't want to have. She has never registered here.'

'You know they don't allow that.'

'True, but it can be done, in secret. Not, mind you, that it would have made much difference. I don't want to seem brutal, Harold, but the first thing you should have made clear to her is that by marrying this chap, she virtually put herself beyond our protection.'

'That's been clear to her from the minute she arrived here.'

'All right. It's as well her eyes were open. What about her husband? Is he going to make trouble? Does he know she's at your place?'

'He does. I telephoned him at his work this morning.'

'And what did he say?'

'Damned little. I didn't give him the chance. I did all the saying.'

This was the Harold Moffatt, Wint thought, who, despite his intelligence and knack of getting on with people of all races, could never have been a diplomat. He was almost melting and spluttering with anger; whereas he, Alan Wint, had seldom felt so cool and resourceful. Yes, there were at least a dozen things to be considered before Mrs Mohebzada was allowed to kill herself.

'And what did you say to him, Harold?'

'I told him she was at my house, and as long as she wanted to stay there she could.'

Wint smiled. Rash, extravagant, indiscreet words, but not disastrously so. Still, there might have been others.

'And I also told him that if he made any attempt to come and take her back by force I'd kick his teeth in.'

And doubtless, thought Wint in a spasm of that kind of irrelevance into which his mind, confronted by threat of disaster, loved to retreat, Mohebzada had excellent white teeth. Then reality had to be faced. 'Good Lord, man surely you weren't so foolish and provocative!'

'And I'll do it, too! She was in a terrible state.'

Here was the crux, Mrs Mohebzada's state, and the reasons for it. Had cruelty been inflicted on her, or was her desperation caused by the too painful contrast between the life she'd led in Ealing and that lived here? If the latter, then it might well be that her husband was hardly to blame, except insofar as he had wilfully deceived her with stories of his wealth and position.

'Does he insist she wear a shaddry?'

'No, but the rest of his family do, and because she refused they make her life a hell. She's kept more or less a prisoner. She's not allowed to visit other foreigners. She never has a penny of her own.'

'Can't she get work here? Other women married to Afghans do.'

'Why should she go out to work and keep his whole family? In any case, they're so bloody prejudiced they won't allow her. And what work could she do here, anyway? She can't type, teach, or nurse.'

Wint reflected that in the whole country, of twelve million people, there wasn't one woman serving in a shop.

The telephone rang. He picked it up cautiously, thinking it might be the Ambassador. But it wasn't; it was a woman's voice, as quiet as the lascivious schoolgirl's but sweeter and far more sane; it was, in fact, Mrs Moffatt's. She wanted to know if her husband was there. 'Yes, Mrs Moffatt, as a matter of fact, he is. Do you want to speak to him?'

'Please.'

He handed the telephone over. 'Your wife, Harold.'

Moffatt's anger vanished as he took the receiver. Wint, uxorious himself, was almost embarrassed by the effect upon the other man of merely touching a telephone, knowing his wife in a moment would speak to him through it. The smile on Moffatt's face was too unadulteratedly happy. No matter how deep and genuine his love, a man ought always to keep in it a grain of scepticism for purifying purposes.

'Hello, Lan darling. Harold here.'

It was interesting thereafter to study Moffatt's face. The happiness never faded, yet at the same time it expressed surprise, anger, and anxiety, while at least once he muttered: 'Christ!'

'Now don't you get upset, Lan. It wasn't your fault. How could you have prevented her? No, I couldn't. I'll be home as soon as I can, in about twenty minutes, I hope. You can tell me all about it then. Don't worry.'

He put down the receiver, his plump face radiant and furious.

'So she's gone back?' said Wint.

'Yes. He stood outside the gate with the baby. It cried, as if it was in agony. Maybe the bastard was squeezing its leg.'

'Now, Harold! I shouldn't be surprised if he was crying himself. You know how prone they are to tears. She's his wife, after all, and in his own way no doubt he loves her.'

'She went, breaking her heart. Lan's pretty upset. I'll have to hurry back. Strange as it may seem, Alan, it wasn't Mrs Mohebzada I originally meant to speak to you about this morning. She arrived last night, a bolt from the blue. This letter' – he threw it on the desk – 'was given to me yesterday afternoon. Lan brought it home from the International School. You'll notice it's addressed to the U.N. Tom Lorimer passed it on to the Principal, Mrs Mossaour, who wanted my opinion. I telephoned her that I thought you should be consulted. She thought it was a good idea.'

'Did she?' Wint's smile was a wince. The English wife of a Lebanese U.N. official, Mrs Mossaour was caustic about British diplomacy in the Middle East.

He took the letter out of the envelope. It was typed. The writer's own address was Manchester.

DEAR SIR,

As I intend shortly to come to Kabul to marry my fiancé, Mr Abdul Wahab, of the Ministry of Education, I should be much obliged if you could let me know what employment, if any, you could offer me on my arrival.

I am thirty-three. I have a B.A. (Pol. Econ.) of Birmingham, and also a teaching diploma. Though not professionally proficient I am able to type. At present I am employed in the British Civil Service, in the administrative branch of the National Insurance Department. I have also had two years' teaching experience.

I hope you do not consider this an impertinent request. I shall be most grateful for any help you can give me.

She signed herself: LAURA JOHNSTONE.

Wint looked up. 'I'm afraid we couldn't employ her here. Even if she got a transfer to the Foreign Service, she'd be automatically disqualified through marrying an Afghan.'

'Wouldn't she just! Finding a job for her's easy enough. Tom Lorimer would give her one. Mrs Mossaour would grab at any trained teacher. But neither is keen to take on the responsibility of encouraging her to come here and marry this Abdul Wahab.'

'Do you know anything about him?'

'Just that he's a teacher at Isban College with a salary equivalent to between seven and eight pounds a month. It would be another case of Mrs Mohebzada all over again.'

'I don't think you can say that. In the first place, this woman's educated, probably intelligent, and old enough surely to know her own mind. Mrs Mohebzada on the other hand is only twenty-one or so, and mentally is rather dim. I shall admit to you, in confidence, that I'm puzzled as to why a woman enjoying a good standard of living at home – she should be able to run a car and have a flat of her own – should want to come out here. Why can't she find a fellow of her kind to marry?' He thought, but was too chivalrous to say it, that likely she was either physically unattractive or mentally awkward.

'Will the Embassy write to her, warning her of the consequences of marrying an Afghan with little money?'

Strange, thought Wint, how Moffatt, socialistic despiser of snobbery at home and reviler of our mercenary civilization, should so hard-headedly emphasize the importance of money in this instance. It would have been tedious to point out the inconsistency.

'No, Harold, we won't write to her,' he said. 'But I expect we could arrange for her to see someone in London with recent experience of Afghanistan.'

'Anyone in mind?'

'Well, there's Pierce-Smith. He was here less than a year ago. But of course you knew him.'

'Yes, I knew him.'

'You don't sound enthusiastic, old man. From what I know of him, he's a very sound chap.'

'He's too optimistic.'

'Hardly a fault, surely.'

'Here, it is. He enjoyed every minute of his time here: parties, skiing, riding, tennis; it was like a prolonged holiday. Besides, there's a tendency for everyone to look back and remember only the pleasant aspects.'

'True. And it could be, Harold, that what is recollected in tranquillity is the truth of experience, whereas the irksome present is full of petty falseness.' Even as the thought was forming, and being uttered, he wasn't sure whether it was wisdom or bunkum.

Moffatt stood up. 'It won't do any harm to get him to talk to her. But we'll get in touch too.'

'Who are "we"?'

'Lan, Mrs Massaour, and myself; and perhaps Josh Bolton.'

'I was wondering if he came into it. He's an American.'

'He's a human being, and he's the expert on the position of women here.'

'I wonder what he'd say if an Afghan went to Mississippi, say, to write about the conditions of Negroes.'

'Josh would wish him luck.'

Wint too had risen. 'I wouldn't get involved too deeply with him, Harold. His visa exists from day to day. He hasn't the approval, either, of his Embassy. Give my regards to Lan.'

'And mine to Paula.'

On that wifely note they parted, Wint to sit down again and ponder, Moffatt to go out into the hot noon sun, climb into his hotter car, and drive past the long hedgerow of yellow roses, out of the large gates with the gilt crests and uniformed guards.

Three

As HE motored along the macadam road from the Embassy
into the city, Moffatt had to admit that he too, like Pierce-
Smith, liked this country and was very happy in it; when he
left, his memories, though assisted by Lan's paintings and
his own colour slides, would not be any happier. At the
University where he taught English, though his classroom
had a mud-brick floor, desks of unseasoned, unvarnished
wood, a cracked slippery blackboard, and chalk like stone,
and though the books supplied to his classes were insuffi-
cient in number and out of date in content, he enjoyed every
minute of it. The students were so splendid, not so much on
account of their attitude for English, though some did learn
quickly and well, as on account of their dignity. Yes, he had
to use Wint's word, though by it he hoped he meant
something different – their courtesy, both individual and
communal, and their hospitality. He was their teacher and
their friend, and he was also their guest, and their sense of
fun which showed itself in many ways but especially in
questions asked unexpectedly in the middle of a lecture,
with the gravity of a priest, as to the precise meaning of
certain four-letter words. In his attempts to avoid answering, or to give an answer in academic terms, he would be
pursued with a grave, brown-eyed relentlessness. When the
episode was over and the lecture was chastely resumed, he
was never sure that his leg hadn't been delightfully pulled;
and that uncertainty of course was good for him as a teacher.
Such episodes occurred at least once a week.

He liked the countryside too, so that now, though he was
anxious to get home to Lan, he found himself involuntarily
decelerating. There were the vines at the side of the road to
look at to see how the grapes were ripening; the nomad
encampment with its black tents, flock of sheep and goats,
camels, dogs, merry children, aloof men, and women with
their faces boldly uncovered; the native village, like so many
mud boxes flung down higgledy-piggledy on the hillside;
the holy man's tomb, sticks festooned with rags protruding
from it like flags of humility; and the tea shop, with its brass
samovar, its blue-beaded, hubble-bubble pipe, and its customers, relaxed in the shade, puffing, or sipping out of their
small handleless cups, and remarking, no doubt, on the
foolishness of the rich foreigner hurrying past in his small,
hot, noisy car. Others, he knew, would have seen and
smelled only squalor; but though he was well aware of it
he felt it was more than redeemed by the mountain sunshine, by the bright green of the irrigated fields, by the trees
that dripped like rain, by the tawny hills that crouched all
round the great valley, the most distant eternally snow-
capped, but most of all by what many called the indolence of
the people but which to him, was again, dignity. Possessing
it, a man in rags, with less than a sixpence in his pocket,
defeated his poverty. All possessed it, so that though all,
except a tiny few, were poor, poverty was never here the
degradation it so often was in India or Pakistan.

Why then, it occurred to him as a question Lan might
have quietly asked, had he made such a fuss about Mrs
Mohebzada, and why was he determined to make so great a
one about Miss Laura Johnstone that she would be discouraged from coming here? Surely it was simply that they,
brought up in England, and therefore lacking that dignity,
must inevitably be degraded and made desperate by the
poverty and squalor? He knew many European and American women, married to their own kind, as Wint had put it,

and so enjoying an even higher standard of living than they would have at home, who hated living here and counted the days till, their husbands' terms over, they could return to fresh milk, unboiled water, and television. At the Embassy Katherine Winn, in other things so staunch and intelligent, was an example; and the other women there, especially Mrs Rodgers and Mrs Gillie, made existence tolerable by staying as much as possible with the Embassy compound which, with its flowers and trees and houses planned in English style, had been made to resemble a village at home.

On the road junction at the entrance to the city the policeman had moved over with the shade until he was now in a position where he could not interfere with the traffic which he was supposed to be controlling; his gestures, usually ambiguous, were now merely somnolent. Under some trees ghoddy drivers and their horses dozed together, sharing the flies. This was the new part of the city, Shahr-i-nau, and many of the houses had been especially built to be let to foreigners. The main street leading to the new mosque was tarred, but most of the side streets, though wide, were of mud, dusty but tolerable now in summer, but in the spring wet season and the snowy winter, quagmires or ponds. Every street was unnamed and unnumbered, and had at its side the 'jowey' or open ditch, which was a complicated means of diverting water from the river into the gardens, but which was frequently used as a dump for rubbish, including, it might be, a dog poisoned with someone's sly gift of strychnined liver.

Every house had its high compound wall, in some cases of plain mud, in others of painted mud-brick and wood. Inside, the gardens were usually a pleasant surprise, with grass, flowers, and fruit trees. The gates were kept locked, with a variety of bells, from up-to-date electric systems to nests of tin cans dangling on a wire behind the door. One rang, by pressing the button or, more often, by tugging the piece of wood attached to the wire, and waited until the door should be opened an inch or two, and a pair of suspicious brown eyes, surmounted by a turban or karakul cap, should inspect you, beam if you were recognized, or cloud over if you were not. If you knew the language fairly well you could be admitted quickly, but if your Afghan was as pidgin as the bacha's English, he might entertain himself by exasperating you for about five minutes before reluctantly letting you in. To add to the difficulty some foreigners kept large fierce dogs which the Moslem servants themselves neither liked nor trusted. Yet crime in Kabul was surprisingly rare, at least as far as it affected the foreign community. A house might be burgled, or a woman whose face, arms, legs, and neck were too provocatively bare might be attacked by some fanatic during Ramazan when tempers were touchy. But generally most foreigners were left in peace, thanks, according to some, to the innate hospitality of the people or, according to others, to the ubiquity and brutality of the police.

To reach the street in which he lived Moffatt had to pass a small bazaar consisting of a few shops: a baker's, with the word 'Cacks' proudly painted above; a pharmacist's in which the latest drugs, obtainable only on prescription in Britain, could be bought freely; a furniture maker's, with labourers outside sawing by hand a great beam of wood into thin boards; and a post office where the regulations were printed in French and the attendant was so Afghan that a customer might have to wait until he had completed his prayers.

On one side of Moffatt's street was the public park where on holidays hundreds of men and youths gathered to fly kites. Now on the grass some shrill small boys were kicking a football with bare feet. A number of men slept under trees, undisturbed by the wailing, from the café in the centre, of Indian and Afghan love songs, which went on all day from morning till midnight. Twice Moffatt, unable to sleep through the gigantic ululations, had telephoned the café to request that the volume be turned down. The apologetic owner had agreed, and had obliged, at least for the next four or five minutes. Moffatt had once rushed across to protest in person, only to find that the fault was not the café owner's, but that of his wireless set, which was so old and defective that the volume control pleased itself – turn it down, and two minutes later it was up again, louder than ever. The solution, the owner had charmingly hinted, was for him to get a new set; unfortunately he could not afford to buy one; if Moffatt had one to spare, then both of them could so easily be made happy. The other solution, to turn the set off altogether, would have meant depriving about ten thousand people of free music; it was unthinkable.

Outside Moffatt's gate a small boy squatted, playing a pipe; about him were his six skinny cattle, grazing on the grass that grew in and around the ditch. He grinned in neighbourly fashion at Moffatt and resumed playing. When Sofi, the small zealous bacha, came running to open the gate, he at once shouted to the herdsboy to take his beasts away from Sahib's door, as their droppings caused a stink; but his shout was more comradely than hostile, and he would have been offended if the boy had obeyed him. Indeed, it was more than likely that after lunch, with the dishes washed and the other chores done for the time being, Sofi would come out, squat beside the boy, and chat with him about country matters. For Sofi too, not so long ago, had lived and worked on the land, in a village about fifty miles from the capital. In three or four years, after saving his wages and all illegal additions to them, such as his percentage of what Abdul the cook fiddled from the household accounts, he would go back home, buy a wife, live at ease while she worked hard, and then, when his wealth was spent, return to seek another job, with the help of the chitties that Moffatt and other employers had given him.

Sofi was excited that morning. He was in a fidget to tell

Moffatt about Mohebzada's visit but was inhibited, not at all
by the knowledge that as a servant he had no right to be
concerned, but rather by doubt with whom he should side –
Moffatt who was his employer, or Mohebzada who was his
countryman. Since he could not possibly endure being left
out of it, he did what he usually did, which was to blurt out
whatever came into his mind, no matter how contradictory,
impertinent, or unhelpful. Laughing heartily, and trying to
swell his five-foot nothing into ferocity, he kept pointing to
Moffatt and crying that Mohebzada was an Afghan and that
Afghans were, the whole world knew, the fiercest and
bravest of fighters.

Genially Moffatt remarked that if he had any more cheek
from him he would kick his backside. Far from insulted,
honoured indeed, and immensely amused, for not every
foreign master could speak the vernacular, Sofi held open
the screen door and yelled in: 'Memsahib, Sahib come.'

Cool and composed, Lan came into the tiled hall to greet
him. She was beautiful in her green silk, high-collared dress,
and with jade combs in her black hair. To Sofi's delight and
embarrassment Moffatt kissed her, and hand in hand they
went into the large lounge floored with red Afghan carpets
and hung with half a dozen of Lan's paintings of Afghan
scenes. All the furnishings were Afghan except for a few
ornaments brought from Indonesia.

He had not been deceived by her composure; it was not a
pretence, nor was it merely skin-deep; but it by no means
meant that since sympathy or grief or love ruffled the mind –
she had learned to dispense with them. He knew that if her
heart ever broke, she would be calmly smiling.

'So she went with him?' he said.

'Yes. She left this.' She held out to him a snapshot that
showed Mrs Mohebzada holding her baby tightly, as if
afraid it might be snatched from her.

He looked at it for almost a minute. She knew more

clearly than he did himself what his thoughts were; conclusions which he was afraid to reach she went resolutely beyond. The baby was very dark, in contrast with its fair-haired mother. By gibing so bitterly against racial prejudice, Moffatt more than helped to keep it in existence; he also kept himself infected with it. His rage against poor Mohebzada was really against himself, so polluted. Knowing this his wife loved him all the more.

'Did she forget it?' he asked, handing the photograph back.

'No. I asked if I could have it.'

'Why, Lan? For God's sake, why should you want this?'

She gazed at the photograph. On her small faintly yellow face slowly appeared first a faint blush and then a shy smile. Raising her eyes, she stared at him with that frankness which could see into the secretmost crannies of his mind and yet, flushing out the shames and fears, never leave him resentful.

'I do not see her child, Harold, but ours.'

Theirs, though, had not yet been permitted to be conceived.

'Whatever it'll be like, Lan, it won't be like that. Tell me what happened.'

'Perhaps you should take your shower first. I shall tell you while you are taking it.'

He grinned. 'Do you want to drive our Sofi out of his mind?'

'He was assuring me that when we have a child we will not need an ayah; he will look after it himself.'

'And feed it on bazaar sweets.'

'When you say that, Harold, it becomes very real.'

'What about a drink?'

'After your shower. One sherry.'

Again he grinned. She was right as usual; he drank too much, out of conviviality he would have claimed, but there was another reason too. He kissed her and murmured:

'Don't expect her, Lan, to be small and dainty and sweet-natured like you. No, she'll be fat and cross like me.'

'He will be like you, and I shall love him more than my own life.'

As he stood with his lips against her brow he remembered her young brother in Djakarta, who had not been like her at all, but neither had he been in any way repulsive.

She felt him shiver and understood why.

'I'm sorry, Lan.'

'Why should you be sorry? I am very happy.'

'This would be as good a place as any for our child.'

'Any place in the world would be good.'

What he meant was that here in Kabul, with so many nationalities and with the host nation considered unimportant, racial prejudice was not so stark or rife. One glance, even of pity, at the child would enrage and hurl him into a dejection out of which even Lan would find it hard to raise him. Both knew that this ineradicable pride blemished his love for her; often in private she shed quiet tears, and he among his friends got drunk.

At lunch, for once, they were alone. Sofi, cheerful and clumsy, served them. Several times Abdul the cook looked sorrowfully in, to solicit and obtain approval. Outside, the café radio shrieked and wailed, and in the midst of it was the quieter, melancholy piping of the herdsboy.

They spoke about Mrs Mohebzada and then about Abdul Wahab who, Mrs Mossaour had telephoned to say, was going to the International School that afternoon to discuss the prospect of a post for his fiancée. She had suggested it might be advisable for Harold to be present, ostensibly as her educational adviser.

'I'll be there all right,' he said grimly.

'Not to frighten him, dear.'

'Why not? If it's the only way to make him give up this scheme.'

'What scheme?'

'First, find a woman who'll cost him nothing; second, find a job for her; third, live easy on her earnings; fourth, keep taming her all the time until she's another Mrs Mohebzada.'

'Would that be wise of him? Mr Mohebzada isn't happy to see his wife in such despair. I do not think we should judge without knowing.'

'If you mean knowing Wahab, I'm afraid these fellows are all the same.'

'Sofi isn't the same as Abdul, and they're both Afghans. And you think so much of your students.'

'In your opinion then, Wahab is doing it all for love?'

'He may be, Harold.'

'No.' Moffatt stubbornly shook his head. 'I'd like to believe it, darling, but I just can't. If he really loved this woman, he wouldn't let her come out here. He knows the conditions. You've seen Mrs Mohebzada. You've heard her.'

'Yes. I agree she is very unhappy.'

'Wahab must know of such cases. According to Josh Bolton, who's made a study of them, there must be at least a dozen in Kabul at this moment. There was the French-woman who did kill herself.'

'But no one knows why, for certain.'

'Everyone has a good idea. No matter what his own intentions may be, Wahab's intelligent enough to realize that all the pressures are against him. Unless he's a very strong-minded character he'll pretty soon give in to them; and nice though these Afghans are, in many ways, you wouldn't call them strong-minded under pressure.'

'Love can make a mind strong.'

'What about Mohebzada? Didn't he love her, to begin with? For that matter, to be fair, doesn't he still love her?'

'Yes, Harold, we must be fair. He does love her, I think. He was very distressed; they were both weeping.'

'Afghans weep easily, Lan. The point is, he crumpled

under the pressure. I'm not blaming him. God knows in the same circumstances I might not do any better myself.'

She smiled down at her plate.

Outside, the boy's piping suddenly became merry.

After a long pause Moffatt said: 'So I'm going ahead to persuade him to leave her at home.'

'You will be the first of the pressures, dear.'

For a moment he felt angry; then, smiling, he put his hand on hers. 'What should we do, Lan? Wint, as I've told you, thinks we should mind our own business. You don't think that: if anybody's unhappy or in trouble it's your business, and I love you for it. But what should we do?'

'We should talk to Mr Wahab, yes, but with open minds; or better, with minds prepared to sympathize.'

'Of course we sympathize.'

'He may surprise us, Harold.'

'In what way?'

'Well, we may get the feeling that in him at any rate his love for his wife will truly resist the pressures.'

'And if we do get that feeling, do we stop interfering?'

'We do not stop helping.'

'But how can we help, Lan? We can't even help Mrs Mohebzada. We could pay her fare home, but she'd have to go without her baby, which she won't do. Surely the best way to help Miss Johnstone is to prevent her from coming.'

'We can befriend Mr Wahab; we can let him see he is not alone in his struggle, if there is to be a struggle; and, most of all, we can welcome Miss Johnstone when she arrives.'

'So you think we should do nothing to stop her coming?'

'What Mr Wint suggests should be sufficient. Mr Pierce-Smith is a warmhearted man. I think he will do his best to dissuade her if he feels she will not be equal to it. You see, Harold,' she added, with that smile which even to him was inscrutable, so deep a humour did it reveal, 'even if I were to live in an Afghan house of mud, in a compound of other such houses, and there were many relatives daily troubling me, and there were many restrictions and suspicions, and if I were very unhappy, I should still prefer it, if to escape from it were to lose you. It may be that it is the same with Miss Johnstone and Abdul Wahab.'

Moffatt smiled too, and for a few moments they were silent.

Then from somewhere outside, a donkey began to bray its prodigious, prolonged disgust.

'Unfair comment, don't you think?' murmured Moffatt.

'Not so unfair, darling,' she cried, laughing.

Abdul came rushing along, to see if it was his proud blancmange, of a peculiar purple colour, that they were laughing at. When he saw it wasn't he went away, hardly assuaged, and left them laughing louder than ever.

When they began to talk again it was about the kebab dance to be held soon at the International Club to celebrate the opening of the swimming pool.

Four

THE International School was in sight of the new mosque with the light-blue dome on top of its high pillar. Proximity to godliness did not here, alas, guarantee cleanliness. Near the school, at a corner no one claimed, was a dump where the servants of all the houses around about threw the daily refuse, including soup cans and hens' heads. The flies and bluebottles that buzzed there were well fed, numerous, and aggressive. Close by too, making the place a hygienist's nightmare, was one of those peculiar Afghan public lavatories, consisting of a niche in a wall, with no door, where only the passer-by's sense of propriety or his disgust kept the shameless squatter private.

Mrs Mossaour, principal of the school, had protested to every quarter she could think of, using her husband's influence with the Government which he was adivising on financial matters. She claimed that owing to her energetic complaints the matter had once been mentioned by the king himself. No doubt all those dignitaries and officials, if they could, would have got rid of those abominations to convenience the school; but apparently they could not. In the same way most of them would have liked to abolish the laws whereby a murderer was handed over to the victim's family for public vengeance, or an Afghan woman would be arrested by the first policeman if she appeared without a shaddry. They seemed to be helpless in the grip of tradition and also of that something else, national pride perhaps, which, not quite so powerful in the poorest, made them all resent their country's role of beggar on the world's high road, receiving alms from opulent America and designing Russia. It might well have been, as had been argued more than once at meetings of the Board of Governors of the school, that a small outcome of that national resentment was this inability or refusal to remove dump and jakes from the precints of the school that served most of the foreign community. No Afghan or Russian child attended, but children of twenty other nationalities did.

Since the nuisances could not be removed, removing the school itself had been considered. Unfortunately, money was sometimes so scarce that teachers' salaries fell in arrears, and a great deal was invested in improvements to the rented building. Besides, it would not have been easy finding a new site that was central and salubrious. So in the end Mrs Mossaour, tall, stout, fair-haired, and Junoesque, had had to decide, prompted by her dry-witted husband, that there was after all educational value of some kind in those vile stinking heaps. They kept the pampered children of the West aware that here was no suburb of Washington or London or Paris, but the unprivileged East; and no doubt the parents too, usually the ambitious mothers, who drove their offspring up to the gate in expensive cars, appreciated the lesson.

When the Moffatts arrived that afternoon they noticed, among the cars outside, the red Hillman Minx of Bob Gillie, the British Consul. Though he was the British representative on the Board of Governors, he was seldom known to visit the school itself. He had no children, and took every opportunity to advertise the advantages of being so un-shackled; but perhaps he thought that the sight of some hundred and fifty of them, of all sizes and various colours, would be too poignant a test of the sincerity of his reiterated satisfaction.

In the compound the children were playing before the bell rang to summon them in. English was the language of instruction, with French the subsidiary, but during play others, such as Swedish, Dutch, Javanese, Hindi, Urdu, and Polish, could be heard, shrilly and on the whole amicably commingled.

As Moffatt and Lan walked along the paved path toward the building, a number of children, catching sight of her, came scampering up in affectionate glee. She was their Art teacher and the best disciplinarian on the staff. Classes, rebellious with others, were not only biddable with her, despite her daintiness, but also eager to work. Yet she never so much as raised her voice. As a result she was a favourite with the American mothers, who all shared the belief that a sharp word to Junior in his impressionable and mystical childhood might leave him unadjusted till he attained gray hair.

Now this clamour of welcome had all the rowdy competitiveness taken out of it by a smile and a few quiet words.

Mrs Mossaour and Gillie, seated on the veranda in front of the principal's office, watched the enchanting scene. The Consul, with grunts of wonder, took a brief holiday from fidelity to his own gray-haired, so English wife, and imagined himself married instead to this small, fragile, fascinating Chinese woman from Indonesia. One of the consequences, and by no means the least, of that exchange would have been that his love of clothes, of fine materials and splendid colours, would be fully indulged, at any rate in the exciting privacy of their home; for he could not see this small beautiful princess of a woman going off into Muriel's shocked giggles at his experimenting with underwear of mauve silk.

Mrs Mossaour's thoughts were not so fanciful. She was thinking what a pity it was that Lan, so marvellous with children, might find having a family of her own difficult, if not unattainable, because of the narrowness of her pelvis, but chiefly because of the narrowness of her husband's views

on race. Harold Moffatt, outspokenly liberal, had not deceived Mrs Mossaour, who was the mother of children not
the same colour as herself. Moffatt still had in his throat the
pride she long ago had swallowed and found after all easily
digestible. There were still times, though, when attitudes
like Harold Moffatt's, outwardly for and inwardly against,
revived a little of her former anguish and made her wonder
bitterly by what freak of nature or quirk of God her son and
daughter were darker even than their father. Sometimes, in
her bath, she would sit and brood over the whiteness of her
breasts and belly; these, like Harold Moffatt, were traitors.

Mrs Satti, Indian, sultry in a sari of crimson and gold,
came out and rang the hand bell. When the playground was
empty at last, she remained on the veranda, clasping the bell
and gazing along to where the Moffatts had joined the
principal and the British Consul, as if she were minded
to glide up to them. They were aware of her half-intention
and knew its reason. A move was afoot to force her resigna-
tion. In a letter to an American parent she had mispelled
three words, and other examples of her lack of scholarship
were being gathered. She maintained, in her quick, sing-
song, priestess's voice, that it was not her bad spelling which
was the trouble but the colour of her skin. Counting her,
there were three Indian teachers at the school, too many, she
contended, for the Americans to stomach. Behind her in the
classroom her class was raising a din and probably causing
damage. Why should she hurry in to subdue them, when
Mrs Moffatt, not white either, was calmly hobnobbing with
the principal, while her class too waited? That it was quiet
and getting on with the work she had set them to do, did not,
in Mrs Satti's opinion, alter the case.

At last, however, she went in. No diminution of the
hubbub followed.

'She's lost heart,' said Mrs Mossaour. 'It's been most
unpleasant for her.'

'I know Howard Winfield tells me John Keats couldn't spell,' said Gillie. 'But I do think a schoolteacher ought to be able to. Why doesn't she just resign?'

'I'm not keen that she should, at any rate not till the end of the session. Her contract doesn't expire till then. If she insisted we'd have to pay her salary, and of course the salary of the teacher replacing her would have to be paid too. That's to say, if we could find a suitable replacement. After all, even if she can't spell "believe", she does have a degree.'

'Indian, I believe?' said Gillie, with a grin. 'So, apart from other considerations, you could do with this Miss Johnstone to strengthen your staff?'

'I certainly could. But not, of course, at the expense of the poor woman's happiness.'

'I hope you do not mind my waiting?' asked Lan. 'My class knows what they have to do. You see, I wish to meet Mr Wahab.'

Mrs Mossaour glanced at Moffatt. 'By all means, Lan. You know how much we respect your judgment.'

'You wouldn't have Miss Johnstone on your staff for long,' said Moffatt, 'if she married Wahab.'

'How d'you make that out?' demanded Gillie. Regarding this probable marriage his own mind was open. When Mrs Mossaour had telephoned him that morning he had agreed to come to this interview for two reasons: first, he had been rattled by that silly – and he couldn't help feeling, sinister – business of the empty cigarette pack in the flower bed; and secondly, when he learned that Wint and Moffatt had been discussing Miss Johnstone at length, without troubling to consult him, although as Consul he was the Embassy official who would be responsible for her, his pride had been jarred. So, though coming had been inconvenient and, to tell the truth, against his inclination, he had nevertheless come and was determined to say his proper share, though he had not yet, five minutes before the expected arrival of Wahab, decided what that say was going to be.

He waited for Moffatt's answer, with the appearance of a man requiring justification of a remark just uttered by another, his junior in years and position.

'I'm convinced,' said Moffatt, 'that if she married him she'd soon lose heart so much she'd be of little use, even to herself.'

'That's a hard thing to say. You mean, this fellow Wahab would knock the initiative and spirit out of her?'

'Yes.'

'Why? Is he a bit of a brute? Do you know about him? Has he a reputation?'

'None of us has ever met Mr Wahab,' said Lan, gently. 'We had not even heard of him until yesterday when Mrs Mossaour showed us Miss Johnstone's letter to Mr Lorimer.'

Moffatt smiled at his wife. 'It's really got nothing to do with Wahab himself, as a person. Whether he's a good sort, or merely a creep with a scheme for acquiring a wife for nothing who'll keep him and his family, makes no difference. It's the situation here that will knock the initiative and spirit out of her, as it has out of every European wife of an Afghan.'

'Every one?' cried Gillie. He knew Moffatt's opinion of the Embassy, that, tucked away in its suburban compound, it knew little of what went on in the city. It was an absurd and impudent opinion. Gillie was sure he knew far more than Moffatt did; after all, if he didn't, it meant he was useless at his job. 'That's a wide statement to make. Are you sure of your facts?'

'Sure enough. Whether he's a rebel or a conformist, no Afghan at the present time in the country's development can be a suitable husband for any Western woman. The pressures are all against him.'

'Unless he happened to be a very remarkable man,' said Mrs Mossaour, convinced that no such man existed.

'Or the woman a very remarkable woman,' added Gillie.

'No, Bob,' said Moffatt. 'She'd just take longer to succumb, that's all; but in the end her surrender and degradation would be all the greater.'

'You seem to feel damned strongly about it, Moffatt,' said Gillie, with a direct glance at Lan. As he'd expected, she obviously did not agree with her husband, but unlike most wives she was contented to express her disagreement with a smile in which love for him did not aid and abet humiliation. A wife in a million, thought Gillie; and flowerlike though she was, if ardour was needed, he felt sure she had it in plenty.

'And rightly too,' cried Mrs Mossaour. 'A wrong marriage is always hell; here, as Harold indicated, it would be hell within hell.'

Gillie turned his heavy gaze upon her. Frequently her fitness as principal had been debated at meetings of the Board; he had always championed her, on the simple grounds that her qualifications were British. Detractors accused her of being an assiduous disseminator of news never false, but never wholly true; of forming her judgments quickly, delivering with confidence, and thereafter beginning to distrust. They thought her an educator having too many ideas in her head, some alive, some dying, but most of them dead. Challenged once by the American Consul, Chairman of the Board, as to her views on discipline she had flung the gauntlet back at him. No doubt, she had said tartly, he in theory saw love as the perfect guider of children but instinctively felt that strictness was better and in practice, paralysed between theory and instinct, just left the children to grow up according to nature. It had been a devastating reply, much appreciated by Gillie, especially as his brother Consul's own kids, all four of them, were terrors at home and away.

Now, remembering all that, Gillie recalled that she too had married someone of different race and colour. Was she agreeing with Moffatt because both of them were actuated by the same subconscious grudge against Miss Johnstone who was about to do what they themselves had done? They would never acknowledge that they themselves had made a mistake, but there was always a danger that some unfortunate newcomer such as Miss Johnstone would produce a fiasco, giving the world a chance to hoot: 'Told you so!' True enough, Mrs Mossaour and Moffatt were happy in their marriages, at least so far as any outsider knew. It was an interesting human situation, but the Consul decided that he was neither subtle, nor indeed misanthropic, enough to ponder over and analyse it. Kabul, though, was full of people who were.

'Here is Mr Wahab now,' said Lan.

The others came from their thoughts to look toward the gate. A few yards inside it, under an acacia tree in full blossom, a man was standing, with his karakul cap held in his hand as one might carry a nest containing eggs. He wore spectacles; indeed, the sun suddenly glinted on one of the lenses, giving the watchers the impression of the vividest of winks. It was rather a grotesque impression, out of all keeping with the rest of Mr Wahab's appearance, which was of a slightly comic solemnity. He stood, for instance, with his heels together and his toes as far apart as he could get them; it was as if, in a moment, he were about to spring into some ludicrous dance of sorrow, in which the so delicately held woolly cap and the flashing lens would play parts. From that distance it was not possible to make out if, like the majority of Afghan men of his class, he were handsome, in a jejune way, with brown eyes too melting and full lips too slyly sensual.

Mrs Mossaour stood up. 'Mr Wahab?' she cried.

He gave a little bow and came forward. At that moment a

class in the school began to sing a French ditty. The contrast
between its cheeky jauntiness and Wahab's cat-footed caution was so funny that Gillie had to grin. Moffatt, though,
could not help scowling, as if this young man approaching
with such ridiculous decorousness were his enemy. Mrs
Moffatt, on the other hand, smiled in a way so welcoming
that it made not only hers, but the human face in general,
beautiful. Again it crossed Gillie's mind what a damn shame
it was that she had been excluded from the British wives'
sewing circle.

'Please come up, Mr Wahab,' called Mrs Mossaour.

Knees stiff with politeness, he climbed the three steps. He
was handsome enough; a few faint pockmarks in his cheeks
and some blemishes in his teeth were advantageous rather
than otherwise – they gave an unexpected touch of manliness. His eyes were another surprise: brown certainly, but
not melting, not hangdog, not sly, but candid, intelligent,
and plucky. If there were a flicker or two of self-seeking in
them, well, in what eyes, man's, woman's or cat's, were those
not to be seen? Gillie was inclined to approve of him – not
the kind of man one would want one's white-skinned
Westernized daughter to marry of course – but in himself
worthy enough. What Miss Johnstone of Manchester saw in
him was another matter.

Mrs Mossaour introduced them. He did not, like most of
his countrymen, make a fool of himself with a display of self-
effacing ostentation but contented himself with returning
Moffatt's nod and Gillie's with similar brief nods, and Mrs
Moffatt's smile with one as friendly. There was no hand-
shaking, which was really remarkable, since the Afghans
were the most indefatigable handshakers Gillie had ever
known.

Wahab sat down in the chair Mrs Mossaour indicated.
His cap rested on his lap, with his hands lightly upon it. His
brown suit was far from new but well-kept and neat. His

shirt and collar were fresh and clean, his tie not grubby. His shoes had recently been polished. Gillie, connoisseur of dress, judged that Wahab, like most of his contemporaries with Afghan salaries, had to keep himself respectably clothed by a discipline of tidiness. It was a point heavily in his favour.

Mrs Mossaour was explaining why the others were present. 'Mr Gillie, who is the British Consul, is one of the Board of Governors of the school. Mr Moffatt is a teacher of English at the University; he is also an expert on the English educational system. And Mrs Moffatt is one of my most valuable assistants.'

'It does not matter,' he said. His English accent, like his smile, was pleasant. He might have been thinking that they had no damn right to be present at what he'd intended to be a private interview, but it was hard to feel offended. So Gillie at any rate thought.

'You have seen the letter which my fiancée wrote to Mr Lorimer of the U. N. Mission here in Kabul?'

'Yes, I have it here.'

'Mr Lorimer advised me, madam, that you might be able to offer my fiancée more suitable employment. She is a fully trained teacher.'

'Miss Johnstone doesn't seem to have taught for a number of years,' said Moffatt.

'That is so, Mr Moffatt. She has been a civil servant.'

'Does she prefer that to teaching?'

Wahab smiled. 'It is a comparison I have not discussed with her. I think we must have discussed every other subject under the sun, except that. Since we were in Manchester, perhaps I should say, under the rain. But do not misunderstand, please. I liked Manchester very much; I liked every place in your beautiful country that I visited. If it had been possible I should certainly have remained there, though Afghanistan is my native country.'

The others, except Moffatt, smiled with uneasy sympathy. Behind those lightly spoken words had been an anguish.

'Did you,' asked Moffatt, breathing heavily, obviously restraining himself, 'ever discuss the advisability of her coming here?'

Wahab met his gaze. 'Many times, Mr Moffatt.'

'You gave her a truthful picture of the conditions she could expect?'

'You mean, have I told her about our women wearing shaddries, and our little shops, and our earth streets, and the smell of our people in the bazaar?'

'Yes, all those; but something else.'

'What else? She knows we are very poor. I made it clear. It was easy for me, Mr Moffatt, for you see I am myself an example of my country's poverty.'

'What were you in England for, Mr Wahab?' asked Gillie.

'I was doing a post-graduate course in science, sir, to enable me to become a better teacher of the subject to our pupils here. Not only our pockets are poor; our minds are too.'

Gillie nodded.

'Wahab turned to Moffatt. 'What else, Mr Moffatt?'

'Do you know a man called Mohebzada who's a clerk in the Ministry of Works?'

'Mohebzada? I know someone of that name, but he does not work for that Ministry.'

'Has he an English wife?'

'No.'

'The Mohebzada I know has. Yesterday she ran away from home and came to my house for shelter. She was so desperate she spoke about killing herself. She hadn't been treated brutally, by your standards.'

'My standards, Mr Moffatt?'

'I meant the standards of your country. Everything you mentioned, and a lot more, have combined to remove first, every scrap of her self-respect, and then of hope. She's got a baby, which she hates one minute, because it's the symbol of her captivity here, and loves the next because it's hers. There's nothing her husband can do to help her. What she wants is to go back home, taking her baby with her. This, neither he nor the Government will allow. And you know as well as I that Mrs Mohebzada is not the only European woman in that position in Kabul, at this moment. It seems to me, therefore, that we have a duty to any Englishwoman likely to make the same mistake.'

'And what does your duty tell you to do?'

'I can only speak for myself. I think it's my duty to warn Miss Johnstone not to come, to point out to her the example of Mrs Mohebzada.'

Wahab turned to Gillie. 'You are the British official, Mr Gillie. Do you also think it is your duty to warn my fiancée not to come here?'

The big Consul rubbed his chin. 'Of course, like Mr Moffatt, I am concerned about Miss Johnstone.'

'Yes, sir?'

'But whether she comes here or not seems to me her business and yours, not mine. I take it you have also talked it over with her people?'

'She has none, sir. Her parents are dead. She has an aunt, whom she seldom sees; that is all.'

Though interested in this cross-examination of Wahab, Mrs Mossaour felt it her duty, as principal, not to lose sight of the main purpose of his visit. 'Do you happen to have a photograph of Miss Johnstone?' she asked.

'I have a photograph.' That was all he said, and indeed all he seemed willing to say on the subject. He was now showing his agitation, so much so that Gillie hoped he wouldn't start to cry.

'Sometimes an applicant for a post is asked to submit a photograph,' said Mrs Mossaour.

'Yes, yes. I know. But here two matters have become mixed. If you wish to consider my fiancée for a post in the school, I should be very pleased to show you her photograph; but if you wish to see it, to judge of her suitability for marrying me, then I am not willing. It is not that you insult me; it is that you insult her. Please understand I do not wish to be unpleasant. When Laura comes she will need your help. It would be foolish of me to make it difficult for you to give it to her.'

'Do not be afraid of that, Mr Wahab,' said Lan. 'We will help her.'

'Thank you, Mrs Moffatt.'

'And I'd like to make my position clear,' said Gillie. 'I'm not here to sit in judgment upon you and Miss Johnstone. I'm here to help Mrs Mossaour to decide whether Miss Johnstone would be a suitable teacher for the school.'

Moffatt said nothing, though his wife smiled an appeal at him.

'In that case,' murmured Wahab, 'I shall be pleased to show you the photograph.' From his inside pocket he took out a wallet with the name Manchester on it in gilt letters, and the city's coat of arms. His fingers were so nervous that he was more than a minute in finding the photograph. It was passport size. A glance at it seemed to reassure him, for he handed it to Mrs Mossaour confidently and proudly.

'Where do you live, Mr Wahab?' asked Moffatt.

'In Karta Char.'

That was a district where some of the newer houses were as good as Moffatt's own; others, according to Western standards, were slums.

Mrs Mossaour was gazing at the photograph. She could not have explained why she felt disappointed. Perhaps she had been hoping that Miss Johnstone would look so un-prepossessing, so dull and thwarted, that to reject her as a teacher would be a legitimate move in the endeavour to prevent her from coming to Kabul. But no, on the contrary, she was disconcertingly as bright and eager and pretty as Mrs Mossaour herself had been fifteen years ago when as Maud Barndyke she had married Pierre Mossaour despite the opposition of her parents and friends. Yet somehow Mrs Mossaour did not feel like sympathizing with her, not then at any rate; it would take time, privacy, and perhaps tears, for it would mean a review of Mrs Mossaour's own marriage which, happy as most, nevertheless had had and always would have, its peculiar griefs.

She handed the photograph to Lan, without the word of praise that Wahab had been waiting for so hungrily.

Moffatt watched his wife closely. She knew it and glanced up to smile, indicating that whatever her judgment it would mean no disloyalty to him.

'She seems very sure of herself,' she murmured.

Gillie was next. He had expected Miss Johnstone to be not eccentric exactly, but to show signs revealing why, with thousands of eligible young men at home to choose from, she should prefer this dark-skinned enigmatic chap who had had smallpox in his childhood. There were no such signs at all. Miss Johnstone, as Lan had said, was very sure of herself; she held her head high, and her smile was no simper. His test, that of the small close-set eyes of the person who acted with furtive difference from his fellows, she passed easily; her eyes were wide, frank, and particularly well-spaced. She had a well-shaped nose too, not a characterless blob. Altogether, she was the kind of woman at whom in the tube in London he would have glanced at least twice, but might not afterwards have remembered. He did not like to think of her in the same bed as Wahab, but then, as he had admitted, that was none of his business. Going about the world pulling ill-assorted couples out of their beds would be a task for a modern Hercules.

Moffatt accepted the photograph, almost with aversion,

and yet, reflected Gillie, he was supposed to be championing the woman.

'My fiancée wanted us to be married in England,' said Wahab, 'but I said no. It was best for her to come first and see.'

'A sound idea,' agreed Gillie.

Moffatt handed the snapshot to Mrs Mossaour who returned it to Wahab.

'When do you expect her, Mr Wahab?' she asked.

'In about six weeks. Do you think you can give her a position?'

Moffatt interrupted. 'She'll be paying her own fare?'

Gillie grunted in protest, but Moffatt waited pugnaciously for an answer.

Wahab, after a long pause during which he failed to hide his humiliation, whispered: 'Yes.'

'I'm not asking because I want to be rude. The air fare to Kabul is expensive. It's important Miss Johnstone should be able to return if she decides that's what she wants.'

'I agree, Mr Moffatt. I have written that she should buy a return ticket. The money can be refunded afterwards.' He turned to Mrs Mossaour. 'When will you be able to give my fiancée an answer, madam?'

'Very soon, I should say. I must of course discuss it with the Board, but I think it will be all right.'

'She is highly trained.'

'Yes.'

'Will you write to her, madam, or do you wish to leave it to me?'

Mrs Mossaour looked for and caught Moffatt's nod. 'I shall write.'

'Thank you.' Wahab rose. 'You will excuse me, please, if I go now. I have some work to do.'

Again Lan spoke, quietly. 'Mr Wahab, do you at present meet any of the foreign community?'

'I am sorry I do not have the opportunity.'

'But when your fiancée comes, she will associate with them?'

'Yes, of course.'

'Wouldn't it be better then if you started to do so yourself? There is to be a party at the International Club next Wednesday. Many foreigners will be there, including most of the British. My husband and I would be very pleased to see you there as our guest.' She looked at her husband for support.

'Of course,' he said.

Wahab was minded to refuse; he didn't, perhaps because he felt he could not manage the high-mindedness without which his refusal would have sounded like the whine of the humiliated. 'I should be greatly honoured, Mrs Moffatt. It is very kind of you.'

'Please come to our house first and then go with us to the party.'

'I do not wish to make trouble for you.'

'It will be no trouble. I shall come with you to the gate and point out to you where our house lies. It isn't far from here.'

'You are too kind.' Then he took a dignified farewell of each of them.

Gillie jumped up. 'I'm afraid I'll have to be pushing along, too, Mrs Mossaour.'

The three of them went down the steps and along the path.

The two left on the veranda watched them.

'Too smooth by half,' said Mrs Mossaour.

' "My fiancée!" ' whispered Moffatt. 'As if she were property he'd bought.'

Had it really been like that? Mrs Mossaour hadn't thought so, but now, in swift retrospect, she decided it must have been. 'Yes. The trouble was he was acting a role. He's been in England long enough to have a good idea how

we would think a man in his position ought to act; so he tried
to act like that. Not very convincingly, though he did seem
to take in Mr Gillie.'

'Gillie wanted to be taken in. He's satisfied himself that
whatever happens nobody can blame him.'

Again Mrs Mossaour wondered. Had Gillie been so
selfish? He had tried at least to show understanding; in
Mrs Mossaour's view his fault was not selfishness, but
obtuseness. Fifteen years of exile had taught her it was
the characteristic British failing – obtuseness, the centu-
ries-old, irremovable unawareness that other people in other
countries ordered some things better. It flashed through her
mind that even the Afghans might be in one or two respects
superior. Wasn't Moffatt himself fond of praising his students for their courtesy and the peasants for the way in
which, by dignified acceptance of it, they kept their poverty
from degrading them?

In some British people, such as the Wints, the obtuseness
was aggravated by conceit; in Gillie, to be fair, it was
alleviated by his brusque good nature.

'Of course,' she said, laughing, 'we can exclude Lan. With
her it's never a matter of being taken in. Likely she saw
through him further than any of us, but that would seem to
her all the more reason for showing compassion. A person as
good as Lan is really out of the game; or perhaps I should say
she's playing a different game from the rest of us.' All the
same, she wondered what the Moffatts would have to say to
each other next time they were alone. Goodness had the
fatal habit of being obstinate to the last degree. Consider
martyrs. Moffatt was the one who deserved pity. The stake
and faggots for the destruction of his wife would be provided
by him; and yet, according to the ordinary human view, he
would be more or less innocent.

'I'd be obliged for your help in drafting that letter to Miss
Johnstone.'

'You intend to offer her a job?'

'I don't see how I can avoid it. But with the offer can go a list of deterrents as long as you like.'

They watched as Lan came into the compound again, waved to them, called that she must go now to her class, and hurried into the building. Moffatt returned her wave and kept smiling after she had gone.

What was it like, thought Mrs Mossaour, to be married to a paragon? Then, malice having slipped the rein, she found herself hoping that before long Moffatt would be condignly punished for that particular sin, committed every time he met Mrs Mossaour's two children, of showing them a defiant affection, while in his heart he was strengthening his resolve to have none of his own, for fear their yellow skins and dark slant eyes would evoke a similar response.

'I wonder, Harold,' she mused aloud, 'what Britannia and her court would advise.'

That was her name for the Embassy sewing group, presided over by the Ambassador's wife with needle for trident. Mrs Mossaour, amazingly, was one of the court. The invitation had been so long delayed, while her fitness was debated, that she had put off accepting for the same length of time, not so much out of spite as because otherwise the hurt to her pride would have shown itself in an un-diplomatic screech. The meetings were held in the Embassy dining room, hung with portraits of Royalty and ancient Afghan swords and rifles. There, with much fatuous tittle-tattle, nightshirts were fashioned for patients in Kabul's hospital. Several times Mrs Mossaour had hinted that Lan Moffatt, British by marriage, ought to be invited. So stony was the ground that her hints had never even grown into shoots of discussion but had withered immediately. Suppose at the next meeting she put forward the suggestion that if Miss Johnstone became Mrs Wahab, one of the best ways of saving her from Afghan despair would be to let her enjoy the society of the foremost British ladies, engaged in so typical an occupation as sewing for charity and whispering the most cautious of inanities. A stink bomb would hardly cause more elegant disgust than that suggestion.

Moffatt rose. 'Ask them and find out. You'll give Lan a run home as usual?'

'Of course.'

'I think I'll go and seek advice too.'

'From whom?'

'Prince Naim, for one.'

'His views should be interesting. And for another?'

'Josh Bolton. As you know, he's been collecting information about all the cases of Western women married to Afghans.'

'For what purpose, except sensationalism? A less likely Sir Galahad I can't imagine.' Her dislike of Bolton was one of the few things she had in common with the sisterhood of the sewing circle.

'You wouldn't expect to see a modern Sir Galahad clad in shining armour, would you?'

'No, nor with a three days' growth on his face, and an Afghan odour about him.'

Moffatt laughed as he went down the steps. 'How often did Sir Galahad have a bath?'

She sat and watched him walk plumply across the compound. He too, with his woman's bottom, was rather a ridiculous deliverer of fair maidens from Afghan dragons.

Five

JOSH BOLTON called himself the only poor American in Kabul and so his country's best ambassador. Certainly, he could not afford the new Chevrolet and marble-floored house which every one of his compatriots had, paid, so the Afghans cynically whispered, out of money officially designated as 'Aid to Afghanistan'. Bolton lived in Kabul Hotel, where the toilet seldom flushed, the bath was rusted, and the food greasy with germs. When he went visiting, or inquiring, he walked or rode in ghoddies, two-wheeled gaudily painted carts drawn by bony horses. He shaved every second or third day, like the Afghans themselves, and he dressed in loose, vivid shirts and slacks marred by travel.

He was in Afghanistan for a year to write a book. His poverty had turned out to be his best asset, for, fascinated by his uniqueness – a poor American – the Afghans, from servants to cabinet ministers, had been very willing to grant him interviews and load him with information, which was not always quite accurate. Seeing him so earnest and so gullible, they had told him dramatically about events that had never happened, achievements that had never been accomplished, and reforms that had never been contemplated. Particularly was he susceptible to stories about the diabolical influence of the Russians, and it so happened that the Afghan imagination was especially prolific in inventing these; therefore many an interview, conducted in whispers, ended with satisfaction on both sides, even if the amusement was only on one.

He had written two other books, one about Thailand, called *The Sickle and the Poppy*; and another about South Korea, punningly entitled *The Soul of a Nation*. Neither had sold well. Indeed, he had arrived in Kabul with a trunkful of them and had insisted on presenting signed copies to various quarters, including the British Embassy library, where revenge was taken by hiding them away in a cupboard along with a copy of Stalin's speeches, presented by the Russian Embassy. Harold Moffatt had also been a recipient. Liking the author, he had tried to like the books but had found the prose so flat-footed as to make tedious even a description of a Bangkok brothel. Nevertheless he thought that, after Lan, Bolton was the sincerest friend the Afghans had among the foreigners in Kabul.

The melancholy-eyed Italian manager of the hotel met Moffatt in the vestibule and readily gave him permission to use the telephone. All he asked in return was for Moffatt to listen to a further instalment of the tribulations of a hotel manager in Afghanistan. It appeared that two days before he had sacked a waiter for persistent unhygienic practices. 'Some of the things I can't tell you – too horrid! But he licked the butter off the plate, and he didn't wait till he was out of the dining room. So I sacked him at last. I was angry, I tell you. Bugger off, I said, very quick, and damn to you and your friend who is a friend of a friend of a friend of the Minister of Transport, who is chief over all hotels in Afghanistan. So off he went, with a smile like a cat that has stolen the fish. This morning, out of that telephone, whose voice did I hear? You are right; it was the Minister of Transport's, telling me to reinstate the licker of butter. He is reinstated, but I, I am saving up to fly home to Naples.'

During that recital Moffatt had dialled Prince Naim's town house, to be told by a servant there that the Prince was at present living at his country cottage at Istalif, ten miles out of the city. After some hesitation Moffatt telephoned there. Naim, he was informed, was swimming in the pool; no, he had no guests with him; yes, he would be told Moffatt Sahib wished to speak to him. Three or four minutes later Naim was drawling in the Oxford accent he practised so regularly that he spoke Afghan in it too: 'Is that you, Harold old fellow? I thought it must be from Abdullah's description. No, I won't repeat it to you, for it wasn't a bit flattering; your corpulence entered into it. But don't be offended, old chap, he approves of you. Anything on your mind?'

'Yes. I'd like your advice.'

'It's yours for the asking. What's the trouble? Are you writing a new poem?'

'No. I don't think I'd care to discuss it over the telephone.'

'I doubt if you could. I'm amazed that our conversation has survived so far, without some bazaar nafar breaking in to harangue the goomroc about some merchandise they've held in bond for weeks. The wind must be in the right quarter today. Why not take a run out, if you've got time to spare?'

'Thanks. I'd like to. By the way, do you mind if I bring Josh Bolton with me?'

There was a pause. 'Ah, our worthy Herodotus! Yes, by all means. Perhaps I shall have thought up another outlandish anecdote for him to copy into his fat notebook. Lan won't be with you?'

'No, I'm sorry. She's teaching.'

'I too am sorry. Lucky children. Well, Harold, I shall expect you in half an hour.'

Upstairs in his small room with the grubby bedsheets and rusty stove, Bolton was busy typing. Ants kept running across his paper and into his machine; he flicked them away with the patience and compassion of a Buddhist.

'Sure, I'd like to go with you, Harold. Just let me finish this page. The Prince is one of the most interesting guys in the kingdom. He told me the most amazing yarn about a pilgrimage to Ali's two-headed dragon – that's the big rock where there's a spring of natural soda water.'

'Are you putting it in your book?'

'Sure. Like a kind of Moslem Canterbury tale, only a darned sight more fantastic. O. K. That's it done.' He got up and looked at himself in the cracked mirror. 'Hell, I guess it's true; I'm not as particular about my appearance as divers of my admirers think I ought to be, particularly Her Britannic Majesty's Consul in Kabul.'

Moffatt grinned. 'I didn't know Gillie was an admirer of yours.'

'Sure. Was I not at the Garden Party last June?'

'I believe you were.'

'And I shall be again, this June; thanks to the fact that my neck in the intervening months has lost none of its brass.'

'You weren't invited?'

'I was not, despite the risk to Anglo-American solidarity. Be candid, friend. Am I fit to visit a prince?'

'He'll be dressed only in swimming trunks.'

'That gives me an idea. I'll pull on my other pants. I'd shave, if you've got a couple of hours to wait. It would take me all that time to descend to the kitchen for hot water, and I'd need the magic of Orpheus himself.'

As Bolton was taking off the dirty, and putting on the grubby pants, Moffatt said: 'I want to ask the prince's advice.'

'What about?'

'And I want to ask yours. It's about an English girl who's coming here in a few weeks to marry an Afghan.'

'Break her legs first.'

'You think she should be advised not to come?'

'She must be forcibly prevented. See this notebook.

Listen to it. Don't you hear the breaking of hearts? Do you
know that there are Western women here in Kabul who
walk about the streets in shaddries, ghosts indeed, as far as
we are concerned.'

'I had heard there were two or three of them.'

'And did you know that there are some relegated to being
the second or even the third wife?'

'I thought polygamy was a thing of the past.'

'Don't you believe it, friend. It still flourishes. How do I
look?' He had drawn a comb through his gray hair.

'Fine. Let's go.'

The road from Kabul to the beautiful little mountain resort
of Istalif climbed through a dusty, sunny landscape. Some
nomads were seen, tending their sheep and goats. Bolton
said he envied those dark mysterious men, so independent
that their wives could walk through the capital with their
faces bare, while even the queen in her limousine had to have
hers completely veiled. At one point the road was being
repaired by conscript soldiers, men of Mongolian appearance from the north; and at another three men trudged
along, bearded, bare-legged, and bowed under great heaps
of thorn bushes gathered from the desert.

'What are those guys thinking about?' asked Bolton.

'Weariness.'

'That all?'

'And rest.'

'Sure. They look as if they'd dropped from another
planet, yet I guess that's just what they're thinking about:
weariness and rest; and the price their fuel will fetch in the
town; and their chances of getting a ride in a lorry, without
the driver looking for too much baksheesh; and their fa-
milies left behind in the village. Human beings. Men. These
guys will never have heard of Eisenhower or Khrushchev.
That's something now that makes me personally darned

humble, and hopeful too. Yes, sir. We just have got no
conception at all of the extent of responsibility that men
should have for one another. I'm thinking of a millionaire I
once saw, a silver-haired dynamo he thought he was; and I'm
thinking too of those poor guys under those piles of thorn
brush. Now should that comparison make me love God, or
marvel at His notion of justice, or reject Him altogether as a
nuisance?'

'Why not consult Manson Powrie?'

Bolton frowned: Powrie, the minister of the American
Church in Kabul, came calling on him in his hotel bedroom
and, gently brushing ants off his knees, spoke earnestly
about Jesus. 'It doesn't do to laugh at Manson P.,' he said.
'It's more than likely that those three guys we passed know
him. He visits as many villages as he can with his pills and
ointments. I went with him once. His wife Thelma was there
too. You see, the men won't allow him to treat their women,
so he's had to train poor Thelma to do it. It's hell for her, for
she just can't see Christ in syphilitic sores, as he can. I've
seen her turn green because there was a small beetle in her
soup.'

By this time they had turned off the tarred road and were
bumping along an earth track between great fields of vines.
At a corner two boys were standing with bunches of flowers
in their hands; they shouted and waved to them.

Bolton asked Moffatt to stop the car. The bigger of the
boys raced along with bare feet to hand in the bouquet. Bees
came in with it and a lovely fragrance. 'Tashacour,' cried
Bolton, and held out a handful of coins. The boy, tempted,
made as if to accept but pulled back his hand. Bolton
dropped the money into the dust.

As the car drove on they looked back and saw that the
smaller boy was squatting to collect the coins. His shaved
head glittered in the sunlight.

'One of the nicest things about the people of this country,' said Bolton, 'is their love of flowers. See a real tough guy down from the hills, six feet high, with a scowl like a gorilla's, and gun across his back; ten to one he's carrying a rose in his hand and dusting his beak with it.'

'Yes.' Often Moffatt found roses lying on his desk in the morning.

The policeman at the gate scrutinized them, with a yawn. As he waved them on with one hand, the other failed to reach his cap in a salute.

The house, built of stone, overlooked the wide expanse of vines. Behind, the mountain slopes were green with pine trees, out of which rose the blue cupola of a small mosque. Nearer, on an adjacent hill, was a round tower with pointed roof; it was painted red, and hundreds of white doves flew and crooned about it.

Near the house was a small swimming pool lined with blue tiles. Beside it, seated at a table under a large striped awning, was Prince Naim, wearing red swimming trunks. As his visitors approached he rose to welcome them. He was a small, skinny man of about thirty-five, with large nose and prominent teeth. His dark glasses were so large they looked like a disguise. He was not, as Bolton muttered out of the side of his mouth, the handsomest guy in the realm.

'Good afternoon, gentlemen. Welcome to Istalif. Did you bring your swimming trunks?'

'I'm afraid not,' said Moffatt.

'Ah no, you have come on business.'

'Not quite business, Naim.'

'With Mr Bolton now, every glance of his eye, every sniff of his nose, every quiver of his ear, is business. Even when they are sound asleep, I understand, authors are hard at work; problems baffling to them while awake are solved by their subconscious during sleep.'

'I guess I'm not that kind of author, Prince,' said Bolton. 'I'm the donkey kind; it's hard work for me all the time.'

'Please be seated, gentlemen. I am drinking orange squash, as you see, but there is beer for infidels.'

'Beer would be just dandy,' said Bolton.

When it had been brought and tasted, the Prince smiled at Moffatt: 'I'm glad to see you looking so composed. You sounded so upset on the telephone. Lan, I hope, is well?'

'Yes, thanks.'

'Of course since speaking to me you have had the consoling society of Mr Bolton.'

Bolton grinned. 'I guess I've been about as consoling as a cement mixer. I talk too much.'

'And of course when you talk you do not have the opportunity to prune, delete, condense, as you have when you write.'

'Well, to tell you the truth, Prince, that's a thing I can't bear to do. Once it's down on paper I think it's good. Afterwards critics assure me it's long-winded, verbose, repetitious, and tautological; but I just can't see it like that. Maybe I'm scared to admit they're right. You see, if I thought they were, I'd be like the guy in the story who was determined to leave in only what was essential, and so he started to cut out what wasn't. In the end he was left with a blank sheet; even his name seemed superfluous.'

'I like that story, Mr Bolton. The moral seems to be that of the many thousands of books published every year, very few are necessary. That is a comforting thought to me, an Afghan, because I doubt if there is any civilized nation that publishes fewer books than we do.'

'It is kind of disappointing, Prince, that your literature is so sparse.'

'But you are helping to remedy that, Mr Bolton. By the way, have you unearthed any interesting stories recently?'

'I was rather hoping you'd supply me with one, Prince, like the one about that pilgrimage to Ali's two-headed dragon.'

'Yes, that was a strange tale. In your researches into our history, Mr Bolton, I don't suppose you will have heard of Said Hasruddin.'

'Can't say I have. Who was he?'

'Some call him a patriot, others a brigand.'

'What would you call him, Prince?'

'I am biased. You see, his ambition was to seize the throne and, I suppose, cut the throats of all my family.'

'Said Hasruddin? No, can't say I remember the name, though I've read all the history I can lay my hands on.'

'Not much of our history has been translated into English, Mr Bolton. Would you like to hear about this Said Hasruddin?'

'I certainly would.'

'Said Hasruddin was as astute as he was ambitious. He had to get a number of men into Kabul secretly if his coup was going to have any chance. Even if they came in twos and threes they would be suspected. So he had the bright idea of buying up as many shaddries as he could – four or five hundred, I should say – and disguised in these his men began to enter the capital. It is difficult to see how such a ruse could fail. As you know, the shaddry is not only an inviolable garment, it is also voluminous, a shoplifter's boon.'

Bolton laughed. 'That's good. A shoplifter's boon!'

'Under it a man could be armed literally to the teeth. Unluckily – for Hasruddin, I mean – one man passing a policeman let his rifle clatter to the ground. Courteous though our policemen are instructed to be to ladies properly shaddried, this fellow on reflection decided he had grounds for investigating. He did so, and received, I am sorry to say, a dagger wound in his stomach.'

'Did he die?'

'No, he recovered. Well, that was the plot unmasked. For weeks afterwards there were many unfortunate scenes when shaddries were torn off suspicious-looking characters, only to disclose that these were genuinely, though in quite a few cases not meekly, female. Indeed, the confusion and uncertainty were so great and the complaints so numerous, that for a time the shaddry was in danger of being abolished out of hand. You might say, a pity it wasn't.'

'Remarkable,' said Bolton. 'You'd have no objection, Prince, if I printed this story?'

'I should be delighted. Only I should like to offer some advice. Treat the whole affair as humorously as you can. Make a farce of it. Ridicule is the weapon which will in the end rid us of the shaddry.'

'I believe you're right there, sir.'

While Bolton was completing his notes, Naim turned to Moffatt: 'And now, Harold, how can I help you?'

During the hoaxing of Bolton, Moffatt had listened with a smile, and even with an outbreak or two of laughter. Yet most of his mind had been concentrated on something else, by no means funny: Lan's belief that he refused to have children because he would be ashamed of them, half-English, half-Chinese. Mrs Mossaour believed that too. So, he suspected, did Wint. No doubt there were others who talked about it behind his back. But there was one person whose apparent sharing of that belief astonished him: himself. Yes, he believed that he was frustrated by that shame; yet surely it could not be true. It was so absurdly against what he had always professed, and indeed had observed: that the most beautiful and interesting children were of mixed parentage. Besides, such a shame on his part was utterly treacherous to Lan whom he loved; it might even destroy her. Most of his friends would have said too that he was betraying himself. They would have expected him in this matter of Miss Johnstone and Abdul Wahab to take the opposite view, to be favourable rather than antagonistic. Yet as, in as matter-of-fact a voice as he could manage, he explained to the Prince about Mrs Mohebzada and then about Miss

Johnstone, he felt seething deep within him that unreasonable and inexplicable hatred.

'So my own inclination is to warn her not to come here at all,' he said. 'I think most Western people here, especially women, would support me.'

'No doubt about it,' said Bolton.

'But I thought I'd like the opinion of some Afghan who isn't personally involved and is acquainted with both ways of life.'

'Am I not personally involved,' murmured the Prince, 'if the reputation of my country is in question?'

'Yes,' said Moffatt, after a pause. 'I have no right to ask you.'

'On the contrary, Harold. I am deeply interested. This is a matter I have been considering for some time. I mean this comparison between the two ways of life, ours in Afghanistan still so primitive, and yours in the West so advanced and scientific. And I have decided that I much prefer ours. For one reason. Here it is still possible for us to have simplicity in our lives; in the West that is now quite impossible. Yes, we have aeroplanes and also simplicity. I admit that we may in time be so foolish as to throw it away, as you threw it away, but at the moment we still have it, and as a result progress is not for us the dead end that the West now sees it to be. We may be deluding ourselves, but we are still able to dream of achieving industrial advancement and a high standard of living, without necessarily destroying this sense that life is still open, that the simple relationships between people are still green.'

'You've certainly given it a lot of thought, Prince,' said Bolton, but as he spoke he was thinking of the ex-Minister of Finance who, suspected of embezzling government funds, had vanished without a trial. Rumour had it he had been beheaded in a dungeon under the king's own palace. Well, that sure was simplicity.

'I read the Western newspapers and journals,' said Naim, 'and I am constantly appalled by how complicated and yet infantile your society has become.'

'Aren't the terms contradictory, Prince?' asked Bolton.

'I don't think so. You would agree that there is a breast fetish in the West?'

Startled, Bolton nodded and then laughed. 'Guess you could call it that. Put a bare bosom on your dust jacket, and you don't have to worry about your sales.'

'Such a fetish is surely infantile. Yet no one could deny that your civilization is also very complex.'

'I guess I see what you're aiming at. You think you've got a chance here in Afghanistan of acquiring the benefits of materialism without being destroyed in your souls by its evils?'

'Yes, I do.'

'Is it because you think the Moslem religion's a surer safeguard than the Christian has turned out to be?'

'Partly.'

'And the Eastern mind is basically wiser than the Western?'

The Prince smiled. 'I believe so, yes. And of course, Mr Bolton, we have the West's example to profit from. We, so far along the road, can look ahead and take care that what has happened to you does not happen to us.'

'By "you" you mean all undeveloped countries?'

'Certainly. Well, Harold, have I given you your answer? Let me reduce it to personal terms. Do not warn Miss Johnstone not to come. Do not scare her off with tales of stenches in the bazaars and lecherous Moslems who will pinch her behind.'

'I don't think it was the stenches and the nips in the behind that have sent Mrs Mohebzada nearly crazy.'

'Oh, if your Miss Johnstone is like Mrs Mohebzada, a foolish young girl lured by materialistic ambitions, by all means save us from her. But if she is as intelligent and brave as she appears to be, even from your rather prejudiced account, then please, for my country's sake, do not discourage her. Let her come; let her help us to advance and yet preserve our simplicity.'

Bolton was not quite convinced. All right, he thought, all right, Prince; just give us a minute or two to sort this out and apply a few tests. You aren't what I'd call a typical Afghan; you don't really represent. This Abdul Wahab, though, might; he isn't a peasant and he isn't an aristocrat. What green relationship, for example, exists between him and Your Highness, or even between him and those three guys we saw limping along the road, with donkey loads of thorn bushes on their backs? Or between the cops and their suspects in the jails where, so I've heard, the blood's kept on the walls to encourage confessions?

'Of course,' said the Prince, smiling, 'to appreciate the force of what I have said you must love us. Few of our Western guests do; they think we are dishonest, stupid, cruel, untrustworthy; in their history books we are always referred to as "the treacherous Afghans". But this Miss Johnstone, she loves us; or at any rate she loves one of us, which is a beginning. She will therefore see us differently. She may even see the truth of what I have been saying at such thirsty length.'

Laughing, the Prince clapped his hands and ordered the servant hovering by to bring more orange squash and beer.

'I am afraid, Harold,' he said, 'I have disappointed you. But after all is it not consistent to believe that a people which can bear poverty with dignity, as you've so generously claimed for us, can also bear prosperity in the same way?'

'But,' said Moffatt, 'this Wahab is already corrupted. If he could, he would have stayed in England.'

'I can see that a lot depends on our friend Wahab. I must find out what I can about him. You say he's a teacher of science at Isban College? Excellent. What you call corruption may only be his progressive outlook.'

Bolton had now arrived at his conclusions. He tapped his notebook with grimy nail. 'I guess I may have been in too big a hurry over these women. Very likely they did come here with the wrong ideas; they thought they were going to live – if you'll pardon the expression, Prince – like princesses. So they brought their materialism with them, and their closed minds. No wonder the shock's been too much for them. Now this woman who's coming, this Miss Johnstone, she may be different, her mind may be wide open. If it is, then her response could be darned interesting to watch. As a writer I'll be very interested in her reactions.'

'So shall I be, as an Afghan,' murmured Naim.

They waited for Moffatt to speak; but he had been thinking more about himself and Lan than about Wahab and Miss Johnstone. Indeed, he had made a discovery: his own marriage was still an experiment, at least for him. If he were ever to decide it had failed and wished to break with her, Lan would make no fuss.

'I'm afraid,' he said, 'you're both being too optimistic.'

'I am surprised, Harold,' said the Prince, 'that the husband of Lan Moffatt should ever be pessimistic about the future.'

Remembering the many lunches, dinners, and even breakfasts he had enjoyed at her gracious table, Bolton said heartily: 'I couldn't agree more.' All the same, he was thinking, he could never have married her himself; not just because she was Chinese, and to him her race was a greater menace to humanity than Russia even, but also because when he eventually settled down in Vermont, say, or if he were lucky, California, her very presence, however delightful, would make his fireside too exotic and somehow too disturbing.

'Let's change the subject,' suggested Moffatt, smiling.

They noticed how his hand trembled as it picked up the glass of beer.

'By all means,' agreed the Prince. He began to chat about the forthcoming visit to Kabul of Mr Voroshilov, President of the U.S.S.R.

Six

DURING the journey back into Kabul, Bolton delivered what amounted to a monologue. Moffatt had often heard it all before and disagreed with it for reasons inexplicable to the American, who saw everything that the Russians did in Afghanistan as well-planned evil, whereas everything his own people did was mismanaged philanthropy. Besides, Moffatt felt that when he got home that evening the crisis between him and Lan, threatening for months, might break out, not accidentally but provoked by him. Therefore, although so calmly contained, he could not bear the painstaking but commonplace sanity of his companion's views.

So Bolton droned on unheeded about the diabolical astuteness of the Russians in sending to Afghanistan, not professors of morphology and university librarians, as the Americans did, but cloth-capped engineers who worked with their hands alongside Afghans and lived in native villages where the conditions were too primitive for other Europeans. There was, too, the scandal of the bread. Dominating Kabul was the silo, a twelve-story granary built by the Russians, with a bakery attached. From this bakery came supplies of good cheap bread, preferred by many Afghans to the traditional unleavened *nan*, and called by everyone Russian bread. But as often as not the flour used was supplied by America, either as a gift or on generous terms; so with every bite of bread an Afghan took the Russians took a bite out of his mind. The trouble was, Bolton concluded, Americans back home were so pacifically minded that they were not even willing to wage war by unloading their surpluses on the underfed, uncommitted nations like Afghanistan; it could be, too, he conceded, that they were short on compassionate foresight. And now Voroshilov himself, the Russian President, was going to pay a State visit, which of course would be very flattering to such a small, uninfluential country as Afghanistan; a few waves of his soft hat would be worth a million roubles.

Remembering Prince Naim's story about Said Hasruddin's shaddried men, it occurred to Bolton that here was someone's chance to get his name in capital letters into the history books. Why shouldn't that someone be himself? Disguised in a shaddry – how simple to stand near enough to the dignitary to shoot him dead. There were, though, three drawbacks: first, no woman was ever allowed upon the streets during public celebrations; second, Voroshilov was nowadays a mere figurehead; and third, it was very improbable that there would be any history books afterwards. Still, that picture of himself in a shaddry – black would be the most fitting colour – with his small automatic clutched ready, fascinated him. He might not live long after it but what an MGM entry he would make into paradise.

The car stopped outside the hotel. He was disappointed, for he had hoped Moffatt was going to invite him to dinner; but he was fair and supposed he had talked himself out of a good meal.

'Thanks for the ride, Harold,' he said. 'Give Lan my regards.'

Moffatt nodded and drove away.

Bolton rushed upstairs, locked his bedroom door, dragged out from under the bed the suitcase in which he kept the shaddry bought as historical evidence, struggled into this, and then, half blind, stumbled to the chest of drawers for his gun, took it out, and stood crouching in the

centre of the room, in potentiality the most sinister figure
since the history of the world began.

Lan was in the gul-khana, or flower room, working on one
of the designs for the Kabul marble factory. As Moffatt
kissed her he thought that the three Afghan huntsmen in her
painting resembled Wahab. He had not thought that yesterday.

'Mr Najibullah rang me up,' she said, smiling. 'He's very
impatient. According to him the Afghanistan's going to be
the best pavilion at the exhibition, though he did admit,
sadly, that the Russians will have a model of a sputnik in
theirs, and an operating table. By the way, Harold, Mrs
Mossaour has invited us to dinner this evening. I said we
would go. Is that all right? I thought you and she would have
something to discuss.'

That might have been the moment for him to speak, but
he let it pass; perhaps because he felt, from the way she
smiled up from her painting, that she was prepared and
would not submit, despite her love for him. Indeed, perhaps
because of that love she could not. Again he realized that in
her were rarer and more valuable qualities than those he
already loved her for. She was so superior to the members of
the Embassy group from which she had been excluded that
the exclusion was more ridiculous than offensive. But the
exclusion that he himself was inflicting on her all the time
could not be laughed at.

'Were you at the Club?' she asked.

'No. I picked up Josh Bolton, and we went to Istalif.'

'Did you see Prince Naim?'

'Yes, he was there.'

Gazing down at her glossy black hair and at her small
skilful fingers creating the tigers that menaced those Wa-
hab-like huntsmen, he found himself tormented by his love
as by an enemy who knew him profoundly. His weakness

and unworthiness were cruelly revealed. He saw himself as a self-exiled Englishman of thirty-five, proud of principles as fat and out of condition as himself, a writer of verses whose brave irony after a month or two decomposed into clever petulance, an internationalist with a wife five years older whose Chinese loveliness he dreaded to find repeated in his children.

'Was he teasing Josh? I think he makes up silly stories for him.'

'Yes.'

'Josh's book should be very interesting. Of course people will say: this or that isn't true; this wasn't done in Kabul when I was there; and so on. No one's picture can be complete. But Josh's will be charitable.'

'Except to the Russians.'

She smiled. 'It is not even Christian to be charitable to them.' For a few moments she was silent as she painted the tiger's claws.

The gate bell tinkled.

'This will be the young man back again, Harold. I forgot to tell you. He came about an hour ago. It was about his diploma. I'm sorry he's going to be disappointed. He's got such a merry face.'

Rahman's voice too was merry. Shown into the lounge by Sofi, he could not keep from laughing as he apologized for being a trouble. In his brown eyes inquiry was pessimistic, though he was smiling.

'No trouble,' said Moffatt.

'Oh yes, sir. Last time I was a trouble to your wife. Perhaps I ruined her beautiful painting.'

'I don't think you did that.'

'You will not be angry, Mr Moffatt, if I tell you that we all think your wife is beautiful also, like her painting? Two things we say about Mr Moffatt; one is that he is our friend because he understands our position and has sympathy; and

the other is that his wife is very beautiful. She is more than
beautiful, she is good. When I talk to her I feel happy.'

Moffatt took the diploma out of his brief case and handed
it over.

Beaming, Rahman examined it as if for some mystical sign
which would convince the Minister of Education of its true
value.

'I'm afraid the Embassy can do nothing,' said Moffatt.
'They think it is purely an Afghan matter.'

'But this diploma, it is English!'

'Yes. I don't promise anything, but I'll see the Minister. If
it's just a move to save them from paying you the extra salary
you're entitled to, then, as you know, nothing I can say will
change their minds. In that case you'll just have to keep on
applying.'

Rahman shook his head and laughed. 'If I do that I
become a nuisance to His Excellency.'

'In my country, that's the way to get things done.'

'Here, it is not so.' He glanced round and dropped his
voice. 'It says in the official book Afghanistan is a democ-
racy. Of course it is not. If you speak to His Excellency, must
you mention my name?'

'I'll keep it general, if you wish.'

Rahman's smile was at its jolliest. 'And you will keep calm
also, sir? We know that any injustice makes you angry, and
we admire you for it; but here in Afghanistan it is always best
to be polite, whether you are speaking to a Minister or a
peasant. It is perhaps our politeness which has helped to
keep us backward, but it is our way of life.'

Moffatt grinned. Translated, the appeal meant: for God's
sake say nothing to exasperate the Minister, who can dismiss
as well as promote. 'I'll be very discreet.'

'Thank you, sir. Now I shall go and not trouble you
longer.'

'No, sit down. There's something I want to ask you.'

'I shall be delighted to help if I can.'

'Do you know an Abdul Wahab, teacher of science at Isban College, recently returned from England?'

Rahman's smile was suddenly preyed on by fear. 'I know him,' he whispered hoarsely, and again glanced about.

'What's the matter?'

'There is nothing the matter, sir.'

'Is there any mystery about this Wahab?'

Rahman shrugged his shoulders. 'They say he is in trouble.'

'You mean, with the Government?'

Rahman nodded.

'Why? What kind of trouble?'

'You are glad, sir? You do not like him?'

'Why should I be glad? I don't know him. Why is he in trouble?'

'They say he tried to escape. He wished to stay in England. He married a woman there.'

'No, he didn't.'

'That is what they say, sir.'

'Who are "they"?'

Rahman smiled and shook his head. 'Just people in Kabul, sir.'

'Why did he return to Afghanistan?'

'He has parents here, and brothers and sisters. Perhaps it would not have been pleasant for them if he had refused to return. They say he is a strange man. He has abandoned his religion. He does not pray. It is even said that he is a Communist and speaks about revolution.'

Disconcerted, Moffatt remembered the small cautious prim man with the cap held in his hands like a nest or a Koran. 'I don't believe he is a Communist.'

'Perhaps he is not. I do not know. Others have said it.'

'I didn't know there were any Communists here.'

Rahman smiled. 'They do not wave red flags, sir. They would be dragged off and killed.'

'Yet Voroshilov is coming here soon.'

'That is different.'

'Wahab didn't strike me as the kind of man who would risk his life for a cause.'

'I do not know, sir. Perhaps he is a spy.'

'A spy?'

'If a man tells you he is a Communist, he is a spy. Kabul is as full of spies as a Hazara's jacket is full of fleas.'

'He is going to marry an Englishwoman.'

Rahman grinned. 'We say that is the best way to get a wife. You pay nothing. Here in Afghanistan a wife will cost you more than ten years' salary. Do not be offended, sir. It is a joke amongst us.'

'It's not much of a joke.'

'Really it is not. It is very serious.'

'Do you approve of your countrymen marrying women from the West?'

'You do not, sir?'

'I asked you, Abdul Rahman.'

'We are not inferior, sir, though we are backward. We are not like Negroes, though our skins are darker than yours and our eyes are brown.' He turned slyly to glance towards the gul-khana where Lan, whose skin was yellow, sat painting. 'It is possible for an Afghan to love an Englishwoman and wish to marry her. That is possible?'

'Yes. But is it wise?'

'I do not understand, sir.'

'There are Western women at present in Kabul married to Afghans. Most of them are very unhappy. Some are so miserable that they speak of killing themselves.'

'Why is this so, sir? We are not cruel to our wives.'

'You keep them in shaddries.'

'It is not necessary for a Western woman to wear a shaddry. Soon it will be necessary for no woman.'

'It seems to me that what Wahab wants is a woman who

will work to keep him and his family. He's a man I wouldn't trust.'

'He must be very careful, sir. I can tell you everything which is in my mind, for I am a simple man, satisfied if I get the small increase which my diploma entitles me to. It is therefore easy to trust me.'

Moffatt shook his head: this picture of Wahab as an Afghan rebel and probable martyr he just could not accept.

'You do not like him, sir. But please, when you speak to the Minister about my diploma, do not mention Abdul Wahab.'

Moffatt flushed. 'I'm not one of the fleas in the Hazara's jacket.'

But when Rahman left a few minutes later, though he was smiling, he still seemed unconvinced that Moffatt would not, for the Englishwoman's sake, denounce Wahab to the authorities.

As she sat in front of the dressing-table mirror in their bedroom, fixing her long jade earrings with what he thought a provocative fastidiousness, Lan said quietly: 'Harold, I've decided to write to Miss Johnstone myself.'

Seated on the bed at her back, stooping to tie his shoe laces, he now rose, red-faced, with the smell of the shoe polish overwhelming that of her scent. A moment ago he had been thinking of Sofi who had recently confided, with much satisfaction, that in another year he would have saved up enough to buy a wife who would do him credit.

He tried to smile: 'You don't have to do that, Lan. Mrs Mossaour and I were counting on you to collaborate with us.'

'No. I see the whole matter differently.'

Her manner was just too calm, too wise, too sure of itself. Over her shoulder in its green silk dress he stared angrily at her reflection, and read disloyalty in the narrow eyes, arrogance in the high cheek bones, and stubbornness in the small dainty mouth. It was, he told himself, a vision of madness; this stranger he was seeing, hostile and hateful, was not Lan. But it took him a long difficult minute to dispel it. During that minute he heard, his heart crumbling with dismay, the café loudspeaker emit, in a spiral of harsh shrieks, a Persian love song sung by a woman.

She must have noticed the resentment on his face, for she waited until it was gone before turning.

He met her with a puffy flushed grin of appeal. 'This isn't important enough for us to quarrel about, Lan.'

She was so motionless that even her earrings were still. He was reminded of idols he had seen in temples; her strange perfume too helped the recollection.

'After all, Lan, it's bound to be different for me. She's a countrywoman of mine. I can't just sit on my backside and let what's happened to Mrs Mohebzada happen to her, too. You'd be the first to despise me if I did.'

'She is also Mr Gillie's countrywoman. Indeed, it is his official duty to protect her. Yet he does not seem at all appalled by her prospects.'

'Nor is he by what's actually happening to Mrs Mohebzada now. As you say, he has the official mind; that's the way he's trained himself to see people.'

'And how do you see them, Harold?'

He was astonished by the question, as if by an act of treachery. How often for the past three years, in poetry as well as prose, had he poured out to her all his humanitarian ambitions and scruples. Sometimes her appreciation had been short of perfect, but he had been able to respect her reservations. Now, though, he was apparently discovering that she had understood nothing at all and had completely failed to sympathize.

'You don't have to ask that, surely? You know me well enough.'

'Yes, Harold, I think I know you well enough. But I must still repeat my question: How do you see Miss Johnstone?'

He laughed. 'Don't be silly. There's no mystery about this. I see her simply as a gullible, lonely, rather foolish woman, who's deceived herself, or let herself be deceived, into thinking that life in Afghanistan as Wahab's wife will be exciting and romantic.'

'No, Harold. You have not yet seen her as a woman at all.'

He was puzzled. 'You know I've only seen her photograph.'

'I did not mean that. I meant you have not seen her as a woman, as a human being, in your mind.'

Though he knew his position was weaker than he liked, and though he expected Lan to be able to reveal that weakness easily, he was surprised by the apparent lack of perception and unfairness of her accusation. It enabled him to recover some of his dignity and assurance by replying quietly: 'I don't quite know what you mean, Lan. When I think of Miss Johnstone I think of Mrs Mohebzada too, whom I've seen weeping, breaking her heart, in this house. My hand's been wet with her tears. Surely that's real enough?' Yet he had to restrain himself from crying out: 'And let it be enough, Lan, for Christ's sake. Leave it at that. Don't try to dig any deeper. Don't humiliate me. Don't really run the risk of breaking us apart.'

She was watching him with the closeness, he thought, of an enemy. He remembered a remark that Josh Bolton had once mumbled and then in confusion withdrawn: it had been to the effect that, sweet-natured though Lan normally was, he wouldn't like ever to be at her mercy. Moffatt had been angry at what he had taken to be another of Josh's crass anti-Chinese prejudices.

'Why is it, Harold, that your hatred of Mr Wahab is making you so strange that I can scarcely recognize you?

This afternoon at the school I did not know you; I did not want to know you.'

He tried to laugh. 'I don't seem to be the only one who's acting, and talking, strangely. But I don't hate Wahab. I've no reason to. I admit that if it's a case of choosing between him and Miss Johnstone, then I'll certainly choose her. No, far from hating him, I'm sorry for him.'

'Please, Harold.'

He saw that, quiet though her voice was, she was really angry. Her breast rose.

'I am not the only one who was left with the impression that you hated him. Mrs Mossaour and Mr Gillie were too; and so was Mr Wahab himself.'

'Nonsense. Gillie says he's never been able to understand me ever since he tried to read some of my poetry.'

She did not smile back.

'As for Mrs Mossaour, she's never deeply enough interested in anybody to know enough to be surprised whatever any person says or does. If she's ever going to make discoveries about human nature, she'll make them in herself; no other sea is worth voyaging in.'

'She thinks the same about you.'

'I know, but she's wrong. I've got you as my mysterious ocean of discovery, Lan; and this, I must say, is a strange island I've run aground on.'

She looked at the sweat breaking out on his brow and trickling like tears down his cheeks. Love for him stirred in her, but it could not be expressed in the way he wished it.

'I think, Harold,' she said, with characteristic graceful deliberation, 'you see personified in Miss Johnstone and Mr Wahab the mistake you and I made.'

'That's absurd, Lan.' Yet when, laughing, he leaned forward to take her hand he suddenly stopped, with his face turned hard.

'It is not absurd. Please admit that you feel, in your heart, our marriage had been a mistake.'

Though she was wrong, for he had never felt that at all, he still could not deny it as utterly as he wished. He jumped up, clutched his head with his hands, and groaned half-humorously, but there was a noticeable incompleteness in his every gesture.

'You have tried not to show it, Harold, to me or to anyone; but you have shown it.'

'To others?'

'Yes. Your friends know it.'

'Who?'

'Josh Bolton. Prince Naim. Howard Winfield. Alan Wint.'

'Christ, I must have yelled it from the top of the minaret if Wint knows it, whatever it is.'

'He is not the fool people say he is. Sympathy helps him to see.'

'If there's one man's sympathy I can do without, it's Wint's. Though what I need sympathy for I just don't know. It isn't true that I feel our marriage has been a mistake; it just isn't true. I loved you when I married you; I still do, more than ever. All these percipient bastards,' he burst out, 'do they see that too?' He crouched beside her. 'They must, Lan, for the very birds in the garden must see it.'

'It is more important that I know it, my dear.'

'But surely you do!'

'Yes, I do.'

'Then, for God's sake, what's all this about a mistake?'

'You see, Harold my dear, I love you too, very dearly; and yet sometimes I have wondered if our marriage was a mistake.'

'No, no!'

'I wondered again today when you were looking at the

photograph of Mrs Mohebzada's baby, and also when you were talking to Mr Wahab at the school.'

He felt so guilty, he could have struck her for her judicial calmness.

'A year ago you would not have been so rude to him. A year ago you would have looked at the picture of the baby with pleasure, not with loathing.'

'Not loathing, for God's sake.'

'It seemed so to me. In spite of yourself, Harold, you are not the same person now.'

'We all change, Lan.'

'So now, without consulting me, you have imposed a condition on our marriage. I do not think I can accept it. I have tried to, but I have been afraid.'

'Afraid? Of what?'

'Of finding our love for each other turned into contempt. How could it do otherwise if you despised yourself, and I myself?'

He raised his head and met her eyes. 'Many married people never have children, Lan. Yet they don't stop loving each other.'

'It depends on why they do not have them. If it is because they cannot, then it is different; they may love each other all the more. But if it is because they are afraid, then they must surely come to despise each other as well as themselves.'

'Not in our case. Is it so outrageous, after all? You know as well as anyone what a bloody unfair thing life can be to children whose parents are of different races. Why is Mrs Mossaour so bitter?'

'If she is, there must be another reason. Maud loves her children; they are her life; she could not be happy without them.'

'Of course she loves them, but the more she does the bitterer she's bound to feel. She can't help it. Do you think she's not aware that whereas she herself is particularly fair-skinned, they, especially the girl, is almost African dark? Do you know what she once said to me? She said: "My breasts are traitresses. There's a phrase for you to make a poem about."'

'And you made it.'

'Yes, I did.'

'You made it comic.'

'No. Ironic, not comic. Lan, it's a fact of nature. Birds and animals join together to mob to death one that's different from the rest. Human beings are civilized; their killing's more subtly done, and it takes longer. It may take a lifetime, but, Christ, how much crueller it is. You know that's true. Well then, what's so shameful about a couple facing up to the fact boldly, and making up their minds not to provide the bastards with more victims? Yes, it means giving up a kind of happiness that's irreplaceable, but it would also mean avoiding a great deal of the most unbearable kind of suffering.'

'I do not agree,' she said, after a long silence, 'that people are as cruel as you say. The Mossaour children are happy. Other children play with them. There is no mobbing. Their colour makes no difference.'

'Yes, here.'

'We are here, and Miss Johnstone would be here.'

'We can't be here for the rest of our lives.'

'She could be.'

'In her case,' he said stubbornly, 'there's more to it; it's not only difference in colour that makes Mrs Mohebzada's child so unfortunate. But, Lan, none of them is important, while there's this thing between us.'

'I see it represented by them.'

He shook his head angrily. He could not bear having the egregious Miss Johnstone with the starry eyes, and the pockmarked ridiculous Wahab, invade this narrowing circle of anguish in which he and Lan now found themselves imprisoned.

'So, Harold, I am going to write to her, and tell her that if she decides to come to Kabul, she will be welcome to live here as my guest until she has had time to settle down.'

She was like a small Mandarin princess as she sat smiling and waiting, having offered him a condition that he must accept. He felt resentful but fascinated too, and curiously proud. Was she at last going to assume that dominion and authority which up to now her persuasive and mysterious charm had made unnecessary?

'Do you agree, Harold?'

'Am I allowed to disagree? All right. If she does come, I suppose it would be as well to have her where we can see to it that Wahab at least plays fair by her. But I shall still try to dissuade her from coming.'

'He will try to play fair. If he does not succeed, it may be because others have not tried to play fair by him.'

Chief among those others, she implied, might be himself; and her smile, warm with love, was a warning.

So at any rate he interpreted her smile; and his own smile in return, though loving too, had deceit in it. Her remark about playing fair had given him an idea. When he went to see the Minister about Abdul Mir Rahman's diploma, there might well be an opportunity, by a little initial unfairness, to make unnecessary any further display of it. If the Minister could be induced, by whatever argument, to arrange that Miss Johnstone was not to be given a visa, then she would just have to stay at home and Wahab would have to look under some shaddry for a pair of brown eyes to greet him as lord and master. There would still of course be this crisis between himself and Lan to get over, but with the complication of Miss Johnstone removed he would feel much more confident.

It seemed to him that for an instant a look of sad contempt appeared in Lan's eyes, as if she had read his thoughts; and when, the moment after, she took his head between her small cool hands and kissed him on the brow his doubt was turned into a certainty.

'It's time for us to go to Mrs Mossaour's,' she said.

Seven

H.E.'s WIFE, Lady Beauly, at the inaugural meeting of the Sewing Circle, had suggested crisply, as if disagreeing with some previous speaker, though no one else so far had spoken, that in the circumstances, considering the work they were meeting to do – sewing cheap cotton nightshirts for patients in Kabul hospital – for the hour and a half during which the needles would ply distinctions of protocol (a phrase at which she smiled) should be suspended. As no one dared contradict (Mrs Mossaour at that stage had not been invited) the suggestion was accepted in theory, but in practice, as everyone anticipated, it was immediately ignored by H.E.'s wife herself, who could not have presided with greater punctiliousness if she had been wearing her husband's official three-cornered hat. With silver-thimbled finger she would tap on the table if a conversation started of which she could not approve. Of all the reasons for disapproval vulgarity came first, which she would have detected, so Annie Parry said, in a discussion on angels among a group of nuns. Annie, the white-haired mother of Tom Parry, one of the 'junior' staff, was a devout Catholic, but saw no harm in a remark or jest just a little on the blue side, especially when no men were present.

There was, however, a reason for Lady Beauly's hypersensitiveness. Her husband, as everyone knew, liked nothing better after a dinner, in that very room as a matter of fact, than to send the women away and remain behind with the men, each of whom had to sing a verse, while the rest sang the choruses, of songs so rollickingly and inventively filthy as to be unknown outside universities. His wife's prudishness may have been to compensate, but even so it was thought she carried it to eccentric lengths, so that innocent remarks about gallstones or birth or the minaret of the new mosque would quickly find that thimble of silence enfolding them. Discussion of any kind therefore was never easy. As Mrs Mossaour put it in private to Jean Lawson, an atmosphere was created in which everything in that room, from the thimble on one's finger to the shuttle of the sewing machines, became a phallic symbol or practice. Jean, a frank Australian, agreed. Often her husband Bill, a U.N. veterinarian and a fertile mimic, would invent conversation of the most shocking impropriety, using Lady Beauly's primmest voice, or Helen Langford's contemptuous snorts, or even Maud Mossaour's high tones of scorn.

Helen was the Commercial Attaché's wife. Gloved and galoshed, like a grim-faced Ceres, she tended her garden in the Embassy compound and, so Bill Lawson jested, suffered neither worms nor butterflies to make love amid her flowers or roots. Among strangers she and her husband John were civil to each other; when alone, it was rumoured, they were like worms themselves, writhing in an ordained separation.

Paula Wint took the part of head prefect to Lady Beauly's housemistress. There were times, though, when she astonished and displeased her superior by displaying a fierce and tenacious interest in what all the others thought very natural for so healthy and bed-worthy a woman.

Muriel Gillie, on the other hand, never transgressed. To her husband, Bob, she could venture a timid joke, sometimes a little blue, but in the presence of others she had always found demure listening safer.

The remaining diplomatic wife, Sarah Rodgers, custodian of the soul of the Military Attaché and chronicler of his army of model soldiers, would sit and sew and smile with such concentrated vacuity that she often, as Mrs Mossaour put it, brought all their minds out in an itch.

As for Rose Lorimer, wife of Tom Lorimer, Canadian head of the United Nations Mission to Afghanistan, she as often as not played truant. An amateur actress, she thought her best part was that of Lady Macbeth, to whose prowess as a seamstress Shakespeare had made no reference.

Such then was the company, Mrs Lorimer again being absent, that chaste Tuesday afternoon when Mrs Mossaour recklessly decided to resurrect a subject already more than once buried, and to broach a new one altogether; the first was the inviting of Lan Moffatt to the Circle, and the other the proposed coming to Kabul of Miss Laura Johnstone.

'I was looking at Mrs Moffatt's designs for the marble factory,' she began, in her sharpest voice. 'They are beautiful. She is a most talented woman.'

Annie Parry had a painting by Lan in her bedroom. After her jolly knock-kneed son, it was her proudest possession. She, who had had experience of three embassies, never hesitated to give her opinion that natural ladies were as rare as snowballs in hell, but that Lan Moffatt was one. She gave it again.

'A natural lady,' she said, loud enough to be heard at the top of the table.

A glance shot from Lady Beauly to Paula Wint, who, with her fine teeth revealed in an amused smile, cried: 'And how, pray, would you define a natural lady, Mrs Parry?'

'Nothing could be easier. When I just see her I feel good.'

'Such a definition would surely suit a saint better?'

'Well, if anybody's going to call her a saint, I'll not argue, though she is in a way a heathen, I suppose. For instance, here's a marvellous thing: I've never heard her speak ill of anyone. Of anyone!' That little shriek of incredulity at the end sounded spontaneous enough, but was shrewdly managed.

'What designs do you mean, Mrs Mossaour?' asked Lady Beauly.

'For marble table tops, ash trays, screens.'

'Chinese in motif?' asked Mrs Gillie, who painted herself.

'Afghan too. More than any other foreigner I know, she has the feel of this country.'

'That's something I don't envy her,' said Helen Langford.

Mrs Rodgers woke up. 'She's truly Chinese, isn't she? I mean, she was born in Indonesia.'

They waited but she said no more and returned into the asylum of her simper.

'A natural lady,' said Annie Parry, 'could be an Eskimo.'

'If you had told me in Melbourne,' said Jean Lawson, 'that the day would come when I would think the most beautiful woman's face I had ever seen was Chinese, I'd have said you were mad. But Lan's is. Not just pretty, like hundreds of faces; really beautiful, and so rare. I agree with Annie, you feel good just being in the same room with her.'

Lady Beauly showed agitation by snipping a thread with her teeth, instead of the little pair of gold scissors H.E. had given her – as a kind of sceptre, Mrs Mossaour had said.

'Paula, have you anything to add to these eulogies?'

Paula swung out a judgment like a hockey club. 'She's a quaint little thing. Not very robust really, too fragile for my taste.'

'Thank you, Paula. You are beginning to make her recognizable, human like the rest of us.'

'Why I introduced Mrs Moffatt's name,' said Mrs Mossaour, 'was to suggest that, since she's British, it might be a kindness if we were to invite her to join us. Most of us like her. We visit her house and she visits ours. Moreover, she sews beautifully.'

They waited for Lady Beauly to speak. First, she blushed and was annoyed.

'Utility is what we seek to achieve,' she said, 'not beauty,

I'm afraid. As to your proposal, I'm afraid it cannot be discussed again.'

'May I ask why?'

'No, Mrs Mossaour, you may not. But I shall tell you this much: the decision is not only mine, and it is irrevocable.'

As she spoke she looked round them all, trying to look as benign as a schoolmistress without a shadow of doubt that the children trained by her would understand the necessity for a regulation that, to ignorant outsiders, might appear a trifle harsh.

Only Paula could manage the jolly grin called for.

Annie Parry let her fingers go on strike for fully a minute.

Muriel Gillie, kindhearted, clung to her husband's precept: 'Muriel, not your business!'

Jean Lawson recalled a description Bill had given her two days ago of an Afghan burial he had seen in a poor village. She did not know why it should have come into her mind just then, except that at the time she had felt a great sadness for the body of the young wife lowered, uncoffined, into the shallow grave on the hillside.

'I would like to say,' said Mrs Mossaour, 'that I very much regret that decision.'

Lady Beauly's fair lashes fluttered. Her mouth, so resolutely lipsticked, could not quite hold its confident smile.

'I understand,' said Paula heartily, 'that this barbecue dinner at the International Club is going to be a really tremendous affair. Everybody seems to be going. I forget how many sheep they're going to roast as kebab.'

'If there is no objection,' said Mrs Mossaour, 'there is another matter I would like to raise. It concerns us, as British women.'

Annie Parry, who thought there was a place for nuisances like Mrs Mossaour, gave her a wink; such a place, for instance, was any embassy where H.E. was not a bachelor.

'I was under the impression,' said Paula, laughing, 'that *I* had raised another matter too.'

Mrs Mossaour refused to apologize or yield. She was, thought Annie Parry in admiration, working for her ticket.

'I think,' said the schoolmistress, 'this concerns us more deeply than a barbecue dance.'

'I do not think,' murmured Lady Beauly, 'that this is either the time or place to discuss anything that concerns us deeply.'

'Mrs Gillie may know about it.'

'Me?' bleated Muriel. 'I assure you I do not, whatever it is.'

'I thought your husband might have mentioned it to you.'

'If it is official business, he certainly would not. I prefer it that way.'

'I prefer not to call this official business. It is not a matter of papers to be read and signed. It concerns a woman.'

'What woman, Maud?' asked Jean Lawson.

The thimble was hopping half-heartedly on the table.

'A Miss Laura Johnstone, from Manchester.'

'Never heard of her,' said Annie Parry, 'and I thought I knew every white woman in Kabul.'

'But is she white?' asked Paula with a brilliant smile. She too was defying the thimble. 'You can never tell nowadays from a name.'

Mrs Mossaour's daughter, Madeleine, would look often enough at a pretty face in a mirror, but never at a white one. Mrs Mossaour's own grew whiter. She tried on Paula a Medusa look.

'Yes, she is white,' she said. 'She is an Englishwoman, who has written to ask me if I can give her a post in the school.'

'Is she a trained teacher?' asked Jean.

'Yes, and a university graduate.'

'You could be doing with her, then.'

'Yes, Jean, I could. But there is an objection, or at any rate it appears to me an objection. Her primary purpose in coming to Kabul is not to teach in my school.'

They waited, and she let them wait.

'Well, what is it she's really coming for?' asked Jean.

'To get married.'

It was Annie Parry who first saw what was wrong with that. 'Not to an Afghan, surely to God?' she cried.

Mrs Mossaour nodded.

'The silly fool,' whispered Helen Langford.

Mrs Rodgers tutted.

'Someone else been reading the *Arabian Nights*!' cried Paula.

'For heaven's sake,' said Jean, with some sympathy and much impatience.

'It isn't right, I agree,' whispered Muriel, shaking her gray head.

But each of them too, in her own way, was thinking that Pierre Mossaour, charming man though he was, was dark skinned, more so indeed than many Afghans, some of whom were lighter in complexion than Italians or Spaniards. Hence the disconcerting duskiness of the Mossaour children.

She knew what they were thinking and met each one's eyes in turn. Only Annie Parry and Paula, for different reasons, did not glance away.

'Well, of course,' cried Paula, 'to be realistic about it, only one thing could make it tolerable.'

'And what might that be?' asked Mrs Mossaour.

'If he's rich!'

'Not even that,' said Annie. 'Look at Gerd Najib. He's rich enough, or at least his father is.'

'There's a difference,' pointed out Paula.

'Even the queen's got to drive about in a shaddry,' said Annie. 'I hope I've got as few prejudices as most, but I'm convinced these Afghans haven't yet learned how to treat a woman. Until they do, my advice to this Miss Johnstone, as it was to poor Liz Mohebzada, is to keep well away from them. Of course in Liz's case it was too late; she was already married by then, and pregnant into the bargain. A nail, you might say, through each hand.'

'The man in question is not rich,' said Mrs Mossaour. 'On the contrary, he's a teacher in Isban College.'

'Where he'll be lucky to get eight pounds a month,' said Jean Lawson.

'Have you met him, Maud?' asked Annie.

'I have. Once. He called at the school. Mr Gillie was there too. So were the Moffatts.'

'Now I remember,' said Paula, still defying the thimble. 'Alan said something about this, a few days ago. I'm afraid I didn't listen very attentively, but I did gather that Harold Moffatt felt pretty strongly about it.'

'It is my opinion,' said Lady Beauly, at last, 'that we have no right to be discussing this here.' It was wrong, but she could not resist adding: 'Certainly we have no right to interfere.'

'No legal right, of course,' said Mrs Mossaour.

'And no moral right, either. This kind of thing is happening every day, all over the world. Every consulate in Middle East and African countries has similar stories to tell. The official opinion, arrived at after much experience, is that the wisest course is simply not to interfere. One's instinct may be all for warning the wretched girl; but one has another instinct that warns one that she will more probably than not interpret your well-intentioned warning as unwarranted interference. I take it, this particular girl will have parents who will already have tried all the dissuasion there is.'

'Miss Johnstone's parents are both dead.'

'Relatives, then. Or friends. Or acquaintances. Or even colleagues.'

'Into none of which categories,' said Helen Langford grimly, 'does any of us come.'

'We come into the category of her countrywomen,' said Mrs Mossaour.

'Rather a large category, Maud,' said Paula Wint. 'At least fifteen million, I should think.'

'There is a larger category into which we also come. Nearly a billion, or thereabouts. She is a woman; so are we.'

Muriel Gillie saw a chance here to change the subject gracefully. 'And nearly a third of them Chinese,' she said. 'Bob often says they are bound to dominate the future by sheer mass of numbers. I know they have been misbehaving of late, but he says that one point in their favour as a nation is the respect they have always shown to the beauty of dress. We must agree, for instance, that Mrs Moffatt dresses beautifully.'

'Today they all wear blue boiler suits,' said Jean Lawson.

'True, Jean, but Bob maintains that if a man has the right attitude to dress he can wear even a boiler suit with more dignity than some other man can wear a dinner suit complete with decorations.'

It was, to their astonishment, Sarah Rodgers who recalled them to the subject of Miss Johnstone.

'What have you done about her, Maud?' she asked.

'I have written and offered her a post.'

'Isn't that tantamount to inviting her to come here?' asked Jean.

'I have also given her a very frank picture of the situation in which any Western woman who marries an Afghan must find herself.'

'I hope you didn't forget to warn her that if she ever has a child she'll never be able to take it out of the country.' It was Annie who asked that, thinking of Mrs Mohebzada.

'Everything pertinent was told her.'

'Nothing could be more pertinent than that.'

'It was underlined, Annie. Mrs Mohebzada's example was quoted.'

'What age is Miss Johnstone?' asked Paula. 'Or didn't she say, being a coy spinster?'

'She is thirty-three.'

'Well, for goodness' sake, she's surely old enough to know her own mind. There may have been an excuse for Mrs Mohebzada. She was too young to have any sense but this woman, thirty-three and a university graduate – I would say she's had plenty of time to think the thing out. Besides, I really can't see that it's any of my business. If she were at home in Manchester and I in Lymington, I would never dream of trying to interfere. That I happen to be in Kabul and she's coming here really makes no difference. Mind you, if she were to ask me for help and advice, I'd be glad to do what I could. Otherwise I'm afraid I'm just not interested.'

'I am interested,' whispered Mrs Gillie, 'but I agree. There's really nothing we can do. After all, as Annie has said, there was precious little we could do for Mrs Mohebzada; indeed, what can we do for her even now?'

'Her case,' said Lady Beauly, 'is being discussed at the policy meeting tomorrow. I think that being so we need not discuss it here any longer.'

'I was not discussing Mrs Mohebzada's case,' pointed out Mrs Mossaour. 'I was discussing Miss Johnstone's.'

'Yes, and I would like it ended.'

'A woman's whole happiness—'

'Mrs Mossaour, please.'

That Mrs Mossaour contained her rage was marvellous; it extended in her as fierce, barren, and illimitable as the Sahara. Tears came to her eyes; to hide them she bent her head to sew savagely. Then she thought of one of Harold Moffatt's poems, and felt consoled.

In it a young man, a diplomat of some kind, though his nationality was obscure like much else about him, advanced with slow, curious dignity into an immense, empty marble hall hung with paintings that seemed to represent history, and pillared with enormous, sculptured columns. When he had found the exact centre, he had stood staring about him, like someone about to be sacrificed, and then, without raising his voice he remarked: 'Go and b— yourselves!'

Previously, like others, she had thought the poem obscure and vulgar; now she saw its point.

Eight

THE policy meeting was almost over. The last item, the case of Mrs Mohebzada, had just been dismissed by Sir Gervase with the observation that, in the struggle for the mind of an uncommitted country like Afghanistan, Britain's role, as former would-be conqueror and present unwilling lender, was difficult enough.

'I'm afraid,' he said, picking up his pipe, 'the girl's made her bed – or should I say charpoy? – and she's just got to lie on it. Dammit, at home there are any number of women leading miserable lives, married to the wrong men.' And not only at home, he could have added. There was Helen Langford, for instance, living less than a hundred yards away in a large house surrounded with rose beds. 'Of course it's open to any of us to give what help we can as individuals, always bearing in mind we do nothing to offend the susceptibilities of the authorities here, who in a matter like this are liable to be, not the legs of the snail, but its horns.'

He had now filled his pipe and was pushing at the matchbox, trying to take out a match with one hand. With the first puff, the meeting would be over; gossip and bawdry might take its place.

Both Alan Wint and Bob Gillie did not want it to be over just yet. Each had a matter he wanted discussed. Alan had decided his not important enough to go down on the agenda, but at the same time not trivial enough to be altogether ignored.

Gillie got in first. 'There's one thing, sir.' He spoke

gruffly. Yet he was dressed with his usual suavity, and had a fresh red rose in his lapel. Sweat, profuse as dew, beaded his big brow. Outside the noon sun was bright and warm.

'Yes, Bob?' The match, lit, hovered over the pipe, happy as a firefly.

'It's about this cigarette pack.' The words shot out, as if to match the speed with which he produced the pack from his pocket. He thumped it down on the table.

On the table, too, but gently, was placed the pipe. The match, blown out, was carefully dropped into the ash tray.

Howard Winfield, always a little ahead in everything, had a cigarette already lit. Now, his brows up, he stubbed it out.

Colonel Rodgers, chin supported by hand with elbows on table, moved dramatically to his other elbow. It was his favourite sign of interest and was usually followed by a contribution of painstaking fatuity.

John Langford, his thin dark face gloomy, wished to Christ he could have a drink. To hell with Gillie for prolonging this weekly farce. The trouble with Gillie was he had a crass mind, costive with conscientiousness – so much so that he went about calling his marriage to his mouse Muriel happy and successful. Whatever success in marriage was, it certainly wasn't represented there. Where then in Kabul? Not by Alan and his Paula with her bar girl's bum. Nor by Bruce and his simpering Sarah who made love, he was sure, in curlers. Nor in the Big House, despite the rumour that another little ambassadorling was on the way. Perhaps by Harold Moffatt and Lan.

Meanwhile Gillie had been waiting, not so much for permission to proceed, as for the moment when saliva would be bitterest in his mouth – or so his expression indicated.

'What about it?' asked H.E.

'You sent it to me, sir, with a note attached, to the effect that it had been found in your flower bed.'

'I did.'

'I'm afraid, sir, I wasn't quite sure what I was supposed to do with it.'

'I see.' Sir Gervase looked round at them all. 'Did you seek advice?'

The First Secretary glanced sternly up. 'I was consulted, sir. I suggested to Bob that obviously you intended him to find out who had been using your flower bed as a little bin.'

'And you, Howard, what did you suggest?'

'Well, sir, I believed I said you may have meant it as a kind of intelligence test.'

'Everything I send down to the Chancery could of course be so regarded. In what particular way did you think this was such a test?'

Howard reached forward and started to pick up the pack, to examine it; but Gillie snatched it away from him. Howard's hand was much amused by its rebuff.

'I believe I mentioned Freud, sir, but to be candid I don't quite remember how I put it.'

H.E. grinned. He liked Howard and appreciated Freudian witticisms.

'If I may butt in, sir,' said the Colonel, 'I've been passing the word around among those who have American friends, and also among the Americans themselves, to be a bit more considerate where they drop their empty cigarette packs.'

'And what about you, John? Have you exerted your wisdom upon the mystery?'

'Only to the extent, sir, of comparing the prices of American cigarettes with British.'

'I see. The commercial aspect?'

'Yes, sir.'

Gillie then spoke, with some difficulty; rage stuck in his throat. Veins stood out under his eyes. 'It happened to come, sir, when I was overwhelmed by work.'

A little pink with suppressed annoyance, H.E. said: 'Yes?'

'So I'm afraid I've not been able to do anything about it.'

'That's not quite so, Bob,' said Alan Wint anxiously. 'You've been round the staff, you've made inquiries, you've made it clear to everyone that that sort of thing mustn't happen again.'

'I have done nothing of the sort. I have made myself a laughing-stock; that is all. I want to know, sir, what precisely I was supposed to do about it. If it was intended as a joke, very well, I shall laugh with the rest; but if it wasn't, then obviously I'm too obtuse for my job. That's what it amounts to.'

Then red-faced as his rose, he sat scowling, with his big fist sprawling like a spider over the cigarette pack.

Silly bastard, thought Langford, in sullen sympathy: this isn't just costiveness of intellect, this is complete stoppage. Muriel's haverings these days are said to be menopausic in origin. Can a dutiful husband be affected too?

The Colonel narrowed his eyes shrewdly, to discover when they were almost closed that he didn't know why he had done it.

Wint was swiftly examining his own position and rushing up reinforcements of arguments where he felt it to be weak. As always, during a crisis, he felt his bowels ache in gratitude that he had Paula to run to soon and make consoling love to.

Howard Winfield grinned behind his face. It was his opinion that the matter was trival, and he was determined to treat it as such. It was also his opinion, derived from a study of history, that kings, dictators, prime ministers, and generals had often behaved in a childish manner. Therefore he was not surprised that an ambassador and a consul should do so too; indeed he was moved by it a little, for if it did not excuse his own incorrigible childishness, it at least made it less remarkable.

'You see, sir,' said Gillie, 'I am well aware that I am not given the credit of being as quick-witted as others.'

H.E. decided to adopt a kindly tone. 'I think, Bob,' he

said, 'you and I had better discuss this in private. In front of the others I shall say this, though: I'm sorry you've taken my little jeux d'esprit in this way. When I saw that damn thing among my flowers, I felt really annoyed. Why? Because it seemed to me to symbolize an indifference to what's beautiful, what's dignified, and what's worthy of respect.'

In other words, they saw now, it was a symbol of his anti-Americanism.

There was a silence, neither deep nor wide, but enough for so astute a diplomatic swimmer as Alan Wint to slip in quietly.

'Something I ought to mention, sir,' he said, 'if I may?'

'You may not, if it's still about this.'

'Oh no, sir. Not at all. Something altogether different. Moffatt came up to see me about it.'

H.E. frowned. He was thought not to approve of Harold Moffatt, who had, besides, American friends.

'I might have mentioned it while Mrs Mohebzada was under discussion, but I didn't want to confuse the issue. It appears that another Englishwoman, a Miss Johnstone from Manchester, is coming out here to Kabul, with the intention of marrying an Afghan.'

H.E. toyed with his pipe on the table. He had already heard of this Miss Johnstone; indeed, she had been in bed with him and his wife last night. He had been given instructions about her. The circumstances had been such, though, that he was now hazy as to what he had promised.

'Well?' he demanded.

'The point is, sir, very briefly: should we do anything, in an official way, to dissuade her from coming?'

'What in particular have you in mind?'

'Nothing really, sir. Except that I thought of asking Pierce-Smith to see her in London and make sure at least she's got no illusions about the kind of life in front of her if she does marry an Afghan here. You see, sir, it might well develop into another Mohebzada case. This man she's proposing to marry, Abdul Wahab's his name, isn't any better off than Mohebzada. I wouldn't be surprised if he's turned her head with tales of his wealth and importance. In point of fact, he's a teacher of science at Isban College, with eight pounds or so a month. Moreover, he has his family to help to support. I may say Moffatt was quite upset about it.'

'Why?' asked H.E.

Alan was about to answer confidently when he suddenly stopped and let a few words of hesitation dribble from his lips. For the first time he was considering Moffatt's motives, and he could not be sure what they were. Simple compassion was hardly enough as an explanation. In spite of his fat bonhomie Harold Moffatt was a complex fellow, full of twists and complications; and of course being married to a Chinese woman, however charming, must surely contribute to any man's eccentricity.

'He doesn't know the girl, does he?' asked H.E. testily.

'No, sir.'

'Well, what's his interest?'

'I'm afraid I couldn't say, sir.'

'I think I could,' said Langford. 'He's a good sort. His heart's in the right place.'

'I think I agree with that,' said the Colonel. 'I know he writes poetry. There was one that might have been about me; he got it into that rag, the *New Statesman*, too. Rubbish about toy soldiers. But apart from that he's quite a decent type.'

H.E. turned to Howard, whose judgment he trusted. 'What's your opinion?'

'Of Harold Moffatt, sir?'

'Yes.'

'I'd rather not say, sir.'

'Why not?'

'I don't think I understand him well enough.'

'You're surely being very coy?'

'No, sir. Just careful. I really don't understand him. This woman who's coming may be associated in some way in his mind with his wife.'

'She's Chinese, isn't she?'

'Yes, sir.'

'An admirable race in many respects, but I'm damned if I would ever have married one of them.' He remembered a joke about Chinese women and grinned.

'In any case, sir,' said Wint, 'he was really furious when I refused to promise to take any official action to prevent her from coming. It's common knowledge of course that he thinks diplomats are ineffective creatures.'

H.E. grunted.

'I'm afraid so, sir. He boasts he does more for British goodwill than the whole Embassy combined.'

'Infernal impertinence! I take it he thinks the Afghans would be flattered to be informed that marriage to one of them is a fate worse than death for a schoolmam from Manchester?'

'The curious thing is' said Wint, 'he's always praising them, the Afghans, I mean.'

'Don't expect consistency from a fellow that dabbles in poetry,' remarked the Colonel wisely.

'You're all missing the point,' said Gillie ponderously.

All were astonished. H.E. in addition was indignant.

Even Wint, eager to rescue the Consul from his own savage ill-humour, could find nothing to say; true, he was also busy examining his own position. After all, to be charged with irrelevance was a bit much when his every remark had been a model not only of tact, and helpfulness, but of aptness too. In the nursery, at school, University, and all during his career, he had made a point of keeping to the point, no matter what seductions had tried to lure him away. As a consequence he had earned himself nicknames, and had left shoals of exasperated infants, schoolmates, fellow students, colleagues, and especially subordinates, in his wake.

'Is there a point, old man?' asked the Colonel affably. 'I mean, it's jolly simple. Here's a silly female going to sacrifice herself on the altar of romance, or some nonsense like that, and here's Moffatt, not to mention the rest of us, damned sorry to see her do it. And all the sorrier, you might say, because there's really nothing we can do.'

'As far as Moffatt is concerned,' said Gillie, 'there's a lot more to it.'

'What d'you mean?' asked Langford.

'I shall tell you what I mean.' Gillie picked up the carton and held it at his chest, as if it was a microphone. 'I have met this Abdul Wahab. In my capacity as Consul, I was invited by Mrs Mossaour to meet him one afternoon when he visited the school to discuss the possibility of his fiancée's – he called her that – getting a post there. I may say I thought him, for an Afghan, pleasant enough and possessed of some dignity; but if you were to ask me if I would consider him a fit husband for my daughter, if I had one of marriageable age, I should without hesitation answer in the negative. I have ordinary instincts in such matters. But that is by the way. What really interested me was Moffatt's reaction, not so much to this Wahab fellow in himself, as to Wahab championed by Mrs Moffatt. For she went out of her way to take Wahab's part, even when she saw how opposed her husband was to him. It was not a very wifely thing to do and left him exposed in a way I would not have thought possible with so astute a man. I saw very clearly that the reason why he is so opposed to this marriage is because it would reveal his own as the miscegenation that he undoubtedly thinks it is. I am expressing no opinion of my own or adopting any attitude; I am merely describing what I saw revealed in his mind. If you were to suggest that my perception may have been sharpened by his rather obvious scorn of my personal obtuseness – in which he was partnered by Mrs Mossaour – then I would not deny it. I have noticed this before in those intellectuals: they work out their racial broadmindedness as if it were a Euclidean proposition. It is not really in their natures, for after all do they not despise the rest of us who never read Proust, who consider Picasso a charlatan, and who prefer Edward German to Bach? They are by nature narrow-minded, but until they are touched personally they are able to keep up their sham of a breadth of outlook of sympathy. Moffatt, by his marriage, is touched personally. I know what some of you are inclined to tell me, that Moffatt loves his wife and is loved in return by her and so, consequently, their marriage is a happy one. That is what I believed myself before I saw him exposed, as I say, by what he regarded as her treachery. I do not say he hated her at that moment, but I do say that he hated the idea of her. She was, as I have since reflected, a poem which had gone wrong, which could never be finished and which represented the falseness of so many of his previous high-minded declarations. I used to think that was as happy and successful a marriage as I had ever seen, despite its superficial unlikeliness, but now, now I would not give an empty cigarette pack for its chances of survival.'

Perhaps the fascination of that speech was best shown by the Ambassador's removing of his eyeglass during it, and his inability thereafter to screw it back into place again.

Wint too paid it open-mouthed homage; from beginning to end it was the most remarkable exhibition of culpable obtuseness that he had ever listened to.

Its effect on Howard Winfield was quite contrary. He realized that that devastating conclusion had been planned right from the outset, in the dark cavern of Gillie's brain, and so revealed there a cleverness and resource that he had never dreamed existed. Therefore, for the rest of his life, he was to look upon pompous fools with warier eyes.

John Langford, impressed, saw it as a confession that marriage to Muriel was hell too, as marriage to Helen was. Marriage to Lan Moffatt seemed to him to have nothing to do with it, except perhaps by provoking, with its happiness, this revelation of poor Gillie's misery.

Only the Colonel had anything to say: 'Well, by Jove, Bob, all I can say is, you certainly took a jolly deep look at him.'

Nine

MOFFATT's appointment with the Minister of Education was at three. Usually at quarter to three Lan left the house to stroll across the park to the afternoon session at the school. Though it would have been easy for him to take a route close to the school, he did not offer to give her a lift. If he had, he told himself, she would not have accepted; she liked her solitary walk among the flowers and praying men.

That afternoon she was wearing European dress. At no time did he think this became her, but then in particular it did what two weeks ago he would have thought impossible: it made her look squat, coarse, unintelligent, and even shifty. As he furtively watched her get ready to leave, he was well aware that, in some sort of revenge, he was betraying her, not only by his intention of discussing Wahab with the Minister, but far more by this systematic exclusion and denigration which he had begun and could not stop. That she was as cheerful as ever, as she gave Sofi and Abdul their instructions, and that they laughed merrily at her shrewd Persian, served only to accentuate the isolation into which he was deliberately forcing her. If she was aware of any peculiarity in his attitude to her, she gave no sign of it, but at last, carrying her books in a yellow straw basket, she kissed him as trustfully as ever and set off, with a white rose in her hair.

He meant to stay in the house but could not and hurried out on to the terrace to watch Sofi unlock the gate to let her out. She turned and waved; he did not wave back. For a

moment she stood still, as if her very heart were still, and
then, with a last friendly remark to Sofi, she crossed the road
into the park.

That refusal to wave back had been, he realized, the first
open sign of the breaking up of their marriage. Now, trying
to imagine what life without her would be for him, and also
what without him it would be for her, he walked about on
the terrace among the pots of blood-red geraniums, as
agitated as any of the ants whose labours his feet kept
interrupting or destroying. He knew that if he looked for
her in the park he would not yet be able to see her as she
wouldn't have advanced far enough into it. Every second he
waited was a separate agony.

At last he swung round and looked. When he could not at
first see her an instant and shattering pang of fear smote
him; it was as if he knew he had killed her and yet expected
her still to be alive whenever he wanted her to be. He
muttered her name aloud and had to restrain himself from
shouting it. Then he saw her, not on her usual path, but on
one that twisted under some tall shady trees, as if she
understood the need to hide from him.

His fear grew more painful and urgent. Most of the time
he could not see her. She seemed to be walking very slowly,
as if she had divined his betrayal and, with her usual calm
courage, was thinking what to do about it. He wanted to run
after her shouting reassurances; but he knew that if he did so
and came upon her so small and resolute under the trees, he
would not be able soon enough to find anything to say that
would reassure either himself or her. Even if he were to
gasp: 'Oh Lan, to hell with this Miss Johnstone and her
Wahab. What have they got to do with us? What matters is
that we love each other,' it would not do. It was their love
itself which, in him at any rate, was creating this strain that
must soon break them irrevocably apart; and he did not
know what could ease it. Not surely the success of his efforts

to prevent Miss Johnstone from marrying Wahab. No, but if those efforts involved him in degradation which Lan was willing to share with him, perhaps they might be able to keep going, having made the necessary adjustments to the world's level.

Then she came out from under the trees and walked in the bright sunshine among the flower beds. Beyond her were the khaki-coloured mud-brick buildings of the town, and in the distance the high vague mountains. An aeroplane, from Delhi he thought, came roaring overhead, turning to land at the aerodrome. Its pilot, Captain Mabie, an Indian, was a friend of his and Lan's. Sometimes he would bring his silvery Dakota swooping over the house to let them know he was back, bringing perhaps a bunch of bananas as a present. Mabie was a mixture of irresponsible hilarity and conscientious solemnity. His fiancée waited in Calcutta until he could make up his mind to marry her; but he could never do that, he had told Moffatt and Lan many times, until the astrologer in his village at home declared that the time was auspicious; twice already a time, provisionally approved, had turned out days before not to be auspicious after all. He had shown them her photograph. She was years younger than he and very beautiful. Moffatt had thought then that it might be better for her if the stars remained adverse; now, gazing up at the plane, and knowing that Lan would be gazing up at it too with similar thoughts, he felt a sense of involvement like a sentence of doom. Laura Johnstone too, when she came by aeroplane across the mountains, would find her place here waiting for her. If she did not come, perhaps they could all escape.

Lan had stopped and was chatting with some Afghan children in their brightly coloured pyjamas. He watched for a few moments and then hurried into the house where every article of furniture, because of its association with her, increased his confusion and anguish.

*   *   *

He drove slowly on his way to the Ministry and chose the wide, tree-lined avenue that took him past the Chinese Embassy. Its diplomats never mixed socially with the rest of the foreign community, and of course from its official functions the representatives of most other countries, following the lead of America, stayed away. He and Lan were always invited, and always went. Lan refused to call herself a Communist, but considered the capital of her country to be Peking. Moffatt had enjoyed those occasions and he had been pleased that Lan was given the chance to meet, even if only at official level, some of her country-women, and speak with them in her native language. Now as he drove past the gate, with the Afghan policeman yawning outside his little striped box, he recalled those conversations and realized how inadequate they must have been to a woman so spontaneously friendly as Lan. Yet their polite exclusion of her would not hurt her nearly so much as the one he himself was deliberately imposing on her. The price of their admitting her as one of themselves would merely mean her surrender to their ideological beliefs; the price he was demanding was much higher. To satisfy him, she must assist in his scheme to keep Laura Johnstone from coming to Kabul, and she must accept his motives as humanitarian and just. She must also accept their own marriage as it stood now, with no further blossoming, and so, inevitably, with a kind of withering ahead, which compassion for each other would not help to disguise but might, in his own case anyway, make toler-able. She need not become different, she need only degen-erate to a level that, being human, she had in her; she would find him there. Everywhere married people were being forced into such necessary restrictions of their happiness, either by the pressure of outside circumstances or by their own personal weaknesses. There were many too, such as the Langfords, who had not been able by their ruthless pruning of marriage to save it; these continued to live on with their hopes dead in flower and root.

It would, he thought, make a poem; and as he drove past the armed soldier at the gate, into the courtyard of the Ministry, he was already seeking phrases. 'The slant-eyed penny mercenary; the bright Russian rifle and the Afghan rags; the clerks huddled over their desks, with their bicycles padlocked beside them; the corridor with its mud-brick floor; the murmured greetings: "*Salaam Alekhom*"; and the hoarse sudden shout of treachery, like this camel's, far away in the mind's desert.'

He kept thinking of the irony of that greeting: 'God be with you.' Here, he wondered, at the Minister's door; here, on the red carpet leading to the desk, here in the soft handshakes, first with the tall hook-nosed sad-eyed Minister, and second with Mojedaji, the important mullah, with snowy turban and plump, lewd thighs.

The Minister had formerly been headmaster of one of the four high schools and had been shot up to his present eminence by the Prime Minister himself, whose portrait, bald and saturnine, hung on the wall alongside the King, with a dusty flag between.

Mojedaji's eyes glittered behind his spectacles, with a peculiar kind of derision. Moffatt had seen it once before, in the eyes of an old white-bearded mullah seated at the entrance to the famous blue mosque at Mazar in the north. Moffatt had asked if he might be allowed to enter; a shake of the head and that glitter had let him know that there, where God was for them, he wasn't welcome. He had the same feeling now, though Mojedaji was smiling and chatting amiably. His family, all of them mullahs, was one of the most powerful in the country; even the Prime Minister, it was said, had to be careful not to offend them. Mojedaji himself was in charge of the religious education in the schools but he was known to be more influential than the

Minister in many matters. Certainly it was the latter who
showed nervousness and diffidence.

'I happened to mention this matter to Mr Mojedaji,' he
said, 'and he expressed interest. So I suggested he should
join us in our discussion.'

Moffatt smiled and nodded. He felt himself trembling at
this stroke of luck; whether good or bad he could not yet say.
On the subject of the respective merits of foreign diplomas
Mojedaji's opinion might not be of much consequence,
though his decision would be; but on the subject of Wahab's
intended marriage with a feringhee he would be able to
speak with vindictive authority.

'Please explain, Mr Moffatt,' said the Minister.

Briefly Moffatt did so. 'I don't want to belittle the
diplomas and certificates of other countries,' he said. 'All
I want to do is to give you a true estimate of the value of
those awarded by British colleges.'

The mullah had listened with urbane attention. One fat,
ringed hand kept caressing a thin ankle clad in a green silk
sock; the other, black with hairs, stroked his thigh.

'Do you British still maintain,' he asked, 'that your
educational system is the best in the world?'

'I don't. I'm satisfied with saying that it's as good as any
other.'

'As good as that of the Soviet Union?'

'On the whole, yes.'

'But I read that the Soviet system is turning out many
times more scientists every year. However, this is by the
way. What exactly is your own personal interest in this
matter, Mr Moffatt?'

'I'll be frank. Some holders of British diplomas have been
coming to me and asking my help to get them recognized at
their proper value.'

'You mean, of course, Afghans?' said the Minister.

'Yes, Excellency.'

'May we inquire who they were?' asked Mojedaji.

'I'm sorry. They came to me in confidence.'

'Ah yes, I was forgetting the British code of honour; a promise must not be broken. But of course there is another way of looking at it. Were these men ashamed to let their names be known?'

Moffatt smiled. 'Perhaps.' No need to say they were far more afraid than ashamed. The two men at the other side of the desk knew that better than he.

'We know their names,' said the Minister.

'Yes, indeed.' Mojedaji reached out the hand that had been cuddling his ankle to pick up a sheet of paper on which was written, in Persian script, a list of names. 'All of these gentlemen are the holders of British diplomas or certificates. As you see, it is quite long. Shall I read you a few?' Sure enough, Mir Abdul Rahman's was among the half dozen he read out. Wahab's, though, wasn't.

A curious lisp had come into the mullah's voice; it struck Moffatt as malevolent. 'We all know, Mr Moffatt, that you and your beautiful wife are among the best friends we Afghans have.'

'We hope so.'

'But everyone knows it. All of your students at the University praise you enthusiastically. We are grateful. Not only do you teach English well, but you also inculcate a spirit of independence which is truly admirable. I can assure you that your efforts are appreciated, not by the students only but also by the authorities. Nevertheless, you will agree that in this small matter of which diplomas to consider of higher value than others, we must be allowed our own opinion, even if we do make mistakes. Among us are men educated in various countries. I myself, for instance, spent two years in Germany. His Excellency here studied for a year and a half in France, and as you no doubt know he has recently returned from an inspection of the educational system of the Soviet Union. Others have acquaintance with America, Great Britain, Italy, and Scandinavia. You are not to think that we spend all our lives among these bleak mountains of Genghis Khan.'

Moffatt smiled at his fellow phrasemaker. How great the distance, he wondered, from Genghis Khan to Abdul Wahab?

'So, Mr Moffatt, His Excellency has decided not to make any changes at present.'

'I shall keep the matter in mind,' said the Minister.

'Does that satisfy you, Mr Moffatt?'

'It will have to, I am afraid.'

'But there is something else you would like to mention? I have seen it several times on the tip of your tongue. I think His Excellency and I could spare a few more minutes.'

The Minister glanced at his large gold wrist watch. 'Of course,' he muttered.

Then both of them waited, contemptuously, so it seemed to Moffatt. He was again trembling, and his throat was dry. Glancing at the white turban he remembered the rose in Lan's hair.

'I believe there's a teacher of science at Isban College,' he said.

The King in the portrait looked suddenly very like his son Naim, Moffatt's friend.

'That is so,' replied Mojedaji. 'I know him. I visit that school frequently. His name is Abdul Wahab. Is he the same man?'

'Yes. Please understand, I know nothing at all to this man's discredit.'

'I'm sure no one does,' murmured the mullah. 'Wahab is a very serious young man, and a most conscientious teacher. I may say he is a fervent advocate of English methods.'

'Yes, he's not long back from England. That's really what I want to talk about.'

They waited.

'He met a young woman there.'

'One?' Mojedaji laughed. 'I thought England was much more hospitable than that.'

'This was more than a passing acquaintanceship.'

'They fell in love?'

How lewd the expression sounded under those glittering eyes. 'Yes, I suppose you could put it that way. He would have married her and remained in England, if that had been possible. It wasn't, so he came back to Kabul. She was to come after him. They were to be married here. That was their plan.'

Again they waited.

'I think, from our point of view, it would be a mistake if they were to marry.'

'Whose point of view, Mr Moffatt?'

'I meant, from the point of view of the English.'

Mojedaji shook his head; his eyes appealed to the Minister. 'I'm afraid I don't understand. Do you, Excellency?'

'No.'

'I don't mean of course that the Afghan way of life is inferior to the English. But it is different, and I know from my own experience that they don't mix successfully.'

'From your own experience, Mr Moffatt? I did not know you were married to an Afghan.'

'I meant, from the experience of people I know personally.'

'I see. Your own wife of course is of Chinese origin?'

'Yes. So I have written to this woman advising her not to come.'

'Well then, surely she will take your advice? I mean, being a poet, you would be able to paint a truly terrifying picture of our primitiveness. An admirable race, the Chinese, so industrious, so shrewd at business very unlike us lazy backward inefficient Afghans.'

Moffatt thought it might be safer to stop; but he could not. 'If she were refused a visa she could not come.'

'I am surprised, Mr Moffatt. A poet trying to place obstacles in the path of true love.'

Mojedaji giggled, but the Minister's smile was sour.

'Why are you so certain that the two ways of life will not mix?' asked the Minister. 'Men are men, are they not, and women are women?'

'Ah, but Excellency,' chuckled Mojedaji, 'perhaps Mr Moffatt thinks that children are half-castes. Do you?'

Moffatt nodded. 'It's not a matter of opinion. It's a fact.'

'I'm surprised to hear you say so, all the same,' said Mojedaji. 'We thought of you as a man of progressive outlook.'

'Progressive enough,' said Moffatt dourly, 'not to like shaddries.'

Mojedaji's family, he knew, was powerful among those who favoured the retention of the shaddry.

'Foreign women are exempt, as you should know,' said the Minister.

'Even if married to an Afghan?'

'Yes. You know instances yourself.'

'Of course, Excellency, Mr Moffatt has his tongue in his cheek when he uses the shaddry as an excuse. He has much stronger objections to this marriage that he hasn't yet divulged.'

'Yes, I have.'

'What are they?' asked the Minister coldly.

'I'm well aware that many Afghans would make good husbands for Western wives. But this one wouldn't.'

'Wahab?'

'Yes.'

'And why do you say so?'

'I have heard that he meddles dangerously.'

'Did you not say at the beginning that you wished to say

nothing to this young man's discredit?' The Minister's smile grew sourer.

'I am sure,' whispered Mojedaji, 'that Mr Moffatt wishes only to speak the truth. In what does Wahab meddle dangerously?'

'I am only saying what I have heard. He's supposed to be communistically inclined. It's none of my business, I know, but it is my business to try and save this Englishwoman from a life which might be full of hardship and misery.'

Mojedaji rubbed his hands together. 'Communistically inclined? What does that mean exactly, Mr Moffatt?'

'Even a rough-and-ready explanation would help,' said the Minister.

It occurred to Moffatt that perhaps Wahab was a remote relation of the Minister's. 'He sympathizes with Russia,' he said.

Mojedaji laughed. 'Do you, Mr Moffatt?'

'In some ways.'

'So do I. So does His Excellency. So does the Prime Minister. So does His Majesty. Russia is our neighbour. It is good to sympathize with one's neighbour. As a matter of fact, Mr Voroshilov, President of the Soviet Union, is paying us a State visit soon. Thousands will cheer him, among them Mr Wahab no doubt.'

Laugh as you like, thought Moffatt, but the bait and the hook both are stuck in your throats.

'Will you stop her visa?' he asked.

'Really, that is surely a most impertinent thing to ask,' said the Minister. 'We have authorities to consider such things.'

Mojedaji turned to him. 'Perhaps we ought to see to it that the lady does get one, Excellency, because how better to tame a wild revolutionary than to get him safely married?'

The Minister suddenly got up and held out his hand. 'It was good of you to call, Mr Moffatt. We shall certainly consider this matter of the diplomas. Good afternoon.'

Mojedaji, with great cordiality, accompanied Moffatt to the door, holding his hand moistly all the way.

'And the lady's visa,' he whispered. 'It will be kept in mind too. A country is lucky when its friends act voluntarily as its spies. Good afternoon, sir.'

Sick at heart, Moffatt tried to grin; and as he went along the corridor he pretended to slink like a spy. But in the midst of the game he stopped, muttered 'Oh Christ!' and pressed his mouth against the filthy wall. If Wahab disappeared, transported to some camp of correction in the barren north, or imprisoned in some dungeon here in the city, with marks of brutality on his face and body, he himself would be the chief guard and torturer. There would be no way now of escaping that responsibility.

The soldier with the fixed bayonet and string for boot-laces gave him a cheerful gap-toothed, slant-eyed grin, and somehow, despite his uncouthness, looked very like Lan and would look even more like her as he ripped his bayonet into Wahab's belly.

He sat in his car for almost ten minutes, trying to convince himself that his imagination was exaggerating what could happen to an Afghan suspected of political subversion. There were many rumours in Kabul, but no one knew the truth. The walls of the room in the prison where criminals were interrogated were said to be splattered with blood. Not so long ago the Minister of Finance had been caught smuggling large sums into other countries in his own name. No one was sure what had happened to him; but in all the embassies and legations were horrified whispers of his having been seen with all his teeth missing and his wits askew. Mojedaji had not mentioned Genghis Khan for nothing.

When at last he drove out of the gate he turned right and headed, not back home, but out into the country, past the Embassy with the Union Jack fluttering above the Residence, where a few weeks ago the Judas trees had been in blossom, and past the holy man's cave where Afghan travellers always took care to fling down a few coins to win his blessing. Moffatt too flung some down and looked back to see the ragged, skinny, bearded hermit come creeping out of his hole and scramble about in the dust.

About half an hour later he stopped beside the river, at a spot that was a favourite of his, or had been previously. There the wide water sparkled shallowly over a multitude of round smooth pebbles that chimed against one another, as if the river indeed was singing. On the banks were hundreds of young poplars with silvery trunks and green leaves that glittered and rustled in the breeze as the stones did in the water. From there the city could not be seen, only desert with one village in the distance; far beyond, across the great plain of shimmering sunshine, were the high mountains where he had gone climbing a year ago.

Close to the water was a large, warm boulder, dappled like a seal. Here Moffatt usually sat, and Lan too, when she came with him to paint. As he did so this afternoon, the feeling that had been growing stronger every minute now became an illusion: he was not alone, and his companion, though he had been thinking about her all the time, was not Lan, nor Wahab whom he had so recently betrayed, but rather someone whom he had seen killed thirteen years ago in a Burmese jungle. Then twenty-two years old, Moffatt had been a lieutenant in the army, in charge of a patrol of which this man had been a member. But though Richardson had been killed, machine-gunned from an aeroplane, and had been buried, inadequately in a great hurry not far from a river, there seemed no reason why, such a long time after, he should now undergo this peculiar resurrection by this river in a country so dissimilar, thousands of miles away. He had not been an outstanding personality, or at least Moffatt had not known him to be; he had done what he had to do in that quiet, dogged, self-preserving way which among soldiers makes for anonymity. He had laughed, cracked a joke, and grumbled like the others. Why then should it be he who seemed to be standing here beside the dappled stone? The reason could not be that it was his having been so suddenly killed; others whom Moffatt had known better had been killed too, even more bloodily, and so were also eligible for resurrection. He did not think he had ever wronged Richardson or even done him any special service. Certainly they had never saved each other's lives, and though he had been very near Richardson when the aeroplane had swooped he could never have been held responsible, not even by Richardson's wife. Nor had there been anything unusual about her, either. She had not been, for instance, foreign or even noticeably pretty. She would never have been looked at twice in any street in Liverpool where she had come from and where no doubt she was still living. There had been a photograph of her in Richardson's wallet, which Moffatt had had to look through. There had been blood all over her, and she had been holding a baby.

Could that be it? he wondered. Was it possible after all these years that Richardson should come to haunt him here by this quiet river because of that blood and the baby in his wife's arms, a baby that would now be a boy or girl of fourteen unless it too had died? And what stresses in Moffatt's own mind could cause so strange a ghost to haunt? Supposing he were ashamed of his betrayal of Wahab, why should shame take this form?

But he had not yet admitted to himself that he was ashamed. What he had done had been to protect Miss Johnstone, and if Wahab were to suffer as a consequence then it was a pity, but no man who had approved of Hiroshima at the time, as Moffatt and his fellow soldiers had done, most profanely, could be expected to be too squeamish about the means taken to achieve a necessary end, particularly when the issue was so infinitely much smaller. Even if Wahab was as honest as Lan too readily gave him credit for being, he must still be sacrificed; and it was more than likely that, being an Afghan on the make, he was selfish, cynical, and mercenary.

Lan of course would have to be told, but there seemed no reason why she should not be convinced that the betrayal, if it could be called such, had been justified. After all, whenever anyone in her presence, such as Josh Bolton, condemned the idealistic excesses of Communist China which had resulted in hundreds of thousands of innocent peasants being slaughtered or starved to death, did she not always keep silent and hide behind a smile of such faith and beauty that it was almost, but not quite, an answer? And in private whenever Moffatt had discussed the question with her, she had always shown such agitation and sorrow that he had been only too willing to change the subject. All the same, she ought to show the same consideration for him in this matter of Wahab.

Ten

WAHAB, hat on head, was so engrossed in squinting through the lens of the microscope and in crying out a description of what he saw to the boys crowding round him, that he didn't hear the rattling at the door.

A boy had to touch him on the shoulder. 'Sir, there is someone at the door.'

Wahab straightened up, blinking. 'Who is it?'

'We think it is the Principal.'

'The Principal!'

'Do not be frightened of him, sir,' said another boy. 'Everyone knows he is not important.'

Wahab licked his lips nervously and tried to smile. 'Do not be disrespectful, Aziz.' Then suddenly he rushed to his desk where he usually kept his hat and searched for it to put it on. The Principal was very orthodox; he liked his teachers to show an example to the boys by wearing their hats in the classrooms.

'It is on your head, sir,' said a boy.

Most of them were not really boys, but young men; two or three had moustaches. Few wore hats. Most were rebels against the imprisoning traditions of their country. Now they stared at Wahab in sympathy that had a sneer of contempt in it.

The door rattled again and the Principal's shrill, plaintive voice was heard: 'Wahab, are you there? It is important that I speak to you.'

'Stand back from the microscope,' whispered Wahab. 'Go to your desks. Write in your notebooks.'

'What does it matter, sir?' asked one. 'He will never know what we were looking at.'

'He is not interested,' said another.

'All the same, return to your desks.'

They obeyed, their shoulders hunched in disappointment at what they so plainly considered his timidity. Chewing at his knuckle, he could have wept: those boys should be his allies in his fight against the ignorance and prejudice which were holding his country back; yet here he was once again betraying both them and himself.

'The time's not ripe, do you not see?' he muttered. 'We must go forward carefully.'

The Principal was kicking the door. 'I hear you, Wahab,' he cried.

Wahab hurried over and unlocked the door.

The Principal, Abdul Mussein, fidgeted outside, one hand in his pocket, the other clutching the knot of his tie as large as a goitre. His suit was threadbare, and the collar of his shirt badly frayed. 'Why do you keep the door locked?' he asked.

'It is the regulation.'

'Sadruddin's?'

'Yes.'

Sadruddin was the Custodian. His salary was lower than any teacher's and he wore native clothes. Nevertheless, in his zeal to protect all the property in his charge he would defy the Minister of Education himself and be respected for it.

'But surely it is only necessary,' suggested the Principal, as he entered cautiously, his hand nervous in his pocket as if it held a gun there, 'when the room is unoccupied?'

'No, when it is occupied too. Even when I am present.'

The Principal stretched out his long neck to look at the equipment. 'This is valuable, of course,' he muttered. 'We dare not have it stolen.'

'I agree.' In the first place what was stolen would never be replaced; and in the second place every teacher's salary would have deducted from it an amount that, in aggregate, would be worth more than double the value of the stolen article. Wahab like all the others dreaded such deductions. 'Nevertheless,' he added bravely, 'these boys can be trusted.'

The Principal shook his head, meaning there wasn't an Afghan in the whole country, including himself, who could be trusted.

'Yes. They respect this equipment; they know its purpose is to bring to them the secrets of science.'

The Principal sighed. 'Perhaps it is too expensive. Perhaps it would be safer to keep the room empty and the door locked.'

Wahab pouted scornfully. That had been the situation when he had come to the school after his return from England. This science laboratory had been kept permanently locked; the microscopes had not even been taken out of their boxes. It had been opened and furnished with students only when some foreign official, such as the Egyptian Minister of Education or the Russian Cultural Attaché, was paying a visit. After a long exhausting struggle with Sadruddin, Wahab had been allowed to teach pupils there. At first the condition had been that the Custodian should always be present, but though a special chair had been installed for him at the end of the teacher's dais, he had soon given up the arrangement as tedious and had substituted this other of keeping the door locked. Wahab had had to agree. Sadruddin was such a power in the school that if he were absent, either ill or on leave, nothing could be issued from his store, books or chalk or stationery, until he returned. Not even the Principal could afford to offend so officious an underling. Wahab's resistance had not been forgiven by Sadruddin, who maligned him every day at the Ministry, where he reported like a spy.

The Principal glared sadly at the students. He did not like

or trust them, but he could not have said why. They, on the other hand, knew very clearly why they didn't approve of him: he was too scared of authority above him to have any fresh ideas himself or any tolerance of them in others; his only concern was to keep his position, which he had got by nepotism. It was impossible for them not to sympathize with him, for they knew the abyss into which a man who had lost favour could fall; but that very sympathy made them all the more bitter. Wahab, who had returned from England bold and enthusiastic, they had at first idolized. He had seemed to them not only a clever but also a brave man, daring to oppose forces that had dominated their country to its detriment for centuries. Frequently, however, under their eyes made sharp by admiration, his courage had faltered or even completely collapsed. He was for instance, like all his colleagues, terrified of the mullah Mojedaji. He had tried to explain to them in confidence that as he had given up most of the religious beliefs instilled into him when a child he was more vulnerable to the mullah's spite than the other teachers were, who were afraid only out of habit. But most of the boys were themselves much more critical and outspoken than he, and so refused to take his excuses. As an unmarried man he should have been able to show more independence. What they were looking for, they had told him, were heroes, not the same kind as of old when invaders such as the British had to be repelled, but a new kind whose weapons were ideas. In tears, he had agreed.

With a kind of indignant loyalty they protected him against his superiors. Now, for instance, when they heard him stammer to the Principal that they had been looking at some microbes on a slide, they did not add that the microbes were those that caused syphilis, a disease rife in all the country villages as well as in the city itself. Nor did they mention that in the drawer of Wahab's desk were real photographs showing syphilitic sores on men, women,

and children in some of those villages. They knew that the
Principal would be shocked and terrified, not so much by
the sight of the chancres as by his subordinate's rashness in
giving such a lesson.

Wahab, well aware that he was at their mercy, gave them
little comradely smiles that kept dying on his lips.

'No one can say that we are not advancing,' said the
Principal as he gazed round. 'Every year the Ministry
spends hundreds of thousands of afghanis on school
equipment.'

'True, but don't let us forget that compared with school
laboratories in England, this room is nothing.'

'Compared with Saudi Arabia?'

'Yes, indeed, and the aborigines of Africa. We used to be a
civilized people.'

'Are we not still civilized, Wahab?'

'In many ways we are not.' Wahab's teeth chattered as he
spoke; here he was again blurting out truths that could
destroy him.

The Principal gaped at him and suddenly remembered
why he had come downstairs. There were two reasons – to
relieve himself, and to tell Wahab that someone wished to
speak to him on the telephone.

There should be, no doubt, in a civilized school a W.C.
for the principal alone, or at least for him and the senior
teachers. But there was none, and to relieve himself he
would have to slink outside, round the back of the building,
and find a corner which others would have found before
him; or else he would have to set off across the playground
for two hundred yards or so to the latrines which were
indeed only aboriginal holes in the ground and smelled
atrociously.

'You are wanted on the telephone, Wahab,' he said.

Wahab looked worried. 'Is it the Chinese woman again?'

'No.' The Principal realized he ought to have been

smiling with excessive friendliness. 'It is the secretary of His Highness Prince Naim.'

'Prince Naim!'

'Yes. I did not know you knew the Prince.'

'But I do not know him.'

The Principal was not surprised at thus being excluded from Wahab's sphere of influence; but he was also by no means discouraged. 'It is his secretary of course, but I think it is the Prince himself who wishes to speak to you.'

'There must be some mistake.'

'I thought so, too; but the secretary gave your name and described you as a teacher of science at this school. Prince Naim is, I understand, interested in education. He is also, I am told, a friend of the Prime Minister.'

'I do not know who is a friend of whom.'

The Principal grinned sadly. 'It is wiser to say so,' he whispered.

'Perhaps, if the Prince is waiting, I should go at once?'

'Yes, of course. You must hurry.'

'What about my students? Will you stay with them until I return?'

The Principal remembered his rank. 'I cannot. I have so much other business to attend to.' Indeed, he had now to keep one knee pressed tight against the other.

'Then they must all come out. The agreement is that they must not be left in the laboratory without someone to supervise them.'

'A very necessary agreement.'

Wahab addressed the boys and apologized for having to put them out. They dawdled, resentful at the lack of trust.

Outside in the gloomy corridor Wahab was locking the door when around a corner, his fat thighs impeding each other, waddled Mojedaji, Koran conspicuously in hand. His little black moustache glittered with scent. It was his method of defeating the stenches of the city.

The reaction of the boys to his approach was curious. Some smiled warily but drew back; a few bowed towards him, with hands pressed against their breasts, and two went cringing forward and kissed his negligent hand.

Knock-kneed, the Principal smiled with affable obtuseness. Wahab held his head up and did not smile.

'It is necessary, you see,' cried the Principal, 'for the students to come out and wait in the corridor; otherwise they might steal or break the microscopes.'

'I think I should like to help them do that,' said the mullah, with a sly grin. 'Scientists are such dangerous people.'

'No, no,' said Wahab. 'They want only to enrich the earth.'

'Ah, but we have seen in the West that to enrich the earth means also to impoverish the soul.'

'Not necessarily so. One day scientists will give everyone enough to eat, and they will also abolish disease.'

'No, no,' said Wahab. 'They want only to enrich the earth.'

'Are they Gods then?' Mojedaji turned to the boys. 'And with what experiment was Mr Wahab showing you how to enrich the earth this morning?'

At first none was willing to answer.

'We were looking at some things through a microscope,' said Wahab.

'What things?' Mojedaji glared at one of the boys who had kissed his hand. 'What things were you looking at through the microscope, Mansour?'

Mansour, a boy with shaven head and thick lips, looked at the mud-bricked floor. 'Microbes,' he muttered.

'What kind of microbes?'

'I shall tell you,' said Wahab, in agitation. 'They were the microbes of syphilis.'

'Syphilis!' yelped the Principal and thought he had wet himself with the shock.

With delicate forefinger the mullah dabbed at his perfumed moustache. 'A strange experiment for schoolboys, surely?'

Wahab stubbornly shook his head but kept his mouth shut. If he tried to explain he might lose control of himself and start screaming at Mojedaji that it was he and his like who kept their country imprisoned in ignorance, disease, hunger, and stupidity.

'I did not know,' wailed the Principal. 'These microbes were dead, I hope?'

'Yes, but people are alive,' cried Wahab.

They waited for him to explain what otherwise need hardly have been said; but he had his mouth shut again.

Thinking of dead microbes and living people and angry Mojedaji and his own painful need, the Principal suddenly remembered that the Prince was still waiting.

'It is necessary for Wahab to go up to the telephone,' he explained to Mojedaji. 'Prince Naim wishes to speak to him.'

'Prince Naim?'

'Yes, indeed. I was surprised too.'

'Well then,' said the mullah, patting Wahab on the arm, 'you must certainly not keep the Prince waiting.'

'One ought never to be discourteous,' said Wahab, as he moved off with sad smile, 'to prince or beggar.'

They all watched him as he hurried along the corridor towards the stairs. The Principal noticed that in Mojedaji's eyes surmise was taking the place of disapproval; he noticed too that the mullah's scent was conjuring up the stink of the latrines.

Yet when he took leave of them all he did not go out into the playground but rather followed Wahab up the stairs, although each step he took was now a danger and an agony. To go and make water, in so filthy a place, while the Prince was actually telephoning, seemed not only disrespectful, but also somehow absurd.

*　　*　　*

Going up the stairs, Wahab had glanced out of the window and caught sight of two shaddried girls skulking along a street at the back of the school. Instantly he was reminded of Laura, and the times when, hand in hand, slowly to suit her, he and she had walked fearlessly through the widest streets in Manchester. As he remembered, the coolness of her hand came upon his, so that his heart ached with a longing that would have brought tears to his eyes if he hadn't for her sake vowed never again to be so unmanly as to weep. With his other hand he stroked the fingers where he had felt hers, and thus, like a man manacled, he went up the stairs into the Principal's room. The clerk, with bare feet and shaven head, was stretched out on the sofa that matched the chairs. He had a headache, he whispered; and indeed he looked ghastly as if he might have some fatal disease which Wahab would catch and die of, without ever seeing Laura again. 'Do not,' whispered the clerk, 'talk loudly on the telephone.'

The telephone lay on the table, upon a copy of *Time* magazine. As Wahab approached it, he saw out of the window which looked on the main road a caravan of camels pacing along, so far from Manchester that again the ache tortured him.

With a sigh he picked up the telephone. 'Hello,' he said cautiously. 'Abdul Wahab speaking.'

'Ah, at last.' This must be the secretary; no prince would sound so rude.

'I am sorry to be so late. I was teaching.'

'On the top of a mountain?'

'No, in a laboratory.' But to explain would have been more exhausting than to climb a mountain. Once he had climbed a hill with Laura; she had surprised him with her agility.

'You have not been keeping me waiting, you understand. You have been keeping His Highness waiting.'

'I am very sorry.'

By this time the Principal had come in and was standing by the desk, fidgeting with a long melancholy finger at his lips. The gesture confused Wahab still more; he did not see how he could speak even to a prince if he were also to remain silent. Behind him the clerk moaned.

'Well, I shall inform the Prince. Do not go away.'

'No, no.'

'In this country—' But the secretary did not finish it. A moment later he said, with such a change of tone, all cordiality now, that Wahab was almost astonished into handing the instrument to the Principal: 'Here is His Highness to speak with you now.'

'Good morning, Mr Wahab.'

So English the words and voice, Wahab gaped in stricken nostalgia. If he waited a little longer at this street corner Laura would come along. The Principal had to poke him with a finger conscious of its altruism.

'Good morning, Your Highness.' Wahab spoke in Persian.

'I say,' said the Prince, again in English. 'Do you mind if we speak in English? I like to practise as much as I can, and I have reason to believe you are in a similar position.'

What did that mean? Had those great men, chief mullah and prince, been conspiring against him behind his back? But why should they? Though in his own dreams valiant and important, he knew that in reality he was insignificant.

'Yes, thank you,' he whispered, 'English would suit me.'

But it did not suit the Principal, whose second language was French. He believed himself deliberately and cruelly excluded.

'I hope this call out of the blue hasn't upset you, Mr Wahab. You see, you and I have a mutual acquaintance.'

Impossible, thought Wahab; he knew no one who frequented palaces.

'Yes, his name is Harold Moffatt,' said the Prince cheerfully. 'He's an Englishman. He teaches at the University here.'

'I have met Mr Moffatt.'

'Like yourself, he is an admirer of Afghanistan.'

'Sir, it is my native country.'

'It is mine too.'

'But it is not Mr Moffatt's.'

'He speaks our language pretty well.'

'Even so.'

'He is on our side, Mr Wahab.'

Wahab smiled sadly and shook his head. 'He is not on mine, I am afraid.'

'Have you any special reason for thinking that?'

'He said something to me, sir; but really it is not very important.'

'Yes, it is. I want to have a chat with you, if you don't mind.'

Wahab blinked. 'It would be a great honour, sir.'

'Nonsense. It will be a pleasure for us both. I am in my town house. It's in the Palace grounds. Enter by the side gate near the mosque.'

Even at the side gate the guards were huge and fierce. 'I shall be on a bicycle, sir.'

'That doesn't matter. Just give your name. I'll see that you are expected. By the way, I'm assuming you will be along this afternoon. Is that all right?'

It wasn't really – it was very inconvenient – but Wahab murmured: 'Of course, sir.'

'Good. When does school finish?'

'Twenty past one.'

'I'll expect you then about two.'

'Certainly.'

'That's fine, then. There may be someone else coming who is in a position to give you some valuable advice.'

'I should be grateful, sir,' he said, although he had no idea what kind of advice was meant. As he replaced the telephone he saw on the road a donkey being whacked by a white-bearded old man; some children stood by, jeering. Any one of those, he thought in a fit of pessimism, the donkey, the cruel old man, and the vicious children, was in a position to give him advice; everyone in the world was, for surely he was the stupidest man alive. He had dreamed that because of his endeavours and those of men like him Afghanistan would soon leave all its cruelty, poverty, ignorance, and disease behind; he had dreamed too that Laura would come and help in the flowering of the desert. He too was flogging a donkey, only in his case it was dead.

He became aware that the Principal's melancholy brown eyes were gazing into his. He could not resist holding out his hand.

The Principal took it. The gesture meant nothing. In a day a man might shake hands fifty times; not once would it indicate cordiality; *that* would be indicated by embracing, and perhaps not even then. The Principal did not feel like embracing Wahab who was obviously plotting to oust him from his position. In a struggle between his own relative, the Minister of Education, and Prince Naim, third son of the King, there was no doubt who would win. The Minister, wisely mindful of his own place, would yield at once.

'I really do not think,' said the Principal, in a sad defeated voice, 'that this country will ever be civilized.'

Then with as much dignity as he could manage he scooted from the room.

Wahab waited. In another five minutes the bell would ring – No, to be accurate, in another five or six or seven or eight or even twenty minutes the urchin whose job it was would appear downstairs in the hall and strike with a stone brought in from the playground the metal disk suspended from string. That would be the signal that the fourth lesson was over. The pupils would stream out into the sunshine. It was as he imagined them there, laughing, playing, or gravely discussing, that he was able to throw off his own gloom. Yes indeed, his country would be civilized one day. If he did not live to see it his children would; and they would all have blue eyes.

The clerk groaned on the sofa and pressed his hand against his head. Someone, he gasped, had driven a nail into his brain.

'Not at all,' said Wahab. 'You have a headache.' He felt in his pocket and took out the small bottle of aspirins he always carried. He spilled two into his palm and did not let them fall in dismay at seeing how brown by comparison with their whiteness that palm was. No, his hand remained steady. 'Please take these,' he said, and forced them into the clerk's mouth. 'Swallow them quickly, or they will have an unpleasant taste. Here, drink some water.' He got the water out of the large earthenware jar that stood leaking in a corner. The cup was a beer can to which a tin handle had been soldered. Many others had drunk from it. Besides, the water itself would have given an Englishman sickness and diarrhoea in less than an hour. Here were microbes in millions. Nevertheless the war against them would in the end be won.

'Keep your eyes closed for a little while,' he told the clerk. 'The pain will soon go.'

'I shall die.'

'Do not be foolish.' Wahab was scornful. Since his return from England he had made up his mind never again to humour this readiness on the part of his countrymen to succumb to despair and tears. Nevertheless, as he looked down at the clerk's dark unhappy face, with its three days' growth of beard (this was forgivable, razor blades were dear, and in the hovel which a clerk's salary could afford hot water would be hard to come by) his own breast heaved with compassion. His and this clerk's ancestors, in the past wars against Moffatt's imperialistic Britain, had slaughtered many thousands of those arrogant usurpers. Well, such massacres of history were regrettable, but still the insolent Mr Moffatt must not be allowed to forget them. What ought to remind him daily was, not the violence, but rather the brave forbearance of the present-day Afghan. Next time he met Moffatt he was going to stand up to him, not with any hysterical resentment but with the calmness of a man strong in the confidence that God, if there was a God, was on his side. After all, what right had Moffatt to object to his marrying Laura? Was not the fat fair-haired Englishman married to a woman whose skin was yellow and whose eyes were narrower than a Mongol's? (At this point Wahab turned so that the sunlight shone on his hand; once again he saw that his skin could easily be taken for that of a European, nicely sunburned; indeed, he had seen many Europeans much darker.) But as he kept turning his wrist his sneer of triumph suddenly changed to a frown of dismay. Here he was, in the way that British history books described as characteristic of his nation, making a cowardly attack on a woman because he felt himself incapable of tackling her husband. He had no reason to despise Mrs Moffatt; rather he had reason to admire and be grateful to her. In any case how ridiculous for him, whose skin was brown, wishing to marry a woman whose skin was pink, and at the same time having contempt for another woman whose skin was yellow. Surely, if any man should, he should regard the colour of a person's skin as of supreme unimportance. Yet was it not true that, though shuddering at the risks involved, he intended to walk about the bazaars of Kabul and show off his wife's fair skin, as a man from Mazar might flaunt the carpet that he and his family had taken months to make?

The door opened and the Principal stumbled in. He too looked more confident. Downstairs the boy banged the gong again. Pupils streamed back into the classrooms.

Wahab started to leave. The Principal called, 'No more microbes of syphilis in the meantime, Mr Wahab, please.'

'That was a lesson for the Twelfth Class,' replied Wahab. 'Now I have the Tenth Class. I shall demonstrate to them the principle of Archimedes.'

The Principal nodded, glanced at the telephone, sighed, and shook his head. He had been thinking that perhaps Mojedaji would consider this principle too, whatever it was, as unfit for Afghan youth. But really, if every lesson Wahab taught had to be so approved, by telephone, life would become impossible. Not only was Mojedaji often hard to find, but it might be that, when found, he was in the Prime Minister's office, and it was not likely he would be pleased to be interrupted there by such a query. Besides, sometimes when one lifted the telephone one heard the conversation of merchants in the bazaar, discussing the prices, perhaps, of karakul skins. One would wait politely until they had finished, and then two others, from somewhere else, would start talking angrily about German electric pumps. One needed a great deal of patience.

Eleven

CYCLING into Kabul, on his way to the interview with Prince Naim, Wahab found himself escorted by a flotilla of Twelfth Class pupils. Unlike him they were all daring and expert cyclists, and took risks that made him nervous; front wheels kept grazing back ones. All the time too they chattered, asking questions whose purpose might have been sincere desire for information but might too have been to make fun of him. On this occasion, laughing like conspirators, they kept dangerously close to him and asked him when he thought Afghanistan would be able to manufacture her own hydrogen bombs.

'Never,' he replied, and wondered wistfully if he could therefore regard himself as morally superior to Moffatt, whose country made and exploded such bombs. He thought not.

'But, sir, no one will ever consider us civilized if we cannot.'

'I would say, Majid, the converse is true. We will never be considered civilized if we do make such bombs.'

'But, sir, no one will listen to us if we have no bomb.'

'On the contrary. Everyone will listen. They will understand we do not speak out of fear and hatred, but rather out of wisdom and love.'

For some reason they thought that very funny and shrieked with laughter. Yet at the time they were approaching the narrow bridge over the Kabul, which was the hub of the city's traffic. The policeman on his stone dais in the centre gave the impression he was up there to be out of danger. He kept stubbornly making the gestures he thought appropriate and blowing his whistle, but no one dared heed him. All – cyclists, bus-drivers, motorists, donkey and camel drivers, pedestrians, and ghoddies – entered into the fray with wits and voices lively, and though collisions were frequent and altercations more so, still most people got safely over. Sometimes Wahab got off and wheeled his bicycle, but today those conquistadors, with hands on each other's shoulders, whizzed him around with them and even kept up their hilarious discussion of the hydrogen bomb.

'You see, sir, it is like having fireworks. We shall be like the little boy who has none.'

'I cannot agree, Mohammed Ali, that a hydrogen bomb can be compared to a firework. It is estimated that one alone could kill a million people, that is more than twice the population of Kabul.'

'But are there not already too many people in the world, sir? You told us yourself that overpopulation is also a problem facing mankind.'

'Yes, Rasouf, but I do not think that the solution is to kill millions with hydrogen bombs.'

'How do you know, sir? Perhaps that is the best solution.'

'It would be the quickest, sir.'

'I know you are joking, boys.' Wahab was sweating. In another minute they would turn into the avenue where the side gate into the Palace grounds was situated. He had not been given the leisure to prepare himself, to consider who this other person the Prince had mentioned might be. Still, he had been discussing some of the most urgent contemporary problems with Afghan youth.

'Sir,' said one called Farouq, a mischievous boy with close-cut hair and enormous whites to his eyes, 'when you were in England, why did you not marry a wife?'

'They are very cheap and beautiful there,' said another.

Wahab felt brave and strong and adventurous. He had indeed gone forth like a conqueror to the West and had returned with one of its beautiful fair-skinned women as a prize.

'Here you must save up for ten years.'

'It is a barbarous custom,' said Wahab. 'But do not despair. It will soon be abolished, like the shaddry itself.'

'There are no women here, sir, only shuttlecocks!'

'Moving tents!'

'Clothes pegs!'

'Please do not be so disrespectful of Afghan women, boys. They do not want to walk about in these disgraceful shaddries.'

'Oh sir, they do. It gives the ugly ones the same chance as the beautiful ones.'

Again they laughed. Wahab was terrified. They were bright, intelligent, and eager; but they were also irresponsible. Of course they were still boys, but he had found that most Afghan men carried their irresponsibility with them into manhood, and even into old age. It was easier to laugh than to face up to grim difficulties, and certainly if a man laughed when humiliated it saved him from having to weep.

He had cycled past the side gate. A guard with glittering helmet and bayonet had been standing there.

Now he stopped at a corner where there was a pharmacy.

'I must go in here,' he muttered, 'for aspirin.'

'We shall wait for you, sir.'

'You forget, Farouq, we live in different directions. Please go home. Think. Keep thinking.'

'What shall we think about, sir?'

But they were cycling away, without waiting for his answer. He heard one cry: 'We shall think about girls,' and for a moment he was bitterly shocked, thinking them lecherous. Then he smiled, because of course for a young man to think about a young girl, even in shaddried Afghanistan, was not lechery. No, no, it was only the surge of the divine life force, irresistible and beautiful, which one day would people their country with children as hopeful as they would be healthy.

He turned and cycled slowly back to the gate.

Though it was a side gate it still had the royal crest worked on it in large gilt signs, and the guard's boots shone like his helmet.

'My name is Abdul Wahab. I have been summoned by Prince Naim. I understand he has advised you that I was coming?'

He might have been a bird chirping for all the heed the guard paid him, so he began to push his bicycle along the avenue towards the policeman he could see lurking under a tree. He felt sure he would be stopped this time, and he was right. The big tough-faced policeman shouted so fiercely that Wahab's heart jumped. Once, years ago, Wahab had had an encounter with the Kabul police which had left him with a permanent fear of them. It was an occasion of holiday in the city and the King was on his way to the stadium to see a game of buz-kashi. To make sure no assassins got near enough to shoot him, as his father had been shot, all the streets which his car took were closed by the police; and as the maximum amount of inconvenience was thereby caused to the ordinary population the police, liking the taste of tyranny, kept the streets closed long after the King's car had passed. Wahab had innocently turned the wrong way into one of those empty prohibited streets. Instantly half a dozen burly policemen had rushed on him, flung him off his bicycle, had shaken him so that his spectacles dropped off and were broken, had kicked his machine, and then, with hundreds watching in silence, had taken the valves out of both his tires. As he had pushed his bicycle away with its flat tires, hardly able to see for myopia and fright, he had heard the policemen behind him roaring with laughter. When he had got home, after walking for two miles, he had found his bowels loose for days afterwards. Now, this afternoon, accosted by this thug in policeman's uniform, he felt loose again and was afraid he might have a most demeaning accident. But behold, when he stammered his name, he was astounded to find the big official brute smiling and saluting. Overwhelmed by another kind of terror altogether, Wahab hurried on: this time he was afraid because he himself had for a moment felt the taste of privilege and power and had found it delightful. It was, he saw, quite possible that he too, if he ever rose to eminence, might not use his opportunities for the betterment of his country but rather for his own. He imagined himself a prince's friend, with a villa by the river and a country estate full of melons and vines. There he and Laura, with their blue-eyed children, would live in luxury, attended by ill-paid servants.

He had to stop, lean his bicycle against a tree, and wipe his spectacles with his handkerchief. The act was symbolical. He was wiping away not only the steam of sweat but also that vision of temptation. His fingers trembled so much that they could scarcely put his glasses on again; they seemed to have forgotten where his ears were.

The Prince's house, half of marble, half of sandstone, stood in a private garden of flowers. To reach it Wahab had to pass two more policemen, both armed, and each time the uttering of his name had produced that miracle of respect. Perhaps, behind his back, they sneered at one so obviously out of place there, so poor, so down at heel, and wearing the cheapest kind of karakul hat; but to his face they were marvellously respectful, or rather to the Prince's for the time being reflected in his. That thought made him wonder again what motive the Prince could have in inviting him. Once, during an examination in his student days, he had been faced with a question which try as he might he could not answer, and he had felt then the same dizzy despair that he was feeling now. Failure at that stage might have meant the end of his scholastic career, and now if he did not satisfy the Prince in whatever it was he had to satisfy him, there would be the same dreadful danger. A word from the Prince to the Minister, and Abdul Wahab, patriot and dispassionate disciple of Newton and Einstein, would have his microscopes, pupils, and ideals torn from him, and he would be given a clerk's job in some dark poky Government office where there would never be a shade over the electric bulb and where if the bokhari smoked it would be sealed with mud. What would become then of his dreams of happiness for himself and Laura? What, indeed, would become of Laura? Moffatt would have his wish. She would stay at home in Manchester, and marry some Englishman after all, who would, it must be admitted, be a much less hazardous husband.

He was so confused by these miserable forebodings that when he suddenly awoke out of them he found himself standing among flowers and gathering a large bunch of them. 'For Laura,' he kept murmuring. Then, struck by guilt as forcibly as by a policeman's fist, he whimpered and let the flowers drop on the grass. The trouble partly is, he told himself, I have not eaten for six hours; I am therefore rather lightheaded, because the supply of blood to the brain is not sufficient.

He tiptoed out of the flower bed, picked up his bicycle, and humbly finished his journey to the broad marble steps of the house.

A servant in a white uniform embroidered in red came out. He was as brawny and contemptuous as a policeman. He grinned rudely at Wahab and at the crown of his hat where, indeed, the fur had grown thin. As Wahab entered he wasn't sure what he should do with his hat, whether to wear or carry it. The Prince had spoken English and it was of course the polite English custom to remove one's hat on entering a house; but this was Afghanistan, where a man kept his head covered even in a mosque. He decided to take it off, and discovered with relief he had made the right decision, for in the big, quiet, sunlit room into which he was shown the Prince was standing, bare-headed, wearing trousers and shirt of immaculate white, and dark glasses so large they gave the impression he had three faces, two smooth and one by contrast very wrinkled. Or at least they gave Wahab, so embarrassed he could scarcely force one knee past the other, that impression. His trouble was, as he informed himself in the tiny chamber of his mind where only the truth was spoken, despite fear of subservience or despair outside, that a kind of shame was clamped round each leg like an iron band. Here he was, in a Prince's presence, that was to say, more accurately, in the presence of a man whose grandfather had become king through a successful military coup, and he was being as abject as the most illiterate coolie in the bazaar. As a scientist, as an Afghan, as Laura's future husband, he should have his shoulders back and his head high, he should have felt his knees glide past each other with smoothest confidence, and his hand should have gone out frankly to take the Prince's as one honourable man to another. Instead, he slunk, he gaped at the floor, he skidded on the marble, his knees clanked, and his hand, stretched out as if to a red-hot fire, was as flabby in the Prince's as a lump of new bread. In the midst of his humiliation too, he heard Laura cry: 'I *hate* a man with a flabby hand.' When he had first heard her say that he had gone home to his lodgings and for half an hour had rubbed his palm with the back of his hair brush. Indeed, he had made that a habit for weeks afterwards. Now he was betraying her, as well as himself, with the worst display of flabbiness in his life.

The Prince was inspecting him. 'So you are the famous Abdul Wahab?'

'I am Wahab, Highness, but I am afraid I am far from famous.'

'But you may be some day. Please sit down. You look tired. You must be exhausted cycling in the sun. We shall have tea.'

Wahab knew it was polite to demur, but he could not; his mouth was too parched with shyness. He did manage to sit down safely on the edge of a bright blue chair with slippery seat, although to bend his legs needed an effort that brought him out in a fresh sweat. Yet the Prince was a small man, in physique punier than Wahab, not much older, and certainly no handsomer.

A servant came in carrying a tray with tea-things. The cups had handles and had the royal crest in the national colours on them. This, realized Wahab, was an experience he ought to be able to tell his children about with pride; but somehow, as he raised the cup to his lips, he felt that the first sip would prevent those children from ever being born. Unless he quickly recovered his manliness, a sterility would blight him, body and soul. Bravely therefore, he set the cup down again, took another spoonful of sugar, his fourth, crossed his legs, slid back a little in his chair, smiled in Laura's direction, tasted his tea again, found it sweet enough, and then smiled straight at the Prince.

'Feeling better?' asked Naim. 'You were looking awful, you know, when you came in.'

'You will appreciate, Highness, that it came as a shock to me to be asked to come here. You see, I am completely in the dark.'

'Not completely. I told you we had a mutual friend, Mr Moffatt.'

'On that point, sir, I must be candid. Mr Moffatt is not my friend. I should say rather he is my enemy. No, that is too strong, perhaps. He does not wish me well. Yes, I think I can truthfully say that. If he has prayers, he does not remember me in them. Yet I wish him well and his charming Chinese wife.'

'Have you any special reason for thinking he does not wish you well?'

'Oh, yes, sir, a very special reason. You see, I have recently returned from England. There I fell in love with a beautiful Englishwoman.' He paused, gravely, for the Prince was smiling. 'Laura really is very beautiful.'

'I do not doubt it for a moment. Her name is Laura?'

'Miss Laura Johnstone. What is, I agree, much more incredible, she fell in love with me. I find that very difficult to believe myself.'

'I do not see why. Englishwomen, no matter how beautiful, are still human.'

'Agreed. And Laura is very human.'

'And how does Mr Moffatt come into this?'

'That is what I do not quite see myself. On the only occasion I have met him he made it very plain that he disapproves strongly of my marrying her. I do not see really what business it is of his.'

'Perhaps he thinks that as her countryman he has a duty to protect her?'

'From me?' Yet Wahab's smile was eloquent. It meant: from me, so deeply in love with her? From me, so timid an idealist? From me, who would give my life for her? From me, a poor Afghan living with my family in an overcrowded house built of painted mud bricks?

'Yes, Mr Wahab, from you. But not only from you. From me also. From all of us. From Afghanistan.'

'Yes, yes. But here is what he does not understand: Laura loves Afghanistan.'

'Has she been here before?'

'No, but I have described it to her.'

'Truthfully?'

'As truthfully as I could. I admit I spoke also with enthusiasm. Why should I not? I love my country, though I am impatient with its faults. But do not for a moment think, Your Highness, as Mr Moffatt evidently thinks, that I deliberately deceived her with falsehoods.' He spoke with intense conviction, although he knew he was telling lies. 'As a scientist, I must revere the truth. Is it true that Mr Moffatt is a poet?'

'He writes poetry.'

'I thought that poets also revered the truth.'

'A different kind of truth perhaps.'

'Sir, there is only one truth.'

'Do you think so?'

'I do.' Though really he didn't. To begin with, he sometimes in that small inviolable chamber thought that Moffatt was right in trying to keep Laura from coming. It was very likely that if she did come the reality would be as Moffatt's truthfulness pictured it, not as his own extravagant hopes desired. Her life and his would both be ruined.

'Please have another biscuit, Mr Wahab.'

'Thank you, Highness. I shall. They are delicious.'

'Do you mind if I ask you some questions? No, don't give me sanction until I have warned you that you may consider them too personal and indeed too dangerous to answer.'

'Sir, I have nothing to hide.' Another lie. He had as much as any man to hide. Did he not spend a good part of his mental life in hiding from himself?

'You have a clear conscience?'

'If you mean, sir, do I pray and visit the mosque regularly . . .?'

'Well yes, I could mean that too. Do you?'

'No. I do not think I am an atheist, but I find it very difficult to accept the idea of God forced into me in my childhood. Our prayers have become too materialistic. We beg from God and rightly He scorns us.'

'These are unorthodox opinions, Mr Wahab. You do not try to communicate them to your students?'

'On the contrary. I find myself combating their unbelief. They are too young to be disillusioned.'

'Are you interested in politics, Mr Wahab?'

'When I was in England, sir, I studied their Parliamentary system. I even visited the House of Commons.'

The Prince smiled. This man, he saw, was a fool all right, but an engaging one and harmful only to himself. Perhaps also to his Laura? Harold Moffatt might well be right.

'I meant, the politics of our own country.'

'I did not know those existed.' Then Wahab paused, saw the enormity which he had let escape from his mind, tried to get it to return by gaping, failed, and waited, with a grin whose foolishness he was well aware of, for this small, prim, wrinkled, three-faced representative of the ruling oligarchy to blast him with anger. In would thunder policemen. They would not beat him there where his blood would sully the beautiful furniture, but they would drag him off quickly through the flowers to some underground cave where in half an hour he would have forgotten Laura and wish only to die. Farewell, my darling. Moffatt, I forgive you. As for myself, I have been mad to bleat out the truth, but it may be that years later when freedom of thought and speech have triumphed in my country my name will be held in honour. A pity, perhaps, that our religion forbids statues.

'Are you a Communist, Mr Wahab?'

'No.' Wahab lifted his head indignantly. 'I know there are many who secretly think it would be better for us if Russia took us over, by force if necessary. Yes, they would bring tractors to plow our fields; they would build great irrigation schemes; they would provide food for those of us who often have to go hungry; they would hasten the elimination of disease; they would build schools and equip them with magnificent laboratories. Yes, they would do all those things, but in the end Afghanistan would have disappeared. That is too high a price. I want all those things, but I want them to be Afghan. We must work for them ourselves. We must not pay for them with our souls.'

The Prince clapped his hands. Ash fell from his cigarette in his long holder. 'Well said, Mr Wahab. I understand, nevertheless, that you have stated you would have remained in England if you had been allowed to.'

Wahab scratched his chest ruefully. 'I was in love,' he murmured.

'So you were. And now she is coming to Afghanistan, and you hope, with her encouragement, to help to achieve all those fine things you have so fervently described?'

'Laura is more idealistic than I am, sir.'

'You do not associate with politically minded people, here in Kabul?'

'Sir, I am a dreamer. Since I returned I have had very few friends, I am sorry to say. You might think a man dedicated to the improvement of his country would have many friends, but I seem always to be alone.'

'You do not discuss your dreams with others?'

'I used to. I wished as many as possible to share them. But no one was interested, I am sorry to say. So now I keep them to myself. Laura will share them with me.'

'I am sure she will.' From behind his dark glasses the Prince stared at his earnest, naïve compatriot. He did not know whether to love or hate him for embodying so absurdly all his own enthusiasms and hopes. This reliance upon a woman, too, was ridiculous. Women were sharp in seeing that their menfolk were making dangerous, idealistic fools of themselves, and insistent upon putting a stop to it. What Laura might do the Prince's mother was already doing; every day she was warning Naim to be content, to accept the ease of wealth and avoid making vindictive enemies. But if Wahab's Laura stifled his idealism, what could she put in its place? Their life together might quickly degenerate into the hell which Harold Moffatt prophesied and in which poor Mohebzada at present roasted. And if idealists defeated themselves in this way, what victory could Afghanistan ever have?

The Prince rose and came across to take Wahab's hand. Wahab rose too, and was astonished by the fervour of the Prince's clasp. He was not to know of course that inwardly the Prince was resolving, with equal fervour, never to get married.

'I believe you are a sincere patriot, Mr Wahab, and I regret to say there are not many of us. You are one, I too, and my father is a third.'

Wahab blinked. The Prince's father was king. To call him a sincere patriot, on the one hand seemed superfluous, for the country belonged to him; but on the other hand it seemed dubious, because surely if there were many forces which for their own personal advancement kept the country in its medieval backwardness, he was the one with the power and opportunity to sweep them out of the way? Of course it was true that his father before him had been shot by a fanatic for initiating reforms.

'Like yourself I dare to be optimistic,' said the Prince. 'It is my belief that if there are enough men of vigour and good will in Afghanistan we can show an example to the entire world, by achieving material prosperity without at the same time sacrificing our spiritual dignity.'

'That is precisely my belief too,' cried Wahab.

They were beaming into each other's faces when the servant entered and announced, with a grin, that Mr Mohebzada had arrived. Behind him came Mohebzada, explaining and even excusing the insolence of that grin.

Wahab was ashamed for him. It wasn't just that Mohebzada was shabbily dressed, with the cuffs of his trousers frayed and his left sleeve stained with ink; it wasn't either that he was unshaven and dusty. No, it was because he looked so cowed, so defeated, so ready to lie down and be kicked. He carried a tattered brief case that, unlike himself, was fat, as if it was stuffed with the appurtenances for his own funeral. He had, too, a mouthful of shockingly bad teeth, reminding Wahab of his own, bad too, but not nearly so bad as these. And yet this pitiable, apologetic specimen of Afghan manhood slept every night with a woman whose breasts were white. That really was why Wahab could neither forgive nor pity him; he was the living, miserable proof that what had been sustaining Wahab's dream for months was a foolish myth: making love to a Western woman did *not* confer courage or confidence. This fellow Mohebzada looked as if he had crept out of a kuchi's tent, or indeed from under a kuchi woman's filthy skirts.

The Prince meanwhile was receiving Mohebzada hospitably, inviting him to sit down, and urging him to take tea.

'I am not thirsty, Your Highness,' said Mohebzada, in a croaking voice. 'I am also not hungry,' he added, when pressed to eat a cake.

'I am sorry,' said Mohebzada suddenly, hoarser than ever.

They looked at him. Tears grew big in his eyes. 'I am sorry,' he kept croaking.

Wahab was so ashamed he could look no longer. He wanted to rush into a corner and hide his own face. This fellow's feebleness was, in an inescapable way, his own. It represented, far more than any governmental tyranny, what had kept Afghanistan backward all these hundreds of years; it was the reason for that tyranny.

'My child,' said Mohebzada, 'is very sick.'

Wahab then, as it were, rushed back from the corner where he had been hiding his face, and sat again on the chair by Mohebzada's side, with a puzzled scowl of sympathy.

'I think he is going to die.'

The Prince glanced at Wahab. Neither knew what to say. Both were men, but not fathers. The child, wondered Wahab, had it blue eyes?

'And I do not know,' went on Mohebzada, 'if my wife wishes him to die or not.'

'But that, my poor fellow,' said the Prince, 'is surely wrong?'

'No, Your Highness.'

'Surely she loves her child?' asked Wahab.

'It is because she loves him that she is not sure whether or not she wishes him to die.'

'This is strange, Mr Mohebzada.'

'If he lives and grows up to become a man, he will be an Afghan.'

They waited, while he mastered his sobs.

'And she hates Afghans because I, his father, am one. Besides, if the child dies, she will be able to return home to England.'

Though full of grief for Mohebzada's sake, Wahab found himself glaring at the Prince. So this was why he had been brought here this afternoon, to meet poor Mohebzada and be terrified into giving up Laura. The Prince was in league with Moffatt. All his talk about sincere patriotism had been deception. It was a cruel plot, and the bitterest part of it was that it had succeeded. Wahab wanted to dash home and write a letter to Laura; it would be wet with his tears and almost indecipherable, so flabby would be his hand, but it would be resolute in commanding her never to be so foolish as to come to Afghanistan or even to want to come. He would be heart-rendingly truthful on the shortcomings of his country and of himself. Moffatt would be delighted with that letter. It would be as good as one of his own poems.

'I am very sorry, Mr Mohebzada,' said the Prince. 'I did not know your child was ill. If I had known I would not have asked you to come. Why were you at your work? I should have thought you would have been at home.'

But Wahab knew why Mohebzada had preferred to go to

his work. At home the sick child would cry, and its demented mother would scream.

'You should have told me,' said the Prince.

'Sir, when you said you wished me to meet this gentleman who is contemplating marrying an Englishwoman, then I felt it was my duty to come. You see, I did not require to speak. All he needed to do was to look at my tears.'

The first stirring of rebellion was felt in Wahab's impulsive breast. Why should he be so ready to drown his own happiness in this little man's too copious, craven tears? What kind of woman was this Mrs Mohebzada anyway, who hated her husband and half wished that her only child would die? He did not wish to judge her because it was obvious she must have suffered greatly in her mind, but there was also no need for him to think her as brave, unselfish, and determined as Laura. When he had been in England, other girls had tried to make friends with him, thinking at first, thanks partly to his own silly boasts (uttered on his country's behalf, rather than on his own) that he was a wealthy man's son; but when they had found out, which they had been embarrassingly skilful at doing, that he was much poorer than themselves, they had dropped him like a hot potato. Indeed, there had been a time, just before he had met Laura, when he had bitterly called himself 'the hot potato'; after all, had there not been a similarity in colour? He did not wish to be unjust to Mrs Mohebzada, about whom he knew nothing except what her husband had just said, but it did not seem unlikely that she too had been one of those scheming for luxury and riches. To some extent, therefore, this disappointment had been deserved; but still, confident that Laura's attitude was altogether nobler, he felt he could afford pity.

'I am sorry, Mr Mohebzada,' he said, 'for you and your wife.'

Mohebzada had been looking at Wahab with what now

struck the latter, to his amazement, as intense malice. Suddenly he said: 'If you are rich, Mr Wahab . . .'

Ought not a man drenched in grief to have sympathy for all human beings, themselves also mortal and liable to disaster?

'As you can see, I am not rich,' replied Wahab calmly.

The malice remained. It merely changed direction. 'Perhaps your family is not old-fashioned in its outlook?'

'My family, I should say, is typically traditional in its views.' That was an understatement, in the case of his mother; she was almost reactionary.

'Will your mother object if your wife does not wear the shaddry in the street?'

Trembling, Wahab reflected. 'She may.' The truth was, she vehemently would.

'In your home do they eat with knives and forks, or with their hands?'

'Frequently with their hands.'

'Will you be able to afford a house for yourself and your wife, apart from your family?'

Wahab smiled. 'I think so. Laura, you see, is a trained teacher. She has been promised employment here in the International School.'

'How much will she earn?'

No Afghan could be offended by that question. On the contrary, Wahab welcomed it. 'I understand, about five thousand afghanis per month.'

Mohebzada's eyes almost dried instantly, so warm was his astonishment. 'Five thousand!'

'Five thousand.' Wahab's lips were of silk. Within, his heart sang. There was no doubt those five thousand afghanis would be like five thousand horsemen galloping to his and Laura's rescue.

Mohebzada tried again. 'Will your people allow her to go out and work for feringhees?'

It had not of course been discussed. How could it have been, since Laura's coming had not been discussed. Her mere existence had once been briefly mentioned.

'They may object, but, though I am a believer in filial loyalty, I do not think I can allow their disapproval to stand in my way. They know I am a scientist, with forward-looking views. I have informed them repeatedly that my vocation is to help bring about improvements in our country. They must therefore expect some unorthodoxy in my own personal life. I would remind you, Mr Mohebzada, this is the twentieth century.'

'How old is this woman?'

Not only anger at the rudeness of the question, but also fear at having to answer it truthfully caused Wahab to speak with a rather shrill voice. 'You mean, my future wife?'

'Yes.'

Wahab found himself rubbing his finger tips together. Why should he do that? Did he wish he had some holy beads? Was he appealing to God?

'Is she old?'

'Old? Don't be ridiculous, my dear fellow. Of course she is not old. She is only thirty-two.' Though his tongue stumbled over that 'only' he got it out challengingly enough. Yet it was a lie. Laura was thirty-three

Mohebzada's sneer was radiant. 'But you yourself are younger than that?'

'Three years. A trifle.'

'My wife is only twenty-one now. She was nineteen when we got married.'

'Yes, Mr Mohebzada, I was wondering if that could have been partly the explanation of your present trouble. Surely your wife, for a Western woman, was too young and inexperienced to face so drastic a change?'

'My brother married a girl of fourteen. They are very happy.'

'Because she does everything she is bid, like a slave? A girl of fourteen is a child.'

'A wife should obey. It is the law of nature.'

It was obvious that Mrs Mohebzada did not respect that law, as her husband thought she should.

'I see. Mr Mohebzada, I am grateful to you for having come here specifically to warn me. I appreciate that your motives are, to some extent at least, altruistic. But I love Laura, and am more than ever resolved to marry her, though the whole world should queue up to shout reasons why I should not. Others have given me the same advice as you, and no doubt it will be given again. I hope, however, that after we are married such advice will cease. But let me say this, in all sincerity: If Mrs Mohebzada is still in Kabul when Laura comes, I would like them to meet and become friends. Laura is wise and mature. She could comfort and advise your wife.'

The Prince then, like a wise referee, decided the contest had gone on long enough. He made the verdict a draw.

'Mr Mohebzada,' he said, briskly, 'you will wish to get home to your wife and child. If you let me know where you live I shall see to it that the best doctor in Kabul, the one who attends my father, goes to your house and does everything he can for your child.'

'Is he an Afghan?' asked Wahab.

'No. A German.'

'I thought so. Some day it will be different.'

Mohebzada described where he lived (no streets in the city had names or numbers) and the Prince noted it down.

'As for you, Mr Wahab, I can always get into touch with you at the school.'

'Certainly, Your Highness.'

Thereafter it was all done with such expert courtesy that in less than three minutes they were both outside, mounting their bicycles and riding away.

*　　*　　*

Meanwhile the Prince had gone straight to the telephone. It was Lan who answered.

'Is Harold at home?'

'Yes, Naim, he is. He's just going off to a Club committee meeting. Just a moment, please.'

During that moment Naim thought of her. She reminded him always of the water lilies in the pond at his country house. He would sit there alone for hours, staring at them and thinking about her. Nevertheless he was quite sure that he himself would never marry. That she and Harold loved each other he had no doubt; but sometimes he had felt that between them was an antagonism as tragic as that between poor Mohebzada and his silly little wife.

'Hello, Naim. Harold speaking.'

Yes, and speaking too as if on the defensive. He is my friend, thought the Prince, and I know he is a good man; but Wahab is my countryman and he is in this instance the one betrayed. 'You remember our conversation at Istalif about Abdul Wahab? Josh Bolton was there.'

'Yes. What about it?'

'Well, I thought, my dear fellow, you were going to play fair.'

'In what respect?'

Had his voice been lowered so that Lan would not hear? Or had shame lowered it? Naim was sure that she had had no part in her husband's rather mean and treacherous attempt to stop Miss Johnstone's visa and get poor Wahab into trouble.

'Didn't we decide that this marriage between Wahab and his Laura was going to be a kind of experiment?'

'You and Josh may have had that idea, Naim. I certainly didn't. You know my views. I take a much more serious view of it.'

'Didn't you use to have contempt for those who put ideas before people? Harold, Wahab and his Laura are people.'

'You never heard me say people never made a mess of their lives. I'm trying to save Miss Johnstone from making a mess of hers.'

'Does Lan agree with you?'

'I'd rather we kept her out of it.'

'Why? You used to say you would put her judgment before anyone else's. You were right, too. I still believe it. If Lan assures me she thinks Miss Johnstone ought not to come then I shall personally see to it that no visa is issued.'

'No. I want Lan kept out of it.'

'Does she wish to be kept out of it?'

Moffatt was silent.

'All right, Harold. I had a telephone call from Siddiq, the Minister of Education.'

'Well?'

This fellow forgets, thought the Prince in a spasm of indignation, that my father is the King of this country where he is a guest and employee.

'He told me you had been to see him, Harold.'

'So I had.'

'I understand Mojedaji was also present.'

'Yes. I didn't know he would be.'

'But Harold, my dear chap, the truth about Wahab is simply that he's a true Afghan. A bit of an ass, and like the rest of us too full of enthusiasms that shoot up like rockets, are beautiful for a few seconds, and then leave the heart darker than ever. You may therefore be right in trying to save Miss Johnstone from him.'

'I know I am.'

'Yes, but for the wrong reasons. Good God, man, don't you know that men have disappeared without trace who had the misfortune to displease Mojedaji and his friends? Was it really your wish to have poor Wahab transferred to some school in the northern desert?'

'Don't they need education there too?'

'You know what I meant, Harold. I was speaking euphemistically.'

'You mean he might be dragged off some dark night to spend the next twenty years making a road across the desert?'

'I can't commit myself, old man.'

'Such things do happen, Naim. I agree. And it strikes me as all the more reason why I should try to save Miss Johnstone from them, or at any rate from their effects.'

'You're puffing against the wind, Harold. She'll come in spite of you.'

'She may. But it doesn't mean she'll marry him.'

'You know nothing about the woman, Harold.'

'None of us does, Naim; not even Wahab.'

'Oh, come now. There's no need to question the sincerity of the poor fellow's love for her.'

'Naim, you must dream your own dreams. I think it's pretty obvious what's going to happen to Afghanistan.'

'Please remember you are speaking on the telephone.'

'I remember all right. It's going to fall into the clutches of the Russians. They'll build you mosques with minarets that stay up.'

'Well, supposing that is what happens, couldn't Wahab and his Laura, and their children, find happiness together in such a country? You're not one of those, I hope, who think that everyone in Russia cringes about in terror from morning till night.'

'I wish to Christ, Naim, you wouldn't keep saying: Wahab and his Laura. It sounds obscene to me. But you're right: this isn't a conversation for the telephone. So if you don't mind, I'll ring off.'

And he did, leaving Naim gazing in dismay at the instrument left crackling in his royal hand.

People, thought the Prince as he put it down, are always disappointing in the end. I would have sworn that Harold

Moffatt would have been enthusiastic in helping a man like Wahab; instead of which he seems to hate him, revengefully. Yet what conceivable harm can Wahab have done him? Always there was this disappointment – he had experienced it in all kinds of men, from servants to cabinet ministers, and of course in women too. As likely as not Wahab's Laura was coming to Afghanistan with the same kind of expectations as those which had lured Mrs Mohebzada. She was older and so more crafty; therefore she was coming unmarried, to take a look first. She wouldn't need a very long one, if her ambitions were materialistic. Before she was in the country a week Wahab would get his ring back. Why was Harold Moffatt, the renegade poet, so concerned? Didn't he realize that greed and selfishness and the brittleness of human affections were his most mighty allies? Having Lan as his wife might delay that realization, but couldn't prevent it altogether.

His heart heavy, Naim went out to try and lighten it by walking among his flowers. There, however, he saw old Ahmad and the boy picking some up from the grass.

He rushed across, furious. 'What has happened? Who has been destroying the flowers?'

They bowed before him. Ahmad's white beard almost touched the ground.

'I did not see it happen, Your Highness,' he said. 'The boy did.'

The boy was no more than ten. Some of the flowers were taller.

'Well?' cried Naim.

'It was the man with the spectacles, Highness,' he whispered.

'Wahab?'

'I do not know his name, Your Highness. He came first to the house.'

'But why did he pick the flowers?'

The boy could not say, and Naim, seeking reasons, found one that was ridiculous; Wahab had wanted to take the flowers to some shrine that he had at home, dedicated to his Laura.

'Did he do it before or after his visit to me?'

'Before, Highness.'

'Before?' That was inexplicable. If they had been intended for Laura, though she was thousands of miles away, how coolly impudent of Wahab to pluck them before his visit; but surely such cool impudence was quite uncharacteristic of the fellow? And impudence would never have left its fruits lie ungathered. No, there must be another explanation. Could it be that this strange wanton pulling of the beautiful flowers by Wahab was in some mysterious way symbolic and prophetic? Was Laura coming, not as Wahab's inspiration and counsellor, but as his destroyer?

In his sadness at that thought he remembered his promise to Mohebzada.

'Tie the flowers together,' he said. 'Make them into a bouquet and have them ready. I shall send them to someone who is ill.'

He rushed in and telephoned Dr Steeb. He found him at the hospital about to perform an operation.

The doctor mentioned, not too meekly, that the patient was lying unconscious on the table.

'Yes, yes, Steeb. I'm very sorry. I want you, as soon as you are finished, to go to a friend's house.' He described its whereabouts. 'His baby is very ill.'

'But, Your Highness, this operation may take hours.'

'As soon as you are finished. I shall send my car to take you straight there.'

There was some loud peeved Teutonic breathing. 'Very well, Your Highness.'

'Thank you, Steeb. You see, I gave my word.'

The doctor grunted and said good-bye.

Naim rang for a servant. While waiting for him to come he thought that he himself would go with Steeb and see Mohebzada's wife and child, but he remembered that Steeb had said the operation might take hours. Besides, had not his mother warned him not to rush into anything indiscreetly? Perhaps it would be more judicious if he let the flowers convey his sympathy.

He was not deceived. Worse than finding disappointment in others was finding it in oneself. There was a map of the world on the wall, in a silver frame. He had had Afghanistan proudly coloured bright red so that no one would guess his real purpose in having the map there in his drawing room. This was to stand in front of it, in moments of depression, and wonder to what country he should exile himself. Usually England was his favourite, but this time, as he stood and gazed, he did not wish to go there. Germany perhaps, in honour of Steeb at that moment slicing with saviour's hands into the entrails of some Afghan. Or Switzerland, home of neutrals. Or South Africa, where the darkness of his skin would cause him to be persecuted, for the good of his soul.

As always his eyes, dim with emotion, returned to that small bright redness, like a blot of his own heart's blood. He believed that, like his grandfather, he would die in serving his country; but in his case it was not likely to be an assassin's bullet that would kill him, but a broken heart.

Twelve

PEOPLE often dropped into the Moffatts' before going on to some party or other. It was looked upon as one of the most hospitable houses in Kabul, with a hostess everyone admired, and a host who, diligent at handing out whiskies to his guests, still managed always to have a companionable glass in his own hand. The sing songs there were celebrated, with most of the singers seated on the carpets. Moffatt himself, and Bill Lawson, were the leaders and seemed to know every song, sad or comic or serious or bawdy, that anybody wanted sung. The Embassy people, in from their ghetto three miles away, as Katharine Winn called it, were especially grateful. Often members of the junior or non-diplomatic staff awoke there in the dawn to find themselves lying in armchairs or on the floor or in charpoys in the garden, amid the debris of empty bottles and dirty glasses. With a last toast, drunk out of imaginary glasses, to their sleeping host and hostess, they would rise and stagger off home.

That evening of the barbecue dance at the Club the house was again full, with people coming and going. Tom Parry put in an appearance, chaperoned by his mother Annie; Jean and Bill Lawson; Paula and Alan Wint; John Langford and Howard Winfield; Josh Bolton and several other Americans, among them Helga Larsen, with one breast Swede and the other Yankee, as she put it herself; an elegant, bearded Frenchman and his petite wife; the Japanese First Secretary and his wife, to both of whom Moffatt taught English; the

Mossaours; the Sattis, she in a brilliant yellow sari, he in a purple turban; Captain Mabie and three other Indians, air crew of the A.A.L., the Afghan Air Line; and various others, all of them dropping in to pay their respects to Harold Moffatt, thanks to whom the swimming pool was ready in time, or at least only three months late, considered marvellous for Afghanistan where even the new mosque had been under construction for two years and still wasn't finished. For weeks Moffatt had come every day to supervise and encourage the workmen and bully the contractor. It would be a good idea, wonderfully appropriate, cried Captain Mabie, in his shrill happy voice, if everyone would take along a bottle of whisky and pour it into the pool as a kind of libation. Then Harold should be heaved in for the first swim, in an element much more congenial to him than water. Normally that would have been taken as a passable joke, at which most of them, including those biased against happy, drunk Indians; indeed, some did take it as such and laughed; but others, such as the Wints for example, and the Lawsons, and the Mossaours, frowned instead and found plausible reasons for slipping off earlier than they had intended.

What caused their uneasiness was their host's unprecedented drunkenness. It wasn't that they hadn't seen him drunk before (he had once slept all night on the Wints' lawn, and on another occasion had come begging to the Lawsons' door disguised in a shaddry) or that he was this evening drunk to an uncontrollable degree. No, it was simply that he was not merely rude to his wife, which any drunken man might on occasion be, but rather viciously antagonistic to her. What made it all the more embarrassing was that Lan, aware of every insult, remained uncannily calm, and in her Chinese dress of black and gold so exquisitely beautiful that any man's hostility toward her seemed inconceivable. Some of the guests of course, advanced in their own drinking or impregnably happy, remained unaware that there was anything strange between host and hostess.

John Langford had come from a particularly arid scene with Helen, whom he'd left dandling, as if it were a dead baby, a gin bottle he'd emptied that day. He not only quickly noticed Moffatt's attitude but was also so shocked by it that he took the first opportunity to grab Moffatt by the arm and pull him protesting through the kitchen to the bathroom, where he locked the door.

'Now Harold, what the hell's wrong?'

Moffatt answered by using the pissoir. 'Might as well, seeing I'm here.'

'I asked you what's wrong.'

'Nothing. There's damn all wrong, old man. Did you know there's going to be the biggest barbecue seen in Kabul for donkeys' years? A dozen sheep going to be roasted.'

'I'm a lot more concerned about the way you were roasting Lan out there, for the delectation of those bastards.'

'You're talking about my friends, not to mention my guests. Besides, Mr Commercial Secretary, what bloody business is it of yours anyway?'

Langford knew his own eyes were bloodshot, which made him all the sadder when he looked into Moffatt's. The rest of the pink, plump, sulky face was hardly recognizable.

'What are you trying to do, for Christ's sake?' he demanded. 'Yes, I've got a right to talk. You know what a hell of a stupid life Helen and I lead. If one of us were to die, it'd be no relief to the other; that's how bad it is. Granted there are others all over Kabul not much better. But you and Lan, my God, you've always been there to show what could be done. I'm not joking either, when I tell you that meant a hell of a lot to me. So why this public crucifying of her?'

Moffatt scowled. 'If you came to piss, go ahead, otherwise, let's get out of here.'

There was a hearty thumping on the door. 'Don't hog the

can, you in there, whoever the hell you are. I'm drinking cold English beer.'

Moffatt drew the bolt. Outside stood Dean Moriss, crew-cut Cultural Adviser to the U.S.I.S. in Kabul. He recoiled in mock horror. 'What's this, gentlemen? Or am I getting the sex wrong?'

'It's all yours, Dean,' said Moffatt.

'You say amen to that?' asked Moriss, looking at Lang-ford. 'You seemed embittered.'

'Go to hell.'

'No, no, merely to leak. But I may also shed a tear or two at the moral depravity of English gentlemen of the twentieth century. I was warned about this when I left home, but I laughed it to scorn. Pity the poor American marine on Hampstead Heath.' He went into the bathroom and could be heard joking lewdly to himself about his inability to slide the bolt home.

Going through the kitchen Langford tried again. 'If you want to be sadistic,' he said, 'why not try giving that bitch Larsen a kick in the tail? She's got that drag-you-to-bed look in her eyes, and you're her bone tonight. Must Lan watch that too?'

'Mind your own bloody business, John. I know what I'm doing. Isn't there a lot to mend between you and Helen?'

'There is.'

'Then for Christ's sake go and mend it, and leave me to do my own mending.'

'If that means you and Lan have quarrelled, all right. Any man and his wife can quarrel. Look, Harold. Let's leave the whole shower of them and go for a walk in the park.'

Moriss appeared, on his way back. 'So it's a walk in the park now? What has Mom's innocent boy from Chicago wandered into? And two such virile specimens of manhood too!' Chuckling, he pushed past to join the throng.

'There's nothing like a walk in the fresh air for restoring things to their right proportions.'

'They tell me you've worn a moonlight track round the Embassy compound.'

'They're right. So I should know what I'm talking about. Let's go over to the café among the Afghans; that's another way of seeing things straight.'

'John, you're reputed to have corkscrew vision. Don't forget I'm host here, with duties to perform.'

'But one of your duties, you miserable sod, surely isn't to humiliate your wife.'

Moffatt had moved away and didn't hear that. He stood in the centre of the sitting room and clapped his hands.

'Here's one you've heard before,' he shouted.

'That's right, Hal boy. Nothing like the old ones.'

Langford saw Lan, apprehensive but still resolutely self-contained, too much so and obviously in love with her husband. Whatever the cause of the quarrel he felt sure she was in the right; but what difference did that make, once the pair of you were lost in the labyrinth?

They had gathered round him to listen. Helga Larsen was at the front. Glass in hand, large bosom thrusting up out of her low-cut green silk dress, and red lips glistening with whisky, she once turned and gave the small demure faintly smiling Lan a sneer of contempt that dared to have pity in it. Langford felt like shouting: 'You brazen bitch, keep your pity for yourself.' Then, in horror, he began to listen to Moffatt.

It was a silly, unwitty, and grossly offensive story about two American sailors, visiting Shanghai, who had been told in their boyhoods that Chinese women were different from all other women in the world, in one anatomical respect.

Even those prepared, in whiskied good humour, to find laughter in anything found it difficult to laugh then. There were some embarrassed titters, and one shriek of appreciation, from Helga Larsen, that shocked everyone. Some slipped away, during the telling of the joke, and others as soon as it had been told; but most remained, fascinated by the sight of the fat unhappy clown in the centre with sweat like vitriol on his brow, yelling out his stupid filthy joke as if he were a priest haranguing a mob of unbelievers. What in Christ's name, wondered Langford, is he trying to convert us to? Not surely to a contempt for Lan, because the more repuslive he, the more marvellously unsullied she. Perhaps she was flushed a little more than usual, and she seemed not quite able to control a slight restlessness in her fingers. Langford thought, and some others thought it too, judging by the curious glances they gave her, that she was just too composed, too ready with her defences, and too resourceful with that smile. They wondered if the trouble could be that she was too icy in her affection, in her love-making more like a temple priestess than a wife full of faults and warmth; and more than one remembered that their feelings towards her had always been of respect and admiration, rather than of liking. Having a Chinese wife might perplex any man; but, telling that hideous joke, Moffatt had been anguished too.

People soon began to take their leave to go to the Club. Among them were Langford and Winfield who travelled round to the Club in the latter's Land Rover.

'Remember Gillie at the policy meeting?' asked Langford.

'I'll never forget it.'

'Do you think there was something in it?'

'What do you mean?'

'Well, the big bugger did sound inspired. I thought his eyes were going to pop out and land in H.E.'s pipe bowl. But good God, Gillie as prophet!'

'Why not? The Lord never chooses as we would choose.'

Langford shuddered. 'That's true enough. There was sweat on Gillie's brow too. What do you think's behind it, Howard?'

'You mean, our Consul's being chosen?'

'No, dammit. That shocking performance of Harold's. Is their marriage breaking up?'

'I would say it looks like it.'

'Don't be so bloody smug, Howard.'

'I'm not being smug. I like Harold.'

'And Lan?'

'I'm not sure. Does she want to be liked?'

'Yes. I know what you mean. But, God Almighty, I thought they were the perfect married pair. What's gone wrong?'

'I think we'd better wait till the mantle falls on Bob again.'

'It's not a joke, Howard.'

Winfield did not answer. The whole of life was a joke; otherwise what was its point? But of course only a fool tried to explain a joke, and he had vowed never to be a fool.

About half a dozen guests remained when Prince Naim arrived, accompanied by Abdul Wahab, smelling strongly of gasoline. They had met outside the gate, the Prince stepping out of his chauffeured Daimler, Wahab jumping off his bike. Naim, like most of the other men, was in evening dress. Wahab wore the suit in which he went to school, since it was his best; it had been at the dry-cleaner's, hence the smell of gasoline.

Moffatt, talking to Helga Larsen, noticed the two late-comers. He did not hurry forward to greet them; instead, with his free hand gently bumping against her soft rump, he whispered: 'Do you see these two Afghan gentlemen who have just arrived?'

'One's the Prince, isn't he?'

'Yes. But look at the other.'

'Why? What's special about him? Is he the Prime Minister's son? Looks to me like any ten-a-penny Afghan.'

'If you think that, you must be lacking in percipience.'

She giggled. 'I'm sure I am, whatever it is. What you're lacking in, Hal boy, is sobriety; but don't get sober too soon.'

'That dusky gentleman, I would like you to know, is Mr Abdul Wahab.'

'Is he now? And who the hell is Mr Abdul Wahab? Lan seems to have a fancy for him.'

'Look closely, dear Helga. This is a matter in which I value your judgment. Look closely.'

'For God's sake, at him?'

'At him. At the soul of Afghanistan.'

'Is that what he is? I must say he looks it.' Then Lan came across with Naim and Wahab.

If I stink of gasoline, thought Wahab, he stinks of whisky, and this woman beside him, with her arm through his, is a drunken whore. My poverty has been making me squirm with shame, despite the friendliness of the Prince; but surely poverty becomes honourable in the face of all this squandering of money on drink which makes a man boorish and pugnacious, and a woman undignified and salacious? The whisky which has depraved this man, my self-appointed enemy, and this woman, rubbing herself against him in front of his wife, cost money that would have kept an Afghan peasant and his family in what they would have called comfort for a month. No doubt our mullahs are too strict, with their many out-of-date taboos; but it is equally certain that these degenerates from the West represent a licence that is even more harmful.

I shall not of course attempt to retaliate, no matter how he insults me; not for his wife's sake, or Laura's, or my own, but for Afghanistan's. They would all laugh if they were to know that three times I had to visit the dry cleaner's to make sure he would have my suit ready in time, and the third time had to sit and wait while the work was done. They would laugh still louder if they knew that the dry cleaner, a man with a misshapen foot and eleven children, was a remote cousin of mine. Nevertheless, it is still possible for me to achieve a superiority over them all simply by showing the kind of humility which they call Christian; but I must take care it is not interpreted as servility. Therefore I shall accept this glass of whisky, and drink it as manfully as Moffatt himself does, not in timid sips, but bold gulps, even though it burns my throat and turns my guts instantly sour. I shall smile too, indomitably, and though this fair-haired woman with the large bosom keeps winking at me in an incomprehensible way, and asking me if I am conversant with Afghan history, I shall remain cool and courteous. See, she is not really interested in our history, for as soon as I begin to talk about it she laughs and struts off on her very high-heeled shoes. I notice – it is impossible to avoid noticing, so tight is her dress – that she has plump buttocks; and I reflect again how strange it is that though I am naturally attracted to women with big breasts and plump buttocks, I have promised to marry one plump nowhere. Laura is skinny.

But really I had better stop drinking this whisky. As the Prince has just whispered, it is not like orange juice. Yet I feel courageous. I am certainly not afraid of Mr Moffatt, glaring at me all the time like an enemy. Shall I tell him what I, the meek and subservient Wahab, have been thinking here, on his own carpet, in his own house? Would he put it all down in a letter and send it to Laura? Well, what if he did? Better that she find out in time she is going to marry a man who, though not claiming to be a lion, passionately denies he is a mouse.

'No, Harold,' said Lan. 'Mr Wahab doesn't want any more.'

'Let him speak for himself. What do you say, Mr Wahab? Your glass is empty, like mine. Shall we fill them both up?'

'By all means, Mr Moffatt.'

'That's right. You and I have lots of sorrows to drown.'

'No, I assure you, I have no sorrows; no personal ones, that is. For my poor country, yes, I weep for her.'

'So you do. These are noble tears. Lan, go and attend to our other guests. Mr Wahab and I are going into the gulkhana for a little chat.'

Wahab found himself laughing, in an excess of confidence. He felt so like one of the warriors of old he half looked for the proud horse under him. As he followed Moffatt into the flower room he did not know yet what he was going to say, but he knew he had in his mind a vast treasury, with jewels of wisdom for any subject the Englishman might choose.

'I understand, Wahab, you've met Mohebzada?'

So the 'Mr' was already dropped! 'Yes, Mr Moffatt, I have had that privilege.'

'I wouldn't call it that myself. A nasty spiteful whining little runt with a mouthful of rotten teeth.'

'It is possible his wife has a different view of him.'

'I doubt it. You knew their child was ill?'

'Yes. I also know it is now recovered.'

'But it will get ill again.'

'It is mortal.'

'Have you seen it?'

'No.'

'You should go and have a look at it.'

'For what particular reason, Mr Moffatt?'

'So that you can see for yourself what a miserable unlucky little bastard it is.'

Wahab felt exalted, rather than angry. For poor Moffatt, so angry, with specks of foam on his lips, he had not only sympathy, but love. Even when he put out his hand to pat him and had it savagely knocked away, he still loved him.

'You have no children yourself, Mr Moffatt,' he said, with a sad, loving smile.

He continued to smile when Moffatt with a vicious oath flung what was left in his glass about his face.

'Why did you do that?' he asked, groping for his handkerchief. In spite of his spectacles some of the whisky had got into his eyes and blinded him.

The incident had been seen. There were cries and titters. Someone shouted: 'For God's sake!' It sounded like Naim.

His eyes were now on fire. He kept them tightly closed. A cool hand touched his, and a voice, calm but sympathetic, murmured: 'Please come with me, Mr Wahab.'

It was of course Mrs Moffatt. She held his hand and led him.

'This is ridiculous, I am afraid,' he said, as he stumbled into a small table and knocked over a glass. 'I hope I have not broken it?'

'Never mind it.'

'I also hope this pain is temporary.'

'Is it very painful?'

'I must confess it is.'

She led him into what certain noises informed him was the bathroom and made him sit down on a stool.

'You must bathe your eyes.'

'Of course.'

She took off his spectacles for him. 'Here is a piece of cotton wool.'

He stooped over the basin and tried to bathe his eyes. The pain was still intense.

She whispered something, but he could not make out what it was. After a long pause she said it again: 'Why did he do it?'

'I really do not know. I merely remarked that he had no children. You see, we were discussing Mr Mohebzada's unfortunate child, which was ill a few days ago. Perhaps, madam, you did once have a child that died? If so, I am very sorry.'

'No.'

'You mean, you have never had a child? Perhaps then being without one is a great sorrow to your husband. It would be a great sorrow to me.'

A voice spoke in the doorway, polite but sulky: 'How are you, Wahab?'

He recognized the Prince. 'Thank you, Your Highness. In a minute or so I shall be as good as new again, thanks to Mrs Moffatt's kind attentions.'

'If I may say so, her husband's weren't very kind. Why did he do it?'

'A foolish impulse, shall we say?'

'That's not what he says.'

'Mr Moffatt?'

'Yes, yes. He said that he did it because you insulted Miss Larsen.'

Wahab opened eyes and mouth in astonishment; he quickly shut the former again; they were still fiery. 'Miss Larsen?'

'Yes, yes. Please do not say you do not know who she is. You were talking to her.'

'Is she—' he almost said 'the woman with the plump buttocks,' but changed it in time to 'the woman with the fair hair?'

'Yes. Now why did you insult her? Was it because you had drunk too much whisky? For you had, you know.'

'I do not think I insulted her.'

'Surely in such a matter you can be sure? Your eyes may be closed, Wahab, but your memory, I suppose, is still open.'

Wahab tried to remember. Of course he had admired her buttocks and breasts, and perhaps in his imagination he had fondled them; but he had reason to believe that was a normal and permitted degree of lasciviousness. Still, it was true he had drunk too much whisky. Had he dared to speak his admiration?

'You see, Wahab, you are not sure. He's gone to spread it all over Kabul, and everyone will believe him.'

'It is not true, Naim,' said Mrs Moffatt, 'and I shall tell everyone it is not true.'

'They will say you are only doing it to protect this foolish fellow.'

Wahab nodded and sighed. He could not deny that he was foolish.

'I think they will know that Miss Larsen is not the kind of woman to be insulted.'

'Ah, but you forget, Lan, that she is Western, and poor Wahab here, and myself, are ignorant dark-skinned natives from the East. It just isn't good enough, you know. Even if Wahab did say something he shouldn't have, because of the whisky, Harold had no right to do what he did. What's wrong with him? Is he ill? Has he gone mad? Do you think it's time he went home? I must look upon this from a selfish point of view. Consider my position. It will be said I brought Wahab here. I didn't, of course; I merely met him at the gate. But it will be all over Kabul by tomorrow that I brought him here, he got drunk, he insulted this woman, and Harold threw whisky in his face. My mother will hear about it; my father; the Prime Minister; Mojedaji. If it had been tea, even scalding tea, it might not have been so bad; but you know the absurd prejudice they have against whisky. I'm afraid, Wahab my dear fellow, your goose has been cooked. I've been trying to use my influence on your behalf, but after this I'll have none left.'

'It wasn't in any way Mr Wahab's fault,' said Mrs Moffatt.

'He drank the whisky, didn't he? I warned him, and you warned him. Yet he drank it as if it was water.'

Wahab was suddenly sick. Mouth full of sour vomit, and eyes still tightly closed, he tried to mumble apologies.

'It's a bit late now for repentance. Lan, I must push off now. I may say the house is empty. Discretion has swept the

last of your guests away. The servants have gone too. Harold
took them with him in his car.'

'Yes. We had promised to lend them to the Club.'

'There's nothing I can do to help? You're not blind,
Wahab, are you?'

Bravely Wahab opened his eyes long enough to see how
peeved the Prince was. 'I am not blind,' he muttered.

'For heaven's sake!' cried Naim. 'I did not ask to be a
prince. I would have been happier as a simple gardener. But
I must go and consider what my line of action should be. I
would advise you, Lan, to get along to the Club as quickly as
possible; for reasons that ought to be obvious. Good night.'

'Good night, Naim.'

'I am deserting, I know it; but who will be surprised?
Wahab, have you learned this: no one is to be trusted, not
even your Laura?'

Wahab heard the footsteps receding along the tiled
corridor, and a minute later heard the car move away.
For a moment he wondered what it was to be a prince.
Then he opened his eyes, determined to keep them open.
They smarted painfully, and streamed tears; but they func-
tioned well enough to let him see that Mrs Moffatt standing
beside him, with a wad of cotton wool in her hand, was
weeping too. Her tears were new and rare. Only he was
seeing them; not even the Prince had been privileged.

He put out his hand and touched hers. 'Please do not
weep on my behalf.'

She tried to smile.

'You are a brave woman. I am not a brave man. I am little
better than a coward. Like the Prince too I will desert;
nothing is surer. They will send for me. Mojedaji will be
there. "Wahab," they will say, "no more syphilis microbes,
no more Laura." And I will reply: "Yes, masters, I promise."'

'No, you will not!'

He was startled by the fierceness with which she cried that. Yes, small and dainty though she was, she could also be fierce.

'You will not let them insult you, persecute you, and defeat you.'

'Mrs Moffatt, do not distress yourself for my sake. I assure you I am a weakling. I have been deceiving myself even about Laura; and I have been deceiving her too. Never once have I really been convinced she would come here and marry me. She was to come and marry a man proud of being an Afghan, devoted to advancing his country, unafraid of the reactionary forces now in power, prepared to face insult, prison, torture, even death. But who was that man? Not Mohammed Abdul Wahab, not me. He was a dream. She cannot come and marry a dream.'

'You can make the dream come true. You must. How are your eyes now?'

Fearfully he examined them in the mirror; bloodshot, tender, wet, they were recognizable as his own; he saw and hated their brown furtiveness, their servile meltings. Mrs Moffatt might as well ask him to pluck them out of his head as to expect him to become the hero he had dreamed himself to be.

In the mirror he noticed the lavatory pan. The sight terrified him. He ought not to be there with this Chinese woman.

'You and I will go to the Club together,' she said.

He let out a squeal of alarm. 'No, no. I am going to find my bicycle and go home.'

'If you do that, you will have lost Laura.'

'I tell you, I have already lost her. For weeks I have been carrying a letter in my pocket, stamped, ready to send. Do you know what it says? It says that she must not come, that I never was in earnest, and that she must be a conceited English fool to think that I, an Afghan, would ever condescend to marry her, a skinny cripple! Yes, it is addressed to Laura. Look, here it is.'

He took it out and showed it to her; but it was at his face she stared.

'She is a cripple?'

'Yes. I have told no one. I have tried to hide it from myself. It is shameful. Only one foot, of course; her left. When she was a baby she had some illness; her leg too is very thin. But she can walk; she can climb hills. She is very courageous about it, not bitter as I would be. I have a relative – you see, there are no princes in my family – who has a small shop. He too is a cripple, and he has eleven children. You see, Mrs Moffatt, how ridiculous my dream has been.'

'You love her.'

'Yes, yes, I love her. I weep for her in the darkness. Would I have written this letter if I did not love her?'

'And she loves you.'

His face grew radiant. 'Yes, it is wonderful, impossible, but she does. I am sure of it. Why should I care if they cut out my eyes with knives? Laura loves me.' It was true he had desired Miss Larsen, but only in thought. All men had such thoughts. Women should not feel insulted.

'I think Laura will come here and you will get married.'

'Why not?' he cried. 'I am a coward, but I should not be afraid to die for her sake.'

'We will go to the Club together.'

'They think I insulted Miss Larsen.'

'You and I know that is a lie.'

But he did not know that at all. 'They will hate me. Perhaps they will not allow me in. Mojedaji will be there. But you are right,' he went on shrilly. 'I must not let them defeat me. I will go and perhaps I will dance too. You will not think it possible, but twice Laura and I went dancing in Manchester. She can dance well enough, if one is slow and gentle. Yes, if they laugh, I shall think of her. If they hate me,

I shall remember that she loves me. Even if she does not come to Kabul, have I not known her, and shall I not remember her all my life? No one will be able to hurt me; at least not very much.'

Thirteen

ON THEIR way down to the main road where they hoped to find a ghoddy to take them to the Club, they passed one of the policemen whose duty it was after dark to patrol – some said, to spy on – that street where all the houses were rented by foreigners. Light from a distant lamp glimmered on his broad, sullen face.

Lan wished him good evening. In reply, he made a harsh noise in his throat, like an animal, and crashed the club he carried against his leather leggings.

'In his native village,' said Wahab, 'you would see him play with his children. He would give you his best carpet to sit on, and his best mutton to eat. Here in Kabul it is different.'

'Why?'

'He is afraid. He has seen you are foreign and I am Afghan. He has been taught to consider that unnatural. He feels his superiors would have liked him to stop us.'

'I think he was much happier in his native village.'

'Oh yes. Much, much happier.' He sighed. 'Sometimes I wish I had been born a simple villager, with a river beside my house and trees behind it.'

'He would be conscripted?'

'Yes. His pay is the equivalent of one English penny a day.'

'Listen. I think he is following us.'

'Yes.'

'Why?'

'It is simple. He is lonely and far from his people. We are human beings.'

'Yet he would not speak to me.'

The soldier had stopped again.

'What was there for him to say? Nothing, I am afraid. Perhaps he does not understand Persian very well. They have their own dialects in the north.'

She felt a desire to go running back and stand in front of the soldier until at last he said something, no matter what. It seemed very important that he should speak to her. If necessary she would wait for hours; and so demonstrate still once again, she told herself as she moved on, that patience and imperturbability which characterized her in Kabul just as unshaven Josh Bolton's credulity characterized him. Lan Moffatt, they said, has the secret of time. She never has too much of it or too little, and so none is ever left over for regret or heartbreak. Therefore her life is so tidy and well-arranged. Perhaps, though, that legend of imperturbability had ended that evening. Surely those with sympathy must have seen through her mask.

They passed a man, shrouded in a blanket, crouching to make his water against the wall.

'Barbarian,' muttered Wahab.

But she shook her head. Tears were again running down her cheeks. She remembered her childhood in Djakarta, where in the canals in the middle of the street folk side by side washed teeth or urinated. Even then she had been learning to assemble, as if it were a work of art, this thin, delicate shell of dignity, but within, no one's heart had remained more sensitive and easily bruised. During the Revolution, when soldiers hung with grenades were swarming about the city, burning buildings and firing their rifles even at the birds in the air, her young sister Ling had been found dead under a tree with many bullet wounds. She had wept then, quietly and often, but her grief had seemed to the rest of her family incomplete, for there had been no hatred in it or desire for revenge. Kneeling beside Ling's body, touching it, she had not been able to see the necessity for hatred. Sometimes she had wondered if she would be incapable of love also. Harold's coming had proved that wrong.

'Here, at last, is a ghoddy,' said Wahab.

She awoke from her memories. In front was the mosque, its dome gleaming in the moonlight, but it was thousands of miles from that other temple in the jungle where Harold had first asked her to marry him. She had said no.

'As you would expect, it is filthy; but if we wait for another we may have to wait for an hour, and in any case it will be just as filthy.'

As she took his hand to step up on to the soiled cushions, she found his shy, timid face under the gray karakul hat as terrifying as a creature's out of the jungle.

'It will be all right,' he assured her, as he sat down beside her. 'At least the horse is docile. It is too tired and hungry to be otherwise.'

She had been terrified because he had been helping her up, not into this Afghan ghoddy which would rattle and bump along the bleak earth roads of Kabul, but rather on to the ancient, high, brassy American car that would take them back to Djakarta along the jungle track; and his face had been Harold's, huffed and angry at her refusal.

She had a vision of life without him.

'Please hold on tight,' advised Wahab. 'This bit of the road is full of holes. They dig it up, you know, and use it to mud their roofs. No one prevents them. There is no regulation against it. What a ridiculous freedom!'

She tried to remain in this world where people dug up roads to place the mud on their roofs. How could she help Harold to subdue this shame in his mind, which would destroy them both, and which she had foreseen in that temple in the jungle. Many times since then, lying beside him in the dark, she had sensed that struggle in his mind as he had tried to prevent the shame from being born. After he was asleep he had sighed and sometimes had sworn; but always in the morning he had been gentle and curiously grateful. But the shame had been born, had thriven, and now possessed him like a madness.

It was not so simple as Josh Bolton thought: she Chinese and yellow, Harold English and white, different races, different cultures, different ideologies, conflict inevitable. 'It's history, Lan,' the American had said, with his naïve impertinence that thought itself wisdom. 'It's history that's between you, and I doubt if you can fight that.' But it wasn't as simple as that. Yes, history was against them, history represented by the sneers of people who really were shocked in their hearts by this marriage of yellow with white, slant eyes with round. That she had not been invited to the Embassy Sewing Group was no doubt an exclusion to laugh at; but after the laughter a regret persisted, and a feeling, rather than a recollection, that there were many similar exclusions, all amounting to a sentence of isolation.

She would never forget, for instance, the scene in the restaurant in Singapore when an American at one of the tables had told his companions the joke that Harold had shouted out in the house an hour or so ago. Harold had jumped up and rushed across. He would have struck the American if the latter's friends hadn't prevented him. Harold had got the worst of it, and his mouth was bleeding when they were at last shooed out by the manager. But the tears in his eyes had been of shame and anger unappeased. Later he had apologized. 'You'd have to know my story from the day I first knew the thumb in my mouth was my own. And who wants to know that?' She had wanted to, very much; but he had never told her. All she knew was that his mother had divorced his father when he was thirteen. He had mentioned that as a kind of counterbalance when she had told him that her sister Ling had been thirteen when the soldiers had shot her.

'Very jolly, very gay,' cried Wahab, intending to be sarcastic but quite failing, for genuine appreciation was making him laugh.

They had arrived at the Club. From the ghoddy they could see the fairy lights and Japanese lanterns in the trees. Dance music was playing, and people were dancing on the big terrace and below it on the grass. The water in the swimming pool was of many colours, red, blue, green, yellow, from the lights surrounding it. There were two large fires burning in corners and the smell of roasted kebab was delicious. Everywhere were women in lovely dresses, Indians in saris, Japanese in kimonos, Americans and Europeans with bosoms half-revealed. Had Laura been there, wondered Wahab, would she have worn such a dress? And would he have been proud or ashamed of her? It was not really in answer to that last question that he murmured to himself that at any rate the dress, being long, would hide her foot, even if it did show off her breasts, which in any case were less conspicuous than most.

He could not see Moffatt or Miss Larsen. They would be inside the club house, dancing or drinking or continuing their amorous play.

He helped Mrs Moffatt to alight. She too had a small bosom, and yet her dress buttoned right up to her throat. She was, he realized then, very like Laura in other ways too: sympathetic, but demanding in the person sympathized with a degree of resistance that he himself for instance was not always capable of; able to think clearly even when shedding tears, but not shedding them often; physically frail, but in will stronger than many muscular men; and with the ability to inspire friendship, though able to do without it herself.

For a moment or two, without knowing why, he felt a kinship with Moffatt and a timid longing to be his friend.

Several small Afghan children stood outside the gate, not quite begging, not quite jeering, but with hands and tongues out. Wahab was about to feel ashamed of them when he suddenly wondered why he should be, and wasn't; instead, he loved and was proud of them, despite their rags. Pakistani or Indian children would have been as pestiferous as dogs, clinging to clothes and catching hands, whining all the time, and parading what lucky deformities they might have, such as missing fingers, or blind eyes, or twisted feet.

He felt it was foolhardy of him to go in and be among so many antagonistic people; but he had in a way promised Laura to make the effort for her sake.

They went through the gate together and down the fairy-lit path toward the dancers on the terrace. Among these Lan saw Alan and Paula Wint, he debonair in evening clothes, she voluptuous in a blue dress that showed off her fair skin and blonde hair. Heads close, they were laughing, oblivious of everyone else. People called them self-centred, and certainly they had spent much time in cultivating their natural inclinations to ignore or casually notice others; but now it struck Lan that perhaps they had been wise in fashioning a nest out of their cosy selfishness. The Mossaours were dancing too, Maud stately and stern, Pierre compensatingly charming. John Langford had as his partner the little wife of the Japanese First Secretary; they danced sedately, but Howard Winfield, partnered by a pony-tailed American teenager, now and then broke into steps like a Red Indian war dance, with whoops to match. Spectators, with glasses in their hands, sat or stood around, chatting and laughing.

It was obvious it was going to be a successful party. In another hour or two dozens of them would be war-dancing and whooping. Griefs would be forgotten for the time

being. There was one woman for instance, fat-faced and
Dutch, whose child, Lan knew, had been quite ill a week
ago; she shrieked as merrily as any.

Wahab had seen, among the spectators, Mojedaji and
another important Afghan, the Chief of Protocol at the
Foreign Office. The latter, tall, silver-haired, and the handsomest man present, was smiling and sometimes clapping
his hands; but the mullah's grins were sour. Wahab, his eyes
guilty, tried to slink by unseen.

Josh Bolton, dressed as usual in rumpled clothes, was
talking excitedly to the burly Russian Consul, whose evening suit was as immaculate as his politeness.

Josh saw Lan and hurried over: 'Harold's inside some-
wheres,' he said. 'Say, you oughtn't to have brought this guy
with you. Harold's liable to throw him into the pool. He
insulted Helga.'

'And you are all her champions?'

'Hell, I know she's a bit of a tramp, but we've got to draw
the line at letting Dagos insult her.'

'Dagos?'

'You know what I mean. He's coloured, isn't he?'

'So am I.' She walked on.

'That's right, you are,' he muttered as he stared after her.
'And that's just the trouble. For I guess of all the colours
yours is the one we could best do without at this present
time. That, lady, is the inescapable truth.'

Wahab had heard the short conversation. 'An American
gentleman?' he asked, with a little smile.

'Yes.'

Again he had the feeling that she was tired of his company. Already she had gone beyond the call of duty. Well,
from his point of view, her presence beside him was like a
light shining on him; and of course what he wanted was
obscurity.

'Ah,' he said, 'I see a friend of mine, Mrs Moffatt. Do you

mind if I join him? There are many of your friends here, whom you will wish to speak to.'

He had seen no friend and when he hurried away he did not know where to go. Behind a tree, turning, he saw her where he had left her, in a loneliness that only her husband could relieve. Just as only Laura can relieve mine, he thought, as he went on toward the bonfire where the kebab was being roasted. People there were standing about eating the hot mutton off the long iron skewers. Their manners were sufficiently Afghan to make him feel more at home near them than near the dancers. Among them was someone he had met: Mr Gillie, the British Consul. He did not think Gillie would remember him, or at any rate would want to talk to him, so he was slipping past when Gillie shouted cheerfully: 'Ah, Mr Wahab. Come and meet my wife.'

As Wahab went over he tried to keep in mind every lesson Laura had taught him, but he was so grateful to Gillie for noticing him that he found it impossible to prevent his eagerness from overflowing into what he knew was typical Afghan obsequiousness.

He shook hands with Mrs Gillie. He liked her; with her gray hair and ordinary, worried look she reminded him of his own mother.

'Get yourself some kebab, Mr Wahab,' said Gillie. 'It's good. Only an afghani per lump.'

That was fantastically expensive. 'I am not hungry,' said Wahab. 'Everyone looks like cannibals.'

'Cannibals!' Startled, Gillie stared round, and began to laugh. 'You're not far wrong at that. Look at old Weitzler there, chewing somebody's knee-bone.'

'Bob, for goodness' sake!'

'And there's Dave Lipton, head of I.C.A., gnawing his way through an ankle.'

Wahab apologized to Mrs Gillie. 'I meant it really as a joke.'

'Many a true word spoken in jest,' said Gillie. 'Pardon me if I speak rather greasily.'

'Use your handkerchief, Bob, please.'

'See how I'm bullied, Mr Wahab. Do Afghan women bully their men like this?'

'I'm afraid they do, Mr Gillie.'

'But I forgot. You're not going to marry one of them. Maybe you're going to do worse. I mean, these ex-school-ma'ams are usually martinets.'

'Laura is really a civil servant.'

'But she used to be a teacher? And that's what she's coming here to be. As well as of course to get married.'

'Pardon me for asking this, Mr Wahab,' said Mrs Gillie. 'But is the lady still coming? I mean, there has been no change of decision?'

'Not as far as I know.'

'It's a very big decision for a girl in her position to take.'

'Now, Muriel, Miss Johnstone's no impulsive little girl. She's thirty-five.'

'Thirty-three,' murmured Wahab.

He was astonished how even more like his mother Mrs Gillie had become: face sharp and intense with interference.

'I wouldn't feel honest talking to you, Mr Wahab, if I didn't tell you straight to your face that in my opinion Miss Johnstone is making the wrong decision.'

'Muriel, that's not being honest; that's being downright impertinent.'

'No, no. As Laura's countrywoman, Mrs Gillie has a right to speak.'

'Well, if I were you, Wahab, I wouldn't be so broad-minded about it. I'd be telling them to mind their own business.'

'But, Bob, think of poor Mrs Mohebzada.'

'Always,' sighed Wahab, 'I am having Mrs Mohebzada flung in my face.'

'She was happy to begin with, Mr Wahab. Now she talks about suicide.'

'This is hearsay, Muriel; and unpleasant hearsay at that.'

'I have not met Mrs Mohebzada,' said Wahab, 'but I understand she is very young. Perhaps she was too young to face up to so drastic a change?'

'If that is your reasoning, Mr Wahab, I am afraid you are wrong. The younger a woman is the more adaptable. At thirty-five Miss Johnstone will be set in her ways.'

'Thirty-three, please. Do not forget that she is not making the same mistake as Mrs Mohebzada. She is coming here unmarried. If she does not like it she will go away again unmarried. Unless of course—' and Wahab, with a bitter little laugh, looked round at the carefree well-off foreigners—'she meets someone else not doomed to remain in Afghanistan all his days.'

Mrs Gillie nodded, as if she'd already thought of that.

'There's just one more thing I'd like to ask, Mr Wahab, if you don't mind.'

'If you do mind, Wahab, don't hesitate to say so.'

'I do not mind.'

'Suppose you and Miss Johnstone were to get married, who would perform the ceremony? There is a Christian clergyman here, an American of somewhat evangelistic views, but properly qualified. But would not the law of the land demand that a Moslem mullah perform it?'

'Really, Wahab, I cannot allow you to answer that. Muriel dear, this is a party, a dance, a celebration, not an inquisition.'

Among cannibals, as among other people, thought Wahab, were differences of outlook and opinion. Staring at Mrs Gillie's not unfriendly but greedy little face, he had another grimmer vision of cannibalism where not flesh was eaten but souls. Here, in this pretty garden hung with coloured lanterns, was surely a debauch of it. As he gazed round, at the bald German Weitzler and the big-paunched American Lipton, at Mr and Mrs Wint dancing, at Mojedaji and the Chief of Protocol, at Mrs Mossaour and her very dark-skinned husband, and at all these others whom he did not know but who no doubt by this time had heard of him, he felt his self-esteem grow less within him, as all these devourers gnashed at it. On the grass were already dozens of bones flung away; he saw what was left of him tossed aside also, an enticement only to stray hungry curs and flies.

Gillie heard him sighing. 'What you need is a drink, Mr Wahab.' And he clapped his hands for a waiter.

He could not, thought Wahab, have heard of the incident at Moffatt's house; or perhaps he had and this was either his British way of letting bygones be bygones, or his merely human way of helping humiliation to develop.

'What d'you like?' asked Gillie, when the waiter, who turned out to be Sofi, Moffatt's servant, stood grinning beside them. 'Whisky?'

'No, thank you. I find whisky is bad for my eyes.'

Gillie guffawed. 'D'you mean after a few glasses you don't see so well? It's bad for everybody's eyes in that way, I assure you.'

'If you do not mind, I would much rather have orange juice.'

'My God! But just as you wish.'

'You are forgetting, Bob dear, that it is against Mr Wahab's faith to drink whisky.'

In Mrs Gillie's eyes, despite the kindness of her voice, was an accusation that also in his faith were many other things, equally unnatural to a Christian.

He could not tell her that he had no faith, Christian or Moslem; he could not, amid that spree of soul-eaters, remind himself he had no God to pray to. In the sky shone Orion, which could also be seen from England. But for the fact that it would still be daylight there, Laura could at that moment have been watching her favourite constellation too. That she was not, that the sky over Manchester was still light while the sky here was dark, seemed to increase the distance between them so immensely that had she been dead and he still alive they could not have been farther apart.

'Still sighing?' said Gillie, laughing. 'Well, I don't think orange juice is going to do much about that.'

When the orange juice arrived, and their whiskies, they soon made excuses and went off to join some friends, leaving him with Orion for company.

The Wints had seen Lan and Wahab arrive. Unlike the Gillies, they had heard about the joke and the whisky-throwing. Heads close, sometimes with his lips against her cheek, they danced and with the compassion and con-descension of happy lovers discussed Lan, who was standing by herself under one of the Japanese lanterns.

'As cute a little showwoman as you could find,' said Paula. 'First she brings that fellow along, and then she stands pensively under the lantern. All the same, if you had told me that she could ever have looked lonely I wouldn't have believed you.'

'Darling, you surprise me. I think she always looks lonely.'

'Self-sufficient, darling, not lonely.'

'Lonely, dear, and never quite as self-sufficient as she likes to pretend.'

'Is this masculine intuition, darling? Or just chivalry? She's dainty, I admit, but take a woman's word for it, she's a little nugget of purest self-sufficiency. Why are you all looking for an explanation of Harold's admittedly beastly behaviour? She's driven him to it, simply by her Oriental self-sufficiency. Not only does everyone else – with one exception at least, as you'll gather – think the little lady's well-nigh perfect, she's got into the habit of thinking it herself. Really she must be pretty unbearable to live with. I mean to say, darling, that filthy joke, after all it did have a point. I mean, what else could it possibly mean but a revolt against this presumption of perfection? I know I'm a bundle of faults myself, but at least, as you know, darling, I'm normal in that respect.'

'As I most deliciously know, and as I hope to know again.'

'But not quite here, darling. Though from the look of him last time seen I wouldn't be at all surprised if Harold attempted it in our midst with the abominable Miss Larsen.'

'In the pool, perhaps, like seals?'

'Seals? Do seals, darling? How do seals?'

They laughed together.

'Seals do,' he murmured.

Again they laughed.

'All the same, darling,' said Paula, 'in the interests of a world with variety, it's a pity it isn't true.'

' "In the interests of a world with variety." Darling, how delightful!'

That had been a favourite expression of an Ambassador Alan had served under as a raw Third Secretary.

'All the same,' said Paula, 'throwing whisky in the fellow's face was a bit thick.'

'To save the honour of the egregious Miss Larsen.'

'How does one insult the uninsultable?'

'Shush. Maud Mossaour is glaring at us.'

'Why should she?'

'Didn't you know, whenever she's with Pierre she suspects all public laughter?'

'I knew she was sensitive, but not as much as all that.'

'Darling, it isn't sensitiveness; in fact, it's the very opposite; it's the lioness' instinct.'

'But I thought the lioness' instinct was for protecting her cubs, not her mate.'

'This lioness wishes to protect her mate also, as well as her cubs.'

For a few seconds then they danced in silence, smiling, and thinking of their own pale cubs far off in England, in no need of protection by fang and claw.

'Cat,' he murmured, affectionately.

'I see she's got company at last.'

'Who?'

'Little Lan.'

He turned and looked. 'Mojedaji! Now that would be an interesting conversation to listen to. What has the wily mullah got to say to her? He'll have heard what happened at the house.'

'She certainly doesn't look very pleased.'

Then the music stopped and hand in hand they went in for a drink, to find that their neighbours at the bar were Harold Moffatt, and Helga Larsen, he morose and she perseveringly hilarious.

Lan had been finding her loneliness more and more intolerable, but she wanted only Harold's company, anyone else's would be worse even than being alone. Outcast and strangely afraid, she appreciated how Wahab must be feeling; but she did not wish now to take his and his Laura's part. Before, she had not realized Harold's opposition would be so bitter as to endanger his love for her. Now, realizing it, she felt for the first time that she could remember a desire to strike back, to hate, to hurt if necessary, and not be too particular about her victims. There, under that other tree, watching the dancers, among whom were the Wints obviously talking about her, she experienced again the finding of her sister's body with its many bloody wounds; but this time she felt sick with hatred of those who had done it.

When she saw Mojedaji step off the path, clumsily, for his fat thighs gave each other little room, and waddle across the grass towards her, her heart, cold and angry, was glad too. She could practise her new-found hatred upon him. He, rather than the foolish Wahab, represented what in this country was causing Mrs Mohebzada so much sorrow, and Harold so much complicated disgust. With his white turban, black evening suit, gold tooth, and scented moustache, he revolted many European and American women because he emanated a kind of lust that they could not understand and so take measures against. His holy man's eyes, they said, stripped off your clothes, garment by garment, and then at their contemptuous leisure ravished you.

'You are not enjoying the festivities, Mrs Moffatt?' he asked.

'I like to watch.'

'Yes, I think you are like myself, by temperament a watcher rather than a participator. It has its advantages, but we also lose much, I fear.'

He pressed close to her. Turning, she searched for Wahab, and found him talking to the Gillies. Her purpose seemed to be to set Mojedaji upon him. If so, it wasn't successful. Mojedaji looked in that direction too, and no doubt saw Wahab, but merely smiled.

'You did not come with your husband, Mrs Moffatt?'

'I think you saw me arrive.'

'Yes. I was a little surprised. You came with Mr Wahab, a countryman of mine.'

She said nothing, though he waited.

At last he sighed. 'I was very sorry indeed to hear of the distasteful occurrence at your house this evening.'

She could not help shivering.

'You are cold, Mrs Moffatt? Perhaps you should go inside.'

'I am not cold. What was it you heard?'

'It is really a beautiful evening, quite warm. Yet see how bright the stars are. I think our stars are the brightest in the world. We have a saying that we are nearest to heaven. One could believe on such a night as this.'

'What was it you heard that happened at my house, Mr Mojedaji? People distort and exaggerate.'

'That is true. Still, it is never safe to give these young Afghans whisky. They are not used to it. Little wonder they turn pugnacious. When sober their fault is perhaps the very opposite; then they are too humble.'

He took a gold cigarette case out of his pocket, snapped it open, and offered it. She shook her head. He took one himself and lit it with a lighter, itself of gold.

'You will pardon me if I take a very serious view of this, Mrs Moffatt. You see, Wahab in a way represents his country. He is young, eager, educated, patriotic. It may not be too fanciful to say that if he fails, Afghanistan fails too. So I am very anxious to find out the truth about this incident. According to your husband's version, Wahab grossly insulted Miss Larsen, an American. I have not yet heard Wahab's. But we all have a high regard for you, Mrs Moffatt. We know you are completely without prejudice against us, and I believe you have shown friendship for Wahab personally. If you confirm what your husband has said, I shall accept it, without further question.'

'Will you not ask Mr Wahab?'

'Yes. But if he denied it I should not believe him.'

She remembered Wahab's sad puzzled words: 'I merely remarked that he had no children.' And she remembered too his confession that Miss Johnstone was crippled in the left foot. Not truth only, but humanity itself, would be outraged if she supported Harold in his unforgivable lie that Miss Larsen had been insulted.

'I do not think,' murmured Mojedaji, 'that this Miss Larsen enjoys a very good reputation. But of course that does not matter.'

'My husband does not lie, Mr Mojedaji.'

'Then he is most unusual among men. But in one matter any man may tell the truth. I am not expressing myself well, but English is a difficult language. Did you actually hear Wahab yourself?'

'Yes.'

'I see. Well, that certainly disposes of it as far as I am concerned. You see, I wondered if your husband could have some personal grudge against Wahab.'

'Why should he?'

'True. There seemed no reason. But then, why should he come to His Excellency the Minister of Education and myself, and ask us to use what influence we had to prevent a certain Englishwoman from being given a visa to visit Afghanistan? He told us this woman was hoping to come here to marry Wahab. That did not seem to us a sufficient reason for withholding a visa, and so your husband made insinuations about Wahab which could have serious consequences.'

Within, she felt like screaming; outwardly, she smiled and nodded. 'My husband always has good reasons for what he does and says.'

'He accused Wahab of being a Communist, of associating with persons engaged in plotting against the Government. These accusations are being investigated. If they prove to be justified we shall certainly be grateful to your husband.'

She found her mouth dry. 'Mr Wahab is rather a simple person. He might mix in politics without any evil intentions.'

'Such fools are dangerous, Mrs Moffatt. I do not think they are tolerated in your own country.'

'My country, Mr Mojedaji, is my husband's country.'

'England?'

'Yes.'

'I understood you were very proud of being Chinese. And very rightly so, to my mind. Were not the Chinese civilized when the English were still barbarians dressed in animals' skins?'

Suddenly she saw Harold. Some men, Captain Mabie and
Dean Moriss among them, had dragged him out on to the
terrace. Helga Larsen came behind, laughing and holding up
a bottle of whisky that had coloured ribbons round it. At first
Lan thought they were going to baptize him in some way by
throwing him into the pool or to anoint him with the whisky.

'There's my husband,' she said. 'I must go to him.'

'Of course. Please let me thank you for your help.'

As she left him and began to push her way through the
crowd towards the terrace, people began to yell at Harold to
make a speech. All over the large garden they took up the
chant: 'Speech, speech, speech.' She saw the Wints chanting
it and thought they were a little drunker than they had been
when dancing a few minutes before. She saw the Gillies
chanting too, and even the Mossaours; everyone she knew
and liked.

'How the bloody hell can I make a speech when you're
ramming a whisky bottle down my throat, Mabie, you mad
Hindu?'

Everybody roared with laughter, and clapped such a
brilliant opening of his speech.

He had been lifted up on to a high stool by Mabie and
Moriss. His black tie was askew and his hair dishevelled. He
looked sullen and unintelligent.

'All right,' he shouted hoarsely. 'You asked for a speech,
and you're bloody well going to get one.'

It was now or never, she knew, if their marriage was going
to be saved. When people felt her pushing at their backs
they turned to protest, but instead made room for her to
pass. So, before Harold could say any more, she had arrived
in front of him, panting, and looking up at him with an
appeal that sobered Mabie at least, who hung his head and
mumbled apologies in Hindi.

Harold glared down at her.

'If he tells that joke again,' whispered Langford to Winfield, 'and he's drunk enough to try, I'll throw the bastard into the pool.' And when Howard smiled, he added: 'What the hell is there to smile at, old man? If he insults her he insults the whole damned human race.'

'That could be why I'm smiling.'

A hearty voice roared: 'Put her up beside him.'

Langford and Winfield stared at each other. 'Gillie?' said the former. 'Our bold and prophetic Consul himself,' agreed the latter.

'Go on, Captain Mabie. Help the lady up. What would our guest of the evening be without his charming and beautiful wife?'

Someone shouted: 'Hear, hear.' It was Alan Wint, and he began to clap. Paula clapped too, loyally. Others joined in. Soon the whole company was clapping.

Delighted, Mabie and Moriss seized Lan and lifted her up on to the stool. Harold had to put his arm about her to make room.

'Lan, what the hell do you think you're doing?' he muttered.

They noticed she was weeping as well as smiling, and into their clapping came a note of affection. She had always been respected and admired; now those tears were making her liked. Most supposed they were of joy.

She saw Wahab on the outskirts. He too was clapping.

She noticed Helga Larsen also, not clapping, but smiling, as patient as a whore. When he's sober, thought Lan, he despises her.

She looked for Gillie, and saw him standing beside his small wife. People called him stupid, and perhaps he was not very subtle; but she had always considered him the type of Englishman who had earned for his country its reputation for fairness and decency. Under no circumstances could she think of him betraying anyone, of whatever colour or rank, as she and Harold had done Wahab.

'Speech!' they were again chanting.

Someone brought another stool and Lan was lifted on to it. Harold's arm was no longer round her. He turned and whispered: 'Go on. Here's your chance.'

'For what, darling?'

'Telling them what a bastard I really am.'

'I love you. I've got nothing to say to them.'

He flung up his hand. They cheered. Facetious advice was flung from all sides, in a variety of accents, and even of languages.

'I just want to say this,' he cried. 'If you want to give the pool a name—'

In great merriment they hailed that the idea was brilliant and asked him to suggest a name.

By contrast, he was in maudlin, angry earnestness. His voice and mind were thick. If Mabie hadn't kept supporting him he would have tumbled headlong from the stool.

'You can call it what the hell you like,' he shouted, 'but for me it's going to be: The Waters of Babylon.'

Owing to the truculent drunken thickness of his voice most of them didn't catch the name, and those they asked weren't sure either, but it made no difference, he was a good chap, a wit, a poet even, and he was affably drunk.

'Get me down from here, for Christ's sake,' he muttered.

Mabie and Moriss lifted him down and he went staggering into the clubhouse.

Then some fair-haired Germans came sprinting from the dressing room, clad in trunks, and dived into the pool. People gathered around, throwing in coloured balloons, which the swimmers tossed back. Some burst, and everyone cheered.

Lan no longer was alone. Friends sought her out and were painstakingly kind. Paula Wint, in particular, chose to be very friendly, and seemed even to be trying hard to com-

municate some of her own assurance in love. Lan should
have married a diplomat, she said, not a poet. Whatever one
might say about diplomats – and good heavens, didn't
everybody have something nasty to say about them? – at
any rate you could depend upon them to be at their most
discreet when a little drunk. Of course, such discretion was
not nearly as exciting as a poet's extravagance. Who but a
poet would ever have thought of calling a swimming pool in
Kabul 'The Waters of Babylon'? That was the name he'd
suggested, wasn't it? Out of the Bible, or somewhere? Alan
had absolutely no imagination in such matters. The names
he had proposed for the children! He would have called the
pool just The International Club Swimming Pool, or simply
The Mill Pond, after one in Warwickshire where he had
swum when a boy. By the way, had Lan heard anything fresh
about this Miss Johnstone of Manchester, who was supposed
to be coming out to marry Wahab? Surely if she did come
she would never marry him now. A sober Afghan was bad
enough, a drunken one would be the last word in horror.
Didn't Lan agree?

Hours later, after midnight, Wahab, tired and woe-begone,
but undaunted, came looking for her. He found her with
some people who at once withdrew, grinning and winking at
one another. At least, he thought, if I now smell of whisky, it
is a more expensive and fashionable smell than that of
gasoline. But perhaps what I smell most strongly of all to
those people is simple-minded folly.

He had not expected Mrs Moffatt to be pleased at his
taking her away from her friends, but neither had he
expected her annoyance to be so sharp. Reconciliation with
her husband had apparently given her claws. Though he
smiled, his heart sank lower still: he had counted on her at
least as a friend for Laura; otherwise he would never have
told her about Laura's foot. Well, it didn't matter: Laura

wouldn't be coming. It had been a dream, and now he was awake, yawning and shivering.

'I am sorry, Mrs Moffatt. But, you see, it is time for me to go home.'

She found herself resenting his humility. If she lost Harold, this simpleton would be to blame. He was not as harmless as she had supposed. Let Mojedaji deal with him as he deserved.

'I would not have disturbed you, Mrs Moffatt, but I wished to find out if there would be someone at your house to open the gate for me. My bicycle is there. If it is not convenient, I shall walk home.'

'How far away do you live?'

'Not far. About three miles.'

She looked in her bag and took out a key. 'I would ask one of the servants to go with you, but they are busy.'

'It is not necessary.'

'This is the gate key. After you have got out your bicycle, please lock the gate again.'

'And then shall I bring the key back to you?'

'No. My husband has one, and the servants have another.'

'What shall I do with it?'

'Return it whenever convenient.'

'Perhaps I could throw it over the gate, wrapped in a piece of paper?'

'If you like. Mr Wahab, has Mr Mojedaji spoken to you tonight?'

'No.'

'Are you sure?'

He smiled. 'I am not quite so drunk as others are, Mrs Moffatt.'

'What do you mean?'

He just smiled.

'Well, if he has not spoken to you yet, he certainly intends

to. In the meantime, my advice to you now is to write to
Miss Johnstone and stop her from coming.'

'This is a big change, Mrs Moffatt, in such a short time.'

'I did not know then—' she hesitated, wondering which
lie to use.

'That she was a cripple?'

'That, and other things.'

'No,' he said, in a curiously gentle voice. 'You are not
speaking the truth.'

'How dare you!'

'What did you say? "You will make the dream come
true."'

'That was before you told me she was a cripple.'

His smile too was gentle. 'No. After I told you, you said:
"She will come here and you will get married." How do I
remember your words so well? I have been saying them in
my mind all night.'

'I think, Mr Wahab, you will be able to help your country
more if you marry an Afghan. If you marry this Englishwoman you will find yourself involved in too many personal
difficulties.'

'That may be true. You are in a position to know, I
suppose. Good-bye, Mrs Moffatt.'

He did not altogether blame her for this change in her
attitude; indeed, he had been expecting it sooner or later. In
every English person he had met, with the exception of
Laura, he had encountered this change from cordiality to
indifference, in some instances, as here, to active dislike. Mrs
Moffatt, Chinese herself, had inevitably acquired English
characteristics from her husband. Would he, after sleeping
and eating and talking with Laura for years, have become
English in some of his ways, and the possessor of arrogance
and hydrogen bombs? But was not Laura as far away as
Orion? As he stared after Mrs Moffatt the sight of the great
constellation above her head confused him, so that as he

turned away and went down the path between the fairy
lights, and out of the gate into the earth street with its ruts
and holes, he kept staggering and muttering to himself, as if
he were drunk.

Behind him the music and laughter grew more faint, and
soon, coming to a bundle of rags against a wall where some
homeless old man tried to sleep, he had a feeling that, dead,
he had been banished from paradise and sent for the
purification of his soul among the damned. This was the
first of many he would see. It was therefore with a kind of
defiance of God Himself that he cautiously crossed the
ditch, and crouching, sought for the creature's hand to
place in it a couple of coins that would buy at least a slab
of *nan* in the morning.

As he went on again he heard the murmurs of surprise and
gratitude behind him, and tears came into his eyes. Why do
we hate one another? he wondered. Why do we devote our
energies and abilities to it? Why do we take pride and
pleasure in it? You, Mojedaji, with your gold ring and your
secret brotherhood: you, Harold Moffatt, with your poetry
and your lies; you, Mrs Moffatt, with your strange beauty
and mysterious mind; and you, Mr Gillie, with your big, red
face and redder rose: all of you, please remember, good or
bad, are in the eyes of God no better than that abandoned
old man, even if for purposes of His own He has decided to
allow you houses and money and good clothes and always
plenty to eat, while he sleeps cold and hungry against a wall
pissed against in daylight by dogs and little boys. How do
you know, indeed, that the old man is not God Himself?

As he left the main road and turned down the avenue in
which the Moffatts' house was, he was yawning. Several
times he yawned, but when he came nearer the gate his
mouth stayed open, no longer in sleepiness, but in astonishment and alarm. There, outside the gate, stood Moffatt's
little German car.

He thought at first Mrs Moffatt must have got her husband to drive her home. But no, the car faced the way he was walking and must have come from the Club by the same route. It could not have passed him without his noticing it.

Approaching it like a thief, in spite of his fear that the soldier might be lurking somewhere, he saw there was no one in it. The gate was locked. The moonlight shone on the lock. It was easy to find the keyhole. The key fitted. He turned it. There was no rusty shriek. The gate too was silent as he pushed it open. Seconds later he was inside, the gate closed again, his back to it, and his eyes on the house, dark save for a lance of light lying on the terrace.

There, where he had left it, was his bicycle, leaning against the wall. Fondly, he pressed its tyres; they were still hard enough. He searched in his pockets for the key of the thief-proof lock that imprisoned the back wheel. As he put in the key and turned it, he remembered the creak Mohebzada's back wheel had made and hoped that it too, like the baby, had been cured. Then, taking the trouser clips from the handle bars, he fastened them round his ankles. That done, he was ready to go.

But he could not go; that spear of light from the curtained room was deep in his heart; he could not go until it was plucked out, and the curiosity that, sharper than steel, was paralysing his vitals.

What was more likely than that Moffatt had sneaked back to the house with the blonde woman with the big breasts? And what could be a more succulent feast for his own revengeful eyes than to peep in and see the pair enfolded in their guilt?

Those were sinful speculations, and he giggled at them, in shame; but still, they did not stop, the screen in his mind did not go dark, and what kept it bright, with those pictures of illicit love-making, was the most shameful thing of all, his

delight that the victim was Mrs Moffatt who, more cruelly
than her husband, had made it obvious to him that not only
was he unworthy of Laura at present, but also that he would
never have the opportunity to prove himself worthy. At the
heart of the conspiracy to deprive him of his sweetheart, and
of his faith in his country and himself, smiled Mrs Moffatt.
Therefore, taking her imaginary hand in his – he could feel
its coolness as he had done already that evening when she
had helped to bathe his eyes – he took her with him along
the side of the house to the terrace steps, and up these one at
a time, his shoes and knees too squeaking, so great a strain
did his caution impose on them. Luckily his companion
seemed anxious also not to be discovered. She, and her
expectation of horror, were so real to him that if she had
suddenly screamed he would have been appalled but not
surprised.

At last he was on the terrace, along which like a row of
guardian dogs slept the flower pots. He noticed the moon
shining on the mountains beyond the city. The sight was so
beautiful, and so familiar, that he felt sad and guilty. He did
not know where he should have been at that time of the
morning, but certainly he should not have been there, on
that terrace like a thief, holding captive by the hand the
ghost of Mrs Moffatt. It was not yet too late to recover
honour and so be able to face the beauty and grandeur of his
native land without sickening shame. All he needed to do
was to let Mrs Moffatt go and watch her vanish into the
moonlight, and then himself return to his bicycle. Within
two minutes he could be on his way home, pedalling quietly
so as not to invite attack from homeless men or dogs.

But he spent those two minutes in another way altogether.
Tiptoeing up to the French window, he put his eye to the
space where the curtains did not quite meet. His heart
pounded so noisily he felt sure that the two within must
hear it, but he was past caring. Nevertheless, though scruple

was at last trampled on, he kept telling himself that if ever a man had a legitimate excuse for playing Peeping Tom, it was he; not just because Moffatt was his enemy accusing him of foulness, but also because through Moffatt's machinations it was likely that he, Wahab, would be deprived of his natural rights as a procreator. This peeping then was not merely revenge, it was also a kind of compensation.

Was he cheated? At first he wasn't sure. The two persons in the room were the couple he had expected all right, Moffatt and the big-bosomed blonde, but they were not making love. It did not even look as if they had been, a minute or so before. Neither looked satisfied. In fact, the Larsen woman, seated in an armchair with a glass of whisky in one hand and irritation in the other, scowled across at Moffatt as he lolled on a sofa, more than half asleep. A glass of whisky stood on the carpet close to his dangling hand. No cushions lay on the floor to form a bed. The woman was fully clothed; even her knees were covered by her green dress. Moffatt's jacket, though, was off, and lay across the back of a chair. They might have been friends listening to a symphony being played on the radio.

Suddenly, causing Wahab to bump his nose against the glass, she jumped up, set the whisky down on a table, and strutted out of the room. For an instant he admired her plump angry buttocks. Perhaps she was now gone to a bedroom to prepare herself, to take off all her clothes so that when she returned in a minute or two she would be entirely naked. It seemed, however, that if such was her intention, he himself was showing much more interest than Moffatt, and would show more appreciation. Moffatt's hand still hung above the glass of whisky; it had not once lifted it. The situation was altogether absurd, he decided, and was made worse by someone's weariness, not Moffatt's, but someone else's, who yawned, kept closing his eyes and losing interest. For a few seconds he felt indignant at that sleepy intruder, until he realized it was himself. Even if the blond woman did come in naked he would continue to yawn and lose interest, and might even fall sound asleep.

He did not wait to see her come back into the room, but, quite alone now, crawled away, going down the steps like a monkey and creeping round the side of the house to his bicycle. Only once did he fall off, when he ran into a large stone which he thought was a shadow.

Fourteen

To LADY BEAULY and Alan Wint fell the task of bringing up
to date the invitation list for the Queen's Birthday Garden
Party. The previous year more guests had come than there
turned out to be whisky for, either because the Ambassador,
rankling under a recent cut in his allowance, had miscalcu-
lated the number of bottles required or the orderlies had
misunderstood their instructions as to the proportion of
whisky to water; or the guests had consumed more than was
decent or fair. He had afterwards discussed it with his wife
and had left her to decide whether next year more water
must go with the whisky or fewer guests should be invited.
The former practice seemed to her not quite genteel,
whereas the latter was not only perfectly permissible, according to any code of etiquette, but had the advantage of
enforcing the exclusion of those rather exasperatingly on the
fringe of eligibility, such as some educationists from Wyom-
ing. Therefore, with Paula called in to give support to every
decision made, Lady Beauly and the First Secretary met in
the drawing room of the Residence for a whole afternoon,
behind drawn sun blinds, to choose the lucky three hundred
and fifty.

Among those had to be Harold Moffatt and his wife;
being British, nothing short of public sodomy could bar
them, as he had been known to put it himself with typical
disrespect; and the Mohebzadas were included, out of uneasy charity, the expectation being that they would not
come. Among those excluded were Josh Bolton and Captain

Mabie, one white and the other dark, so that the one snub
cancelled out the other with characteristic British imparti-
ality. Among those never considered, either for inclusion or
exclusion, was Abdul Wahab.

The completed list, with as many scoring-outs and writ-
ing-ins as the manuscript of a poem, was handed to Katharine Winn who was to type the names on the cards and
envelopes. First, with what she called her plebeian efficiency, she went through the list and discovered the names
of more than a dozen people who had left Kabul. One
American couple had gone to Bangkok and she was tempted
to send them their invitation there. Two of her friends,
clerks like herself, employed in the American Embassy, had
not been invited, either because they were too low in the
hierarchy or because it was known at the Big House that
they were personal friends of hers. She had once rejected an
invitation to a function there in favour of a shindig at their
house. However, she had suspected that they would be left
out and without much hesitation put them in herself. Every
guest had to be personally presented to the Ambassador and
Lady Beauly in the great hall, by Alan Wint, and there was
no doubt memories would somersault and eyes roll when
these interlopers appeared, assured and radiant in beautiful
dresses direct from New York. They would not know their
invitations had been brazenly forged and, diplomacy being
what it was, no one would ever tell them.

It was easy to explain why she should have risked Ambassadorial lightning – the only danger in her case being that
the monocled flashes might send her into a giggling fit – on
her friends' behalf, but for years afterward, in various parts
of the world, including Leopoldville and Barcelona, she was
often to wonder why she should have done it for the Afghan
Abdul Wahab, particularly as she felt quite sure, while
typing his name on the gilt-edged gilt-crested card and
the College's address on the envelope, that the invitation

would confound rather than flatter him. Perhaps one part of her motive was jealousy of Helga Larsen, voluptuous and blonde, whereas Katherine herself was mousy-brown and, at twenty-eight, as good as virginal. Another part could have been the pity she had felt for poor Wahab at the Barbecue Dance where she had come upon him twice in the space of two hours, still sipping the same orange juice, and dabbing at his sore eyes with his handkerchief. Moreover, she detested his country and sometimes in her heart felt ashamed. But most of all her inviting him represented rebellion against Alan Wint and the Ambassador's lady, who seemed to think that their positions of petty authority gave them the right over her of masters over a slave. Well, just as a slave might get revenge by spitting in the soup, so she got it by sending out that card to Wahab. She did not think he would come, but even if he did and astounded the Reception Committee by his meek intrusion, he would have some kind of right to be there, since he was engaged to marry an Englishwoman; though, to be truthful, she considered that ambition of his a presumption worthy of ten years' solitary imprisonment.

So, one morning about a week after the Barbecue Dance, the Pakistani orderly, with the red Embassy turban and the Rudge Whitworth bicycle, delivered the envelope to Isban College. He handed it on the front steps to the custodian, Sadruddin, who asked what it was. When told it was an invitation to the great party at the British Embassy which was to celebrate the British Queen's Birthday and which the Afghan Prime Minister would attend, he assumed it was for the Principal. In fact, it was the latter himself who, after a minute or two's pride and rejoicing, discovered that the name on the envelope, and worse still, on the card itself, was not his but, impossible to believe, Wahab's – whom everyone knew to be almost in disgrace and who at that moment was teaching the Twelfth Class in an ordinary classroom. The laboratory in the meantime had been closed as a precaution against something, the Principal himself wasn't sure what but believed it had to do with Wahab's unfitness and imminent dismissal.

Looking out of the window at two small dung-gatherers with their kerosene cans roped to their backs, neither of them as old as his own son, he noticed the large stain on the lapel of his silver-gray suit where some rice had fallen out of his hand at dinner. It was his best suit, and if he had been invited to this great celebration he would have had to wear it, as it would have been impossible for him to buy a new one, unless his cousin the Minister advanced him the money. Let this anxiety also be Wahab's. But all the same, why Wahab, an ordinary teacher, not even an under-Principal? No wonder, he thought with sad bitter smile, a British envoy and all his staff had been murdered here in Kabul a hundred years ago.

'This is not for me,' he said, with dignity, handing the card back to the custodian. 'It is for Wahab.'

'Wahab?'

'Yes. I think he must have friends among the British.'

'I have heard,' said one of the other teachers, from an armchair, 'that Wahab is the friend of a Chinese woman who is the wife of an Englishman who teaches at the University.'

'I have heard that too,' said the Principal, and he was reflecting, with the most cautious nose-picks as if each nostril were red hot, upon that extraordinary involvement of Wahab's, when the telephone on the desk in front of him rang. As he picked it up, he kept shaking his head, trying to disentangle poor Wahab from that Chinese wife of an Englishman.

The voice in his ear was sudden, harsh, and anonymous. 'I want to speak to Abdul Wahab.'

Though the accent was much too good for an English-man, the Principal pretended the speaker was from the British Embassy.

'It is all right,' he answered coldly. 'He has received his card.'

'What card? Do not be a fool, Abdul Mussein. I am speaking on behalf of the Brotherhood.'

Swiftly the Principal changed the telephone to his other hand, so that he could drag his handkerchief out of his breast pocket and dab his brow with it. 'Yes, sir,' he said. The Brotherhood terrified him. It was a new secret society, whose purpose was said to be the purification of Afghan life. A week or two before, an Afghan had been found murdered in the street outside his home. People whispered that the Brotherhood had done it. The man had been a known adulterer. Nepotism too, so it was rumoured, the high-minded Brotherhood condemned.

'Is Wahab there?'

'You mean, in the room at the moment?'

'Is he available for me to speak to?'

'Yes, certainly.'

'Then fetch him.'

The Principal shouted. The message boy jumped up from his snooze on the floor.

'Go and tell Abdul Wahab to come here at once.'

The voice in his ear said: 'And I want my conversation with him to be private. You understand? Everyone else must clear out. Yourself included.'

The Principal trembled and frowned; yet, instead of protesting at that rudeness, he murmured meekly: 'You may be interested to know that today, ten minutes ago as a matter of fact, Wahab received an invitation to the big party at the British Embassy to celebrate their Queen's birthday.'

'Did you receive one?'

'No. Yet am I not the Principal?'

'You are a nonentity.'

The Principal blinked. It had occurred to him that the speaker might not be a member of the mysterious Brotherhood at all, but someone from the Twelfth Class playing a joke.

'I am the Principal of one of the chief educational institutions in Afghanistan,' he said, with dignity.

'Your students consider you a frightened fool, and rightly so.'

'I do my duty. The Minister is pleased with my work.' He almost added: 'I have only one suit fit for a man in my position, and it has a stain on the lapel. Therefore it is obvious that at least I take no bribes as other principals do. No matter how wealthy a student's parents may be, he must work to pass the examinations in my school; he cannot use his money to buy marks.' But he kept silent, for though it was true he had accepted no bribes, being afraid to, still he had yielded to please on behalf of the Chief of Police's nephew. Besides, he knew his teachers took bribes. 'I hope,' he said, with trembling magnanimity, 'that poor Wahab is in no trouble.'

'That is our business.'

'I think I can say, with justice, that he is a sincere teacher.'

'Who are you to judge?'

'I am the Principal.'

The other laughed. Perhaps he was a Twelfth Class student, and also a member of the Brotherhood? Youth was the age for reckless idealism.

'You know that many, if not all, of the people in this country, in important positions, occupy these solely because they have been hoisted into them by relatives who themselves were previously hoisted into theirs.'

'I have heard of it. It is not right, I agree; but it is still possible for a corrupt system to appoint a capable man.'

'Such as yourself? We know your history. Is not His Excellency your cousin? When you were at the University you were not one of the brightest students.'

The Principal suddenly remembered that some subordinates were listening. Therefore he dropped his voice to a passionate whisper: 'I was often hungry in those days, and I had no private room in which to study.'

'All the most able young Afghans are hungry often, and have no private rooms.'

'Then surely I was one of them?'

'It does not follow. Your reasoning is illogical. Why is Wahab taking so long?'

'His room is downstairs, at the end of a long corridor. But here he comes, carrying his card, I see.'

'The invitation card?'

'Yes. He must be a friend of the British.'

'Give him the telephone, and then clear out. My conversation with him must be private.'

'I understand.' But he wasn't convinced yet that this wasn't a hoax. He imagined some of the Twelfth Class faces at the other end of the line, and every one, with its impudent smile, fitted; but what he could easily imagine too was the fierce bearded face of some leader of the Brotherhood – fanatical, bloodthirsty, and pro-Russian.

'Wahab,' he called. 'Someone wishes to speak with you.'

Wahab approached the desk. He did not look frightened. Was it the card in his hand that gave him courage? Indeed, he looked stern and important. Was it possible that he was a Brotherhood leader? Certainly he was a rash and fervent advocate of change. Remember the syphilis microbes! Remember the telephone conversation with Prince Naim. Remember, too, this invitation to a party that most of the chief men in the Government would attend.

'Do not speak yet, Wahab,' he said, in a tone involuntarily

respectful. Then he clapped his hands and cried shrilly: 'You must all leave. Mr Wahab's call is a private one.'

All were astounded, none more so than Wahab himself. He gaped at the instrument in his hand. 'Is it from England?' he asked, hoarsely.

The Principal shivered. What kind of man was this who expected telephone calls from England? 'No, no, Mr Wahab. It is local. Hurry, please, everyone.'

Out of armchairs and off sofa, they dragged themselves, insulted and indignant, especially those senior to Wahab.

When they were all out, the Principal whispered: 'I think you will agree, Mr Wahab, that I have done my best to treat you fairly. Remember also that upon my salary many people depend.' Then he crept out and closed the door.

'Hello, please,' said Wahab, into the telephone. Miracles had happened before. Consider the exploits of Ali, the Prophet's son-in-law. Laura could have arrived secretly, by aeroplane, and could now be waiting to speak to him from the airport.

The voice that answered obviously spoke through a beard; it was gruff and as unlike Laura's as a human voice could be. 'Abdul Wahab?'

His belly aching with disappointment, Wahab answered: 'I am Abdul Wahab. Who are you?'

'Never mind who I am. It is enough for me to tell you that I am speaking on behalf of the Brotherhood.'

Wahab's belly got sorer as anger mixed with the disappointment. His eyes glittered. 'And who may the Brotherhood be?'

The other gasped. 'You do not know?'

'I have heard of a gang of grown-up children who skulk in the darkness and yet claim their aim is to bring light to our country.'

'That is our aim.'

'Rubbish.'

'Wahab, I warn you.'

'And I warn you,' cried Wahab hysterically. 'I shall form a brotherhood too, with myself the only member. I shall make it my task to expose you.'

'You must be drunk again.'

'Again? I never was drunk in my life.'

'We have heard differently. I have been instructed to summon you before a meeting of the Council.'

'Absurd!'

'Take care, Wahab.'

'Who are you? You know my name, tell me yours. Let us speak like men together.'

'I am under an oath of secrecy.'

'In that case I have nothing whatever to say to you.' He set the telephone down, and was staring at it, in awe at his own splendid audacity, when it rang again. To his astonishment the member of the Brotherhood, for it was he again, spoke this time in a much less unpleasant voice.

'I am sorry I cannot give my name, Wahab. What I am instructed to do is to summon—'

'Summon?'

'Invite you then, to a meeting of the Council.'

'Who are its members?'

'But, Wahab, you cannot ask that.'

'I have already done so, and I do it again. Who are the members of your Council?'

'They are important men.'

'Give me their names. I shall judge their importance for myself.'

'Really, Wahab, I cannot tell you. The place is Abdul Raouf's bazaar in the carpet serai, at seven o'clock. Do you know the place?'

'I am a native of Kabul. I know every corner of my beloved city.'

'Good. You will be there?'

'Suppose I am not, suppose I dismiss all this as puerile folly, what then?'

'Do you think Hamoudi, who was found dead last week, thought it was puerile folly too?'

Wahab laughed scornfully. 'I know people are whispering that the Brotherhood killed him, but I do not believe it. His wife's brothers killed him. The Brotherhood are merely trying to steal the credit, if you can call it creditable to murder a man in the dark, even an adulterer. But yes, you may tell your Council that I shall be there. Tell them too that I am not afraid of their masked faces and their hidden knives. If it is true, as you yourself have almost admitted, that they employ assassins to carry out their aim of restoring Afghanistan to greatness, then I shall welcome this opportunity of pointing out to its leaders that the methods of Genghis Khan are not applicable today.'

The voice sounded worried. 'No. I shall merely tell them you will be there. Good-bye.'

'Cowards,' muttered Wahab and became slowly aware of the responsibilities and probable consequences of bravery. In the past, secret societies had often flourished in Kabul and had spilled blood with relish. The stab in the dark appealed to the Afghan mentality more than the calm, wise word in the sunlight; or at least had done so formerly. It could very well be that this latest society, the Brotherhood, really did employ skulkers with knives, and in a day or two he would be waylaid by three or four of these in some lonely spot at night and would suffer, not just a ripping of his tires, but also of his belly and throat. He would have died a martyr, but no one would know it. A hundred reasons would be put forward for his murder, but among them would assuredly not be the true one of martyrdom. Neighbours would say he had seduced someone's sister. The newspapers would print that he had died from heart failure. The police authorities, if they were not in league with the Brotherhood, would suppose he had been killed by robbers. What version the British Embassy would choose to send to Laura he could not say, but that they would send one, however false, was indicated by this invitation which he had received and which was, in its way, as disquieting as the summons by the Brotherhood.

Were the new and old forces, tug-o'-warring for his country's soul, using him as a rope? Often these days he did feel as if he were being pulled apart.

There was a soft knock on the door. In slipped the Principal, alone. 'Finished, Mr Wahab?'

'Yes.'

The Principal drew near. 'I know the call was from the Brotherhood.'

Wahab sniffed.

'Who is its leader, Mr Wahab?'

Another sniff. 'Who cares?'

The Principal nodded, in admiration of such an astute reply. 'Some say it may be the Prime Minister himself.'

'Why not the King?'

'Ah, indeed.'

'Or Prince Naim?'

The Principal nodded. 'Yes, yes. All of them. Of course.'

Wahab had not heard from Naim since the evening at Moffatt's house, but that silence did not prevent him now, in a characteristic plunge from selfless idealism to cunning self-interest, from indulging in another dream of power and wealth. The Principal's face, littered with the relics of discarded ambition, inspired him. All his acquaintances regarded him as a man of ordinary abilities and qualities. Most of the time he was inclined to agree with them; but there were other times, admittedly rare, when he felt that he was only waiting for a suitable opportunity to throw aside his disguise of mediocrity and stand revealed as Afghanistan's twentieth-century man of destiny, who by sheer brilliance of intellect and steel-like strength of character had been chosen as his country's saviour. He it would be whom, some Independence Day, the army with its Russian tanks, guns, lorries, and armoured cars would march past, and whom too the MIG's would salute at eight hundred miles an hour. Yes, and the day after, he it would be who would issue an order rejecting all those instruments of murder. Tanks, guns, lorries, armoured cars, and aeroplanes would be sold back to the Russians. The money received would be spent on many irrigation schemes to improve the country's agriculture. Schools would be opened in remotest villages. Teachers would be adequately paid everywhere. The shaddry, and all the other disadvantages at present dishonouring women, would be flung contemptuously aside. Men, who now walked through the streets of the country with roses in their hands and frustration in their hearts, would then find the flowers symbols of hope as well as of beauty.

He awoke from his dream to find on the Principal's face, with its overlarge nose, cunning, typical Afghan cunning, that tried hard to reassemble those fragments of ambition and piece them together in a smile that had hope in it too, but corrupt hope, and ignoble expectation, of the kind that would keep Afghanistan a desert, with oases only for the unscrupulous few.

The Principal was whispering: 'There has been talk, Mr Wahab, that I am not competent. My ears are not made of stone. You know that I have a wife and child, and other dependants. You know also that I am not entered as Principal, but merely as Acting-Principal, the difference in salary being three hundred afghanis per month. It is not difficult to remove a Principal; to remove an Acting-Principal is as easy as blowing a dead fly off a cake. I do not sleep well. For more than five years I have not slept well. I do not wish to be made Inspector-General of Secondary Schools, though some weeks ago my name was mentioned in connection with that post, which is still vacant. All I want is to be established as Principal here, and perhaps to have an office of my own, with a proper W.C. for the convenience of guests and distinguished colleagues like yourself.'

Even while accumulating anger at this selfish and sarcastic request, Wahab suddenly was flooded with love for his foolish countryman. Though powerless, that love was not absurd; what only mattered was that it was genuine and had him looking at the Principal as one man ought always to look at another, with tolerance and sympathy. The Principal's face was not handsome, with its big nose, its slightly bloodshot eyes, and its hollow cheeks, but it was human and therefore precious. In it Wahab saw Laura's, so much more beautiful, and also every face that had ever looked kindly upon him since the moment when, a brown baby on a red cushion, he had distinguished his mother's face from the many blurs that up to then had represented the outside world.

In his joy he embraced the Principal, who laughed too, though anxiously.

'But, my dear Hussein,' cried Wahab, 'I am a person of no importance. I am a hindrance to myself. How can I help another to advancement?'

'It does not matter,' cried the Principal. 'Do whatever you can. I have an old uncle – he lives with us and eats twice as much as other old men – who always cries, with his mouth full of food: "We are God's children".'

'I do not think I believe in God.'

'Sometimes I too have difficulty. And I shall make a confession to you, which I have never made to anyone before. When I try to imagine God's face, whose do you think I see? It is terrible, I know, and blasphemous, but I cannot help it. I see Mojedaji's gold tooth and all.'

Wahab laughed too; and his laughter, like the Principal's, had weeping in it.

'Do not be afraid of Mojedaji,' he cried. 'Do not be afraid of any man.'

'Ah, before I was married, Wahab, I was not afraid. I used to dream of sitting under a tree and letting myself starve to death, in silence and dignity. People would come from miles around to watch and be impressed. The King would send witnesses. There would be consultations at high level, and in the end they would decide that I could not be allowed to rebuke them all with my peaceful but valiant dying in front of them. So in the night their emissaries came, with money, and the title-deeds of an estate in the country, presented to me by the King himself.'

'I too have had such a dream,' cried Wahab. 'Only in mine I was dead when the emissaries came.'

They drew back a little so that they could stare into each other's eyes. Each saw that the other had been, not lying, though what they had said was not quite true, but bravely defying with their dreams the poverty not only of themselves but of their whole country, and the injustice which such poverty surely represented.

At that moment the door opened and in walked Mojedaji, frowning, and looking so like God that the Principal's hilarity and faith instantly degenerated into cringing fear.

'I was congratulating Wahab,' he muttered. 'He has been sent an invitation to the big party at the British Embassy.'

Mojedaji looked surprised. With godlike disdain he took from his folio case under his arm his own invitation card.

Looking from one card to the other the Principal felt more than ever his own exclusion, not from the British Embassy garden, beautiful though that was said to be, but from paradise itself where God bestowed on those, like Mojedaji who impersonated Him, and others, like Wahab, who were not afraid of Him, favours eternally denied His timid believers.

Fifteen

IN THE AFTERNOONS Wahab worked as a clerk for the Bus Company. The work was such simple drudgery, the salary so tiny, and the office so like a hovel with its mud floor and walls and its thousands of flies, alive and dead, that often during those hours from three o'clock to six his ambitions both for himself and his country crumbled into dust which choked his mind as the real dust, drifting in through the broken window from the sun-baked streets, choked his throat. His colleague was a thin consumptive youth called Aziz, whose frequent coughing kept blowing the tickets off the table and bespattering them with germs whose deadliness no one knew better than Wahab, master of microscopes. Yet Aziz was most of the time cheerful and laughed as often as he coughed. Indeed, it was laughter that sometimes brought on the coughing. Wahab was quite shocked by his dying colleague's levity; besides, for Laura's sake, he had to try to protect himself from the disease. This was not easy, in such a small dirty room, with both of them so close together and so many flies buzzing from lip to lip, but he learned to tell when a bout of coughing was about to begin, and had his own handkerchief out, as if in sympathy, but really to cover his mouth and nose. Once, though, when Aziz had been unable to find the coloured rag he usually used, Wahab, with a kind of tragic generosity, had lent his. 'If I could, my poor Aziz,' he had cried, 'I would lend you my lungs too.' Of course he had insisted many times that Aziz should consult a doctor, go into a sanitorium, rest there for

six months or a year, eat wholesome food, and come out
again, cured and strong. But though there were plenty of
doctors, all of whom in Aziz's case good at shrugging their
shoulders, there were no sanatoria, wholesome food, cure,
new strength. Sometimes he saw Aziz dying of a curable
disease as the embodiment of Afghanistan, and that vision of
despair had his eyes warm with angry tears.

Therefore that evening about seven o'clock when he
cycled off the tarred main street along the mud track that
led to the carpet serai, on his way to the meeting with the
Council of the Brotherhood, he felt more indignation on
Aziz's behalf than fear on his own. He supposed they were
displeased with him for proposing to marry a feringhee or
perhaps for having had whisky thrown in his face in a
foreigner's house, thus bringing ridicule upon the whole
nation. But surely, if they really were patriots sworn to
purify their country and protect it from disgrace, it was far
more important that they should use whatever wealth or
power they had to help Aziz and the many intelligent,
admirable young men like him doomed to suffering and
early death?

At that hour the serai was deserted. The moonlight lay
where during daylight the red carpets were spread out for
customers to examine and walk on. Those carpets, thought
Wahab, with their beautiful traditional designs were the best
artistic achievement of his country. Besides, so indelible the
dyes and durable the wool, the more they were used the
better they became. Thus they too might symbolize Afghanistan but far more hopefully than poor Aziz did.

The shutters were down at Raouf's bazaar, but no sooner
had he arrived there than from around the corner slunk two
large men, with turbans on their heads and their faces
hidden to the eyes by blankets, under which no doubt they
clutched knives. Yet he did not feel afraid. One snarled,
asking what he wanted. He answered with a coolness that

astonished himself and impressed the two thugs, one of whom began to knock on the door with what looked like the handle of a knife. In a moment a similar knocking was heard from within.

Wahab was not impressed – neither by this mystery nor by his own danger. Indeed, as he grunted scornfully, he wondered if they could have drunk any whisky within the last few minutes: this exalted feeling of fearlessness was almost the same as the one he had felt seconds before Moffatt had flung the whisky in his face. Yet he had had nothing to drink for hours, except a few drops of polluted water at the office; and he had had nothing to eat, either. Could hunger produce this balloonlike effect of soaring above earthly fears and anxieties? Yes, because it was hunger not only of the belly but also of the soul. He wanted to yell, louder and more confidently than the muezzin from the minaret of the mosque: 'I am Wahab, scientist and idealist. In my lungs millions of Aziz's germs are already at work. I have many other enemies also unseen. But I am not afraid. I dare not be afraid, because, let me warn you, Brotherhood that skulks in darkness behind assassins' knives, if Wahab yields, if he goes down on his knees to you and begs for mercy, then for our country, for our unhappy beloved Afghanistan, there can be no hope. I, Wahab, humbly proclaim that I represent the last hope. Do not forget that. Drag me away, beat me, kill me, strew my bones over the desert; I shall not once whine, but in the distance you will hear the noise of a great lamentation. Do not wonder what it may be; it will be the soul of our country mourning.'

The door had opened. Someone within pulled him, one of the muffled guards outside pushed, but respectfully, and in he stumbled. The room was thickly carpeted; at least half a dozen of Raouf's carpets were spread out on top of one another. It was lit by one electric bulb, shaded with green paper. Several men, green-looking, sat on the floor and gazed up at him. They had scarves draped over their hats and turbans, screening their faces. He sniffed, but there was no smell of hashish; he stooped, but no cards or money were on the carpet; he peered into corners, but the bundles lying or standing there were not women, but rolled carpets. This was not a den of ordinary human vice. Here murder was not done, but merely planned; or much more likely here silly dreams were dreamed.

He heard a scornful laugh, and realized, from the startled swingings of the scarves, that it had come from himself. He knew it would be more discreet to restrain himself, but instead he cried: 'Good evening, gentlemen. I am Abdul Wahab, at your service. You see, I have come; but not because I am a slave to be summoned. I am an Afghan.'

The man who had opened the door for him spoke in what was meant to be a disguised voice, but Wahab at once recognized it as the one on the telephone.

'Hush,' muttered this man, scandalized. 'Remember in whose presence you are. Are you drunk again?'

'Sir, you are mistaken. I may be hungry, but I am not drunk. Sometimes I go deliberately hungry. Do you know why? It is to remind myself that millions of my countrymen are frequently hungry.'

That was a lie, or at least an exaggeration. As he said, he remembered a feast he and Laura had had at Christmas with some friends. There had been turkey, mince pies, Christmas puddings, wine. He had eaten and drunk the most. Everyone had laughed.

'Yes, of course,' the official was murmuring. 'Do not speak so loudly. The Council is in the next room. We know about our people's hunger. It is one of the things we are pledged to remove.'

As if to prove that claim, one of those seated on the floor felt under his wrappings and produced a slab of *nan*, which he held up to Wahab. Without hesitation, the latter took it, calmly broke off a piece, and returned the rest with a dignified word of thanks. He felt the whole action was symbolical, and he performed it therefore with a dignity that brought a lump to his own throat and surely also to the throats of these benevolent murderers.

Meanwhile the man in command had rapped on an inner door, had been bidden to enter, and had gone in. Before Wahab had finished the piece of bread, which he found particularly delicious, the other was back again, whispering: 'They are ready. Please be respectful. I assure you these men are important.'

Men, thought Wahab, in astonishment and disgust, as he boldly entered the inner room. Behind a table there sat three forms, shrouded in shaddries; one, in the middle, the chairman, was as small as any woman, and his voice was almost squeaky enough to be feminine. Yet it sounded familiar.

'Please be seated, Mr Wahab,' he said, courteously. 'We are glad to welcome you.'

'I shall be frank, sir,' said Wahab passionately, as he sat down on the chair at the opposite side of the table. 'I do not know yet if I am glad to be here. I do not approve of secrecy. It is, moreover, my belief that the shaddry should be abolished, and yet I find you, and your colleagues, hiding within them.'

The man on the right, big and burly, spoke in a deep harsh voice. 'It is not for you to instruct us. Please remember your proper station.'

'My station is that of a free-born Afghan.'

'You are a teacher; that is all. Your father is a mere clerk. You are in the presence of your superiors. Please conduct yourself accordingly.'

Somehow Wahab felt that patriotic boldness was still the best policy. 'No man who has to hide his face in my presence is my superior,' he said. 'He is not even my equal.'

Again he wondered where on earth he got the nerve to

speak so audaciously. Usually he took care to avoid such
provocative boasting. Then, in the midst of his amazement
that the present reckless boaster was himself, he realized that
the small man, the one in the middle, the fidgety leader, was
without doubt Prince Naim. The silent one on the left
might be Mojedaji. Perhaps the massive deep-voiced one
was an Army general.

Once for a whole day Wahab had worn his sister's
shaddry in the house. As a male Afghan, he had wanted
to experience for himself the ignominy and discomfort that
he and his like were guilty of inflicting on their womenfolk.
He would never forget how his spectacles had immediately
clouded over with his imprisoned breath, how the cloth at
his mouth had become infantilely wet, how his body all over
had sweated and itched, how slow and difficult scratching
had been, and how, at the end of the day, he had hardly
known who he was or cared to know, identity, personality,
and pride being all darkened and smothered.

No doubt something of the kind was being felt by the
three men in front of him. Did not the Prince wear spectacles? Would not the big man sweat a lot?

Coolly Wahab considered how best to exploit his own
advantage.

'It is not time for us to reveal ourselves,' muttered Naim.

The big man, the General, said suddenly: 'We are considering the case of the Englishman, Moffatt. Last week in
his house he insulted you, and so the whole nation, by
throwing whisky in your face. Is this true?'

Wahab could not deny it, but his admission was wary.
'But, gentlemen, is it not my private business?'

'No. It is ours too. One of our purposes is to restore the
dignity of our nation.'

'An excellent purpose.'

'What we have to consider is whether he ought to be
punished, and if so, what that punishment ought to be.'

'I did not think,' said Wahab, still very cautious, 'that you brought foreigners under your jurisdiction.'

'In future we intend to do so,' said Naim, as passionately as his muffled mouth could manage. 'Why should they come here, live well at our expense, and all the time sneer at us, and insult us?'

But surely, remembered Wahab, Moffatt is your friend, my dear Prince? I had better be very careful indeed.

'Is it not better to answer their insults face to face?' he asked.

'How can you answer whisky flung in your face, Wahab? By throwing some back?'

'No. By remaining calm. By refusing to retaliate. By being more civilized than the insulter.' Not, he had to add to himself with a secret grin, by peeping in the window, hoping to find the whisky thrower engaged in drunken adultery.

'We consider your own behaviour, Wahab, in the affair admirable,' said the General.

The one on the left, who might be Mojedaji, still kept quiet. Perhaps he was someone even more powerful than the gold-toothed mullah; a Minister even; the Chief of Police.

'Well then,' said Wahab, 'why not let me continue to handle it in my own way?'

'Turning the other cheek is a doctrine suitable for the powerful,' burst out Naim. 'The meek cannot afford it. Consider the practice of these Christians themselves. Besides, here the cheek is brown, and the hand white.'

Wahab felt wisdom sliding in to join the compassion already cozy in his heart. Yet, he thought, I am really a villain. This is all pretence. I am a coward, yet here I am impressing important men with my courage. I hate Moffatt for having humiliated me and for trying to deprive me of Laura; yet I am asking mercy for him. What game am I trying to play? Am I myself? Did that whisky in my eyes bewitch me, change my view of the world?

'We must take into account what his students at the University think of him,' he said.

'Yes. We have investigated. It is true enough. They think highly of him.'

'And I believe it is true that he has more Afghan friends than almost any other foreigner in Kabul.'

'So it is said.'

'Influential friends, I understand.'

There was a short silence, broken by a sigh from Naim.

'So all we have against him is this throwing of a little whisky in my face?'

'But, Wahab dear fellow, it might have blinded you for life!'

Yes, this must be Naim, beyond a doubt. I must be careful, thought Wahab again, trembling. I am here like a man who has discovered gold. Before I rejoice and make plans to spend it, I must make sure my claim to it is recognized.

'We should not forget it was his wife who bathed my eyes,' he murmured.

Afterwards, it was true, she had made it clear that she had disowned him and Laura, and her apostasy was even less forgivable than her husband's antagonism from the beginning. Considering that change in her, Wahab had decided that the reason for it must be some personal trouble between herself and her husband. Perhaps Moffatt made a habit of adultery with big-breasted blondes. Then on the point of gloating over his enemy, Wahab suddenly sympathized with him instead. He, too, married to Mrs Moffatt, beautiful though she was, would feel like finding some other woman with whom to make soft-buttocked love. It was not that Mrs Moffatt was Chinese; it was just that as a woman she was too percipient, too able, too remote. No, her breasts were not of gold with rubies for nipples, but somehow, he felt, she would make love as if they were; it would be a precious holy experience but not enjoyable. She was too like an idol in a temple, come to life but never quite human.

'We have no quarrel with Mrs Moffatt,' said Naim. 'She is a good woman and a true friend of Afghanistan.'

'Well, if you take steps to cancel his contract, and expel him from the country – I take it that is the form of punishment you are considering – you will also be punishing her.'

'Why do you say that?'

'Where would they go?'

'To England, surely. That is his country.'

'No.' Wahab found himself shaking his head with a certainty he had no right to show and yet felt deeply; indeed, he knew he had in that moment discovered Moffatt's secret. 'He will never take her back to England.'

'Has he said so?'

It was simpler, and truer, to lie: 'Yes.'

'Why? Because she is Chinese?'

'Partly that.'

'He is supposed to love her very much,' said Naim.

'He does, but their love is complicated.'

'She is a strange woman,' murmured Naim, and sighed, as if he too had to sympathize with Moffatt.

'Therefore, gentlemen,' said Wahab, 'please, I beg you, leave me to settle this business between myself and Mr Moffatt. Of course,' he added, with every word sweet as a grape in his mouth, 'if I find he is irreconcilable and repulses my offer of friendship—'

'In that case,' said the General, 'there would be no further hesitation: he would have to go.'

Wahab bowed his head. He could hardly control his trembling now. Every man on his way up had to begin somewhere. Was this *his* beginning? And how lucky to have Moffatt thus handed over as a prisoner. He touched his pocket in which lay Laura's letter; in it she described indignantly how Moffatt had maligned not only Afghanistan but Wahab himself. 'He sounds a nasty kind of person, Dul,' she had written.

Then the man on Naim's left spoke at last. He was not Mojedaji; but his voice, though soft, was even more accustomed than the mullah's to be listened to with obedience and fear.

'I understand, Wahab, there is an Englishwoman coming to Kabul to marry you.'

'Yes, sir.'

'When is she coming?'

'In three weeks. I have just received a letter telling me so.'

'Are you aware that Moffatt has done his best to have this lady refused a visa?'

Wahab had not known that, but he was not surprised. 'He has not been successful then,' he said, 'because she tells me she has received her visa.'

'It is the lady's intention to come here and see the conditions for herself, before deciding to go on with the marriage?'

It occurred to Wahab that if Laura's decision was no, he would lose not only a wife but also a career.

'Yes, that is so,' he said. 'It was not her wish; I insisted on it.'

That was flatly a lie. He had been all for marriage in England; she had refused. A shiver crawled down his spine as he remembered how intelligent, affectionate, and firm that refusal had been. He had a vision of her limping bravely but determinedly during her investigations. He saw her gray candid eyes as they looked on shaddries, beggars, joweys, men pissing behind walls. Again he saw the resemblance between her and Mrs Moffatt. Her breasts were not of gold; his hand, privileged once only, had ascertained that; but there was nevertheless the same formidable priestesslike quality about her.

'Other foreign women come here,' said Naim, 'already

married to Afghans. They come for shameful reasons. They think their husbands are rich and able to keep them in luxury, with many servants.'

'Laura knows I am poor.'

'She is an educated woman?' asked Soft-voice.

'A University graduate.'

'And she is coming here,' said Naim, 'because she loves you, an Afghan?'

'That, sir, is her only reason.'

Yes, she had loved him when he was in England; and judging from the letter in his pocket she had still loved him only two weeks ago. But when she came and saw how backward the country really was, and how vulgarly poor he and his family were, would she continue to love him? He had always doubted it, and now that doubt, bold and agile in his mind, would not let timid faith pass. In a spasm of despair he blamed Aziz, coughing his diseased lungs all over the bus tickets. He blamed the contractor who had built the new block of offices and had left out lavatories. He blamed Mohebzada's sickly baby. He blamed Genghis Khan for having, a thousand years ago, given civilization a setback in this country. He blamed God for having let the deserts and hills round Kabul, indeed throughout most of the land, crumble away into infertility. Flying over them and seeing how parched and barren they were, in contrast with her green England, Laura would have her mind already made up before she stepped off the plane, or rather before she was helped down the steps.

When they discovered she was lame, would they turn against her? Would they think, as he had sometimes been unable not to think himself, that she was willing to marry him, a dark-skinned, poverty-stricken Afghan, because she knew her lameness would prevent her from marrying an Englishman?

'Loving you, Wahab,' said Naim, 'she will understand Afghanistan.'

Ah, but would she? I am not an expert in the consequences of love, thought Wahab. I do not know if it is the case that love brings understanding. Certainly it does not do so always. My parents do not understand each other after thirty years of loving. Perhaps their love had too many flaws in it. Will mine and Laura's be perfect? Look at Moffatt and his wife. Could a couple be more intelligent? He writes poetry and she is a painter. Yet apparently they too have failed to understand.

Soft-voice was softer than ever: 'There is another thing, Wahab. We feel that the time is ripe for you to consider your personal advancement.'

Naim and the other man nodded. 'You are the kind of young man we need today,' said the latter.

It was impossible not to feel flattered; in fact, self-gratification tingled in Wahab's fingers and ran up from his toes as far as his privates, like an electric shock. He had never felt so delighted with himself in his life before, not even when Laura had first declared she loved him. Even now, in the midst of this greater delight, he remembered the schoolmistressy qualifications in her eyes, and the cool way her hands had stopped his. Here on the contrary was pure bliss; and there was to be more of it.

'There is much dissatisfaction with the Principal of your school,' said Soft-voice. 'There has been talk of replacing him. The students do not respect him. They laugh at his authority. That is not good for a school. Do you agree?'

Even as he was remembering that embrace and the joy and tears shared with Abdul Mussein, Wahab was nodding and replying: 'He is a good man, I think, but he lacks ideals.'

'Surely it is useless supplying a school with modern equipment, if its Principal has medieval ideas?' asked Naim.

These men, realized Wahab, were not merely speculating. They had the power to remove poor Mussein and put anyone they chose in his place – himself, for instance. As

Principal, he could make the school famous for its teaching of science; he was sure of that. So famous, indeed, that he would probably leap from that eminence to one still higher, and then upwards again. With Laura by his side, counselling him, he would be able to reach greatness with far less damage to his principles and ideals than they would sustain if he were to remain a humble assistant teacher all his days. It was a pity about Mussein, of course; but really, had he not properly described himself as a dead fly on a cake? And besides, once degraded to his right level, that of ordinary class teacher in the primary department, he would at last be in a position to discipline the greedy dependants at present ruining him, especially the gluttonous old hypocrite who mouthed, through rice: 'We are all God's children.' That was a useless truism; what was far more worth saying was that God, like all fathers, liked to be proud of His children and rewarded only those who brought Him honour and spared Him shame.

'It is probable,' murmured Naim, 'that you will become one of us.'

'I should be honoured, sir. Your ideals and purposes are mine. I wish to advance my country.'

'We recognize your sincerity, Wahab. You will hear from us again.'

What was that noise he heard in the far distance? Aziz coughing? The soul of his country lamenting? No, no, just a belated donkey objecting to being encouraged by its master's stick. In any case, to help Aziz and all others like him he must first himself, by whatever means, rise to power.

He took his leave with a dignity and restraint that impressed him. Inwardly he was all for yelling his gratitude to them, and falling on his knees to kiss their hands; but outwardly, as if he were the prince, he stood upright, manfully shook the hands thrust out at him from the folds of the shaddries, and left the room like a hero. In the outer room, though the thicknesses of the carpets under his crepe-soled shoes prevented his tread from ringing out as boldly as he would have liked, he strode through masterfully, with brisk greetings in return for theirs murmured respectfully. Outside the two burly guards were holding his bicycle by the handle bars in a way that turned it in the moonlight into a ministerial limousine, an English Daimler or Russian Zis. He could not do other therefore than mount it as if he were entering such a car, and as he pedalled away he caught sight of the moon nodding at him over the roof of a building. Such celestial familiarity did not surprise, and with a smile he nodded back.

Sixteen

LAN and Harold Moffatt were in the sitting room after dinner, she sketching, and he brooding with a glass of whisky in his hand, when the telephone rang.

'I'll get it,' he said and, heaving himself up, waddled out.

She thought that in the past two or three weeks he had got fatter; his stomach was like a man's twice his age, and his rump was like a woman's. Did it represent in some way a diminution of her love, that she should now see him as physically grosser than before? Could a feeling of guilt, such as had been festering in him ever since the night of the Club dance, coarsen the body as well as the mind? Her own fingers, steadfastly drawing, were as delicate and skilful as ever, and this old man's age, seen that afternoon as she walked through the bazaar, was not only as good as anything she had ever done, but also, with its gap-toothed, bearded grin, represented a compassion so tender that she was still new to it, as a mother was to a newborn child. That Harold's concern for Mrs Mohebzada, and for Laura Johnstone too, sprang as much from humanity as from principle, she now not only saw but felt; and also that his fears for their own children, as yet unconceived but now permitted, were based on love. As he had put it himself fondly, she had at last ventured out of her temple; but he had not seemed confident that she would stay out long.

In the hall he was chatting to Maud Mossaour. Suddenly his voice became eager. 'Did you? Yes, of course I'd like to see it very much. No, she hasn't. At least not as far as I know, and I don't think she'd keep it from us. Yes, but she's still sorry for him, I think. Why, God knows; he can look after himself. I heard a rumour that he's to be promoted to principal of his school. There's to be a change at the Ministry itself. Rumour has it that Naim's taking it over. I know he's always fancied himself as an educationist and a leader of youth. We'll be seeing our friend Wahab shoot up. He's by way of being one of Naim's brown-eyed boys. Yes, very good, Maud. I'll let you know my verdict.'

He returned to the sitting room, flat-footed in his native sandals, and took a sip of his whisky.

'You would gather that was Maud,' he said. 'She's had a reply from Miss Johnstone, and is sending it over. According to her, we've got nothing to be afraid of. From the tone of her letter, there are no flies on our Laura. When she sees the number of flies here, she'll be shocked to the bottom of her antiseptic little soul, and she'll rush away from the carcass that attracts them. I mean, this bloody, stinking, corrupt country.'

She knew that the violence of his words was caused by his love of Afghanistan.

He came over and looked down at her drawing. He said nothing, and she kept on, knowing that with every touch of the pencil she was pleading not for Afghanistan, but for herself.

'It's good, Lan,' he murmured. 'It's uncannily good.'

'Do you think so? These faces are so interesting, they draw themselves.'

'Will Wahab smile like that when he's old? I told Maud what I'd heard about him. She wasn't surprised. Like me, she's always thought of him as a slippery one. At the moment his wriggles seem to be upward, but the time's coming when they'll be downward, fast. It's happening here all the time, but I hate to think of that poor bastard the present Principal being kicked backward to make room for our fancied jackanapes. It's Naim's doing, of course. He's got it into his head that Wahab's marriage to Laura Johnstone is a kind of experiment. If it succeeds, Afghanistan will prosper; if it fails, Afghanistan will continue to be backward.'

Lan's hand stopped for a moment. She remembered the bright-eyed smiling face of Laura Johnstone, in Wahab's snapshot; and she tried to imagine the crippled left foot, as Wahab so tenderly had described it. She had not yet told Harold, or anyone else, about Laura's lameness. She could not have said why; after all, the minute Laura alighted on Afghan soil it would be seen.

He had sat down again beside his whisky.

'According to Maud, she sounds as if she were already a Minister's wife. We'll have to tell her about the ex-Minister of Finance and his wife. Where is Farid now? According to the latest rumours round the Embassies, when he was last seen all his teeth had been knocked out and his face was so misshapen even his wife would have hesitated about kissing it. They say he did it for her. All that went wrong with their plan was that they got the money out safely enough, half a million of it, but didn't manage to get themselves out with it. So there's a situation would perplex even our hard-headed Laura: Her Wahab with his face in pulp, she guarded at home by men who won't be eunuchs, and half a million pounds waiting in a Swiss bank.'

He took another sip.

'You hate me when I talk like this, Lan. I don't much like myself. You know why I do it. Because I like the Afghans, because I think, given the chance, they could make something out of their country. You couldn't find a friendlier, keener, more humorous crowd of students anywhere in the world; yes, and more intelligent, too. Yet they'll all become clerks and ill-paid teachers and inefficiently trained doctors and necessarily subservient civil servants, all shifty-eyed and

cringing and afraid to speak their minds; while that creep
Wahab becomes Principal, then Chief Inspector, then
Secretary-General of Schools, and finally Minister. That's
what makes me talk like this.'

'You may be wrong about him, Harold. He was a student,
too.'

They heard the gate bell ring and Sofi dash out to answer
it.

'That'll be the letter now,' said Harold.

He could not wait for it to be brought in but jumped up
and went out.

She heard him laughing affectionately with Sofi, and then
in he padded, the letter in his hand. He held it up.

'By the way, Lan,' he said, 'you haven't had a reply from
her yet?'

He took the single sheet of flimsy blue notepaper out of
the envelope. He held it to his nose and sniffed.

'Scented! I didn't think our Laura was the kind to use
scented notepaper.'

As he slowly read, he took a long sip of whisky.

'Scent and asperity!' he said at last, with a grin. 'Truly a
strange girl is our Laura.

'Listen. "Dear Mrs Mossaour [I bet you her ears bristled
as she wrote that, it's scarcely a true-blue English name, is
it?] "Thank you for your letter of the 21st. I am delighted
that you will be able to offer me employment in your school.
Teaching there, with children of so many nationalities, must
be very interesting." [New paragraph.] "If I have not given
much consideration to the points that you and Mr Moffatt
have felt it to be your duty to bring to my notice, it is merely
because I have so often previously discussed them with my
fiancé, Mr Wahab. That his country has faults is certain; I
have them too; and surely England is not perfect, though
perhaps to exiles like yourselves she does seem so. In my
professional capacity, and also in the course of some vo-

luntary social service work which I do, I am sorry to say I come across quite a number of cases of unhappiness not unlike Mrs Mohebzada's." [Another new paragraph.] "I do not usually appreciate interference in my private affairs, but the circumstances here are sufficiently abnormal to excuse it. Indeed, I am grateful to you both for your concern. Yours sincerely, Laura Johnstone."'

When he had finished he let out a bellow of laughter. 'What have we been worrying about?' he cried. 'What age did she admit she was? Thirty-five, was it? An old maid, a female bureaucrat, with tight lips, massive knees, and a sense of humour like a hospital matron's. Can't you picture her?'

Lan could, and, in spite of the sarcasm with which he had read, her picture was altogether different. She imagined a small slim woman with pale tense smile and, under the table, her good foot firm on the floor. The stiff dignity, awkward pride, snapped gratitude, and schoolmistressy pompousness of the letter were not characteristic of her. Beneath them breathed, like a frightened creature, a profound anxiety.

He sat down on the arm of her chair and placed his hand on the back of her neck.

'I wasn't drunk, you know, when I threw the whisky in his face. I hated him, but I had no right to. Before I saw him at the school that afternoon I was prepared to hate him, and I found it easy. Don't ask me why. If this Johnstone woman had been there too and I'd seen him be actually brutal to her, I couldn't have hated him more. For God's sake, why? I don't think he's up to much, but one usually ignores his kind, one doesn't pay them the extravagant compliment of hatred.'

She waited.

'And he didn't insult that bitch Helga, either. That was a lie.'

'What was it he did say?' Would there, she wondered, be another lie?

'Something about my having no children.'

'Was he taunting you?'

'No. He seemed so bloody happy. Maybe what I was really doing was throwing the stuff in my own face.'

'It was a strange thing for him to say.'

'I suppose so. He was a bit drunk, of course. Anyway, we were talking about Liz Mohebzada's baby.' His hand tightened painfully on her neck. 'If we do have a child, Lan, where do we go with it? We can't stay here all our lives, though I think I would, if they let me. Should we apply for Afghan citizenship? And ask Wahab to be one of our sponsors? Whatever Naim may say or hope, I don't think his country is going to become what's called progressive, for a long time anyway. So we'd have to put up with primitive plumbing and dust in our melons and camel shit outside our door, but we'd never have to be ashamed of the colour of our skins. Perhaps it's not so impracticable. I could ask Naim; and there are others. They'd want us to become Moslems. Well, I could be a bad Moslem just as easily as I've been a bad Christian. What about you? Would you forsake the philosophic Buddha?'

'My children would be my religion.'

'Yes, Lan. I know they would.' He got up and stood in the middle of the room, running his hand through his hair. 'Where today is there freedom to practise that kind of religion? Here, yes, in this country that's still next door to the desert. But not in civilized England; no, not there. You'd be accepted: so quaint, so charming, so beautiful, so purely Chinese. But your children, Lan, and mine, make no mistake about it, would at every stage of their growth be treated – oh, in such kindly fashion – as freaks.'

She did not think people were as prejudiced and callous as that, but she did not argue.

'We could go back to Djakarta,' she murmured.

He seemed to be considering that, for he was silent for

almost a minute. Then he burst out: 'No!' And turned furiously on her, almost as if he were going to strike her. She saw his fears in his face. In Djakarta whom could their children marry? Indonesians, or Chinese, or half-castes like themselves?

'There's just no place at all, Lan,' he said, desperately. 'Even here's been spoiled by my own bloody nastiness. I've managed to do what I didn't think anybody on earth could have done: I've cheapened you. I've given a shower of bastards not fit to lick your shoes the opportunity to laugh at you. Christ, how can you ever forgive me?'

She put down her sketchbook and went over to him. 'I love you. I shall always love you.'

'As the priestess loves her god? Yes, Lan, it's not possible for human love to stay constant, whatever happens. I love you. I never loved you more than when I was standing over there, telling them that joke. I could see your face. Yes, you still loved me, but, my Christ, how humiliated you must have felt. If you don't remember that humiliation on your death bed, I will. So what protection's love? Mohebzada loves his wife; and maybe Wahab loves his Laura, in his own crooked way. And I've often thought that the trouble with John and Helen Langford is that their love for each other's got all tangled up. You see, it's not the bath of syrup for everybody that it is for Alan and Paula. You should go home, Lan, before it's too late.'

'I have no home without you.'

He embraced her and kissed the top of her head. 'And I've got none without you. As long as we keep together, we'll beat them. We'll show them that if they thought they were going to lick their lips over the spectacle of our breaking up, then they're going to be disappointed.'

She remembered how enthusiastic and apparently sincere their acclamation had been at the Club Dance. Most people would be pleased that they were reconciled again. Perhaps a few, like Helga Larsen, would be disappointed; but she wondered if a part of him, a deep uncontrollable part, would be too.

'You knew it all before we got married, Lan. You were well warned.'

Yes, but she had been naïve enough to believe that marriage to her would cure him of despondencies, worries, and forebodings whose sources she now knew lay far back in his childhood, though their causes today might be the cynicism of statesmen, the inadequacy of pity in the face of hunger and disease, or even his inability to express in poetry something he felt deeply. She had been sure that at least she could help him to get over those moods more quickly, and she had been right; but now she was realizing that the cost had been the loss of much of her own self-confidence. As she shivered in his arms, listening to his anguished murmurs of comfort and love, she felt the burden of optimism to be too heavy. Even as he kissed her, angry with himself because of her tears, she was remembering, with longing and regret, the peace of mind she had found on her knees beside the murdered body of her sister. Not only had Ling been killed, but also joy and hope, and hatred of evil and desire for revenge. It was an emptiness to which, in spite of her love for him, she had often been tempted to return; and now that temptation was stronger than it had ever been.

Two days later the reply from Laura Johnstone arrived.

In that mud-built city of nameless streets and unnumbered houses, letters had to be addressed in care of some well-known institution such as an Embassy or Ministry. Previously the Moffatts' mail had been sent to the British Embassy, from which it would be returned in a day or so by the runner; but Moffatt once had intercepted the old postman at the local sub-post office, where he called to drink a cup of tea and say his prayers, and had persuaded him to take his bag of Embassy mail first to the Moffatts' house. The old man, hook-nosed and bearded like an amiable Punch, had agreed without any fuss, though the sub-postmaster, younger and more ambitious, kept assuring them both it was against the law, until a little baksheesh changed his tune. So every three or four days the postman on his decrepit red bicycle arrived at the gate, rang the bell, and when either Lan or Harold appeared, untied the bundle and let them rummage through it. If there were letters for them, he was delighted; if not, he would promise to bring some 'farda,' that was, tomorrow. Indeed, that was the nickname they had given him, because whenever he met them, on the street, or in the park he would wave and shout 'Farda!' He seemed too typically a peasant to be able to appreciate the longing that exiles often have for letters of any kind, and yet a bond had grown between him and Lan especially. If there was a letter from her people for her, he would have it out ready, having recognized it by its stamp. Usually she gave him a copper or two as baksheesh; he took it with a smile and a murmur that it didn't matter. Despite his poverty, his indifference to the money struck her as genuine.

Lan and Harold were still seated at lunch when the gate bell jangled. They knew it was the old postman.

'I'll go,' said Harold.

She got up and watched from the window as he stood in the gateway, joking with the old man and looking through the letters. Three he took out and stuffed into his trouser pocket. The rest he handed back. The postman tied them together with his hairy string, placed them carefully in his dusty bag, put this into the carrier of his bicycle, waved, and cycled away. Lan could hear a dog bark as it dashed after him.

When Harold came in she was again seated at table.

'Three,' he said. 'One an advertisement, another I fancy is a rejected poem, and this, if I'm not mistaken, is what you've

been waiting for. At any rate the postmark's Manchester.'
He still kept her waiting as he pretended to study the
postmark. 'Now I wonder what Laura's got to say to a
sympathetic approach. I've a feeling she'll have been put out
of her stride somewhat. Yes, you'll be rather sternly thanked,
but you'll also be told it's none of your bloody business.'

At last, with what both of them knew was a malicious
reluctance, though both pretended it was meant playfully,
he threw the letter towards her end of the table. It fell
against the butter dish.

'Sorry,' he said. 'It's sugar it could do with, I suppose, not
butter.'

She picked it up, wiped it calmly on her table napkin, and
then tore open the envelope. 'I think you're wrong about
Miss Johnstone.'

He grinned across the table at her. 'Are you basing that on
stylistic evidence? Or does she reveal a heart of gold?'

'Did you know she's lame?'

'Lame? What do you mean?'

'She's permanently lame. She has been since a child.'

He was silent. 'Does she say so?'

'Yes. But I knew before; Wahab told me.'

'When? After I flung the whisky in his face? I've wondered what confidences you shared in the bathroom while
you were bathing his poor brown eyes. Lame? The silly
bitch, if she comes here, she'll soon feel she did it by walking
all the way from Manchester.'

'What do you mean?'

'For Christ's sake, can't you see? Can't you use your
imagination? Lame!'

'You speak as if it were vile.'

'So it is, here. I thought she'd have at least her two feet to
stand on or to kick him with. How does it affect her?'

'He told me she was able to dance, as long as it was slow
enough.'

He hid his face in his hands, not in shame, but rather in a kind of desperate sorrow.

'What does she say?'

'Do you want to read it?'

'No. Read it to me.'

She hesitated, wondering whether she should or not. It was important that their own lives be kept as far apart as possible from those of Miss Johnstone and Wahab. For that reason she now regretted her offer of hospitality, which Miss Johnstone had accepted; but excuses could be found for withdrawing it. The tone of the letter was not emotional, but even if she read it in a flat voice she would inevitably be identifying herself with the writer. Her very hands, holding the letter, had, as Harold had so bitterly pointed out, bathed Wahab's eyes. Now as she looked at them, she found herself wishing she could change them and with them her whole being. Perhaps, she suddenly thought, with a pang that seemed for a moment to stop the beating of her heart, that is the key to the mystery: all I need to do is to transform myself into any shape so long as it is human and my skin is white and my eyes not oval. Even Miss Johnstone's shape would do, in spite of her lameness. In spite of his sneers about Miss Johnstone's massive knees, he had been impressed by her photograph.

'Well?' he said.

'I'd rather you read it yourself, Harold.'

'Why? For God's sake, don't make a fuss about it. It's not important. I don't care if I never see it or hear it. Surely you know that?'

Then the gate bell rang. A car had stopped outside. Lan waited, wetting her lips, as if about to begin reading the letter. They heard Sofi dash out to open the gate. The caller said, in a pleasant American drawl, but excellent Persian: 'Are Mr and Mrs Moffatt at home?'

'Christ, just what we needed,' muttered Harold, getting to

his feet. 'I think I'll go and hide in the bathroom. Descent of the angel. St Manson to the rescue. He's come with the holy secotine, Lan; he's heard we've fallen apart.'

She rose too. 'Don't mock him. He's a good man.'

'How true, and how bloody irrelevant. A damn sight better than me. Do I go out to remote villages to smear ointment on syphilitic sores? Do I pray for hours beside dying babies? Is Jesus my chum?'

She had hurried out into the hall to welcome their visitor.

After a long glance at the letter which she had dropped on the table, Harold went into the sitting room. In a cabinet there was an assortment of bottles – whisky, brandy, gin, sherry. He poured himself out some whisky. The Reverend Manson P. Powrie, minister of the American Church in Kabul, the only non-Moslem church in the country, was a more fanatical abstainer than the Moslems themselves; but with benign grimaces he tolerated the vice in others just as he tolerated other vices, with one exception, it was said: fornication. Yet he was married himself, and in slightly over five years had begot four children. Now in the hall he was warmly apologizing for having come at such an inconvenient time. 'If I've interrupted you good folks at your lunch, I'm awfully sorry. Really you should just open the door, Mrs Moffatt, and show me out again.'

Assuring him that they had finished lunch and that he was very welcome, Lan showed him into the sitting room where Harold rose out of an armchair, with a glass of whisky in his hand.

'How are you, Harold? I've just been telling your good wife how awfully absent-minded I'm becoming. I even forget folks have got to eat.'

With four kids, the eldest four, no wonder you're glad to skip your own meals, thought Moffatt. 'That's all right,' he said. 'We had just finished. A pity, otherwise you could have joined us.'

'No, no. But thank you, thank you indeed.'

'Please sit down.'

The minister did so. 'I don't aim to waste too much of your valuable time. Maybe I'm interrupting masterpieces of painting and poetry.' He laughed. 'The fact is, Harold, I've come because a countrywoman of yours telephoned me and suggested I should come to consult you.'

Harold studied the minister, who was about his own age and whose combination of moral superiority and intellectual simpleness always fascinated him. Ludicrously dressed for an apostle, in mauve open-neck shirt and cream pants with thin black vertical stripes, he was nevertheless the kind of man who, on hearing Christ preach, would have followed Him and, through gold-rimmed spectacles, seen every miracle; whereas Harold himself would have remained in the background, with many clever sceptical remarks. What he had said about Powrie's expeditions to remote villages with medicines was true. And it could not be charged against the minister that he was curing their bodies of pain in order to entrap their souls into Christianity. In Afghanistan, proselytism was forbidden. Let Powrie try to convert one Moslem and he would be out of the country in a week, with his church closed.

'Yes, Harold, Mrs Gillie, your Consul's wife, phoned and told me about some English girl who's coming out here to marry an Afghan. She explained she didn't know what the girl's attitude is about religion, but thought you might know. I certainly would be prepared to marry her, if she wished that, but what's most important of course is that we all unite to give this girl a really Christian welcome. You good folks have begun the good work already, I believe. She's going to live with you until she's found her feet.'

'Her foot, Mr Powrie,' said Harold. 'She's a cripple.'

Shocked, the minister blamed first the whisky, and then Moffatt's too worldly sense of humour; what he was careful to avoid blaming was the callousness and malice of the remark. All this was evident in the smile that kept desperately shining on his face. For an instant he closed his eyes. That indicated a flash of prayer, of consultation, but for whose soul's sake Moffatt could not be sure; his, he supposed.

Lan's reaction, he noticed, was almost as complicated, and for the same reason: whoever was to be blamed, he wasn't. She had made that resolution and knew that if she were to break it once only she might swing to the opposite extreme and blame him for everything. She frowned at the minister, as if she too thought his gush of kindliness provocative.

'I didn't know that!' cried Powrie. 'I had no idea. Mrs Gillie didn't mention it.'

'She doesn't know it. Only Lan, myself, and Wahab, the man she's going to marry, know about it here; and now you, of course.'

Powrie held out his hands carefully cupped, as if the knowledge lay in them like water that kept trickling through. What was the Lord's purpose in inflicting lameness upon Miss Johnstone? The question was as bright on his forehead as the Kabul slaughterhouse sign, neon lit, was above the building.

'How did it happen?' he asked gently. 'Was she born that way?'

'No. Poliomyelitis in childhood.'

'I see.' And it was obvious he did see, with far more perplexed sympathy than Moffatt, how unkind fate had been to Miss Johnstone; only in his case fate had to be called God. 'And does it affect her, the poor woman?'

'It appears she can dance. Gentle waltzes. Not square dancing.'

'No. It's very brave of her coming out here with such a handicap. I must say too I'm a little surprised. I mean, you know the attitude most of these Afghans have towards their womenfolk. He must surely love her very much.'

'I don't think it follows. She'll cost him nothing, she'll have a fair amount of money saved up, she'll get a job here and earn six times what he does.'

'Dear me! Is he that kind of person? Mrs Gillie did mention that she had met him. She said he seemed to her nice enough, but a little on the simple side.'

'She thinks all Afghans, from the King down, are a little on the simple side. Whatever Wahab is, he's not simple.'

'What does he do?'

'Teaches science at Isban College. But I hear he's been promoted Principal.'

'So he does have influential connections?'

'At the moment.'

'I gather from your general attitude, Harold – if you'll pardon my saying so – that you do not think Miss Johnstone is acting in her own best interests by coming here to marry this man?'

'That's it. What do you think yourself? Aren't you opposed to these mixed marriages?'

Again the hands were cupped; in them this time, trickling through also, was the responsibility of guessing what God thought was best. 'In principle, yes, Harold, I am. Christians should marry Christians.'

Moffatt grinned. Christians like the Langfords, he supposed. And what did the minister secretly think of marriage between Buddhists and agnostics? There was no doubt that Powrie had come with another purpose: to place his hand in Lan's; and not just metaphorically, either.

Shyly Powrie turned to Lan. 'I take it you agree with Harold, Mrs Moffatt?'

'Yes.'

'I understand. If I may say so, it makes it all the more praiseworthy that you should be willing to offer her hospitality.'

'We hope to be able to dissuade her from marrying him,' said Harold. 'If you can help, we'd appreciate it.'

'I'll certainly do everything I can to help. Do you have any idea when she expects to arrive?'

'In three weeks.'

'So soon as that! My, we'll have to be getting our welcome ready.'

'The authorities will do that for us.'

The minister did not understand, but smiled, still confident that not only would there be relevance in the remark but wisdom and kindness also.

'I mean, just about that time they'll be putting up the arches for Voroshilov.'

'Yes indeed, so they will. True, true. Well, let us claim the arches for ourselves. Our own little welcome will, I am sure, be much more sincere.' He rose. 'I'll not take up any more of your valuable time. But I would sure be pleased if you would let me know in good time when Miss Johnstone's plane is due.'

Moffatt accompanied him out to the gate. 'Really we know very little about Miss Johnstone,' he said.

'Does that matter, Harold?'

'I meant, she may not want to be married according to Christian practice. From what I know of her, she's the kind likely to go the whole way and become a Moslem.'

'I would consider it my duty to prevent that happening, if I could. We are all God's children, Christians, Moslems, Buddhists, agnostics, atheists; but He loved Christ best of all.'

While Moffatt was trying to make sense of that, he saw a family of kuchis, or nomads, on the main road. The dark-faced men and women, and the shy children, seemed as remote from humanity as their donkeys and camels.

'What about those?' he asked.

'I see our Lord walking with them, Harold. His feet too are bare. These people are His true contemporaries.'

All right, thought Moffatt, I'll accept that. It's phony, but I'll accept it. But what about the ex-Minister of Finance, with his face kicked to pulp? Is he a child of God? Was your Lord watching the kicking? Had He His feet bare then, or did He, like the soldiers, wear hobnail boots?

The minister held out his hand. 'If the spirit ever takes you along to our little church, Harold, we'll all rejoice to see you; and that of course includes your beautiful and charming wife.'

'Lan isn't a Christian.'

'Is she Buddhist?'

'She was brought up one.'

The minister lifted his hand to the blue sky. 'Do you know, Harold, when I think of the wonderful variety of God's children, I feel rich in my soul.'

He walked over to the little Austin car that his congregation had bought for him. After Josh Bolton he was said to be the poorest American in Kabul, and it was rumoured that those of his flock who contributed most to his stipend were the most bigoted and forbade his taking part in the square dancing at the U.S.I.S., although he and his wife were thought to be keen and expert. Nevertheless, it was miraculously true enough that he was rich in soul and proved it daily.

Harold watched the car go dustily down the road and then went back slowly into the house.

Lan had the letter in her hand.

He drank some whisky with a gulp, as if he'd needed it. 'Now, let's hear what she's got to say,' he said. 'I feel my soul is fortified enough.'

To his surprise she jumped up, pale and tense. 'I'm not going to read it to you, Harold. If you want to read it, there it is.' She dropped it on a table, and ran out.

He heard the bedroom door close behind her. No doubt she had heard those last words. What was she doing now?

Not, as Helen Langford once had done, doodling all over
her face with lipstick. And not, as Paula Wint would, after a
tiff with Alan, lying upon the bed and waiting for him to
come with his packet of love. Lan would sit on the stool in
front of the mirror, as still as an idol; and without so much as
a tear she would suffer, so privately and mysteriously that,
unable to share any of it in his imagination, he could not
keep his love and sympathy from being strangled by resentment and a feeling of loss. She had gone again to kneel by
her dead sister.

Picking up the letter and his glass of whisky, he went out
and sat on the terrace. The poem that had been rejected had
been inspired by some remarks of Howard Winfield's, to the
effect that almost any action when analysed, whether it were
a king's or prime minister's or general's or ambassador's,
was found to have in it a high proportion of childishness.
There could be no doubt that the human race was still in its
long infancy. 'I challenge you, Harold,' the young Oriental
Secretary had said, 'to name any action, public or private,
contemporary or historical, by potentate or menial, which is
or was completely and unassailably adult.' Moffatt had not
tried, but he had written the poem and now, with this letter
still unread in his hand, he thought that the present trouble
between him and Lan was not unlike the quarrels of childhood. But by admitting that he was by no means belittling it.
He believed that the emotions of childhood were so intense
and complicated as to affect the minds for the rest of life.

As always, too, he sought the same refuge as a child: he
forgot himself and remembered the world about him. The
afternoon was warm and sunny. In the garden the roses were
in full fragrance, and the grapes on the trellis against the wall
were already forming. Among the cool vines a bird crooned.
A cat slept on the wall, disturbed a little by the crooning; it
seemed to think it ought to make a little effort to keep up the
traditional enmity between its kind and the bird's, but, fed

and warm and sleepy, it preferred this truce. In the servants' quarters out of sight around the corner Sofi sang somnolently a song about hunting leopards. In the park boys were playing football; they kept shrieking all the time, like a horde of birds. He could not see them but knew all of them would be dressed in striped pyjamas and most would be kicking the ball with their bare feet.

He glanced at the letter. The handwriting was small, but, in a way that moved him, it wasn't very neat; in fact, it had the rebellious carelessness he would have expected in a schoolgirl, her tongue out, doing a punishment exercise.

He looked away again. The cat had given up trying; it slept soundly. The bird crooned more happily than ever. Bees buzzed among the roses. Sofi sang now about a river in the north. The boys continued to shriek.

DEAR MRS MOFFATT,

I find it difficult to express my gratitude to you. I have read your wise and generous letter a hundred times.

Hitherto, ever since I made the decision to go to Afghanistan to marry my fiancé, Mr Abdul Wahab, I have been made to feel that no one, not one single person, thinks I have done right. People who do not know me at all have gone out of their way to advise me to reconsider. Friends have urged this from the beginning. That it has all been done out of genuine sympathy and interest, I cannot believe; that it has been provoked by ill will and envy is, I suppose, even more unlikely. I can only conclude that part of the reason at least must simply be racial prejudice. I myself have not always been free of that, and perhaps, in spite of my too conscious efforts to eradicate it, it still exists in me. Nevertheless, I love Abdul Wahab and I am sure he loves me. At any rate no one has ever treated me with greater tenderness and more unselfish consideration. As you may expect, it has been suggested to me that his attitude is not sincere. Some of those who think this have been at pains to impress on me that a man from the East, especially from a country like Afghanistan where women are still kept in purdah, would scarcely agree to marry one, like myself, with a physical incapacity – I have been lame in the left foot since childhood, as a consequence of an attack of poliomyelitis – unless he had some dishonourable ulterior motive. This is to show a degree of cynicism that I find disgusting. I know Abdul Wahab's faults, as I hope he knows mine; and I certainly do not expect to find his country perfect.

I should be very pleased and grateful to be your guest for a little while, until I have settled in; but my acceptance, of course, must depend upon your husband's willingness to receive me.

I expect to be in Kabul in about four weeks from now. I look forward to meeting you and expressing my gratitude in person. Alas, I am not very good at this, perhaps because of my Scotch ancestors. But I will certainly try. I have always had a high opinion of your countrymen, the Chinese, and you have proved how justified it has been.

LAURA JOHNSTONE

Moved in spite of himself, he read phrase after phrase over and over again, trying to build up a picture of the writer. In the end his impression was of someone sensitive and intelligent, sheltering in a shell constructed after years of lonely and resolute thought. Many attempts had failed to pierce it. Yet how easily Wahab had got in.

She lacks humour, he thought; and then, looking at the

letter again, he wasn't sure. If one watched carefully one might catch an ironic smile.

Feeling a hand resting lightly on his shoulder he turned and saw Lan. She was listening to the bird crooning. It struck him afresh that she too lived in a shell, more beautifully and subtly fashioned than the dour Miss Johnstone's, but just as strong. He, whose motives were hardly any more or less honourable than Wahab's, had got in just as easily.

As he placed his hand on hers, he remembered Manson Powrie's pious cry about the wonderful variety of the Lord's children. Not so various, he thought, not so bloody various.

Seventeen

BY A coincidence Wahab was installed as Principal on the morning of the day of the Garden Party at the British Embassy. Luckily the Ministry, now under the thoughtful direction of Prince Naim, sent along with the letter of appointment a coupon which would enable him to buy on credit from the Government Monopoly Shop a new suit, new shirt, socks, and a pair of shoes; payment for these would be deducted monthly from his augmented salary. No information was given him as to when these new clothes should be worn, but he knew himself that, arrayed in them, he would be able more readily to convince all those, foremost among them Abdul Mussein, the deposed Principal, who might otherwise have been inclined to question his fitness for so swift an upward jump. Therefore the very day the coupon arrived at the school he cycled to the shop to make the purchases; but not, unfortunately, before Mussein had been able to confront him.

By a mistake of zealousness, pardonable enough in a new Ministry, the two letters – that to Wahab elevating him, and that to Mussein degrading him – arrived on the same morning, instead of the former being sent a day or so in advance so that the dispossessor, whose role was really the more difficult to play, might be given a chance to rehearse. During the conversation with Mussein, Wahab took note several times of that efficient but nevertheless unwise simultaneity; it was the kind of blunder, he thought, that would instinctively be avoided by the inspired administrator. Prince

Naim would certainly be an improvement at the Ministry, but there was no denying that had he not been the son of the King he would never have achieved so responsible a position; he was, as the English put it, merely a gifted amateur.

This conversation between the two Principals, the one rising and the other falling, took place, at the latter's request, outside the school building, in a quiet corner of the playground near the mud-built communal privy. It was necessary to have it there for privacy's sake. Though the school was in session – babble from a dozen glassless windows proved this – an extraordinary number of boys were in the playground, some reading in the shade, some strolling in the sun, some lying in it, a few playing volleyball, and others kicking a football. Indeed, only that area close to the lavatories was deserted.

Mussein had his letter in his hand. He had called Wahab away from a class to which he had been demonstrating relative densities. Wahab, whose own letter was in his pocket, had of course known why he was being beckoned and, though prepared to pity, was at the same time determined to be thoroughly Afghan in his attitude. This was well described by a traditional legend in which the characters were flies on fresh camel dung. As soon as one flew off another alighted, saying: 'It's my turn now.' Thinking about it in those terms, Wahab had to make conscious efforts to prevent himself from sprouting wings and four extra feet. Mussein's monotonous whines, and also of course the horrid stink, confused him. Nor did it help much to raise his head from the baked cracked clay to look at the distant mountains. Meditations on the grandeur of the country were not possible while these pusillanimous complaints, which sometimes verged on the treasonable, hummed in his ears. What Wahab wanted to do was to stop his pacing, silence Mussein with a calm hand, and say to him, quietly: 'The difference between us, my dear Mussein, is that in your youthful dream you had not the courage to let yourself die. If you remember, you not only lived but had messengers from the king coming to shower upon you riches and distinctions. I, on the contrary, died.' But it would have been risking self-derision to say that to a man whose suit, though badly stained on the left lapel, was still as respectable as his own.

Therefore, as Mussein sang his bitter dirge, Wahab tried not to listen to it, but instead to concentrate on his own future which might well contain more tribulations in its brilliance than Mussein's would in eclipse. To begin with, what would the leaders of the Brotherhood say when they discovered that Laura was lame? And even if they did accept that unfortunate blemish in the wife of a man destined to save Afghanistan, was it not brutally true that Laura, in spite of her many admirable qualities, did lack a family with influence? To marry the daughter of a general or minister would surely be the next move of an Afghan manoeuvring to improve his social position. Besides, under her shaddry, that general's daughter might be beautiful and plump. Of course it was just as possible that she might be cross-eyed and skinny. Could he, he mused, be content with such a wife, for the sake of Afghanistan? Would he in that event remain as resolute as he now was to work for the abolition of the shaddry? And if he were to find himself married, with a fine house, and comfortably off, would the poverty of so many millions of his countrymen continue to anger him? Aziz, his colleague in the bus-company office, had once spluttered cheerfully between bouts of coughing: 'But, Wahab, how can our governors learn to eradicate the poverty of others, if they haven't learned first how to eradicate their own?' Wahab had chided him: hunger and disease, those terrible off-spring of poverty, were not subjects for jokes, even cynical ones on a dying man's lips.

At last Mussein seemed to have vomited the last dregs of his grievance. With sweat on his brow, he gaped at the ground; his eyes were closed, and he was shivering. It was obvious that within he was weeping; at any moment his tears might burst into the open.

'What am I to say, Mussein?' asked Wahab, crossly. 'I do not see it as a personal matter at all. This is a critical time for our country. We must put it first. At present it is very backward. Now to be backward when most other countries are backward too is not a disgrace, but to be backward in this age of sputniks and hydrogen bombs and television *is* a disgrace. Do you not agree?'

Mussein opened his bloodshot eyes. 'I know that television is wonderful,' he muttered.

'I have seen it, and it is *not* wonderful,' said Wahab testily. 'It is a toy. I used it as a symbol. It represents the twentieth century; far too much in Afghanistan still represents the first century. It is not only necessary for us to advance, but we must do so at a prodigious rate. What subject did you teach, Mussein? What did you specialize in at the University?'

'Persian literature.'

'Of course. Well then, why blame me because you have been removed from the Principalship? It isn't Abdul Wahab who has taken your place, Mussein; it is a scientist, a man of the modern world.'

For a few moments Mussein could find no answer. 'Well,' he said at last, 'at least poetry can teach us to be humble.'

'But we do not want to be humble, Mussein. We have been humble much too long.'

'There is a line from Firdausi, Wahab, which has often comforted me. "I am dust on the paw of the lion." '

Wahab frowned: he had not expected so heroic a line. 'Be dust as you wish, Mussein; but do not protest when others prefer to be the lion.'

'I am lucky,' said Mussein, with a sigh and ghastly smile.

Wahab thought grief had softened his companion's brain; he felt a magnanimous sorrow. 'Indeed you are, Mussein.

We are all lucky. God has called upon our generation to rebuild our people.'

'You said you did not believe in God, Wahab. Have you found reason to believe in Him now?'

Wahab said nothing, but since he did it with dignity it was equivalent really to a lion's defiant roar.

'I am lucky,' repeated Mussein, 'because I have a beautiful wife who loves me, and a little son who is very like me.'

Whereas the lion's intended mate was lame, with the thorn of fate in her paw.

'But what is the benefit of having two sound feet?' demanded Wahab bitterly. 'Shrouded in her shaddry, a woman cannot run. Hobbled by ridiculous prejudice, she cannot dance.'

'Sometimes in our home my wife and I dance a little.'

To the music of the munching jaws of the greedy old uncle? But to have said so would have been to yelp like a jackal. 'If, before you are too old to enjoy it, you and your wife are able to dance together in public, Mussein, you will have me, and those who think like me, to thank.'

'We are happier dancing in our own home.'

'Then there is nothing more to be said, Mussein. I must go now. I have an important appointment in town.'

Into the Principal's damp red eyes came a gleam of slyness. 'How can you leave now, Mr Wahab? Have you forgotten you still have two classes to take this morning?'

Wahab laughed: it was amusing when the dust tried to impede the lion.

'At the moment, dear Mussein, I see at least six classes which no one is taking.'

'Their teachers are absent.'

'Something could have been organized.'

'Now you are proposing, without permission, to go off and leave two other classes unattended.'

'Without permission! Surely, Mussein, you cannot have read that letter in your hand.'

'I have read it, Wahab. I could recite it by heart. In twenty years I shall still be able to recite it. It states that from the eighteenth I shall cease to be Principal of this school. Today is only the sixteenth. Therefore I am still the Principal. As such, I am unable to grant you permission to leave early.'

'You have been given these two days, Mussein, to get things in order for my taking over.'

'Then please allow me to get things in order. Evidently I have been considered too weak and amiable to succeed as a principal. Very well. I intend to use the little time left to demonstrate how, had I wished, I could have carried out my duties sternly and unpleasantly. Go to your classroom, Mr Wahab.'

'This is absurd, Mussein.'

The finger quivered but it still pointed towards the school.

'It is not only absurd, it is unwise. You should know by this time that I have influential friends. Think of your beautiful wife, Mussein, and of your little son.'

'Please go, Mr Wahab. Your threats are despicable.'

The lion's tail, as a matter of fact, just wouldn't stay taut and proudly curled; no, it kept wanting to droop and trail in the dust.

'I shall go,' said Wahab. 'But I must warn you that I intend to inform my friends that you have been insulting. I do not think Prince Naim will be pleased. In the meantime I shall be most interested in your somewhat belated demonstration.'

He strode off towards the building, holding his tail up by force.

Behind him Mussein stood for a few seconds as if praying, and then began to run as gawkily as a young camel toward the nearest group of boys, squatted peaceably on the ground. Before he reached them he was shrieking, and then he was punching and kicking at them wildly, causing them to scramble up and jump aside. He howled to them to go inside to their classroom. Some shouted back that their algebra teacher had gone for three days to his village to bury his old father who had died; others asked Mussein indignantly if he had gone mad. He continued to howl that they must go in and get on with their studies. Then he rushed away to the next group. As he was cuffing them the gong sounded, and hundreds of boys began to pour out into the playground.

The Principal stood staring and then covered his face with his hands. A boy or two came a little closer, perhaps to ask if he were ill.

Wahab, watching from the steps, laughed, but not too confidently; in his heart he by no means felt certain that he himself possessed the authority and strength of character necessary to clear playgrounds, compel teachers to attend, dead fathers or no, and enforce in every classroom diligent and profitable silence. To govern a country, he realized, was probably easier than to discipline a school; in the first task one had the help of police and soldiers, in the second one had to use the compulsions only of love and compassion.

As he went upstairs he noticed the dust on his shoes and for a foolish, passionate, heart-sinking moment felt envious of it. To be the lion's paw meant prowling and pouncing dangerously, and meeting in conflict other lions, older and fiercer.

On the morning of the eighteenth, sleek in his new fawn suit, Wahab sat at the desk in his room overlooking the street, sucking a throat pastille. Impelled by an imprudence which seemed to rise spontaneously and yet which kept astonishing and indeed alarming him, he had telephoned the Ministry the day before and invited Prince Naim to be present at his installation. If a new era was to begin, better, he had suggested, introduce it with trumpets. Naim had consented, cautiously; perhaps he was offended a little by this insinuation that the promotion of Wahab, rather than his own assumption of power, inaugurated the new educational era. However, he had agreed to come, and now Wahab was waiting at the window for the big dark-blue Daimler to appear, with the royal flag flying on its fender.

Below, the boys were being arranged in classes in front of the entrance. This was being done by the other teachers, under the leadership of Mohammed Siddiq, the Headmaster, who was next under the Principal and who was well aware he was again on probation, though he was gray-haired and twice Wahab's age. Therefore he yelled at his subordinates who yelled at the boys who yelled at one another. Buses passing sounded their horns. Camels and donkeys brayed. The noise was considerable, but it did not worry Wahab; nor would it Naim. Afghans always took noise to be a sign of vitality. The sports teacher, for instance, when announcing the teams for a game of football, would make a tempestuous harangue of it with furious gestures. Wahab himself, with his own crusading speech to make, hoped his throat would be able to do it justice. Never in his life had his voice been powerful. Now he sucked the medicinal candy.

The Daimler arrived and glittered through the gates. Snatching up his hat, Wahab rushed downstairs. When he went outside on the top of the steps there was no instant hush of awe, or even of respect, as there should have been. Even when he clapped his hands no one heeded. Teachers scowled toward the mountains. The boys were cheering Naim. Perhaps it was a mistake asking him to come, thought Wahab, as he hurried across to the car; I should have waited until the whole school was under my benevolent domination.

The Prince was dressed in a white suit, with a red rose in his lapel. He looked fitter to visit a brothel than a school. I must not be bitter, thought Wahab; or rather, I must not let my bitterness show.

The Prince was very affable and shook hands. 'How can we despair, Wahab,' he cried, 'when we have such magnificent material to work with?'

He meant the boys, who seemed then to Wahab a vast, menacing, brainless mob; but the new Principal had to laugh and shine with enthusiasm.

'Who knows, Your Highness?' he said. 'Perhaps there is among them an Afghan Einstein.'

'Or an Afghan Shakespeare,' added the Prince. 'In our advance, science must go hand in hand with art.'

Which is the paw, and which the dust? wondered Wahab. Aloud he cried: 'How true, Your Highness!'

As he pushed his way through the boys many, bigger and heavier than he, would not budge or move aside. For the Prince they did so alertly and cheerfully. What has happened is easy to see, thought Wahab: the rest of the teachers through jealousy have poisoned their minds against me. Well, it may make my task harder, but my courage to accomplish it will be all the greater. Even as he said this to himself, another voice, even clearer, called it humbug.

He stood on the terrace beside the Prince. The sports master blew a whistle. Everyone was quiet.

'You know why I am here this morning,' said the Prince.

There was a great clapping of brown hands.

'A few days ago I became the Minister of Education.'

Again those dark wings fluttered noisily.

'The Government knows that the welfare of our country lies in your hands. You are our future. The most important task before me is to ensure that your education becomes a reality and does not remain the dream it has been so far. I have many plans, but in the meantime men are being appointed as principals who have vision. This is the quality which most of all we need today. With it we can do marvels;

without it, we are as blind men. You all know Abdul Wahab.'

No one clapped. Wahab broke into a sweat. He saw a teacher grin with malice.

'He is not only a teacher of proven ability; he also has vision, and faith in our country. I share that faith. So, I am sure, do you. If we all work together, who can prevent us from taking our rightful place among the important nations of the world? We may be smaller in numbers than some, but we can make up for that by our sincerity and our uniqueness. Yes, I believe that Afghanistan can astonish the world. Today we see nations advanced materially but spiritually sick. Suicide, divorce, murder, racial hatred, mental sickness – these are rife in countries where the standard of living is very high. What we can do, protected by our traditional wisdom and dignity, is to raise our standard as high as theirs, but at the same time to retain our spiritual health. This opportunity to be an example to the whole of mankind is Afghanistan's today. I call upon you to help me, and your new Principal, to accept that opportunity.'

They clapped so vigorously that it was clear to Wahab the action was purely physical. The Prince might have told them obscene stories and got the same response. Look now, thought Wahab, how they renew the clapping and cheering every time they think I am about to begin my speech. He remembered how when he was a student at the University this was how they had tried to prevent the white-bearded, old Dean from addressing them. He had been known to be a tool of the Government who had approved of every reduction in students' allowances.

Naim held up his hand and, magically, there was silence. Uneasily Wahab entered into it.

'Your Royal Highness, esteemed colleagues, students of Isban College, in one word, fellow Afghans, no one knows better than I what a great honour has been done me by being

appointed Principal of this, one of the best schools in our
country. Yet I do not look on it as a personal honour. There
was a time, not so very long ago, when the Principals of our
four institutions of higher education were foreigners. Habibiah had an American, Esteklal a Frenchman, Nejat a
German, and Isban here an Englishman. It was believed
then that we had neither the knowledge nor the ability to
manage our own schools. Slowly that changed until today,
not only do we feel ourselves competent, we are also
convinced that under Afghan control an Afghan school,
with Afghan teachers and students, will be the equal of
any school anywhere in the world.'

By this time he had worked himself up to the necessary
pitch and was shouting and gesticulating in that impassioned way so convincing to the Afghan mind. A man
speaking calmly was unsure; but a man with spittle of
passion on his lips and with his hands clawing down the
sky was a man worth listening to, even if his subject was
merely the iniquity of a ghoddy horse which had pissed all
over the carpets he had brought fifty miles to the market to
sell.

So the teachers and pupils began to pay heed to Wahab
just at the very moment when he himself completely lost
faith in what he was saying. It did not leak slowly out as
water did from the famous Istalif blue jars; no, it gushed out
as if the bottom had been broken; and during the rest of his
address, which became so impassioned at times as to seem
demented, and which was frequently greeted with roars of
approval, he was working hard far within, first to mend the
bottom, and then refill. This was a task of almost impossible
difficulty, because every howled boast, every shrieked pro-
phecy, was shattering so that he was destroying and mending at the same time. No wonder that when he finished, with
sweat all over and the knuckles of his right hand grazed
where he had struck them against one of the stone pillars, by

accident of course, he felt as if he were inside a cement mixer which had just stopped. When Naim shook his hand and congratulated him he wanted to whimper that he wasn't fit to be Principal, but instead accepted those royal congratulations with firm sincerity, and the others, the professional ones of his colleagues, with an impressive mixture of authority and camaraderie. Outwardly towards the pupils he felt and looked like an elder brother who had been away travelling the world in search of experience and wisdom and had now returned to restore the fortunes of his family. Inwardly he felt them to be hundreds of young lions who would in the next few weeks tear out his guts.

A few minutes later Naim had gone. Wahab rushed upstairs to his room, padlocked it from the inside, and sat down at his desk to bite his nails and brood upon two things: first, the reorganization of the school that he had so vaingloriously promised; and second, the Garden Party at the British Embassy that afternoon, to which it was hardly likely any other guest would arrive by bicycle.

More amazing even than this impudence, gushing up in him like oil in Persia, was his ability to control it. He marvelled himself at this mastery; it must surely be that he was destined for some high and powerful post. For instance, in seeking how to avoid the ignominy of cycling up to the great gilt-crested gates of the British Embassy, choked by the clouds of dust thrown up by the limousines of ambassadors, it did occur to him to appeal to Prince Naim – not to be so rash as to ask him for a lift in his royal car, but to hint that, if a Ministry car were available, perhaps Wahab might have it to take him there and back. Even with his hand on the telephone, ready to pick it up, he smiled and agreed with the astute politician within him that to have invited the Prince to his installation was enough for one day. Where patronage was the ladder to success, it was as well to remember that the rungs were rather widely spaced; where wealth and influence were, they were almost too close together; and of course ability itself was merely the frame, with the rungs missing. Therefore when he did lift the telephone, and dialled a number, it wasn't Prince Naim's, but Harold Moffatt's; and while he was waiting for a reply he shouted to the boy outside to run and fetch Maftoon. Maftoon was the young teacher who had grinned so maliciously when Naim had presented Wahab to the school.

It was Moffatt's servant, the small cheerful one called Sofi, who answered. Wahab spoke to him with such quiet command that there were no impertinent chuckles, only submissive respect, and the information that Sahib had left for the University. 'And Mrs Moffatt?' She had gone to the International School. 'Very well, I shall ring up the University. Thank you.' As he put down the receiver he could have sung as he pictured Sofi, so insolent with the glass of orangeade at the Club Dance, now cringing and cautious. This was surely the sweetest thing about rising in the world: to do nothing, not so much as move a finger, and yet watch those, previously indifferent or rude, be as careful as a cat in the presence of a barking dog. He contrasted the policemen who had humiliated him by deflating the tyres of his bicycle with those in Naim's garden who had saluted him. A thrill pierced him, such as even the thought of making love to Laura could not equal. As he sat thinking of all those, beginning with Maftoon, still to undergo that transformation before him, the thrill kept surging through him.

He telephoned the University, was told Mr Moffatt was lecturing, replied that he was aware of it, and suggested that nevertheless the Englishman ought to be summoned at once. The Dean, for it was he, more doddery and fearful than ever, quavered that it would be done at once. Wahab placed the telephone on the table and went over to unpadlock the door. Maftoon had already knocked three times with gratifying meekness.

'Come in, Maftoon,' he said. 'Sit down. I won't be a minute. I am on the telephone.'

He returned to the desk and picked up the telephone. There were still only the wheezings of the Dean.

Scratching the side of his head with the instrument, Wahab stared at his squirming subordinate, who was not squirming enough.

'Are you married, Maftoon?'

Maftoon, now seen to be intelligent as well as cunning, nodded. He was surprisingly well-dressed, but his face was quite hideously pockmarked, so much so that Wahab's own face grew hot. He hated being reminded of his few faint scars, not merely for personal reasons, but because whenever he tried to imagine a typical Afghan he could not prevent his having cheeks like Maftoon's.

'And have you any children?'

'Three.'

'Three? They must be very young surely.'

'The eldest is three.'

'In that case, I take it the youngest is very recent?' Because, though Afghans bred like rabbits, owing to lust and a lazy refusal to use contraceptives, they still had the same gestation period as other people. Was Maftoon's wife, like Mussein's, beautiful? How shameful it would be to help Maftoon to win promotion and in return demand inter-course with his wife.

'My second son is three weeks old,' said Maftoon.

Wahab saw that morsel of Afghan flesh as if it were his own and Laura's. Yet Maftoon had one of the darkest Afghan complexions; perhaps his wife, like Wahab, had one of the lightest. In so mixed a nation, it was a matter of luck, that was all; but it could also be used as a matter of prestige. He had read, with horror and contempt, of American Negroes buying preparations that would take the kinks out of their hair. Now, as he stared at the almost black Maftoon, he remembered how he himself a short time ago in that very room had admired the paleness of his own hand.

Then the telephone spoke. 'Moffatt here.'

'Ah, Mr Moffatt,' said Wahab, very suave. 'How do you do? This is Abdul Wahab. We have met.'

'Yes, I remember.'

'How is your charming wife?'

'Very well, thank you.'

And how, Wahab could have added, is your fair-haired big-bosomed paramour? You apparently failed that evening, but no doubt you have succeeded since. Instead he said, crisply: 'You must forgive me for taking you away from your class. The truth is, Mr Moffatt, I have a favour to ask of you.' And, Mr Moffatt, he added, though to himself, please understand that I, yes I, Abdul Wahab, whom you despise and into whose eyes you flung whisky, have it in my power to have you expelled from my country.

'Well,' Moffatt was saying, in a surprisingly friendly voice, 'if I can help, I'll be pleased to.'

'Thank you, Mr Moffatt. This afternoon there is at your Embassy the Queen's Garden Party. Is that not so?'

'Yes, but – if it's an invitation you're after, I'm afraid I can't help. I've got no influence there you know; rather the reverse. You could have mine if it was any use to you.

'Are you not going, Mr Moffatt?'

'I'm afraid so. My wife wants to go.'

'Certainly. Why should she not? It is the function of the year. I understand the ladies wear hats and beautiful dresses. But none will be so beautiful as she. I have an invitation.'

'Oh.'

'You sound a little surprised.'

'Well, no. Why should I be?' But in the Dean's room, with the old man cracking his fingers in his white beard,

Moffatt was grinning. Only the day before he had asked Alan Wint if Wahab had been invited, and the reply had been: 'For Christ's sake, Harold old man, this is an important occasion, whatever a bolshy like you may think.'

'An invitation was sent to me,' said Wahab.

It must have been a mistake, thought Moffatt; but such mistakes must be welcomed and cherished. 'Congratulations,' he said. 'How are you going?'

'I have my bicycle.'

Both laughed.

'Would they let me pass the gates if I arrived on my bicycle?'

'Probably not.'

'But it was made in Coventry.'

'Why not come with us?'

'Thank you, Mr Moffatt. Let me, with what you consider untypical Afghan frankness, admit that that was my purpose in telephoning you, to cadge a lift. Cadge is the right word?'

'It'll do.' Moffatt could be heard laughing. 'Why not join us at lunch while you're at it?'

'I should be delighted, if you are sure I shall be no bother.'

Does he know, wondered Wahab, that he is in my power? But surely his affability sounds genuine.

'No bother at all. In any case I owe you some amends. Right, then. We'll be looking out for you about one.'

'I am much obliged, Mr Moffatt.'

'Don't mention it. Well, I'll have to get back to my class now. They'll be writing rude words on the blackboard. Cheerio till one.'

'Cheerio.' As Wahab, trembling with happiness, restored the telephone, he saw those rude English words; he knew them all; he was therefore in the game; he was manly, accepted by men; he was a mature human being, capable of taking his place in any society.

He was whispering the magic monosyllables under his

breath when he turned to stare at Maftoon, the father of three infants, all begotten in lustful haste.

'What subject do you teach, Maftoon?'

'Geography.'

'A useful subject.'

'I think so. But I'm afraid I don't have as much success in my teaching as I would like.'

'Indeed. What teacher does? But what is the particular reason in your case?'

'I have not been allowed to use the map room.'

'Yes, I have heard some talk of this. Why?'

'It appears Sadruddin, our custodian, told Abdul Mussein no one must use the map room, lest maps or globes be stolen.'

'I see. Are there any maps in your classroom?'

'One.'

'Of Afghanistan?'

'No. Of England.'

'England?'

'Yes. I do not know how it came to be there. It must be a relic of the days when the school was under the domination of the English.'

'Do you dislike the English, Maftoon?'

'I suspect them. But this map, it is old and dirty, and I think it must have been used once to cover a hole in the window; there are great patches of damp.'

'Rather appropriate. Some parts of England are very wet. I understand the map room is well supplied with maps.'

'It has maps of almost every country in the world.'

'But not one of Afghanistan?'

'There is a small one.'

'Yes, very small.' The United Nations had for their own purposes drawn a map of the country; it was the only one in existence. At present a team of Japanese geologists was preparing a geological map, showing the whereabouts of the great mineral deposits. 'I understand Mohammed Wali also teaches geography?'

'Yes.'

'Has he been allowed to use the map room?'

'No. But he has not cared. He is not as conscientious as I. He is ignorant of his subject. I asked him to go with me to Abdul Mussein to complain, but he refused.'

'You are ambitious, Maftoon?'

'For my pupils, yes.'

Is he really, wondered Wahab, using my own kind of hypocrisy against me? Is it then not so uncommon? Is the whole country full of young men keen to reform it, ostensibly for others' sakes but really for their own? If so, the struggle might well become bloody.

'Maftoon, when Prince Naim presented me this morning, you grinned.'

Maftoon grinned again; there was slyness in it this time. 'I am sure I did, Abdul Wahab.'

'Why? What was there so funny and contemptible about my being presented as Principal.'

'Oh, but I was not smiling for that reason. I was delighted when I first heard of your appointment. I agreed with every word you said. Did you not notice there were tears in my eyes?'

'No.' This was a cunning fellow indeed.

'There were. What you said has needed to be said for years. It is high time we believed we are as good as any other nation and that our pupils are as gifted.'

Wahab was almost sure this too was hypocrisy. Yet why should he believe it to be so? Did he not want allies?

'I intend to introduce a number of reforms,' he said, rather coldly. 'You and Wali will be allowed to use the map room.'

'I am very grateful; but I do not think he will be. He will only consider that an excuse for inefficiency has been taken away from him.'

'I shall find these things out in my own way, Maftoon. His salary is higher?'

'You should know, Abdul Wahab, that none of us, including yourself, is paid a fair wage.'

'It is not for you, Maftoon, or for me, to question the policy of our superiors. Our country is not wealthy. Granted teachers are not paid high salaries. Are there not millions of our fellow citizens far worse off than we? Indeed, compared with the majority, are we not fortunate?'

'I am thinking of the minority.'

Oh, you black, pock-cheeked scoundrel, thought Wahab. I know what you are; you have been planted here to spy on me, worse, to provoke me into injudicious admissions; you are an agent of the Brotherhood, who do not trust me, who do not trust anyone. Naim, they say, is a lover of flowers. How beautiful and fragrant his garden is with them. Yes, but in spite of that he would not be loath to shed blood redder than any of his roses. I have allowed myself to forget the traditional treachery and violence of my race; only it is not called treachery, it is called intelligent readiness to seize every opportunity, no matter how presented. Is it not written proudly in our history books that when an English envoy, during the British imperial wars a hundred years ago, went under a promise of safe conduct to parley with Afghan leaders one of them stabbed him in the back? In peace or war, whatever was most likely to succeed was best, and only a fool would hesitate to use it.

'May I say, Maftoon, that I do not much like your speaking so disloyally of your colleague. And I have noticed that you did not explain why you had grinned.'

Maftoon looked concerned, as well he might, with a wife, three infants, and a justly displeased superior. Yet it was somehow a spurious concern; behind it, peeping out of every pockmark, was an insolence. Perhaps, though, I am misjudging him, thought Wahab; he may only have an unpleasant face.

'I grinned because I felt uplifted,' said Maftoon. 'I may say I have always been an admirer of yours, Abdul Wahab. Ask the others. They will tell you how I have often spoken highly of you. They will tell you also that I used to say you would make a much better Principal than Abdul Mussein.'

Anxious to accept any ally, however dubious, Wahab still could not forget that grin; if ever a human face had indicated envy and sourness Maftoon's had then. However this, and many other things, would have to be pondered over.

'Very well, Maftoon,' he said. 'You may return to your class. I shall look to you to help me in the improvements I hope to introduce.'

Maftoon rose and came over. 'I shall be very pleased to give you all the help I can.' There was a smell off his breath, but worse was the ruthless glisten in his eyes. Wahab almost shuddered. He might dream of brutality if it became necessary to clear incompetence out of the way – this man, in spite of his three infants, would gladly enact it.

After Maftoon had gone, Wahab sat for a while at his desk, realizing more and more clearly that he was in all likelihood surrounded by men who hated him for his luck in being promoted over them, but who would, like Maftoon, pretend to admire him until the opportunity came for them to tear him to pieces. If the lion grew sick, then was the time for the jackals. Perhaps he would have been safer and happier if he had remained an assistant teacher.

Tears came into his eyes as he shook his head angrily, denying that cowardly retreat. I am really an ordinary man, he thought, even if I have a scientific degree and have studied abroad. I am timid and self-seeking. I like flattery better than abuse. I cherish ideals but have the usual instinct that warns me not to try and practise them. I am proud of my nation but am also irritated by the shortcomings of my fellow Afghans. I love Laura but am afraid people will despise me because she is a cripple. In short, I am hardly any different from that camel driver out there. No doubt he smokes cigarettes of hashish whenever he can get them, but then do I not puff as often as I can at the pipe of vanity, which is just as debilitating? Yes, I have my many faults, and I know them, as a cat knows the mice in its house. But my sympathy for my fellow human beings, however flawed by my own selfishness and however stultified by theirs, does exist, and I do not think that I shall altogether betray it.

It was a kind of dedication, much more sincere than the loud-mouthed public one he had uttered that morning. If he had been religious, he would have prayed. If he had been political, he would have both bowed towards and saluted the portraits of the King and Prime Minister hung side by side on the wall. But since he was none of these, but simply an imperfect lover of his fellow men, he turned and gazed out at the people passing on the street. An old woman, her red bloomers visible under her flowing shaddry, shuffled wearily along, with a bundle on her back. A small dung-gatherer watched passing horses and camels anxiously. Some coolies chatted together in a dialect he would not know; their ropes of their trade were coiled around their tattered shoulders. A tribesman, rifle on his back, pranced past on a fine horse. Several ghoddies clattered by, drawn by horses that were as skinny as their drivers.

To all those, and to the students now under his care, he was dedicating himself, so that he stood at the window, with his arms outstretched, like, he thought with a sudden pang of dismay, Maftoon waiting for his infants to come toddling to him.

Eighteen

EVERY year the Residence was given a coat of white paint for the Birthday Garden Party, though as Sir Gervase himself remarked, this summer it was hardly bloody well necessary so numerous were the starlings and their droppings, and so ineffective, surely he implied, had been all the Administrative Officer's attempts to scare or coax them into defecating elsewhere. Gillie took bitter note, but said nothing; nor did he try to defend himself when the scandal of the Union Jacks broke.

Sir Gervase, prowling on the flat roof, and squinting up at the flag then in use, decided it was too grimy and tattered. Telephoning Chancery, he had supposed there was another one in store. Two, Gillie had calmly replied. But unfortunately when Tom Parry went to the cupboard in which they were kept, it was discovered that mice – at least these were taken to be the culprits – had eaten large holes in them. The results, Howard Winfield had suggested, out of H.E.'s bearing, were surely symbolical: were not many parts of the Empire missing? There was no time to send to London or Delhi for a replacement, and so Lady Beauly, Paula Wint, and Muriel Gillie hurriedly formed themselves into a working party to do some patching. The entire Embassy's resources were ransacked to find material of the right red colour, and the extraordinary thing was that by far the best match turned out to be an old pair of the Consul's underpants, which his wife, anxious to redeem him in his master's eyes, offered without his consent. She did not of course tell her sister patchers the nature of the garment from which the lucky cloth had come. They accepted it eagerly and completed the mending to Sir Gervase's rather churlish satisfaction. The flag then was hauled up the standard, and it was found that the patches, even when viewed through Colonel Rodgers' powerful binoculars – used for examining Afghan Russian-built tanks and aircraft – could not be distinguished.

Flooded for days beforehand, the lawns around the Residence were brilliantly green, and the pet crane as it stalked about on them seemed brighter than usual, as if it had been painted too. Behind the great house the marble staircase, descending by flights to the fountains below, was covered with red Afghan carpets. Down those stairs, after their presentation to the Ambassador and his lady, the guests would slowly walk, enchanted no doubt by the lush English beauty of the garden, and perhaps impressed too by the lofty legendary mountains in the distance. Somewhere on the stairs they would be greeted by John and Helen Langford, and at the bottom they would be received by the Consul and his wife, who would point out to them where, past the rose beds, the marquee stood on the grass, full of tables laden with delicacies and watered whisky.

As they alighted from their cars at the main entrance the guests would be welcomed by Howard Winfield, who would pass them on to Colonel and Mrs Rodgers in the hall, who would in turn give them to Alan and Paula Wint at the entrance of the ballroom. The important duty of the First Secretary and his wife was to carry the guests up to be presented and at the same time announce their names.

The junior or non-diplomatic staff had their duties assigned to them, too. Katherine Winn and Mary Anderson, the clerks, were stationed in the marquee to see that the servants there were zealous about keeping flies off the cakes, and also to encourage people to approach the tables for food and drink. Hats had to be worn. Katherine did not have one, but half an hour's ingenuity fashioned something that would, she felt sure, be eccentric enough to win the admiration of every woman but two: she was not at present on speaking terms with Mary, and Lady Beauly was likely to regard the arrangement of basketwork, gauze, and real flowers, as some kind of insult. Katherine had quite forgotten about her sending of an invitation to Wahab. If she had remembered, she would not have worried; indeed, she might have looked on it as another flower in her hat.

So at quarter past two everyone was in his place, although the invitation had stressed three as the hour of opening. Afghans sometimes came disastrously early, out of gratitude for the hospitality, they would have said themselves, but according to soured foreigners, out of a desire to test the sincerity of their welcome.

Like a general inspecting the position before commencement of battle, H.E., beautifully dressed in striped trousers and dark jacket, despite the great heat, walked about and addressed grunts of encouragement. Alan Wint walked a yard behind. There was time for a short stroll to inspect the garden too.

H.E. paused at a place where, in the midst of immaculate colour and greenness, weeds as tall and ugly as camels' heads grew. He shook his head. Soon he stuck his glass in his eye to squint angrily at the abomination.

'Can't something be done about this bloody thing?' he asked. 'It's an eyesore.'

Wint made sucking noises of concurrence.

'What I mean is,' said H.E. 'all over Christendom, piety is weakening daily. A pity, you might think,' he scowled around at his assistant – who wasn't sure what expression was diplomatically correct, and fell back on simpering pre-paid acquiescence – 'but nevertheless a fact. I am sure the same obtains in the Moslem world. Well then, why this?'

'As you know, sir, it was included in the sale of the ground—'

'Yes, of course I know, Alan. I should know; you yourself have told me at least a dozen times.'

Because, you irascible bugger, thought Wint beneath his sleek mask, you've asked at least a dozen times.

'We should never have agreed to it in the first place.'

'Then they would never have sold us the site, sir.'

'Well, don't they themselves consider the ability to double-cross an indication of maturity? Apart from anything else, I don't much care for the idea of having a holy man's bones buried so close to the house in which I'm living.' He glanced round and saw the crane. 'It sleeps here, you know, right on top of the mound. Often I look out, before getting into bed, and here it is, sleeping in the moonlight, on one leg for all I know. Molly won't look; she says it gives her the creeps. D'you think it *could* be the old boy back again? Don't snigger, Alan. When I was in Leopoldville I heard of queerer things.'

'I wasn't sniggering, sir. It's the orderly at the gate. I told him to let me know if there was anything coming.'

'But it's only twenty to.'

'Some do come early, sir.'

'Alan, I was here last year, if you remember.'

They walked swiftly but not quite breaking into a trot. They took a short cut across the lawn, past the crane. It opened a yellow eye, baleful with hellish wisdom, thought Wint.

They were safely at their posts when the car arrived, bringing a general and his attendant colonel, both fat, noisy with medals and vivid with scarlet braid.

These two, fed into the machine, proved its efficiency, though Katherine Winn cried when she saw them come down the carpeted staircase: 'Oh God, I think he's the one that nips your bottom.' And indeed as the plump general waddled purposefully towards the marquee she noticed that his thumb and forefinger were already close together, ready to nip or, as turned out to be the case, to snatch up a glassful of whisky and empty it fast, before any mullah or pussyfooting Moslem arrived. His colonel could not have been more faithful in his attendance.

So the party began and continued for the next two hours, with the machine, or Ali's dragon as Howard Winfield called it, taking in guests at its mouth, passing them along its alimentary canal (represented by the hard-working Ambassador and his wife), and dropping them out at the other end, with much relief. In all, there were thirty-three nationalities. The Afghans and the Americans were the hardest to digest. Hardest of all were Katherine Winn's three friends, and Abdul Wahab.

The girls, glamorous as models, arrived in a borrowed Chevrolet, pink and cream. Howard Winfield received them with the relish of a small boy stuffing his mouth with toffee. He was slow in passing them on to the Colonel and his wife, with the result that Alan Wint, waiting at the ballroom entrance, hopped from one foot to the other, like the same small boy needing to relieve himself. He knew they had not been invited and knew that Lady Beauly knew. But what could he do, with the Iranian Ambassador hovering behind them, and the Russian Consul and his stout wife getting out of their car at the door? The girls, too, giggled and confused him with swirls of perfume and coloured satin. It was out of the question for him to wink at Lady Beauly to show that he was well aware they were gate-crashing. No, he just had to go through with it: greet them with smiles, shake hands, announce their names, and present them. He had to admit that with their charming consciousness of the honour of being presented, there under the portrait of Her Majesty, they were really more worthy guests than the majority of those with bona fide invitations. Nevertheless he could tell

from Lady Beauly's face that there would be an inquest at
which he would be blamed.

Luckily, as always, his Paula was there and would still be
there at night, more lovely and consoling with her clothes
off even than with them on, which was a marvel causing his
heart several times almost to melt. Through the back door
he caught a glimpse of the Langfords receiving the girls after
the Ambassador and Lady Beauly were done with them, and,
for a moment of terrible but thrilling disloyalty, he imagined
Paula and himself living in the same house but never
sleeping together and never seeing each other's naked
bodies, only each other's naked souls. That terrifying picture was in his mind several times that afternoon, once when
he was presenting the French First Secretary and his wife,
considered the most elegant woman in Kabul. With admirable loyalty, Alan again compared the slim dark French-
woman with his fair Paula, from the point of view of
bedworthiness, and again decided whole-heartedly in favour
of his own wife. The Frenchwoman no doubt would bring
elegance to the act, and that for once or twice might be
preferable to Paula's hockey-girl romp; but only for once or
twice. He and Paula were deeply English, and he knew
enough about modern literature to know that pornography
came from across the Channel, disguised as significance.
The love-making of a happily married couple ought indeed
to be a jolly romp, with nothing esoteric or subtle or affected
about it. Was he not, as a result, a virile well-adjusted man,
and were not his children healthy and sports-loving?

Then the Moffatts arrived, with Abdul Wahab.

From the moment that the perspiring Head of Chancery
received them from the Military Attaché to the moment
when he presented them respectfully to the Ambassador, no
more than thirty seconds passed, and yet through his mind
rushed another torrent of thoughts and impressions. In the
first place, Mrs Moffatt wore a high Chinese dress of light-

blue, decorated with an amazing yellow dragon that
breathed fire and twisted round her body. She had no doubt
designed it herself and wore it with a magnificence that
excited and yet dismayed him. He saw that his Paula, whose
own bosom and hips were gleaming with green tussore, was
almost plebeian and courtesan in comparison. Even Lady
Beauly, who could not keep out of her well-prepared face
the grimaces of pain which her feet gave her, was made to
look common and undistinguished beside the small Chinese
woman. Most astonishing of all, Mrs Moffatt looked happy,
and her eyes were bright with a maturity of love that, try as
he might, Wint could not condemn as frigid and idealistic;
there was in it a sexual quality that he had seen often enough
in Paula's, though there never quite so refined. As he
watched her walk with exquisite dignity, despite the tight-
ness of her skirt, he remembered her husband's drunken
anatomical joke, and felt aggrieved that she, so fundamen-
tally misshapen, could so easily succeed in making his Paula,
so athletic on squash and tennis courts, appear arthritic by
contrast.

These thoughts, and others, cascaded through his mind
during that half minute.

The others concerned her husband, who had the impertinence to appear in his role of poet; that was to say, he
managed, by some miracle, to look worthy of his wife's love.
They would, Wint saw, have children, and those children
would be, in shape, colour and mind, mysteriously beautiful;
beside them his Annette and Paula, so carefully nurtured in
the English upper middle-class mold, would be dully cal-
culable in every thought and reaction. This was, he knew,
the bottommost depth of treachery; but he could not help it.
The effect of that glimpse, however, was not to decrease his
love for his own children, but rather to increase it by a
measure of compassion. Hitherto he had always thought
them fortunate – having himself and Paula for parents, being

educated in the English Public School tradition, and expecting quite considerable legacies from their mother's
people. Now he realized that vast tracts of human experience would all their lives be remote from them.

Those thoughts too added to the river of regret pouring
loudly between his ears.

In that river Abdul Wahab might be regarded as a rock, in
the centre, in a narrow place, causing uproar and congestion.

He had not been invited. Only a day or two before, Lady
Beauly had remarked, with satisfaction, that no invitation
had been sent to him. Wahab had come under discussion,
very briefly, because Pierce-Smith had at last replied, to say
that his attempt to get Miss Johnstone to come to London to
discuss her going to Afghanistan had failed. She had sent
him a letter repudiating what she had called official interference. Pierce-Smith had mentioned that he had felt
amused and touched, but neither Wint, as Head of Chancery, nor Lady Beauly, as protectress of British women in
Kabul, could share his feelings. Lady Beauly had declared
that Miss Johnstone seemed a thoroughly ungrateful, unpleasant sort of person. Wint had agreed. And now here,
wearing a new ill-made suit much too wide at the shoulders,
was Wahab, a little nervous perhaps, but brazenly so. On the
walls of the Embassy hall were hung weapons from past
British-Afghan wars. For a moment Wint saw himself, in the
uniform of an officer of a hundred years ago, with some such
sword driving out this dark-faced, insolent intruder. But
now, in a degenerate time, there was nothing he could do
but shake hands rather coldly, introduce him with a wince to
Paula, and take him with the Moffatts to be presented to Sir
Gervase and Lady Beauly. The latter's handshake, he noticed, was as if she were playing that child's game of
touching one's opponent's palm with one's forefinger without letting him imprison one's hand in his: speed and the
most momentary contact were essential.

Wahab appeared hardly perturbed, thus confirming Wint in his own shrewd belief that Afghans were not as thin-skinned as many believed; he had always believed that beneath their superficial tender skin they had another, thick and tough enough to resist insults deadly as scorpions. So, smiling, Wahab, pockmarked and foolish in his teddy-boy suit, strolled out of the ballroom on to the staircase, at the top of which he lingered, gazing not so much down at the brilliant scene below on the lawn but rather beyond, at the high distant mountains. Perhaps, thought Wint, as he hurried not too urgently to receive the next guests, the Reverend Manson Powrie and his wife – perhaps Wahab, poor fellow, is thinking about this formidable English-woman who is coming to marry him. Her aeroplane would come rocking over those sharp peaks.

About four o'clock the majority of those invited had arrived. Any still to come did not deserve to be received and presented. Lady Beauly went upstairs to wash her hands, change her gloves, and put on more comfortable shoes. Then she accompanied her husband down the carpeted staircase to mingle with the more important guests on the lawn. To her astonishment she arrived in time to find the most important of all, Mohammed Shir Khan, Prime Minister of Afghanistan, talking to Prince Naim, and, of all people, the upstart teacher Wahab, who was present without proper permission. It was not possible to loiter until Wahab should have been dismissed to obscurity, because etiquette demanded that she and the Ambassador should go first to their chief guest. Therefore she found herself being intro-duced for the second time to the sly-eyed, pompous little gate-crasher, and this time her handshake had to have an appearance of cordiality, since the introducer was Shir Khan himself, who, his French being excellent and his English comic, chose to speak in the former language.

'Your Excellency,' he said, 'and Lady Beauly, allow me to

present to you one of our most promising young men. Abdul Wahab is a scientist who has recently returned from your own country to take over the Principalship of one of our best schools. We hope in time to make it a nursery for scientists of the future. Mr Wahab speaks very good English.'

They had then to talk charmingly to Wahab for a minute or two, during which he answered their questions with a skill and delicacy that irritated Lady Beauly though obviously impressed the Prime Minister. She knew what he didn't – that Wahab had come uninvited, and therefore, had he been the Prophet himself, could not avoid, every second, adding to his offence.

That was only one of several remarkable conversations Wahab was to have that afternoon.

In a very short time, after he had discreetly stepped back out of the company of his superiors, but not quite from their sight, he found himself surrounded by some compatriots who previously would not have considered him worth a nod. These were important officials from various Ministries who, while the magic of the Prime Minister's reception was still potent about him, wished to come under its influence themselves. Each had his glass of fruit juice ostentatiously in his hand, but they could not have spoken with more fertile and insincere flattery had it been neat whisky they were drinking. Frequently they peeped around to make sure that the Prime Minister was noticing how attentive they were to the man to whom he had shown favour.

Wahab did not have much to say himself; he smiled, nodded, murmured yes or no, and took plenty of time off to gaze around at the women in their lovely dresses. Those flattering him thought that he was playing the favourite's part with damnable efficiency. So he was, but there was something else they never guessed at. Amid all that masculine wealth, feminine lusciousness, and political influence, with flatterers outvying one another to please him and with his own brain coolly assessing their contributions, he did not feel proud or triumphant. No, he felt rather a sadness that kept possessing him more and more until, catching a glimpse of the far-off mountains between two of the sleek ambitious heads talking to him, he wished that he were there, a simple man in a simple village, pleased to find his plot of land turn green twice in the season.

A few minutes later fear, as of drought and barrenness, was to seep into the sadness. With the approach of a really important lion, those lesser ones slunk away. This was the Minister of Justice, Dr Habbibullah, a big thick-set man, more capable than most of steam-rolling the country out of its backwardness, and using, if necessary, the blood and bones of the peasants as foundation for the road into the future. It was whispered that the Russians looked on him as their man. Certainly he had spent much time in Moscow.

Wahab had not been speaking to this potentate for half a minute before he realized that here surely was the Brother-hood leader, whom he had thought to be a general. The voice was the same, harsh and authoritative. The dress, of course was disconcertingly different from the drab shaddry: a suit of pale-blue, semi-tropical cloth, a white silk shirt, and a red tie with a jewelled pin in it.

The hand that plucked Wahab to the quiet place under some trees was hairy, with a gold ring on the fourth finger, and round the massive wrist a gold watch as big as a dahlia, made in Russia. As he bent over Wahab, he now and then, with the hand not holding the glass of whisky, stroked the front of his trousers, as if to hint that in there, black and hideous, lurked the source of life and violence and blood. But his voice, in spite of its habitual rasp, was friendly enough, though the broad nostrils, with thick black hairs protruding, dilated like some venomous creature breathing.

'Yes, Wahab, things are moving at last,' he said. 'Your

appointment is just one of the signs. Before you're much
older you'll see many others. Those without the brains to
see what's needed, and without the guts to see that it's done,
are going to be thrown out. Like Mussein. And like Mohammed Siddiq.'

Siddiq was Wahab's present deputy Principal.

'You agree that he'll have to go too? He's obstructive, out
of sheer habit. He has never had a progressive thought in his
life. Look how content he was with the stagnation under
Mussein. Out with him too. But it won't be easy, because as
you know there's opposition, and it's frightened; it's unscrupulous, too. For your first assistant you obviously want
someone young, energetic, forward-looking, not afraid to
use some initiative, capable of inspiring the students, willing
to work hard, and with an ideal to aim at. I would say that's
pretty fair description of yourself, Wahab; and it also fits a
young man at present on your staff. You know him.'

'Maftoon?'

'Right. Maftoon. I believe you had a long confidential
conversation this morning? Good. I have an interest in
Maftoon; he happens to be my wife's brother. But if he
were my own son and a spineless creature like Mussein, I
wouldn't lift a finger to push him forward. If I show
partiality, Wahab, it's for my country.'

Fascinated, Wahab nodded. In his nose was the rank stink
of power; he thought he liked it.

'Maftoon's a man who's going far, Wahab; just like
yourself. He'll not stop and turn back because there's a
nasty mess on the road in front. You'll need a man like
that to help you at Isban, and after Isban. Now I think
I've convinced Prince Naim that you ought to be given
the final say in the choice of your colleagues. After all,
it'll be you who'll be called to account if results aren't
produced.'

He laughed and revealed three gold teeth; which was

coincidence, for Wahab had just caught sight of Mojedaji standing, white-turbaned, looking at them.

The Minister turned, saw the mullah, and grinned, like one beast of prey scenting another.

'You know of course,' he said, 'that our friend Mojedaji was so opposed to your appointment he went right up to the Prime Minister, and was thrown out. Don't think he's swallowed all his fury; no, there's still a great lump of it in his mouth, hidden behind that beard; and it tastes very bitter. Siddiq's his man, has been for years, a spy. You don't want a mullah's man planted at your back, do you?'

Wahab, staring over the fence into the wood, saw a tiny field mouse scurry away among some leaves; it had a twig in its mouth.

'Like me, Wahab, and like my friends, you see a sane future for our country. Let those who stand in our way look out. All this is in confidence, of course. Mojedaji isn't as safe as he thinks. Here's something you'll be interested to know. At Jeshan the shaddry's going to be abolished.'

Wahab, a field mouse for the moment, jumped as if a cat had pounced at him. He opened his human eyes to see those great gold teeth glitter down at him.

'Of course they're all against it. Mojedaji's at their head. What a picture of rapes and public copulations he paints!'

'But, Excellency, every Jeshan they say it's to be abolished.'

The Minister laughed. 'Yes. But this is the year. Watch for it. After the march past. In the King's presence. Think of it, Wahab: Next year there will be Afghan women at this garden party.'

They both turned to look at those foreign women. Wahab noticed Mrs Moffatt chatting to the American clergyman, Powrie. There were Pakistan and Indian women in beautiful saris; but they avoided one another. Next year would he have Laura with him? And would the other English women avoid her?

The Minister tapped him on the shoulder. 'Well, I suppose we ought to circulate. We've given Mojedaji enough to think about. If I were you, I should find an opportunity this afternoon to speak to Prince Naim.'

Then he walked away, putting down each great brown shoe on the grass as if indeed it were a paw with brutal claws concealed in it. His buttocks were broad and powerful. From them Wahab glanced at those of other guests. Yes, under all these expensive and brilliant clothes everyone was constructed in the same way as his or her neighbour, Indian women were like American women, save for colour, and Afghan men like Englishmen. In Paris, a friend of his, studying at a French university, had taken him to a brothel. There in the choosing room the prostitutes, wearing nothing at all, had chatted with their prospective clients, pretty much in the same way as the women here were chatting with their husbands' friends. These women were made like Laura, whom he loved, and under his clothes he was like these other men. Now at the British Queen's Garden Party, in his own native Kabul, with Ambassadors and Ministers and Heads of Chancery and their wives present, he remembered that brothel scene and recaptured the feeling of sad compassionate kinship. Not only were bodies alike, minds were too: all were troubled by fears, anxieties, ambitions, greeds, and jealousies; and all were in some measure consoled by love.

Even the Minister of Justice loved his wife.

Some minutes later Mrs Moffatt came through the little groups of people, bringing the bow-tied American parson with her. Wahab had just taken from a passing tray a cake whose chocolate was melting in the heat. He had to wipe his fingers with his handkerchief before shaking hands.

'Look, Mr Wahab,' said the clergyman, 'I know you don't particularly want to be seen talking to me here with so many of your co-religionists about, but I just wanted to let you know that if you, and the young lady who is coming out to marry you, should need my help in any way, please ask.'

'Thank you.'

'I never allow myself to forget, Mr Wahab, that we are all God's children, even if some of us play with the wrong toys. Well, so long. Delighted to have met you. Please keep in touch.' And beaming, the clergyman went across to a group of Afghans to say a word or two to them, so that no one would know he had been saying anything in particular to Wahab.

Wahab was left with Mrs Moffatt. For a few moments they did not speak but stood smiling. He felt happy.

'What did he mean by the wrong toys, Mrs Moffatt?'

'You and I are not Christian, Mr Wahab.'

'I see. Christianity then is the right toy?'

'So Mr Powrie appears to think.'

Still smiling, still happy, and still with that sad compassionate feeling of kinship with his fellows, Wahab looked around to see what effect having the right toy to play with was having upon some of the Christians in view.

'I shall tell you something, Mrs Moffatt, which I do not think I shall ever tell to anyone else, not even to Laura. It is possible I may be at the threshold of a career which I shall do my utmost to promote, whatever dishonesty, corruption, servility, and ruthlessness may be necessary. Yet at this moment do you know what I am wishing, with all my heart? I am wishing I were a peasant with a little plot of land in a mountain village, near a clear river. Is that not ridiculous? Here comes your husband. I think he would make a poem about my predicament if you were to tell him about it.'

'I won't tell him.'

'I have no right to expect a wife to keep a secret from her husband. Tell him if you wish. I do not think his poem would be very unsympathetic.'

Then Moffatt, with a girl Wahab did not know, joined

them. She turned out to be Katherine Winn, a clerk at the Embassy, and she had an apology to make and a favour to ask.

As Wahab listened to her giggled explanation he looked towards the mountains; but there the peasant squatting on his patch of dust was an ignorant reactionary fool, probably chancred with syphilis. Here, at this party, in this beautiful garden, with the great white house above and the imperial flag surmounting all, the only part to play with any honour was that of the Principal whose hand the Prime Minister had publicly shaken, and whose unscrupulous support the Minister of Justice confidently expected.

'It was really a joke,' said Miss Winn, for the third time.

'No harm done,' said Moffatt, smiling. 'The Head of Chancery saw you shaking hands with the Prime Minister. I told him too you were a friend of Naim's. Now he's kicking himself for not inviting you. Katherine here's likely to get a medal.'

'Not, I'm afraid, from me.'

Moffatt glanced at the dark, dour, dedicated face. Lan was right: Wahab was some kind of complicated idealist. He felt liking and sympathy for him.

'I wouldn't let it bother me, Wahab,' he said.

'I'm afraid I must, Mr Moffatt.'

'Oh dear, I'm sorry,' said Katherine.

'Why did you choose my name, Miss Winn?'

She could not answer.

'Was it because you regarded me as a figure of fun?'

'Of course not.'

'I do not find your denial at all convincing. But I accept your apology.'

'Thank goodness for that!'

'But this means I must in my turn go and apologize.'

'To whom?' asked Moffatt.

'To Mr Wint first, and then to my host and hostess.'

'Oh, my God,' said Katherine.' If you do that they'll have me shot.'

In the old days in my country, he thought, an underling so malicious would have been shot. But it was those days he was committed to renounce.

'I am sorry, Miss Winn, if it means trouble for you, but my duty is clear.'

'For God's sake, stop him, Harold!'

'I don't really see why I should, Katherine. It's not my business.'

'You then, Lan!'

Lan smiled and shook her head. 'I think I should want to apologize too if I were in Mr Wahab's place.'

'Thank you, Mrs Moffatt,' said Wahab.

'Oh go to hell,' muttered Katherine. 'You're all mad. What do I care, anyway? I didn't want to be sent to this God-forsaken, dusty hole.'

She walked off on indignant high heels.

'Please excuse me,' murmured Wahab. 'I must find Mr Wint.'

It was easy enough to find the Head of Chancery. He was in the midst of a cosmopolitan group, which he was making laugh with a story told in correctly lisped French and illustrated with Gallic gestures. To facilitate those Paula held his glass.

Wahab approached, waited for a few seconds, and then plucked the Head of Chancery by the tail of his jacket. The latter's red astonished face, with its comic pouting still on it, turned.

'Excuse me, please,' said Wahab. 'I should be obliged for a few words in private, Mr Wint.'

Wint's face was acting in a most agile fashion. First it threw off the pout; then, set to scowl, it suddenly leaped up into a joviality that may have startled but by no means discountenanced Wahab, who, without so much as a flicker of conceit, supposed that the favour shown him by the Prime Minister, Prince Naim, and Dr Habbibullah, as well as others, had caused the British diplomat to take him out of the pigeonhole labelled Nonentities, and put him into that labelled Men to Keep an Eye On.

'And what, Mr Wahab,' asked Wint, affably, 'can I do for you?'

'I want to apologize, Mr Wint; both to you, and to my hosts, the Ambassador and his wife. For being here without a proper invitation.'

Wint remembered he didn't have his glass of whisky in his hand. He went to his wife for it and came slowly back.

'Look here, Mr Wahab,' he said, with his most winning smile, 'there's really no need for you to apologize. I am sure His Excellency understands. If not, I shall explain it to him.'

'Your explanation will not remove my feeling of humiliation, Mr Wint.'

Wint stared through narrowed lids. A moment after he snapped them open again, remembering that for a diplomat to reveal cunning, perturbation, ignorance, or perplexity was dangerous. Good-humoured omniscience was by far the best disguise.

'I see,' he said. 'I'm awfully sorry you feel humiliated, Mr Wahab. There's really no need to, you know.'

'I am the best judge, Mr Wint.'

'Come now. I doubt that. Do you know, I think you have rather enjoyed yourself here this afternoon. For a man feeling humiliated you have associated with very strange company, Prime Minister and Prince and poet and priest.'

'It is because my company has been distinguished that I must apologize.'

Wint poked a finger inside his damp collar: a gesture not only undiplomatic but ungentlemanly, as Paula frequently pointed out. The trouble was, when he was in a quandary and foresaw himself making a wrong decision, which would incur an ambassadorial rebuke, he felt that not enough air was getting into his lungs: hence the dimming of his intelligence and the hesitancy of his judgment. He wondered if he should look for Howard Winfield and consult him.

'I tell you what,' he said. 'Why not see me later about this? At the Chancery would be best.'

'I would prefer to have it settled here, now. It is a simple matter, Mr Wint, from your point of view. You have only to accept my apology. Do you accept it?'

'Of course. Like a shot. But really what's troubling me is, I'll confess, simply that I doubt very much whether you ought to approach His Excellency about it. You see, Mr Wahab, if you'll pardon my putting it this way, it's really rather a trivial matter.'

'I do not regard it so. Lest you should regard me as a monster of conceit, Mr Wint—'

'The last thing I should think of doing, my dear fellow!'

'Lest you should, I would like to make it clear that the humiliation is not merely mine, it is also my country's.'

It is a quicksand, thought Wint. The more I argue the deeper I sink. 'Oh come now, surely you're exaggerating? No one here has done the slightest thing to humiliate your country.'

'I am a simple Afghan. Therefore I represent many millions of my countrymen. To treat me as if I did not matter, as if I were of as little consequence as a donkey, as if I was dust on the lion's paw, is therefore to treat most of my nation as such. This I must never tolerate.'

Dust on the lion's paw? What the hell does the fellow mean? God, what conspiracy is cooking? Is that sinister brute Habbibullah behind it? Is rebellion imminent? Are the Russians going to be invited to walk in and take over? Is it timed to coincide with Voroshilov's visit in a few weeks?

Dust on the lion's paw. Is this the password that this fanatic has blurted out? Christ, and we've been treating him as an ill-paid schoolteacher with the impertinence to want to marry an Englishwoman. It adds up, as the Yanks would say. As sure as eggs we'll find this Miss Johnstone who snubbed Pierce-Smith has been a member of the Communist party for years. All this must certainly be fully discussed at our next policy meeting. But, good God, is there going to be such a meeting? This fellow's showing the kind of calm lunacy that often precedes assassination. Ten to one, he's got a gun about him somewhere.

'When I am saying good-bye to them,' offered Wahab, 'I shall mention it to them.'

Yes, by Jove, quietly mention it, and next second empty your pistol into H.E.'s belly. No, no, that's the wildest melodrama. Let's be realistic about this. All right, Wahab goes up to H.E. What does he say? Something like this: 'Thank you, Your Excellency and Lady Beauly, for your kind invitation. Unfortunately it was false.' No, dammit, he wouldn't say that, for his grievance was that the invitation had been far from kind. This then? 'It has been most enjoyable. I wish to apologize, nevertheless, for being here, as I now realize my invitation was sent me as a silly joke.' Yes, that was more like it; that might even do, provided Lady Beauly didn't decide to be bitchy about it.

'Well, what have you in mind to say to them?' he asked.

'Surely an apology is a private matter, Mr Wint?'

The bugger's mad, thought Wint, quietly but recklessly mad. Look how damp and bloodshot his eyes are. God, what am I to do? Here at the Queen's Birthday Garden Party is the last place we want a political sensation to happen. Was H.E.'s curious reference to the holy man's bones prophetic? Hell, of course not; mustn't let my imagination run away with me. Paula. Why didn't I think of her before? Think not of her warm solacing bosom, but of her influence on other men, on this susceptible Afghan, for instance, who has shown he prefers white breasts to brown.

He turned, and yes, oh wonderful woman, she was waiting for the signal. He gave it, and over she came, not Paula Wint, not the wife of the Head of Chancery, not the daughter of Mr Henry Deverson of Hankley Manor, but Eve, Aphrodite, Helen of Troy, Cleopatra, Eternal Woman, whose very ankles as they moved made a man's heart somersault.

For a man with a somersaulting heart, though, Wahab was remaining very cool. Wint could never have guessed that Eve as she advanced was without a stitch of clothing; Wahab's ambitious admiration rose rather higher than ankles.

'Paula, my dear,' said the Head of Chancery, 'you have met Mr Wahab?'

'Of course.' She smiled, with every wile turned full on.

The wrong man was mesmerized – her husband who stood and gaped at her in his usual transport. Wahab, on the contrary, looked at her with what, after a few blushing blinks, she saw was really some kind of pity. From that moment on she was convinced he was simple in the head.

She recalled Alan. 'Well, dear?'

'Oh, yes. It's just that Mr Wahab feels understandably annoyed at that silly prank of Katherine's. He thinks he ought to apologize personally to H.E. I've been trying to persuade him it isn't really necessary.'

'I see. Well, at least, darling, I hope you've made it clear to Mr Wahab that it's we who owe him an apology.'

Had he? Yes, he supposed he had. But Wahab, damn his mysterious humiliated face, didn't appear to think so.

'Yes, yes, of course. Mr Wahab knows we're awfully sorry about it.'

Wahab made a slight bow.

'Very well then,' said Paula, smiling sweetly, 'The

matter's best considered closed. I'm sure we all agree? By the way, Mr Wahab, what is the latest news of your fiancée, Miss Johnstone?'

Ah, thought her husband, that's it. Why didn't I think of that? Concentrate now about his damned Laura. What the devil can she be like anyway, this female boor from Manchester, this Dago-loving crypto-Communist, this stern-faced hag unable or unwilling to mate with a man of her own race and colour?

'By Jove yes,' he said enthusiastically, 'what about Miss Johnstone? Is she still coming? Or should I say, when do you expect her?'

'In three weeks.'

'So soon! You must be quite excited.'

About as excited, thought Wint, as a shrimp left on a plate at midnight, after a party. Yet did such a shrimp sneer? Look up and around with a long-necked disdain that the Ambassador's crane couldn't have bettered?

'I am looking forward very much to Laura's arrival.'

'Is she coming by air?' asked Paula.

'Yes.'

Wint wondered why. Surely such a formidable female, who scorned the Himalayan barrier of colour, could easily have walked the whole bloody way?

'You really must,' said Paula then, with that one pluck at her left earring which was her signal to him that she was going over the top, that was to say, was about to dash out under fire into no man's land to rescue their reputation at the moment crouching there, 'come to see us when she does arrive.'

After her went Alan gallantly. 'By Jove, yes. We must all rally round to see that she gets a good impression of Afghanistan.'

'Thank you.'

There was no need for him to say any more. By this time

he had said enough to deserve an honour that the Wints conferred on very few: that night in bed they were to waste at least five minutes in discussing him.

With the stealth, patience, and grace of a leopard hiding at a river, Wahab waited for Prince Naim to become separated a moment from his friends. His pounce then, though carried out with respectful gestures, was as deadly and bloody. Naim, fruit juice in one hand, and with the other twirling a flower his hostess had given him, looked with involuntary terror and disgust into his subordinate's submissive but fiercely earnest face, and listened to the latter's reasonable words with little distressed flicks of his head, as if it too were a flower in some great hand.

'Yes, I noticed Habbibullah talking to you,' he said. 'I knew what he was up to. All right, I won't argue. If Maftoon's the man you want, then of course you must have him. I suppose something else almost as good can be found for Siddiq as a consolation.'

'If you will allow me to say so, Highness, I do not think that would be wise.'

'Surely you don't think the poor fellow should be stripped of all promotion?'

'I'm afraid I do.'

'Granted he's inefficient, he's still a man who's given thirty years to the service of education here. It would be needless cruelty to throw him down to the very bottom again.'

'I do not know if it would be cruelty, Highness; but I do know it would not be needless.'

Naim held the flower to his nose for an instant; it seemed to stink of cruelty.

'You are talking like Habbibullah and the others,' he said.

'I am merely expressing the truth as I see it, Highness.'

'Sometimes I have the fear we're on a slippery slope,

Wahab. Let go once, and down we all go, taking our poor country with us.'

'I have that fear too. But it seems to me that if we retain men like Siddiq in positions of responsibility, we will not be able to hold on and eventually climb up to the top of the slope. No, he and his kind will force us to let go, and take us to the bottom with them. Have they not been doing that for generations?'

'Yes, I suppose they have. But my dream, Wahab? You know what it is?'

'Yes, Highness, I should know, for it is also mine.'

'To achieve in our country a high material standard of living, without sacrificing the dignity which you will see in any peasant tilling his land, or in any coolie drinking his tea in the chaikhana.'

'Yes.'

'We see what has happened to the countries of the West, to America, Britain, Sweden, Germany, to them all. They have gained materially, but spiritually are almost destroyed. We can benefit from their example.'

'I think so.'

'But can we, Wahab, if we adopt measures like throwing poor Siddiq on the scrap heap, just because he happens to be incompetent?'

'What dignity is there, Highness, in allowing incompetence to prosper? And how can there be any material improvement?'

'I do not see Siddiq as incompetence, Wahab; I see him as an incompetent man. There is a difference.'

Wahab was silent; then he sighed. 'Yes, there is a difference, Highness. But we are only men; we cannot afford the compassion of God.'

Naim turned and smiled piteously at him. 'We really cannot afford it?'

'I am afraid not.'

'Of course you are right. Other men whose judgment and principles I also trust tell me the same.'

Glancing away, Wahab for a few moments admired an Indian woman with her plump buttocks swathed in a sari of glittering golden cloth. She had a red spot in the middle of her brow, and when she laughed, throwing back her head, he noticed her tongue too was red, as everyone else's was, Laura's for instance, and Siddiq's wife's.

'If you will allow me to suggest it, Highness,' he murmured, 'would it not be advisable to have Siddiq, and Mussein too, transferred to some school in the provinces? I have reason to believe that if they are allowed to remain in Kabul they will try to stir up trouble, out of a sense of grievance. For their own sakes it would be better if they were removed from that temptation. Besides, in the provinces they would be given an excellent chance to redeem themselves with hard and extremely valuable work.'

'Yes, of course.'

Both reflected on the conditions in the provinces. There schools were primitive mud huts without equipment or even windows, and teachers, very poorly paid, found their standard of living lower than that of the peasants whose sons they tried so bitterly to teach.

Wahab was watching Mrs Moffatt. For a moment he imagined himself, deeper than ever in evil, allowing her husband to remain in Afghan on condition that she slept with him. He would not, he thought, make love to her; he would just lie beside her.

'You are a very strange man, Wahab,' Naim was saying. 'I am sure you have a kind heart, and yet you show no pity for Siddiq. You tell me you consider it necessary to subdue your feelings of pity. That makes me sad, but I understand it. After all, do I not have to subdue my own? What I do not understand, and what I would like you to explain, if you can, is why when you visited me at my house you pulled some flowers and then dropped them on the grass. The gardener's boy said you looked like a man in a trance. Do you remember the occasion?'

'Yes, Highness, I remember.'

'Is there an explanation?'

It occurred to Wahab as he stared around that a number of the guests were glancing toward them, and he suddenly realized that etiquette forbade them leaving until Naim had left. It was as if they were waiting for him, Wahab, too, and, with his eyes raised to the mountains, he felt the same intoxicating sweetness which he had felt in the Prince's gardens when the policemen, instead of being brutal, had saluted him.

'Yes, Highness, there is an explanation, a very simple one. I was thinking of the Englishwoman whom I am going to marry.'

'I thought you might be, Wahab. But nevertheless why just pull them and throw them away?'

'I am sorry if I destroyed them. Like yourself, Highness, I love flowers.'

'They weren't destroyed. I sent them to Mrs Mohebzada. You remember, her baby was very ill at the time.'

'Yes.' But Mrs Mohebzada must not be allowed into this conversation. 'You see, Highness, my fiancée, Miss Johnstone, is a cripple.'

'A cripple?'

Cripples were often enough seen in Kabul. There was one, indeed, whom the Prince probably saw every day on his way to the Ministry – a man who sold Russian matches in the street. Both of his legs were contorted, as if God at his birth had seized each foot and twisted and turned it, like a man winding a watch. That they had grown and kept their peculiar contortion was a greater miracle than growth itself.

'Yes, Highness. When she was a small child, Laura had a serious illness. She almost died. When she did recover, her left foot was found to be permanently paralysed.'

'Is she able to walk?'

Wahab's voice rose in triumph and love. 'And dance too. And climb hills. And march across the whole world, if it were necessary.'

'But surely it is a handicap?'

'On the contrary, Highness, it has been a challenge which she has met with great courage.'

'Yet you threw the flowers away?'

Wahab smiled sadly. 'Blame our history for that, Highness. I am an Afghan. We still pay for our wives. My father paid for my mother. We are conditioned to demand that there be no physical blemish in our women.'

'I understand, Wahab.' There was a mistiness in Naim's eyes; he laid his hand on Wahab's sleeve. 'And I now realize why you have the resolution not to waste pity on unworthy men like Siddiq and Mussein.'

Wahab bowed his head; in it he was marvelling that this, his most consummate display of hypocrisy so far, should also be accepted as the best proof of his sincerity.

'I shall be honoured to meet this fine woman, Wahab.'

Wahab looked up and saw other fine women, Mrs Wint, for example, Mrs Gillie, Mrs Mossaour, Lady Beauly, and many others. None was fit to clean Laura's shoes, not just because she was superior to them, but also because she was going to be his wife. Only Mrs Moffatt was excepted.

'It is time to go,' said Naim. 'You came with Moffatt? Come back with me. I should like your views on certain changes I am proposing to introduce.'

Wahab murmured he would be honoured.

So it was that when he did say good-bye and thank you to his host and hostess, it was immediately after Naim and the Prime Minister, and therefore the question of the apology did not arise. He took much pleasure in noticing the many surprised glances he got when, by Naim's side, he went up the carpeted staircase, through the ballroom, and into the gleaming car with the royal flag flying from its hood. He knew he was in too deep now to swim cravenly back. Besides, the shore of ambition and high advancement was near enough to be reached, if he kept his head and mustered all his resources, some of which, he realized with a pang of joy and wonder, were still as yet unknown even to himself.

Nineteen

EVERY August, at Jeshan, Kabul and most provincial towns
and villages were decorated with triumphal arches in celebration of the failure of the British, forty years or so
previously, to subjugate Afghanistan and incorporate it in
their shameful Empire. Their repulse was described at
length in the school history books, and those particular
passages had to be memorized by every pupil, along with
passages from the Koran, understandably so, because seldom had history been written so liturgically. In every bazaar
shopkeepers hung their best red carpets outside their shops,
and also framed photographs of the famous political and
military leaders who had led the fight against the insolent
invaders. But as those bearded worthies had faded a great
deal and now hardly looked glamorous enough for the
occasion, other pictures were hung up alongside, showing
in very gaudy colours Persian and Indian damsels with tiny
feet, breasts as round as balloons, and eyes so mild and
defenseless as to be aphrodisiacal. Sometimes deer or leopards would accompany them, and sometimes men, not
quite so tame, whose eyes, beneath their jewelled turbans,
glittered and squinted with desire. Those pictures, the work
of native artists, were much admired, especially by the young
men from the villages who came flocking in at this time to
the capital, carrying their provisions in bundles on their
backs and their sad lusts on their faces.

Also gaped at in awe were some guns, said to have been
captured from the British during their retreat. These,

cleaned and polished, and adorned with flowers, were always
given a leading place in the military march past the King,
evoking from the populace a fiercer, prouder series of yells
than the far more modern artillery being bought on the
instalment plan from the Russians. However, as if to balance
things, the instruments which the Afghan Army Band played
had been bought in London, though the music was native
and, to Western ears, rather more plaintive than martial.
For two weeks before the Jeshan celebrations it practised, at
four o'clock in the cool of the morning, in the park opposite
the Moffatts' house.

Lying in bed, laughing indignantly at those remarkable
serenaders, whose progress around and around the park
could be told by the music receding and approaching,
Moffatt suggested some facetious ways of getting them to
stop or go elsewhere; but it was Lan who offered the
suggestion that struck them both as funniest.

'We shall have to ask Abdul Wahab,' she murmured, 'to
use his influence.'

What was funny about that was that in those few weeks
since his elevation to the post of principal and his public
recognition as a friend by Prince Naim, Wahab had taken to
boasting incontinently of the various powerful men to
whom he had been introduced and who were now his
colleagues. He would come to the Moffatts', often without
warning, and sit in their lounge, talking excitedly for hours
about his ambitions for his country, his school, and himself.
When Laura came, he vowed, she would not find herself
being asked to marry a nobody, as Mrs Mohebzada had
been, and she would not be asked either to live in a squalid
mud house with lots of mysterious relatives who ate with
their hands and stank of bad oily rice. No, by God, on the
contrary she would find herself not only mistress of a more
beautiful house than any she had ever lived in in England,
but also acting in it as hostess to Princes, Ministers, Gen-

erals, Ambassadors, and other important people of that kind, whom in England she would only see in newspapers or on newsreels.

The Moffatts had sat and listened, laughing sometimes, teasing a little, and disbelieving most of the time. That Naim had found him a furnished house at a very low rent they could believe, and were delighted about for Laura's sake, but that it was half as grand as Wahab maintained seemed hardly possible. They noticed how when describing it he liked to dwell on the bedroom which had, among other opulent features, carvings of swans and lilies on its wooden ceiling.

That the shaddry was going to be abolished at Jeshan they couldn't believe either, though before telling them, in a whisper hoarse with importance, he had tiptoed to the door to make sure no servant was eavesdropping outside. That Voroshilov was going to be conducted round Isban College also sounded more like an Afghan hope than a likelihood, especially as it would mean depriving the pupils of part at least of their usual Jeshan holidays; besides, a schoolful of disgruntled young Afghans might not be the most politic thing to show the Russian president. Yet Wahab spent hours describing how experiments involving the use of microscopes were planned and lessons on geography utilizing maps and globes; while a drama, especially written by Naim, with Wahab's collaboration, would be enacted by the pupils. This would portray the Afghanistan of the future, a land of plenty where nevertheless men were dignified and spiritual. Possibly, Wahab admitted, the acting might not be very well done, as the boys were too young to take the play seriously and in any case wouldn't have enough time to rehearse their parts properly. But there was no doubt it would make a tremendous impact. Every Afghan who saw it would have tears in his eyes. And every foreigner too, thought Moffatt, only here the tears would be of laughter. He had seen Afghan moralities before.

So when Lan whispered that they would have to get
Wahab to speak to the Commander in Chief about the
band, they laughed a good deal, but in their laughter was
affection for Wahab. As Harold said, you could scarcely help
liking a man who said, as a kind of joke that he meant to be
taken seriously, that all the decorations being put up in the
streets, and especially the triumphal arches, weren't only for
Jeshan and Voroshilov, but also for Laura; and who was
completely serious when he claimed that the biggest arch of
all, the great red, green, and black one across the airport
road, with the word WELCOME on it in huge white Afghan
characters, had been erected a day earlier than necessary, so
that it would be there for Laura's arrival, two days before
Voroshilov's.

When Harold asked him if he minded Mrs Mossaour
being at the airport to meet her, he said he did not, although
he felt sure that as his wife, Laura either wouldn't work at all
or else would teach in the Kabul Girls' High School. He did
object to the Reverend Manson Powrie's being present, and
requested Harold to be so kind as to keep that goodhearted
meddler away.

Therefore at the airport that hot sunny August morning
the welcoming delegation consisted of Wahab, Lan and
Harold Moffatt, Mrs Mossaour, and Howard Winfield, who
blandly and mendaciously said he had come to represent the
Embassy. This lie was swallowed by Wahab as naturally as a
bird swallows a worm. It was almost certain, Wahab confided, that Prince Naim would be along too, not in either of
his capacities as Prince or Minister, but privately as a friend.
He would be useful in getting Laura quickly through the
Customs.

Kabul airport consisted of a wide dusty plain, ringed by
hills, about two miles outside the city. Its buildings were of
mud brick, painted white, and there was even a tearoom,
where, as in even the most sinister chai-khanas, only the tea

was safe to drink. Dozens of flies, blown off by the cheerful waiter, arrived with the buttered bread or sticky cakes. Almost as numerous as those flies were the soldiers scattered about, all in shaggy, dusty uniforms, and some carrying guns with fixed bayonets. Side by side, like great mating birds, stood the aeroplane of the American Air Attaché, with the stars and stripes painted on it, and one of Aeroflot's, with the hammer, sickle, and star.

It was already hot. They stood, for there was nowhere to sit, in the shade of the tearoom. Several times Wahab heard the noise of the aeroplane; it turned out each time to be the hum of a fly near his ear. Twice he dashed off to inquire when the plane was expected.

'They say in ten minutes,' he cried, when he returned the second time. 'But I do not think they know. They are Indians. Have you ever noticed how effeminate the Indians are? Really they are a decadent nation. How foolish to see in them the hope of Asia!'

Moffatt grinned. 'Did you ask if she was on board?'

'No, I did not. Of course she is on board. She said so in her letter. You will find she respects the truth.'

'It's a far cry from here to Manchester. If you like, I'll go and ask.'

'No, no, Mr Moffatt. But it is absurd that I should continue to call you Mr Moffatt. Do you object if I call you Harold from now?'

'Of course not.'

'You see?' Wahab grinned at the others. 'Harold one day throws whisky in my face, and the next I am claiming him as my friend. You believe the British are the only ones with a broad outlook. Now you see that so have the modern Afghans. But I shall go and find out if Laura is indeed on the plane.'

They watched him rush off.

'Well,' said Harold, 'I suppose he's got an excuse for being excited.'

'He'll insist on her wearing a shaddry,' said Mrs Mossaour.

'Don't be silly, Maud,' said Lan.

'In fact, I'm surprised he hasn't brought one with him, to clap it over her head the moment she steps off the plane.'

'He'll certainly try,' murmured Howard, 'to stamp his brand on her, whatever that might be. I hope she doesn't let him.'

'She won't,' said Harold. 'We've got the impression that Laura's able to look after herself.'

'It becomes exhausting,' said Mrs Mossaour, 'not to be able to relax.'

They knew she was referring as much to her own position as to Miss Johnstone's.

'I'd better go and see how he's getting on,' said Harold.

He found Wahab in an incoherent rage with the amiable chubby-cheeked Indian radio operator.

'What's up?' he asked.

'He refuses my request,' cried Wahab, 'in my own country, too. Both of you – please excuse me for mentioning this, Harold – are foreigners. This I beg you respectfully never to forget. You have chosen to come here to serve us, remember. Good. You are welcome as servants, as friends, but not as masters; I repeat, not as masters. This dust which is on my shoes, and on your shoes, is the dust of my native land, not of yours.'

Kansab's brown eyes rolled in an inquiry: Harold, is this fellow mad, or is he just being an Afghan? Which one of us should tell him that in the Afghan Air Lines not a single Afghan is employed as air crew, and that the seventeen jets of the Afghan air force are flown by Russians?

'It's against regulations to distract the pilot with private messages,' said Kansab, with a wink at Harold.

'Who is the pilot?'

'Captain Mabie.'

'Oh, Mabie won't mind. Tell him it's me who's asking. We want to know if there's a Miss Johnstone among the passengers.'

'As a matter of fact, Harold, there is. Mabie mentioned it.'

'Why then did you not tell me?' cried Wahab.

'Because, my dear fellow, you did not ask very politely.'

'Is this true, Kansab?'

'Certainly, Harold. An Englishwoman, called Johnstone. With gray hair.'

'Ah, insults now!' cried Wahab. 'She is a young woman. How can she have gray hair?'

Yet it was more than six months since he had seen her, and even then there had been traces of gray in her brown hair. Could love for him in his absence have turned her white? It was for a moment a thought for tears, and then for horror: a crippled foot was bad enough, without gray hair too. He had decided to give her age as twenty-eight. If she had turned gray every hair would scream that he was a liar.

'This must be another Englishwoman,' he said.

'No, there's only one. Her name on the passenger list is given as Miss Laura B. Johnstone.'

The *B.* was for Baxter.

'I suppose Mr Wahab couldn't talk to her for a moment, Kansab?' asked Harold. 'Just to say "hello"?'

As Kansab hesitated, Wahab burst out: 'I do not wish to talk to this woman with gray hair. Please do not unite to make me a fool.'

Then they heard the hum of the aeroplane.

Kansab's earphones crackled. He spoke in cheerful Urdu to the pilot.

'Let's get out and watch it coming in,' said Harold.

They hurried out.

'She has not got gray hair, Harold. How could she have? She is younger than you.'

'Well, I'm sure you could find some gray hair in my head

if you wanted to look that hard. But you'll have to keep a grip on yourself, man. Look, there's Naim. He's come after all.'

'Did I not tell you he would come?' It was almost a scream. 'You think I am a liar every time I open my mouth.'

Harold smiled and caught his arm. 'Keep calm, Wahab. I'd be excited too if it were Lan that was coming. But you'll make a mess of her welcome if you can't keep calmer than that. Remember she'll be tired. She's come a long way.'

They approached their friends.

'Does Mr Winfield know she is lame?' asked Wahab.

'I don't know. I haven't told him.'

'He is a diplomat. He will hide his contempt.'

'Contempt? For God's sake!'

'But Mrs Mossaour will not. She is a bitter, disappointed woman. She plots to poison Laura's mind against me. Ah, but when she finds Laura is lame, it will be different. Mrs Mossaour will refuse to become her friend. That is good. That pleases me very much.'

He was laughing in glee when they joined the others. He shook Prince Naim's hand, and with his elbow gently nudged Mrs Mossaour's soft bosom to plead with her to look up at the aeroplane, glinting in the sun as it turned to make its descent over the low houses and green fields. He bit at his own knuckles as he watched it land safely and then become lost in a cloud of golden dust.

He became rather hysterical, insisting on shaking hands with Mrs Mossaour and appealing to her to be a good friend to Laura, whom in two or three minutes they would all see for the first time.

The plane, visible again, came taxiing into view. Attendants were standing by with landing steps.

'Please excuse me,' cried Wahab. 'I must run and meet her.'

He ran on ahead; they followed slowly.

'I hope he is not going to be disappointed,' murmured Naim.

'Why should he be?' asked Harold.

'Sometimes I have thought this woman Wahab has told us about does not exist. Oh yes, an Englishwoman called Johnstone does exist – she will come out of that aeroplane in one minute – but is she really the woman Wahab has spoken of?'

'I don't see why she shouldn't be.'

'Ah, but you will not see her through Afghan eyes, Harold.'

Soldiers at the barrier were keeping Wahab back. He appealed to Naim.

'Better wait here, Wahab,' advised the Prince. 'There is a good reason for these regulations, you know.'

They watched the activity at the plane. First off were the two pilots, one wearing a red turban; then some men, one of whom stamped joyously on the firm ground; then a woman, who came very slowly down the steps, helped by an attendant.

'Laura,' cried Wahab, waving.

But it wasn't Laura, as he saw a moment later; this woman was slow because she was old.

Next came two Afghan women, in shaddries, which they wore rebelliously. No doubt they had waited until the plane had landed before putting them on.

After them, descending carefully as if she too were handicapped by a silken envelope, came the woman for whom they were waiting.

'She seems to have hurt her foot,' said Mrs Mossaour.

'No, no,' explained Wahab, in love. 'She is lame. She is always lame.'

'Lame?'

'Yes, ever since childhood. A tragic illness.'

'But I had no idea. Did you know, Lan?'

Lan nodded.

'Why wasn't I told?' Mrs Mossaour sounded strangely distressed. Her reflections upon Miss Johnstone would have been different had she known. Now, forced to cancel them, and with no time to replace them, she stood in agitation, squeezing her cheek cruelly.

With a slow, patient, curious gracefulness Laura limped toward them.

She *is* gray-haired, thought Harold.

Goodness, she is as small as I am, thought Lan; I had the impression she was as tall as Maud.

No, decided Naim, in anguished disappointment, she is not any more wonderful than any of them; her coming will make no difference at all.

One thing's certain, thought Howard Winfield, Wahab didn't fall for her because of her prettiness, as Mohebzada evidently had for his red-haired, doll-faced wife.

When she was about twenty yards away the soldiers withdrew their bayonets and Wahab, with a hoarse cry, rushed to meet her. At least he set out at a rush but, remembering where he was, in Afghanistan, where a man might greet another man affectionately in public, but not a woman, he slowed down to a rather stiff walk for the last few steps. They did not kiss, though it seemed to one or two of those watching that she held up her face in expectation, but they did take hands, awkward though it was for her, with her white raincoat over her arm, some magazines under it, and a small handbag in her other hand. He seemed, after the first endearments, to warn her about the people she would soon meet, for she took her eyes off him to stare at the others with what struck some of them as a challenge.

Then he led her forward, with a mixture of love, defiance, and embarrassment.

Harold saw that her hair was really brown, but fast turning gray. She was years older than in the photograph he had seen. But her brow was still as broad, and her eyes, though tired, were alert and intelligent. He imagined he could read her life in her face: much stanchly borne loneliness; inability to find male friends, more because of her own fastidiousness than of their revulsion to her being a cripple; inability to make women friends too; charitable work among the poor and the unhappy; ostentatious befriending of foreigners, especially if coloured. Not his kind of woman at all, but to feel pity for her would be an impertinence. She deserved better, though what it was exactly that she deserved and wanted he could not say.

What a pity, thought Howard Winfield, that the two women meeting her should be, each in her own way, so striking and beautiful. Courageous and intelligent though Laura evidently was, beside Lan Moffatt she seemed obvious and commonplace; while contrasted with Maud Mossaour's tall, fair-skinned, ample beauty, she was thin and sexually quite unexciting.

Wahab, he thought, was making these comparisons too; and he felt sorry for him.

Reserved with the rest of them, including Prince Naim, she was almost warm in her greeting of Lan.

'I have thought a lot about you, Mrs Moffatt. I hope we are going to be friends.'

Then she looked round and saw some Afghans watching.

'Are those your people, Abdul?' she asked.

'No, no. They could not come. Later. You must come now and have your luggage inspected, and also your passport. I shall go with you.'

He almost dragged her away.

None of them at first was willing to speak.

'Nothing in life,' murmured Naim, 'is what one hopes it will be. Please convey to Wahab my regrets. Tell him I am sorry I could not stay. I really must hurry back to my office.' And off he went, almost running, like a man in grief.

Mrs Mossaour laughed. 'If we didn't know our little prince,' she said, 'we might suspect that he had been looking forward to sleeping with Wahab's future wife, as a reward for favours shown.'

'Maud, please,' said Lan.

'Don't be mealy-mouthed, Lan. We know it's done; and my opinion of Wahab, indeed of every Afghan, is that, though the arrangement might offend his pride a little, he would readily enough agree to it, provided further advantages might be expected.'

'That's a terrible thing to say, Maud.'

'It is? What's wrong with the arrangement, if the wife agrees? I doubt if in this case she will.'

'I doubt if she'll ever become his wife,' said Howard Winfield. 'And he's the one who'll decide against it.'

'I was surprised to find she had a limp, though of course for self-pity's sake he exaggerated it,' said Mrs Mossaour. 'But I was even more surprised to find her without, so far as I can judge, a vestige of sexual attraction. Do you agree, Howard?'

'I think so.'

'And you, Harold?'

'Well, she wouldn't be my choice, but—'

'Yet Wahab's the kind of man who looks at a woman as if she had no clothes on. They all are, except the Prince, perhaps.'

'Oh hell, Maud,' said Harold. 'We all are, if it comes to that. Give the poor devil a chance.'

'And give her a chance too,' said Lan. 'She's just arrived after a long journey. The country's strange. We're strange.'

'And she'll find him strangest of all,' said Maud. 'Howard's right. They won't get married, but it won't be she who'll back out. She's the kind who'd go through with it out of a spirit of sacrifice. But Wahab will prefer some Afghan woman whose father's got influence.'

'That's possible enough,' agreed Harold. 'Especially if the shaddry's coming off this Jeshan, as he maintains. Have you heard anything about that, Howard?'

'Only the usual rumours. Who's his source of information? Naim?'

'I expect so. And others of the pro-Russia clique. Wahab seems to have got well in with them.'

'It won't last,' said Mrs Mossaour. 'Look how Naim went away.'

'Yes. He's a kind of visionary, you know. He had some absurd idea that Laura was coming here not just to marry Wahab but also to give her blessing to the whole country. Don't ask me in what way. I doubt if he could explain it himself. You saw how disillusioned he seemed to be.'

'Yes, and Wahab too,' said Maud.

'Well, here they come. For God's sake, let's give them a chance. We'll forget our clever ideas about them, and just help them to become whatever it is they want to become.'

'Do you know,' whispered Howard, as he watched Laura and Wahab approaching, 'I'm disappointed myself, and I'm damned if I know why.'

'Isn't it simple?' asked Maud. 'Laura the oracle has been so unwise as to come out of her cave.'

Two airport servants came behind Laura and Wahab carrying her luggage.

'No trouble at the Customs,' cried Wahab, laughing. 'I explained who she was, and scribble went the chalk. We are really more civilized, you know, than you British. I had hours to wait and the young man was very rude. Here there are no smart uniforms, but there is courtesy. Where is Naim?'

'He had to hurry back to his office,' said Harold. 'He asked us to convey his apologies. Of course you're all coming to our house for lunch.'

'Thank you,' said Maud, 'but I'm afraid I can't. My children are waiting for me.'

'How many children have you, Mrs Mossaour?' asked Laura.

'Two.'

They stared at each other.

'Their father is Lebanese,' said Maud. 'Therefore they are dark.'

Laura smiled, but what it meant no one there, including her fiancé, knew her well enough to say.

'I would like to get a chance to speak to you about the school,' she said.

'Of course. There's plenty of time. We are now on holiday.'

Laura dabbed some sweat off her brow with a handkerchief. 'In sunshine as hot as this,' she murmured, 'everyone must be dark.'

'I'm afraid I'll have to get back to the Embassy, Harold,' said Howard. 'But I'll be pleased to drop off Miss Johnstone's luggage at your house. That'll give you more room in your car.'

'Will you give me a lift home, Howard?' asked Maud.

'With pleasure.'

So that was the arrangement. Howard and Maud went on ahead in the former's Land Rover, with Laura's luggage; and the Moffatts in their Volkswagen followed behind, with Laura and Wahab in the back seat.

She looked out eagerly, and asked quick questions.

'There is no need to be impressed, Laura,' said Wahab. 'It is not impressive.'

She was interested in the great arch under which they drove.

'It isn't always there, is it?' she asked.

'No,' said Harold. 'Your fiancé was telling us he had it put up especially for your arrival.'

She patted Wahab's hand.

'It was a joke,' he muttered. 'It is in honour of Mr Voroshilov, President of Russia.'

'Yes; I heard on the plane that he's expected. When?'

'The day after tomorrow. It will be a great day for Afghanistan. I am bringing my schoolboys to the airport to cheer him.'

'Why? Wouldn't they go of their own accord?'

'The intelligent ones would; the lazy and foolish ones wouldn't. It is important that we are friendly with Russia. She is our neighbour, and she is the most advanced country in the world.'

'Here's one of her products coming towards us,' remarked Harold.

It was one of the small taxis supplied by the Russians. Even the Afghans scoffed at them as shoddy tin cans. Handles, however gently used, soon got wrenched off, so that passengers had to be tied in with string or wire. To sound his horn the driver as often as not had to touch the dashboard with a live wire.

The taxi rattled past. Its hood clanged up and down. Much quieter and steadier was the turban of its driver, but he looked disgusted, as well he might, for the steering did not seem satisfactory.

Laura laughed, to Wahab's indignation.

'No, do not laugh,' he cried. 'Remember that their sputnik is travelling around the earth.'

'That's what makes it so funny,' said Harold. 'You'd think a nation capable of sending up a sputnik would be ashamed of such rubbish. Compare it with the American cars.'

'Be sure we do compare it with those, Harold. The Russians make cars for poor people who have little money; the Americans make them for the rich.'

'Nonsense.'

'It is not nonsense. And something else is not nonsense. It

is not nonsense to point out that most of the American cars
to be seen in Kabul, belonging to Americans of course, are
set down as aid to Afghanistan! Did you know that?'

'I had heard of it,' said Harold, with a chuckle. At least
fifty students had lectured him on it.

'Laugh at the Russians as you wish,' said Wahab. 'You will
see that the future lies with them.'

'You didn't always think that, Abdul,' murmured Laura.

Instead of answering her, he shouted: 'Look at those
unhygienic fools!' He pointed to two little dung-gatherers
who crouched beside recent camel droppings, using their
hands as shovels to throw the dung into the kerosene cans on
their backs.

'That must certainly be prohibited by law.'

Laura was looking back at the small bare-legged boys in
the beaded pill-box hats. 'They're charming,' she said.

'Charming! Oh, Laura, how can they be? They are
picking up filth as if it were gold. It is not charming, it is
degrading.'

'They looked cheerful enough.'

'The most cheerful people in the whole of Kabul,' said
Harold.

'Would you, Harold,' cried Wahab, 'allow your children
to do it?'

'I suppose not.'

'And neither would I. And to every patriotic Afghan of
today every child in want is his own child.' As he said it
passionately, he meant it; but he knew that tomorrow
perhaps he might not mean it quite so much, and the day
after that again he might feel he could not afford to mean it
at all just then.

Laura, however, appeared to think that the sentiment was
as much a part of him as his love for her, and that it was
therefore as permanent as the heart that felt it. She squeezed
his hand, and gave him that public smile of loving approval

which he remembered so well, and which now began that
chilling retreat within him sooner than he had expected.
Here was the danger, anticipated certainly, but not obviated.
In patriotism and altruism, as in every other human activity,
adaptability was essential: rigidity might so easily result in
breakage or total loss. But Laura had always been a fanatic
for principle. In spite of her quietness and physical small-
ness, he had often thought that under torture she would not
yield by so much as a word to her enemies; whereas he –
probably at the first prick of the knife under his fingernails –
would scream withdrawal of everything he had ever said,
even though deep in his heart he would hope later to scrape
up a little courage to resume his beliefs, however inevitably
modified. Here in Afghanistan she would have to be advised
by him, just as in England he had let himself be advised by
her. In the first place the mass of injustice was so much more
enormous than in England that the humanitarianism effective enough there would be worse than useless here; and in
the second place she was not really beautiful or regal enough
to tell Dr Habbibullah, for example, to his big brutal
intelligent face, that his concern for the poor was too
tactical, and therefore insincere.

Twenty

IN THE cold shower Laura reviewed her first impressions of Afghanistan.

As she watched the water stream down between her breasts, zigzag across her belly, and pour off her knees to gurgle down the hole in the dark-tiled floor where she had already seen a cockroach skulking, she warned herself how important it was, when assessing the present, not to let the past and future sentimentalize it.

Scrutinizing her small body, still virginal after thirty-three and three quarter years, juiceless therefore and prudish in every nerve, she attempted once again to see it through the eyes of a man whose sexual appetite was above average but well below bestiality. Abdul's peculiar, longing look at Mrs Mossaour's voluptuous bosom that morning had not been lost on her, and she remembered his every single glance in England at an attractive waitress or shop girl. Ultimately she had not blamed him for that interest; prude though she knew she was, she still did not think she would care to marry a man without it. Once they were married she never doubted she could compel him by methods still uninvestigated not only to confine his amorousness to her but also to restrict it within the limits of decency. Indeed, now, in the shower, her heart missed a beat or two, and she smiled as she realized how near might be those shores of sexual discovery. Intrepidly, and with proper explorer's scepticism, she had studied several books on sex, and after much self-analysis was convinced that she did not really suffer from frigidity as she had once suspected, and as Abdul, she knew, still feared. She was not sure that she would ever enjoy what was rather repulsively called making love, because no matter how conducted, with all the finesse and affection possible, it must still by its very froglike nature lack dignity; but secrecy and moderation could make the best of it.

They would have children. Against the top of her thigh, the whitest and smoothest part of her body, she held the golden sponge with which she had been dabbing herself. With luck her children might be such a beautiful colour, somewhere between her own pallor and his tan; but without luck, as apparently in Mrs Mossaour's case, they might be almost black. All during her long spinsterhood she had been in the habit of reading, sometimes twice, those articles in women's magazines which gave advice on mothercraft, but she had never come across any which advised on this particular problem. If there had been one no doubt its advice would have been as sensible, and as difficult to follow, as if she had written it herself. What she needed was to escape from the prison of her own intelligence, where everything was always in order and surprise was not allowed to enter until, as it were, it had wiped its feet. Afghanistan itself, marriage to Abdul even, might not be enough to drive her out; but having dark-skinned children of her own to cherish and protect probably would.

The question was, would she, like Mrs Mossaour, merely love her children in an environment of bitterness, or would she, because of her love for them, love every other child, whatever its colour?

She considered the glimpses she had got of Kabul on her way from the airport to the house. The sight of the women hidden in shaddries had caused her bowels to quake with a great anger and shame. She had listened without reply to Abdul's explanation that the mullahs, as well as old people,

believed that with its removal rape and indecent assaults and
sexual murders would break out, but she had thought, better
those, than this tame and sordid degradation. They had
passed a ghoddy-driver whose horse was being recalcitrant;
it would not move and he had begun to kick it in its belly.
She had wanted the car stopped and the driver reprimanded
but both Moffatt and Abdul had assured her that interference, especially by a woman, and a Christian feringhee at
that, would only have made matters worse for the horse.
Besides, Abdul had added, with that confidence new to him,
if the horse refused to work, the driver would earn nothing;
no one would eat, neither himself, his family, nor the horse
itself. She had not argued, but she had made up her mind
that if she became an Afghan she would devote a good part
of her life to persuading her countrymen to show kindness
to animals.

There was a soft knock at the door. Instinctively, even
when she recognized Abdul's voice whispering her name,
she pulled a towel round her.

'Are you all right, Laura?'

'Yes, of course, dear. Why shouldn't I be? Is there anything wrong?'

'No, no.' He giggled. 'It's just that you are being a very
long time. Our hosts are waiting to serve lunch.' He pushed
at the door, gently but with force.

As she watched the small brass bolt hold, she felt a proper
relief but also, what surely was not proper, a kind of
disappointment.

'I'm sorry,' she said. 'I won't be long.'

He chuckled. 'Remember in Afghanistan in August you
do not need so many clothes as you do in England.'

She had laid out on her bed her white dress, brassiere, and
panties. Had he seen them on his way through the house to
the bathroom? She imagined him handling them.

'Do you think, Laura,' he asked then, in a whisper so

intimate he might have been making love, 'it is a nice bathroom? For Afghanistan, I mean? For so primitive a country?'

It was adequate, that was all. It lacked a bath, except for the large zinc one propped against the wall. There was a W.C., but the hinges on the seat were loose, and though the cistern did flush, after some persevering tugs, it did so with a sudden roar like a wounded animal, and thereafter subsided through snarls and groans to low quiet sobs. The window looked out on a yard in front of the servants' quarters, which included a dry lavatory. Along the window ledge, inside and out, hundreds of tiny ants were pompously and incessantly busy. No doubt also in the drain that huge cockroach had playmates. Perhaps scorpions paid visits.

'Yes, it is quite nice,' she said.

'A surprise?'

'Yes, a surprise. But not so big a one as the garden.'

She had been delighted by the garden. The gate in the high compound wall had opened, and a sudden vividness of green and of red roses had struck her like joy. When she had turned to smile at Abdul she knew that in him, as indeed in every human being, there were in the midst of so much everyday dreariness visions of joy like this to be seen, but in many cases the door was hard to open.

'Yes, it is quite a nice garden,' he said. 'From the terrace you can see the mountains.'

She had flown over those mountains, indeed among them, for often the red pinnacles had soared above on either side. She had been afraid, not of the bumping and rocking, but of their fantastic strangeness. They had not been like a part of the familiar earth at all, but of some other planet where the customs of the inhabitants must be different from those at home to which, after years of painful rebellion, she had learned at last to conform. It might be that in Afghanistan things would be so ordered that she could quickly and joyfully accept them, but she did not think it likely. So she had thought in the aeroplane. Now she knew that cruelty, lust, jealousy, anguish, and all the rest of the mixture existed here too, beyond the strange mountains. She did not feel disheartened.

Abdul seemed to be stroking the door, as if it were her body. Neither she nor her body knew whether to be affronted or shamelessly thrilled.

'But our house,' he whispered, 'has a nicer bathroom, and a nicer garden, and from its terrace you have a better view of the mountains.'

'Our house, dear?'

'Yes. When we are married.'

'But, Abdul, you must not forget our arrangement. I am to live here for three months, before we decide. It is as much for your sake as for mine.'

'Yes. But you are forgetting something, Laura.'

She smiled, trying to recall. 'I don't think so.'

'Yes, yes. I am not a poor assistant teacher any more. I am the Principal. You saw that Prince Naim was at the airport. I am also the friend of Dr Habbibullah, the Minister of Justice; he is a very important man. I was publicly presented to His Excellency the Prime Minister at the British garden party. Last week I was made a member of the Brotherhood.'

Hearing the pride in his voice, she was proud too. Often in England she had wondered if his bitter tales of poverty at home were true; she had thought that he might be testing her love.

'It is very likely I shall have a distinguished career,' he said. 'Many people tell me so. With you to advise me, I could in time become a Minister.'

Again she felt thrilled, but she said: 'I shall always think of you as my poor student, who liked fish and chips.'

They both laughed, fondly.

'But I am ready to come out now, dear,' she said. 'Please run away.'

There was silence. 'Very well, if you wish.'

As she dressed quickly, she vowed not to be the kind of wife who would humiliate her husband by refusing his advances when they were most ardent, and by encouraging them when his hurt pride made them reluctant. It did not occur to her to wonder how she knew of such wives.

At lunch she was particularly gentle with Abdul. When she remarked that cruelty to animals seemed to be prevalent in Afghanistan, he protested passionately. Bits of food spurted from his mouth. She saw them alight on the tablecloth, and felt at least one on her face. Yet she kept smiling, with pity and fondness.

'But, Abdul dear, you used to tell me so yourself. In any case, please don't let's discuss it now. Mr and Mrs Moffatt aren't interested. Do let's change the subject. Yes, Abdul, please.'

At that familiar sharpness in her voice, he had to swallow his indignation, pride, and food in one big gulp, which brought tears to his eyes. She saw them, stared with her own eyes a little hard, and then turned quickly to her host and hostess, whose relations with each other she wished to examine. Moffatt she already considered a fat, conceited, intellectual oaf; she had been surprised to learn he wrote poetry.

'How long have you been in Kabul, Mrs Moffatt?' she asked.

'Three years.'

'But you are really Chinese? Is this a Chinese dish, by the way? It is delicious.' Really she thought the rice too greasy, the lumps of mutton too fat.

'No. It's pilau. An Afghan dish.'

'Some people eat it with their fists,' said Wahab, rather morosely.

She smiled at him as a headmistress might at a small boy interrupting her conversation with one of the staff.

'Do you think you will be here long?' she asked. 'You must forgive my asking. I want you to be here. I would like very much to have you as my interpreter of things Afghan.'

She noticed them exchange glances. Abdul had mentioned in a letter that he thought their marriage troubled by the lack of children. She now believed he was right. But why had they none? Was one of them sterile? Or did his poet's pride recoil from fathering a half-caste? From his present glowers she thought this more likely.

'We hope to be here for another year at any rate,' said Mrs Moffatt.

'I see. I expect it will depend upon the renewal of a contract, or something like that.'

'Mr Moffatt is much appreciated by his students,' said Abdul, with a sneer that she decided to question afterwards, in private.

'You teach them English, Mr Moffatt?' she asked.

'Yes.'

'I expect you find them apt pupils?'

'Very.'

He suspects I am probing, she thought. Look how he scowls. How he would like to tell me to mind my own business.

Then she had to turn from him for a moment to raise her brows in affectionate reproof at Abdul who, absent-mindedly, was scooping up food from his plate with a piece of bread.

'What is the Afghan attitude to children?' she asked.

Mrs Moffatt smiled carefully down at her plate. Her husband let his knife clatter. The question had shaken their defences.

It was Abdul who foolishly answered. 'But Laura, what

could be our attitude?' he asked, with a grin. 'Do you think
we eat them?'

She accepted the joke. 'What I meant was, does it not have
an effect on them to see their mothers' faces covered in
public?'

'They get used to it. That is what is wonderful about
children. They get used to anything.'

'In a way that is true, Abdul. Is it the case that Mrs
Mossaour's children are very dark?'

'I don't know,' he replied. 'I have never seen them.'

She had not asked him. The two she had asked, still
repairing the damage her first question had caused, were
slow in answering.

She waited.

'They are rather dark,' said Lan, at last.

'So the children have just been very unlucky?' she asked. 'I
believe that happens often. I'm afraid I'm very unscientific,
but it's got something to do with genes.'

'No one here considers them unlucky,' said Lan. 'They
are healthy, beautiful children.'

'In what way is it unlucky to be dark-skinned?' asked
Moffatt.

'I should have made it clear,' she murmured, 'that I was
of course not expressing my own opinion, but rather that
of the world. The world would consider such children
unlucky.'

'Only that part which is white-skinned.'

'I'm afraid not, Mr Moffatt. The part too which is dark-
skinned. We must not think that it is only the white races
who look down upon those who are so ridiculously called
half-castes. I believe the dark races are even more prejudiced
against them.'

Abdul was staring at her, open-mouthed. Mrs Moffatt's
pale-lemon left cheek was twitching. Moffatt, though, was
grinning viciously.

'If Abdul and I get married,' she added, 'our own children will be called half-castes.'

'Please do not use the word, Laura,' said Abdul. 'It is detestable.'

'It is. But we must face up to it. No doubt it is thought oftener than it is spoken. Ultimately all races will commingle. It is inevitable, as the species reaches maturity.'

'You do not think it is mature now?' asked Moffatt.

'Goodness, no. Far from it. Childish rather, in so many ways.'

'Laura and I are going this afternoon to look over our house,' said Abdul.

She smiled at him. If they did get married that was one lesson he would have to be taught: never to change the subject, if she had initiated it.

'Dear Abdul is so precipitate,' she murmured. 'He keeps forgetting that if I marry him, I marry Afghanistan also.'

'And what is wrong with that?' he cried.

'There might be a lot wrong with it, dear. I might not be worthy. Consider Mrs Mohebzada.'

'But she hates Afghanistan, Laura!'

'With good reason,' said Moffatt.

Again she noticed Abdul's peculiar sneer. 'From what I have gathered,' she said, 'she's very young and – shallow.' She deliberately hesitated, as if careful to choose a word accurate enough but not too unkind.

'Her love for her child's as deep as any,' burst out Moffatt.

He looked foolish after saying it, as well he might. Laura laughed.

'I wouldn't doubt that for a moment,' she said. 'Maternal fondness is universal throughout the entire animal kingdom.'

Caught in a trap, Moffatt could find no answer. He scowled with desperate love at his wife, but she, trapped too, could not help him to escape.

What the precise nature of that trap was, thought Laura, could soon enough be discovered, but she was in no hurry. In the meantime it was sufficient to know that it had to do with children. Was it because Mrs Moffatt was pregnant? As, smiling, she inspected the other woman for any signs, she found herself hoping there would be none.

Twenty-One

IN THE taxi on the way to inspect their house Wahab decided that if he did not assert his maleness very soon he probably never would. He had been proud of Laura's performance at lunch; it had been so typically feminine, in its ruthless inquisitiveness; and he had looked on it as an instalment in his own revenge upon Moffatt. But if she was going to continue to be useful in that way, it was necessary that she should act under his control, and be seen to do so. Emancipation was being granted to Afghan women shortly, but it would be ludicrous, and indeed treacherous, for him to allow Laura to wrap him in a mental shaddry. He owed it to his nation and his sex to subdue her.

To try to convince her by persuasion and argument was not quite useless, but almost so; she was much too opinionated and resourceful, not to mention cold-bloodedly patient. Action was needed, and the more direct the better. So, while she was gazing out at the thronged, decorated street along which the taxi was honking and zigzagging, he shot out his hand and firmly planted it on her bare knee. That knee instantly stiffened, and a small fierce hand dropped like a hawk on his, not pulling or tearing away, but holding captive. All his efforts to travel further up were restrained. Yet she continued to gaze out and ask interested questions about what she saw.

He tried hard not to let his heart sink too low in discouragement and humiliation. It might just be that she felt this very public part of the street, with camel drivers

peering in, was hardly the proper place for premarital
caresses. Perhaps this small hand with the remarkable
strength was really counselling patience until they reached
the privacy of the house. He had already told her about the
carvings on the ceilings, especially of the bedroom. She had
pressed his hand then, too.

'The men,' she remarked, 'have magnificent faces, especially those with beards.'

'Those are ignorant tribesmen, uncouth and barbarous.
They do not respect law and civilization. They hold Afghanistan firmly in the past.'

'Almost any one could act the part of Christ.'

'Laura, you would be surprised to know how rife syphilis
is in their villages.'

'If the women are as beautiful, Abdul, I can see I shall have
to keep a very close eye on you, once the shaddries are
removed.'

She laughed, and he thought it a good time to try again;
but it wasn't, for he gained not a quarter of an inch.

'Why do you dislike Moffatt so much?' she asked.

'Really, I should be asking you that,' he said huffily. 'I
have not said I dislike him at all.'

'You do not have to speak, darling, for me to understand
what you are thinking and feeling. You are transparent.
What did he do to you? I like her. Yes, I think she's good-
hearted and honourable, but like many another woman
she's had to subvert her own decency in order to humour
him. She's beautiful, in rather a fragile way; but it was
quite degrading to see how all the time she was in horror
of displeasing him. Their relationship struck me as very
precarious. I think I know his kind: on paper and in
speech, no one could be more enlightened; but in action,
especially where he is affected personally, how evasive and
cowardly. For a time, I suppose, it flattered him to have
this beautiful little yellow creature from Indonesia as his

wife: a poet's gesture, you might say; but now she's pregnant and he's suddenly realized he's going to be the father of a little slant-eyed, yellow-skinned brat. The poetry has gone out of the situation; now it's merely grotesque and shameful.'

Wahab had listened with a grin of admiration, although he felt sure she was wrong.

For some reason his grin irritated her. 'What was it he did to you?' she said very sharply, as if to indicate that this nonsense of evasion must stop.

Out of annoyance this time he tried to advance his hand again, but utterly without success; in fact, if anything, he lost ground.

'Had it anything to do with me?' she asked. 'I suppose it must have.'

All of a sudden her resistance seemed not quite so determined; or perhaps her hand was growing tired.

'He went to the authorities and tried to get them to refuse you a visa.'

'And yet,' she said, 'he's the kind you'll hear saying that visas ought to be done away with.'

She showed her contempt by pressing her lips tightly together, and also, so he imagined, by loosening still more that grip of her hand on his; at any rate, he was able to gain at least another inch.

'But that wasn't all, Abdul?'

'No. He also flung some whisky in my face.'

At that her hand flew away altogether, so that his own, astonished, remained where it was.

'The fat arrogant beast!' she whispered. 'Where did it happen?'

He noticed her thigh, like the rest of her, was trembling with indignation. 'Don't let it trouble you, dear,' he said.

'It is known, and talked about?'

'Oh, I should think so. Everyone in Kabul knows about it.'

She seemed almost to have stopped breathing. The look in her eyes was as frightening as a dead woman's.

He found himself patting her knee. 'It's all right, my dear. He put himself in my power, although he doesn't know it.'

'What do you mean?'

'The Brotherhood wanted to have him expelled from the country.'

'Does it have the power to do so?'

'Oh yes. Naim is a member, and Dr Habbibullah, and other very important men. I advised them, not yet.'

'Why did you? Sometimes forgiveness is neither wise nor admirable.'

'I do not think I have forgiven him. Yet I do not hate him.'

'Your trouble, Abdul, is that you can hate no one.'

He reflected. 'I believe that is true,' he agreed ruefully. 'I do wicked things to people thinking I hate them; but I do not.' It was certainly, as she implied, a deficiency. Maftoon, now, could hate as easily as a child could suck a sweet. Consequently, who in a few years' time would have risen, and who fallen?

'To have Moffatt expelled would not be a wicked thing,' she said. 'How dare he do such a thing to an Afghan in his own country!'

'Yes, that is really how to look at it. But, do you know, Laura, sometimes I think he was not flinging it in my face at all, but rather into the face of his own misery. Do you understand what I mean?'

'No, I do not. Abdul, he must go. I could not live in the same country with such a man.'

He smiled, and squeezed her knee. How many far more wicked men than Moffatt were there in England, where she had lived for thirty-three years; and if Moffatt left Afghanistan, now or later, would there not be many liars, cheats, adulterers, and murderers left?

'I mean it,' she said. 'What were you talking about at the time?'

'His children.'

'But he has none.'

'Yes. I think perhaps that was why he was so upset. Some doctor has told him that Mrs Moffatt can never have any children.'

It was her turn to grip his knee, and she did it painfully. 'That cannot be true,' she cried. 'Mrs Moffatt is pregnant.'

Thereupon both looked back at their hostess at lunch. Wahab could remember no swelling of belly or breasts: such symptoms would be very noticeable in so dainty a woman. Laura, more subtle, remembered the darknesses under the eyes, the secretive smiles, and especially the fond timid glances toward the sulky inseminator.

The taxi now turned off the tarred street down a road shaded with trees and corrugated with great ruts in the sun-hardened mud.

It rocked and lurched, so that Wahab's hand, now quite free of its jailer, slid up and down her thigh. Suddenly, startling him and knocking his hat askew, she flung herself upon him and kissed him madly. It was, he suspected, as much a blow against Moffatt as an affectionate gesture towards him; and it was outrageously indiscreet, with the taxi stopped and the driver staring round, with lewd scowl.

Wahab was so disconcerted and embarrassed that he paid the fare demanded, though it was double what it should have been.

'This is the house,' he said, rather peevishly. 'Do not judge it by the state of the road. All these heaps of mud will be levelled. The ditch will be cleaned. This rubbish will be removed.'

Amidst the rubbish he saw a cockerel's head, with open eyes and brilliant red feathers.

'You see, the house has been empty for some time, so

servants from the other houses dump their rubbish here. This is not Manchester: no garbage trucks come round every second day. But we shall have our revenge when we get a servant, for he will go and dump our rubbish outside those other gates.'

As he said it he realized how primitive his attitude was, and how dishonoured his country was by it. 'I am joking,' he added, sadly.

But she was still thinking about the Moffatts. 'I cannot live with them,' she said.

He was trying to turn the key in the lock of the gate.

'I shall go to a hotel.'

'There is only one, and it is not suitable.'

'Then I shall go and live with your people.'

'No, no. That is not possible.'

'Why isn't it, Abdul?' She seized his arm. 'You never speak about them. Why? Is there anything wrong?'

'The key will not turn. It is very stiff.'

'I meant, with your people and me.'

He stopped trying to turn the key, and faced her with the same kind of sneer he had shown at the lunch table. But now it seemed to be at her expense.

'I must ask you, Laura, not to concern yourself with my people.'

'But why, Abdul? If we get married they will be my people too.'

'If! Always you say if. And in the taxi, were you not saying it with your hand? I am a man of flesh and blood, Laura.'

She ignored that panted reproof and appeal. 'I shall try very hard to make your people approve of me. If it is necessary, I shall become a Moslem.'

He let out a little groan. Clever woman though she was, she seemed to think that a few minutes' intelligent, well-meaning conversation could undo the prejudices of a thousand years.

'We cannot talk here in the public road,' she said, and taking the key from him unlocked the gate.

It was of course luck, yet it was typical of her. Oh yes, he must very soon show her that he was the male, the dominant partner.

The gate shut behind them; they stared at the garden.

'I'm afraid it has been neglected,' he had to mutter.

Yet how beautiful it had seemed when he had come here the first time, a young husband to be seeking a nest for his bride and future sons. Now with that bride frowning beside him he saw how long the grass was, how weedy the path, unkempt the flower beds, and rank the roses. Nor were the mountains after all any more marvellous than when seen from Moffatt's terrace. They were nearer, but that only made more obvious their stony barrenness. No doubt the carvings of the swans on the bedroom ceiling would also be a disappointment. He remembered too, with an inward moan of dismay, that on a previous visit when he had lovingly pulled the lavatory chain to test it, it had come away in his hand. But, for God's sake, had it been a fault to see the house as the beautiful home of his love?

Holding him by the arm, Laura turned from the garden to the house. In her eyes he saw all the shabbiness and dilapidation which his own so pusillanimously had pretended not to notice.

'It needs whitewashing,' she said, 'and a few windows put in.'

A rat moved among the rose bushes.

She saw it, but went on: 'I'm sure we can make it into a beautiful home.' Yes, despite Moffatt, despite this hot mountain sunshine which was making her slightly dizzy and squeamish, despite Abdul's refusal to let her meet his people, and despite his incessant fidgetings of desire which were confusing her. She wanted to sit down somewhere in the shade and discuss all these matters responsibly, so that a reasonable understanding might be arrived at as to how their three-month experiment might best be conducted. She wanted to know too how Abdul had obtained his promotion, and what he had meant, on the way from the airport, when he had referred so favourably to the Russians. But resolution kept melting with her very flesh in this fierce dazzling sun. Under her armpits was dark with sweat, and she could feel it trickle between her breasts. The greasy rice, too, as she had feared it would, was turning sour in her stomach.

She dabbed her brow and eyes with her handkerchief. She had been warned to take Vioform tablets but had refused, believing that her stomach, like the rest of her, must learn to accept Afghanistan. With an effort she smiled fondly at Abdul. He was cool, handsome, and still desirous. She loved him. He seemed to be hoping that her strangeness was caused by desire for him. Perhaps it was.

He took her by the hand and led her toward the house. 'It is beautiful,' she whispered.

'Not now, Laura; but it will be. A man and a woman in love can turn a hovel into a beautiful home. But this is far from being a hovel. It belongs to a friend of Prince Naim's, an important man in the Brotherhood. He is letting me have it for a very low rent.'

She made an effort to stop the drift of her mind. 'What is this Brotherhood, dear? Is it some kind of society? I hope it is not reactionary, or Communist.'

By this time they were in the house out of the sun. It was much cooler. She felt better, but not yet clear-headed enough to admire the pale Afghan furniture and the red carpets, as he led her quickly through the drawing room into the bedroom. She noticed the lampshade there was strange, in the shape of silk wings and that the blue quilt on the bed was embroidered with great butterflies in red and black. The window was opaque with dust; in a corner of it hung a big cobweb with at least a dozen dead flies and insects. For a moment she was filled with pity, but whether for the flies or for herself, she was never to know; next moment she was whirled off her feet on to the bed, with Abdul on top of her, his breath reeking sourly of rice.

She seemed not to be a participant, but an observer, watching from somewhere near the cobweb.

'My dress, please,' she said.

'You mean,' he panted, 'you wish to take it off?'

How mistaken he had been in her! So reluctant in the taxi, so willing now. Yet such swift changes were unfair to him. Surely at her age she ought to know that if a man's passion was played with like this, then at the crucial moment it might be found extinguished, and no amount of fanning could rouse it until hours afterwards.

'It is new. I do not want it crushed.'

'Then it will be better to take it off. I shall help you.'

The observer in the corner laughed. No attempt was made to prevent the removal of the dress; on the contrary, arms were held up, and shoulders wriggled. His help was eager but gentle. He unhooked the brassiere too.

'This is madness,' remarked the observer.

'No, no. I love you, Laura. I have waited for years. Do you wish me to wait forever? This is our house, our bed, darling; our children will be born here.'

'We are not married yet.'

'But we will be. Nothing could be surer. Haven't I suffered for you, Laura my dear? Wasn't whisky flung into these eyes? I thought I would never see you again. Did they not all despise me at the Club? Except Mr Gillie, the Consul, whose wife wants us to be married in the American Church. But at the Garden Party, who shook my hand? Yes, the Prime Minister himself; and the Ambassador and his wife spoke to me. Yet my invitation was false. But then, do I not often have the feeling that I am here in life itself with a false invitation? Your love, Laura, should convince me I am wrong.'

During this panting and tearful speech, the observer had come over, was bending down, whispering: 'So this is love? This is what is called consummation. This is what you have dreamed of, feared, longed for. Do you not find it merely much pain, shameful muddle, outrage, and the worst disappointment of your life? If you do, do not be too surprised or appalled. It is the same with most women, though few will confess it.'

'Yes, yes, yes,' wept the participator.

Wahab could not forgive that sobbed affirmation; with it went absolutely no physical encouragement or assistance. He was left shocked and unappeased. It was not his first attempt at intercourse, but it was by far the least successful; prostitutes had been kinder and more co-operative than this woman who was to be his wife and the mother of his sons. All during the act, besides sobbing 'yes, yes, yes,' she had lain and twitched like an animal stricken to death. Small wonder his own performance had been that of a debilitated Indian clerk, rather than that of a bearded Afghan warrior.

When, afterward, he turned his head to look first at her naked but parsimonious breasts, and then further up at her face twisted unrecognizably, he could not help considering the excellent reasons for not marrying her. In the first place, it would need far too much courage and resolution to make love to her again; in the second place, when she recovered her wits, she would without doubt use them to upbraid him coldly, as if the fiasco had been his fault; and in the third place, when the shaddry was abolished as it would be next week, the streets of Kabul would be thronged with girls younger, plumper, more beautiful, and far more enterprising in the making of love.

Thus three or four minutes passed.

'Please leave me,' she said, at last.

He got up with a snort of hurt pride that quickly degenerated into a sigh of self-pity.

'I just want to get dressed,' she explained, with a softening of her voice that, in spite of all his resolves, instantly softened his heart. As he stood looking down at her she bravely opened her eyes and just as bravely made no attempt to cover her body with her arms. She even smiled, and he found himself smiling back.

When he went out on to the terrace and stood, trembling, watching the rat still playing under the rose bush, he realized that, yes, despite her skinniness, her ignorance of and lack of enthusiasm for love, her wrinkles, and her dismissal of him as if she were some kind of princess and he a gardener brought in for a minute or two to serve her, despite these faults, and many others which he could have enumerated as surely as he could have plucked off those mildewy rose-petals, he still had a great fondness for her, and would have all their lives, even if his was spent here in Afghanistan and hers in far-off Manchester.

He heard her at his back. The familiar, slight scraping of her left foot awoke memories of their happiness together in England. That would have been best, after all: to have remained in England. She had urged that it was his duty to return to his country and help in its advancement; he had consented, with misgivings that now, after his recent successes, were stronger than ever.

She stood behind him and put her hand into his. Each felt the other tremble. She spoke humbly.

'You mustn't look for too much in me, Abdul. You know the kind of life I've led. I'm thirty-three, and I've been deceiving myself for the past twenty years. But if you still want me, I'll be a different woman; or, more truthfully, I'll do my best to be.'

He tried too to keep his voice humble, but it kept rising, in a kind of haughtiness: 'It was my fault, I'm afraid. I brought you here with the intention of making love to you. I had it planned.' He suddenly realized, in awe at his own innocence, that he had neither looked up at the carved swans himself nor urged her to look up at them.

'I knew it,' she replied. 'I thought I would have enough resistance for both of us.'

No wonder then, he thought indignantly, I found the experience not only unenjoyable, but difficult.

'Is it possible,' she asked, so wistfully he hardly recognized her voice, 'I could have conceived?'

'It is not likely.'

'I hope I have. I want to have a child. Whether we get married or not, I want to have one.'

Yes, she was the kind of woman who, if he deserted her, would take back his dark-faced child to England with her, and cherish him nobly all her life. She was too good for him, he decided. Next moment he saw that in that admission lay his most honourable way out.

'You are too good for me, Laura.'

'I am not good, Abdul. I am untried, that's all. Do you know what I have been thinking?'

He was more concerned with not losing his own train of thought.

'I've been thinking I was too harsh in judging Mr Moffatt.'

'And not harsh enough, I am afraid, in judging me, Laura. You must not marry me. For your own sake.'

'There's nothing I want more in the world. I see this house and garden, not now, but in ten years' time. I see our children playing on the grass there.'

'I have something to tell you which will make you change your mind.'

'Nothing you or anyone else could ever tell me would make me do that.'

'What if I were to tell you I was already married? Do not smile so quickly, my dear. We Moslems, you know, are allowed three wives.'

She kept smiling, and it occurred to him that perhaps she was thinking that a quarter of an hour ago he had hardly performed like a man with three wives.

He laughed. 'No, I am not married. But be realistic. After I married you, I might want to marry someone else, someone younger, someone who would not think that making love is shameful.'

'I do not think that, Abdul.'

'But you feel it. Please listen to this, Laura. I have a lot to tell you. After you have heard you will certainly change your mind about wanting to marry me.'

Then he began to tell her, or rather sing to her, so impassioned and shrill was he, about his schemes to have Mussein and Siddiq not only removed from their posts but also banished to bleak villages, of his membership in the Brotherhood although previously he had despised its aims and secrecy, and of his obsequious association with dangerous bullies like Dr Habbibullah.

'The truth is,' he said, in anguished conclusion, 'I have found that I am the same kind of Afghan as the rest. There is no other kind. Trees do not grow on those hills. Neither does idealism grow in our hearts. We are all dust on the lion's paw.'

Tears were in his eyes when he finished. I am not a scientist after all, he thought; like Moffatt I am a poet.

Laura was squeezing his hand. 'You are being unfair to yourself,' she said, and her voice was like the voice of every wife. 'You deserved promotion. You are far too sensitive about such things. If these men were corrupt and inefficient why shouldn't they have been dismissed? You have fine qualities, darling. At last they are being recognized. You can be a leader of your country.'

For a few moments he considered that optimistic view, wishing to accept it; but he remembered Maftoon, with the fanatical eyes and the three infants. No, the truth was much more complex than she, with her woman's mind, could conceive: corruption, fanaticism, fatherhood, love, fear, idealism were all ingredients, and there were many more.

There was half a minute's silence.

'I'm afraid I don't feel too well, dear,' she murmured. 'Shall we go back?'

'To the Moffatts'?'

'Yes.'

'We may have to walk a little before we find a taxi.'

'That doesn't matter. As long as I have your arm to lean on.'

As he was about to open the gate she stopped him.

'Please kiss me, Abdul.'

He was about to seek some excuse for refusing when in her eyes he caught sight of an appeal that had concentrated in it the dozens of times he had kissed her before, in faith, love, laughter, and hope. The wicked part of him, the astute self-interested part, which he had believed to be the most influential, stood by advising him not to kiss but to make instead out of the denial the first step in the necessary withdrawal. The rest of him appreciated that advice as sound now, and likely to prove still sounder afterwards, but nevertheless, with a tenderness so genuine that tears now came into both their eyes, he took her head between his hands and kissed her on the lips.

'No one is worthy,' he found himself murmuring, 'no one at all.'

'You are,' she replied, and though he smiled and kissed her again he was aware she did not and could not understand. This sadness which he was feeling, provoked by the realization of the unworthiness of all, could not be experienced by the female, by the maternal mind. Women loved idlers, rogues, brutes, deceivers, tyrants, adulterers, murderers even; and all the moralizing in the world would not diminish their love.

Twenty-Two

A MOTHER's love is seldom diminished by disapproval of its object; indeed, it is just as likely to be increased, though the addition may be rather sharper than the rest.

Wahab's mother had, he suspected, nomadic blood in her. Two hundred years or so ago her forebears had made those heroic journeys of hundreds of miles every year, in winter down into the warm plains, and in summer up to the cool foothills. She showed it as much by her restlessness about the house as by her swarthy strong face and simple violent emotions. She was not fat, but massive; she had startled more than one coolie into obedience by herself picking up the burden about whose back-breaking weight he was making such a song. Even when seated on a cushion on the floor, which she preferred to a chair, she had presence and authority. In her youth she must have been an exciting girl, which made it a mystery that she had ever agreed to marry Wahab's father, who now in gray-haired middle age was still cultivating the stooped meekness he had had in early manhood. Bespectacled, for consolation, he kept moving his lips, as if reciting to himself passages from the Koran. But really, as Wahab had long ago discovered, what his father was inwardly whispering was some nameless instinctive appeal. He was a fairly responsible official at the Ministry of Mines where his salary, after twenty years' service, was about half that of an English bus conductor's.

As a consequence, the house where they lived, in a grubby dusty suburb inhabited by similar lowly paid professional men, was smaller, much dilapidated, and far less comfortably furnished than that rented by Wahab for himself and Laura. Nevertheless it housed, in addition to his parents and Wahab himself, Gulahmad his brother and his fat girl-wife and their ten-month-old baby daughter, and his two sisters, Karima, aged twenty-two, and Sediqa, still a schoolgirl. Besides these, in the slum-like outhouses lived Yakub with his wife and four children. These were very distant relations, kept as servants; they gave their services with an outspoken grudgingness that outraged pride and paltry wages were considered to justify.

To this scene Wahab arrived home that evening of Laura's arrival in Kabul. He had left her at the Moffatts' in a state of tearful laughter; Mrs Moffatt had diagnosed excitement; Laura herself had bravely blamed a touch of sunstroke; but Wahab knew the unsatisfactory losing of her virginity was most probably to blame. She had gone to bed and soon, dosed with aspirins, had fallen asleep. He had walked the three miles home, loving her steadfastly all the way, but finding that love a burden that grew heavier but could not be put down for a rest, even for a moment. Certainly it could not be discarded on the rubbish heap not twenty yards from the gate. He had not yet told his family about Laura; after all, she might so easily have changed her mind on the journey, and turned at Rome, say, or Beirut. Now that she had arrived he must tell them, but it would be, he anticipated bitterly, like throwing a lump of bloody meat into a cageful of wolves. He was especially afraid of his mother.

In the compound, where there was hardly a blade of grass, two of his little cousins were playing. As usual they wore shirts only, and their behinds were bare. On previous occasions he had stood watching them, until a love, or at least some positive affection, had been forced up out of the desert of his heart. This evening he stood again, but had to dig deeper than ever for that spring of love.

Suddenly from around the noisome corner where the outhouses were their mother darted. Much younger than Laura she was already wizened and witchlike. Seizing him with her talons, she began a long sing-song lament about some work that Karima, his sister, had unfairly ordered her to do. He felt sure her complaint was justified, for Karima each unmarried month grew vainer, lazier, and more embittered. But there was nothing he could do, except sympathize. This was considered so inadequate that as he left her to approach the house her wailings turned against him. Who but a fool, she bleated, would supply the money and tolerate contempt?

The terrace was small, and had dangerous holes in the concrete; but on it, kneeling on a rug, his father was saying his prayers. This piety was customary, and, Wahab believed, genuine; Ahmad though was convinced it was resorted to as a respite from their mother. The latter did not nag; she merely glowered. This evening Wahab felt like getting down beside his father. There were so many things to ask for; but, putting himself in God's place, he saw no reason why any of them should be granted. A man must not beg, even from God; besides, his problems were so complicated that even if he were able to describe them intelligibly, God might not be able to follow; it was not for nothing many parts of the Koran, as of the Christian Bible, were obscure.

Yet as he stepped carefully past his father's stockinged feet he remembered how long ago as a crawling infant he had used to tickle them, and how his mother would snatch him up and cry that he would become a great mullah some day. For years afterward he had thought of those solemn bearded men like Mojedaji as ticklers of feet.

In the living room his mother was seated on her cushion, with her eyes closed. Gulahmad's wife, Racha, embroidered with her baby on her plump lap. Ahmad read a newspaper. Karima sulked with scarlet lips. Sediqa lay on the carpet, studying. There was the heavy oily smell that had distressed him ever since his return from England, but this evening it was at its most repulsive. Seconds after he entered he wanted to rush out again, shrieking that he was never going to return; especially as he could tell from the way they all gave up what they were doing to look at him, that they had been waiting for his return. Even the baby rolled its black eyes in his direction.

Animosity and greed made hateful every familiar countenance. Oh, to be able to live like his mother's simple ancestors, and sit in a black tent with only the bleatings of his fat-tailed sheep to disturb him.

His father came hurrying in, carrying his shoes. In the doorway stood Yakub and his wife, cackling and leering. There was no doubt that a conference had been arranged to begin as soon as he arrived.

'Sit down, my son,' said his mother.

She was in many ways so like Laura, he thought; physically they were altogether different, the one stout, the other frail, but both were strong-willed and domineering. Yet, he remembered in awe, Laura that afternoon had become gentle. All her life his mother never had been; at his conception and birth she must have been hearty and robust. Why then had he been born with so many misgivings?

A cushion was flung to him; he ignored it, and sat down on a stool.

'What is this we have heard?' asked his mother.

He looked at those well-known and well-loved faces; yes, they were like wolves; in each one greed was savage. He looked for, and soon saw, pointed ears, dripping jaws, and cruel eyes. Even his younger sister Sediqa, whom he loved most, was transformed. His father, fresh from prayer, had the foolish grin of the last in the pack, which would eat after the rest had feasted. This is not peculiar to Afghanistan, he told himself; it is the same everywhere; in England too a man's family rends bloodily at his good luck.

'What have you heard, mother?' he asked.

'We know you have become the Principal of the School,' said his mother.

'You should know. I told you myself.'

'We have not yet seen any of the extra money you are paid.'

'The explanation is simple. I have still to draw my Principal's salary. These things take time.'

'Sometimes,' his brother said gloomily, 'they take too long a time. I knew a man who was promoted for six months, and still was given the same salary. When he asked for the increase he was put down again.'

'That is not unusual,' agreed Wahab, with a shudder.

Their father smiled and shook his head. 'Promotion is often given to a man because his abilities are such he should be doing the more important work. It does not always follow he must be paid more money.'

'It should follow,' said Gulahmad.

'If we want foolish speech,' observed their mother grimly, 'we shall fetch in a donkey from the street. In the meantime the money does not matter; we can wait for it. But is it necessary for us to wait for this new house? For of course, Abdul, what we have learned is that you have rented a house in Karta Char. Today Gulahmad and I went to see it.'

'Today?'

'We are not long back.'

So they must have missed Laura by an hour or so.

'We had no key to get in to see it properly, but we sat on the ghoddy and saw over the wall. We saw enough. It is a good house, much better than this. When do we move in? It is foolish paying rent for an empty house.'

Then the others all cried out at once. So alert his brain, he heard every single cry. Sediqa yelped that some of her wealthiest school friends lived in that district; Karima loudly thanked God that at last like civilized beings they would have a W.C. and a bath; Gulahmad growled sourly that at long last he and his wife would have a room completely their own; and Yakub, backed up by his wife, wailed that surely he would be given his rightful place as a member of the family; his father sighed that it was progress for the son to supply what the father had failed to do, after a lifetime of honourable but unrewarded work; and even the baby whimpered that in such a modern house, with flowers in the garden and hot water in the pipes, it would be able to grow up into a civilized man.

He felt like the hero in the legend who, with only one piece of meat for the whole tribe, ate it himself. If he starved, who would carry on the race?

'I am sorry,' said Wahab. 'But you are all mistaken. This house belongs to a friend of Prince Naim's. It is true he has offered it to me, at a reasonable rent, but he has made it clear that if it becomes overcrowded he will take it back. This is written in the contract.'

'There are only fifteen of us,' said his mother. 'He cannot call that overcrowding.'

Yakub and his wife applauded; with their fingers they had made sure she had included them and their five children.

'By civilized standards,' he replied, 'it would be considered gross overcrowding.'

'The Russians,' said Sediqa pertly, 'often have more than twenty living in the same house.'

That was well known in Kabul. The Americans, who believed in one house for one family, regarded it as an unfair political manoeuvre.

'And *they* are civilized,' she added.

'They do not believe in God,' murmured the sister-in-law, but no one listened.

'What is your intention, Abdul?' demanded Gulahmad. 'I

have told them that possibly you have got the house for a very small rent, and you are going to let it to some American for a very high rent. I have pointed out that such a transaction might be very profitable.'

Argument broke out. His sisters preferred to live in the new house. Gulahmad thought the money better, and Yakub agreed, with the proviso that part of it be used to increase his salary.

His mother silenced them. 'Money is not the most important thing. Now that you are Principal and a friend of the Prince's you will get more money. It is better for us to go and live in this house. Every family of any worth moves up in the world. We have waited too long. It is now our turn.'

Wahab still felt confident. He was the hunter with many bullets left; the wolves could be driven off. When one was shot the others immediately fought over its carcass.

'You do not seem to understand that I have been given this house because I am going to get married.'

Uproar again, beaten down by his mother's voice and clapping hands. Then, addressing him, she wanted to know why she hadn't been told before, who was the girl, and how much was he having to pay for her. She hoped he wasn't going to be so inconsiderate as to put the whole family into debt for years paying off a fabulous sum. Moreover, as his mother she knew him better than he knew himself; he was far too likely to choose some silly little creature with big breasts.

At that his sister-in-law began to sob and giggle. She had cost fifty thousand afghanis, and so far, as she had been allowed to know, her only assets were her fertile womb and soft bosom.

Wahab faced his mother.

'I shall tell you how much I am paying for her,' he said. 'Nothing. Not one single afghani.'

'Even a she-goat costs something.'

'I thought this family was opposed to the barbarous custom of paying for a wife.'

So they had been, too, because of Karima. Vain, lip-sticked, crimson-nailed, and thin, she was not likely to fetch other than a shameful price. She was lazy and fierce-tempered. No man buys a lifetime of toil and scratchings; but an eccentric might accept it for nothing.

'Who is this girl?' asked his mother.

It was Sediqa who cried out the answer: 'She is the feringhee.'

Once the snapshot of Laura had fallen on the carpet. Sediqa had snatched it up. He had asked her to mention it to no one. She had kept the promise until now.

'Yes,' he said proudly, 'she is the feringhee. Please remember,' he added, as the storm rose again, 'that it is my business, no one else's.'

Now they raised their heads and bayed.

'Will she take our faith?' cried his father.

'Why should she? Thousands of Afghans have forsaken it.'

'How old is she?' snarled Karima.

'Please mind your own business. I will not answer impertinent questions.'

'I suppose she has blue eyes?' shouted his brother.

Once, years ago, Wahab had mentioned a wish in a country of brown-eyed women to marry one with blue eyes. Some tribes in the north, descendants of Alexander the Great's soldiers, were said to have them.

'Her eyes are gray.'

'Is she rich?' shrieked Yakub.

'No.'

'All feringhees are rich,' screamed Yakub's wife.

'Rubbish. Many are poor men, who have to work with their hands.'

'Silence!' bellowed his mother.

Her eyes, he noticed, were already bloodshot. He had

feared she would not be reasonable. Well, did he not have his retreat prepared?

'Where is this woman, Abdul?'

'Here, in Kabul.'

Uproar of astonishment at his having concealed her from them, silenced by his mother's beating hands.

'How long has she been here?'

'She arrived today.'

'But you have known her for a long time?'

'Yes.'

'You met her in England?'

'Yes.'

'Yet until today you have said nothing about her?'

'I wanted no irrelevant discussions.'

'Are you already married, according to English law?'

'No. If I had been,' he added bitterly, 'I should never have returned to Afghanistan.'

'So there is still time, Abdul?'

'For what?'

'Time for you to wash this nonsense out of your mind. I did not think my son would ever think of forsaking his country, and his family, for the sake of a white belly.'

He winced at that coarseness, so characteristic of his mother when she was angry.

Gulahmad clapped his hands. 'Do not let us get angry with one another,' he said. 'Why should Abdul not marry the feringhee? She can live with us in the new house. And I am sure she will have money. We Afghans are already a very mixed nation. It is a good thing.'

'She is not rich,' said Wahab.

'Compared with us, she will be. You have told us that in England the man who sweeps the streets earns more than the Principal of a high school here.'

So he had told them; and, good God, it was still true, even when he himself was Principal.

'Well?' asked Sediqa. 'Will she come to live with us?'

They waited for his answer.

He gave it boldly. 'She would,' he said. 'She wishes to; but I do not wish it.'

He raised his hand, and for another moment their teeth, already bared, were kept from his throat. These are, he reminded himself again, my people, my father and mother, my sisters, my brother and his wife and child; not only are they of the same race as myself, they are of the same blood. Why then do I persist in likening them to wolves? It is not enough to answer glibly that wolves too are Afghan, roaming in packs through the vast woods in the north and even in winter slinking into the snowy streets of Kabul itself after dark. No, the reason is more fundamental: in the human heart, after thousands of years of civilization and religion, brutish selfishness still reigns.

The verdict of course condemned him too; they who savagely demanded were wolfish, he who tenaciously refused was wolfish too. With everyone involved there seemed no remedy.

Yet was not this a shocking pessimism for a man in love, not with a woman only, nor with his country, nor with humanity, but with the whole of life? Love, outraged, took its revenge; suddenly it dazzled and dismayed him with an unbearable vision. His eyes filled with tears, but the vision would not be obscured. These now shouting angrily at him were not wolves; they were his people, and why should they not be angry, when it was true that, though human beings and in God's image, they were being forced in their journey from eternity to eternity to suffer the degradations and humiliations of poverty? And did they not represent millions of others similarly degraded and humiliated, not only outside this house under the Afghan stars, but all over the world, in Asia and Africa, yes, and in Laura's England too?

Karima was digging her red nails into a cushion as if it was his face. 'Am I to live like a pig, while your milk-faced whore lives in luxury?'

'What about my son?' howled Gulahmad, pressing his cheeks hard with his hands. 'Did you not say yourself it was the duty of us all to see that he grew up in an Afghanistan worthy of him?'

Their mother yelled for silence. She smiled at it when it came; then she said, quietly: 'I am your mother, Abdul. I gave you birth. At these breasts you had your first sustenance. You were my first-born. Therefore I have loved you with a special love.'

He had never thought so; Gulahmad had always been her favourite.

'I do not think you will now throw dirt on my gray hairs.'

They were not as gray as Laura's.

Suddenly she laughed. 'I know what you intend to do,' she said. 'Everyone is certain you will become an important man. You have found good friends, such as Prince Naim.'

'And Dr Habbibullah,' added his brother.

'If you are careful, they will help you to become rich.'

'I would like to remind you, mother,' said Wahab, 'that the salary of a Cabinet Minister is only twelve hundred afghanis per month.' That was about eight pounds.

As he had expected, she laughed again, and the rest joined in. Everyone in Kabul knew that perquisites were better than salaries, and the higher the post the greater the perquisites. That was as much a fact of life as eating or excreting. There was no reason to be shocked. Those who suffered from the swindles were the first to grant the swindler his right to perpetrate them, provided he did it discreetly. After all, had they been lucky enough to be in his place they would have done the same. They were too mature in the world's ways to expect a man to stay poor if he had the chance of becoming rich.

'It should be easy for you in a short time to afford two houses,' said his mother.

'Are you suggesting that I betray my pupils?'

'What do you mean?'

'If I make use of my position, and of my friendship with men like Prince Naim and Dr Habbibullah simply to enrich myself, then I betray not only my pupils but every child in the country.'

'What nonsense, my son!' cried his mother. 'If you become rich and powerful, your pupils will be very proud. They will say afterwards, Abdul Wahab used to be our Principal.'

'No. My students are too intelligent for that. It is no doubt true they expect to be betrayed, because always in the past betrayal has taken place; but there is always hope in their hearts that some day someone, some Afghan who has the opportunity to enrich himself by betraying them, will refuse to take that opportunity.'

'And are you going to refuse?' shrieked Karima.

'You must be mad,' howled his brother.

'You will be thrown aside like melon peel,' wailed his father.

Even the baby, his nephew, began to whimper fretfully. Suddenly he had a feeling, souring his blood and crushing his bones, that they were right thus to attack him like wolves. Theirs was the attitude ratified, if not sanctified, by thousands of years of social relationship, whereas his was that of the bleating lamb deserving to be devoured.

He had to be at school early to organize the distribution of the little Afghan and Russian flags supplied by the Ministry. When he cycled through the gate he was disquieted to find the courtyard almost empty. True enough, the boys had been told to assemble at nine and it was now only eight, but still he could not get rid of an apprehension that few or none would turn up for the procession to the airport to welcome President Voroshilov. Maftoon had already hinted several times that there was an underground movement among the pupils, led by some troublemakers in the Twelfth Class; its purpose was opposition to progress as represented by Soviet Russia, and, so Maftoon also said, it was encouraged by Mojedaji. Wahab had been sceptical: he did not want to believe that the young could ever be the enemies of progress and the friends of conservatism; but nevertheless he suspected many of them instinctively were.

Therefore when, having carried his heavy bicycle up the stairs lest it be stolen, he arrived panting in his office he was alarmed and astonished to find, seated in one of the pink armchairs, Mojedaji, so still and quiet that flies were skiing undisturbed on the slopes of his turban. Ever since his promotion he had tried to avoid the fat, sinister mullah.

Mojedaji opened his eyes, to reveal them bleary and bloodshot. When he smiled, too, his gold teeth seemed dimmed, and as he pointed to the door the gold ring among the black hairs no longer sparkled so arrogantly. The way he sat emphasized the fatness of his thighs and the repulsive bulge of his genitals. His turban was almost grubby.

'Lock the door, Wahab,' he said hoarsely.

Wahab obeyed. Then, avoiding those dark hungry eyes, he hurried to his desk at the window. When he was safely seated in his chair of authority he tried to meet that gaze boldly, but he could not help shuddering.

'You are early, Mojedaji,' he said, trying to smile.

'I wanted to speak to you, Wahab.'

Glancing out of the window Wahab noticed more and more boys were arriving. He felt cheered, until he remembered Maftoon's warnings about subversion.

'I understand,' said the mullah, 'that the Englishwoman arrived in Kabul yesterday.'

'Yes, she did.'

Suddenly cheering was heard down in the playground. Wahab craned to see. A group was being harangued on the volleyball field by a tall youth standing on a shaky pile of bricks; he recognized him as Rasouf of the Twelfth Class, usually an eager boy, with a quick smile.

Wahab pulled the window open.

'We are Afghans,' Rasouf was screaming. 'There was civilization in Kabul when Moscow and New York were inhabited by savages. Now what have we become? Beggars. We are laughed at in the world, because we have sold our independence for roubles and dollars. In our history books does it not proudly tell how our forefathers gave their blood to save our country from the imperial British? Now we are like a beggar with both hands outstretched, one towards the East and the other towards the West. I say, let us rather stretch our hands first upwards, to call on God's help, and then downwards to the earth. Look, it is dry and barren; but we can make it fertile by the sweat of our brows.'

He jumped down and, copied by dozens of the boys, rubbed his hands in the dust. Then all the hands shot up and their owners began to chant 'Afghanistan', many times.

We are all fanatics, thought Wahab: no wonder a cool disillusioned man like Moffatt laughs at us. Then he saw Maftoon, backed by two other teachers, his cronies, running across to Rasouf, with sticks in their hands.

With a groan Wahab closed the window, and his eyes too; when he opened these, he found that Mojedaji had got up from the chair and was standing at the desk, with a fat envelope in his hand. This he now set down and pushed across to Wahab.

'I have been authorized to say, Wahab,' he whispered, 'that in certain circumstances no objection will be raised to your marriage with this woman, not even if she wishes to be married according to Christian custom.'

'What circumstances?' Wahab tried to sound scornful, but the result was a bleat of anxiety and complaint. Outside were shouts, screams, laughter, and more defiant chanting. He lacked the courage to peep down to see what Maftoon was doing to Rasouf.

'Open it,' murmured Mojedaji.

'What is in it?' But he already knew. Had not his family barked the information to him, last night?

'Look and see.'

He ought to have swept the envelope off the desk on to the dusty floor, but instead he picked it up and opened it. Of course it was stuffed with notes. He made a gesture as if he disdained to count. Contemptuously he asked how much it was.

'Eight thousand afghanis.'

About fifty-five pounds, he calculated. Scarcely a fortune.

'And how am I expected to earn this?' he asked. His throat was so dry he had almost to cough the words out.

'By a simple act of patriotism.'

'Yes, I am a patriot.' Nevertheless he wished that insane chanting would stop. 'Better than that, I am an idealist.'

'Everyone knows that, Wahab. You will not spend the money on yourself. You will help your family with it, or you will give it to the beggars in the streets.'

'What act of patriotism?'

'You are to take the boys this morning to the airport?'

'Yes.'

'Do not take them.'

The chanting and excitement in the playground grew louder. He ought to be rushing down to restore order and confidence. His very presence should be enough. As Mojedaji had said, everyone knew he was not inspired by selfish ambition and greed.

He heard himself laughing. 'You are asking me to commit professional suicide.'

'No. Nazrullah of Habibiah College has agreed not to take his pupils. Your reason need not be political. You remember what happened when the Turkish Foreign Minister visited Kabul?'

'Yes.' The boys, then led by Mussein, had marched with flags to the airport road, three miles away. They had taken up their places by ten o'clock as instructed. The aeroplane had not arrived till one, and the visitor, exhausted and ill-tempered, had been taken to the Turkish Embassy by another route. The boys had gone off, singing rebellious songs; many had taken a holiday next day.

'It is the duty of a principal to protect his pupils from exploitation,' said Mojedaji.

There was a sudden clattering of footsteps outside, and someone hammered on the door. It was Maftoon. 'Abdul Wahab!' he shouted, his voice too angry and urgent for a subordinate's.

'Yes, Maftoon. What is it?'

'Don't you hear them?'

'I hear Afghan boys chanting the name of their country.'

'No, no. You don't understand.'

'You are an intelligent man, Wahab,' whispered Mojedaji. 'Show it by choosing the right side.'

'I understand perfectly, Maftoon. Keep calm.'

'Calm! Rasouf and his friends have broken into the store-room. They are tearing up all the books.'

'Do not think victory can lie with Dr Habbibullah,' said Mojedaji. 'Prince Naim is about to withdraw. The King cannot bring himself to trust the Russians.'

Wahab jumped up, with the packet of money still in his hand. 'Tell me, Mojedaji. Is it true the shaddry is to be removed next week, at Jeshan?'

'That has not been decided yet.'

'Does your side approve of its removal?'

'No. Not now. Listen to them, Wahab.'

They listened, and Wahab felt the whole building throb with the passions of his pupils.

'No woman will be safe, Wahab.'

Wahab was about to cry that, thank God, he had more faith in his countrymen when he remembered his own fondness for seeing women with no clothes on, and also, of course, his own so precipitate and lustful violation of poor Laura. Probably all Afghans, all men indeed, were like him; there might well therefore be rapes and criminal assaults and indecent exposures at every street corner for months.

Yet it was not confusion or shame that caused him, with his eye on Mojedaji's pocket, to slip the packet of notes into his own before rushing over to unlock the door and let Maftoon burst in.

Maftoon flew for the telephone.

'What are you doing?' cried Wahab. He had shut the door again, appalled by the angry noises that had come through it. Outside the landing was crammed with chanting boys.

Maftoon had a large lump on his brow; a stone or a whirling heel might have caused it. He spoke with asperity into the telephone, asking to be put through to his brother-in-law Dr Habbibullah.

Wahab at first wasn't sure whether it was a family or a business call.

'What's the matter with the boys?' he asked. 'What has made them so excited?'

'Look.' Maftoon pointed to his lump. 'They're out of control. They've got to be taught a lesson.' Then he was speaking to Dr Habbibullah, demanding that some policemen be sent to quell the riot.

'This is ridiculous, Maftoon,' cried Wahab. 'There is no need for any police.'

'Go downstairs and see.'

'I shall certainly do so,' and off he went, leaving Maftoon

gabbling cruelly into the telephone and Mojedaji seated again on the pink chair, with his sourest, most sinister smile.

If the boys are pacified and calm when the police arrive, thought Wahab, there will be no brutality; and he bravely kept thinking that all the way across the wide landing and down the stairs, though these were thronged with boys who crushed against him, struck and kicked him, and even spat in his face. He kept crying that it was all right, there was no need for panic and anger, he was their Principal, their friend, and counsellor who would give his life on their behalf, if necessary. What were their complaints? Like them he too was proud of his country, and ashamed of its present ignoble acceptance of alms. All that was necessary was for them to work together in faith.

So shouting, and pummelled all the way by fists and jabbed by elbows and tripped by feet, he managed to reach the great hall below where hundreds of boys were gathered. The door of the storeroom was open, and boys were rushing out of it with armfuls of books which they were tearing to pieces. Rasouf stood by, with his arms folded and a foolish triumphant grin on his handsome young face. Two of his classmates kept close to him. Other Twelfth-Class students kept apart, near the door.

So excited that he could scarcely speak, with unexplained tears pelting down his cheeks, Wahab struggled fiercely through the mob till he reached Rasouf.

'What madness is this?' he gasped. 'Why are they destroying the books? Are you for dragging us back to the barbarous times of Genghis Khan?'

'The great khan fought; he did not beg,' cried Rasouf.

'Begging is never noble, Rasouf, but sometimes it is better than fighting. You must stop them. The police are coming. Maftoon has telephoned for them.'

He noticed Rasouf's two lieutenants exchange glances and then slip off towards the door. Along the corridor he caught sight of several teachers armed with hockey sticks, with which they were prepared to defend themselves.

There was a chair beside Rasouf; no doubt he had been fomenting the disorder from it. Now Wahab leapt on to it. Unfortunately, being a typical classroom chair, it had one leg loose, and at once collapsed under him. There were shrieks and whistles of derision, which wounded him like swords, but up he scrambled, ignoring his cut knee, and propping the chair against the wall got on to it again, gingerly. There, shaking, he addressed them. The attention he got was sudden and concentrated, but not the kind he wanted or expected.

'Go back to England!'

'Where is Abdul Mussein?'

'What's happened to Siddiq?'

'Liar.'

'Hypocrite.'

'Coward.'

'Fool.'

Those were hooted or yelled at him, and though the tears kept tumbling down his cheeks, and every accusation stabbed like a sword, he also felt proud of his boys, so perspicacious, so honest, and so resolute in support of what they considered justice.

'Yes, yes,' he cried. 'No doubt I am a liar and a hypocrite, a coward and a fool.'

'Go and drive a camel, Wahab.'

'Go and kiss one.'

'Go and kiss one's behind.'

Now they were becoming juvenile, but they were also beginning to laugh: so many different kinds of brown Afghan faces, thick-lipped Negroid, thin-lipped Caucasian, slant-eyed Mongolian, white-eyed Arabian, and hook-nosed Semitic, all young, good-hearted, courageous, and beautiful in their laughter.

Then from some of the boys at the entrance came screams of warning. Too late, though, for seconds after into the hall charged about a dozen policemen armed with long truncheons and led by a huge officer with a cruel obtuse face. Straight for Wahab they rushed, knocked over his chair, sent him flying, shattered his spectacles, jabbed him with their batons, and kicked him as he lay stunned on the mud brick floor. Yet he was smiling, for the last thing he had seen through his spectacles before they were hurled from his face was Rasouf slinking off to become lost in the crowd.

The boys had gone very quiet and watchful, though a few tittered nervously at the policemen's ridiculous mistake. Some escaped out into the playground, but most remained. Through them Maftoon now came pushing, shouting peevishly to the policemen that the man they had knocked down was the Principal. They looked surprised, but not apologetic; they had never been at school themselves, but had learned to despise those who had.

Wahab was dragged up and planked down on the shaky chair. He felt sick and ached all over, especially in the groin where the end of a truncheon had poked too fiercely. Without his spectacles, too, he had to strain to see, and that seemed to add to his nausea.

The big officer was explaining to Maftoon, whom he knew. His men weren't to blame. They had been urgently summoned to subdue a rebellion. When they had come in Wahab had been on the chair addressing the boys, like an inciter. It was always good tactics to strike at once; now and then the innocent might get hurt, but in his experience they deserved it, as they were always fools.

Wahab's wits were clearing, though he still felt sick. He staggered to his feet, and in a voice that kept rising to a shriek in spite of his efforts to keep it low and dignified he ordered the policemen out of his school.

Maftoon whispered into his ear: 'It would be better if we

let them take Rasouf away and one or two of the others. They wouldn't hurt them; they'd just keep them locked up for a day or two.'

'If they take any of my pupils away,' yelled Wahab, 'they will have to take me away too. You had no right to send for the police, Maftoon. I did not give you permission.'

'You do not understand, Wahab. You are too simple. This is a very critical time. It is important that Voroshilov is given an enthusiastic welcome. The people are with us, but they must be shown that we are with them. Do you want Mojedaji and his friends to win? You know they are against the teaching of science, the freeing of the women, the spread of enlightenment. They want to keep the situation unchanged. Do you want that?'

'I do not want changes produced by fraud, force, and cruelty.'

'Sometimes there is no other way, Wahab.'

'Yes, there is. The trouble with you, Maftoon, and with all those who think like you, is that you have no faith in your fellow human beings.'

Maftoon gazed into the fatuous, earnest, peering, swollen, and bloody face. 'Do you have such faith, Wahab?' he asked.

'Yes, I have. I would not have accepted the Principalship of this school if I did not have.'

Meanwhile the policemen were leaving. They went slowly, grinning but furious. Quietly the boys hissed.

With the help of some Twelfth-Class boys Wahab got up on the chair again. One of them whistled for silence. It was quickly given. Many boys could not help smiling as they saw how he had to keep dabbing at his nose, from which blood kept trickling.

'I am sorry,' he cried, with passion, 'I am sorry our school has been polluted by such visitors.'

They paused, and then began to cheer and clap wildly.

'You know why we were to meet here this morning,' he

cried, when they were quiet again. 'We were to march to the airport to welcome President Voroshilov. Very well, then. Those of you who wish to go to the airport, remain here in the hall; those who do not wish to go to the airport, are at liberty to return home. Do not be afraid. No names will be taken. The choice is left entirely to you.'

They were astonished, excited, amused. Then one cried: 'What do you advise, Abdul Wahab?'

'No. I shall not advise you. The choice must be your own.'

For a few minutes they discued it among themselves. Some consulted Maftoon, others Mojedaji who had at last appeared from upstairs. Other teachers, without the hockey sticks, stood shame-facedly about; no one bothered to consult them.

Finally boys began to stream out. About as many remained in the hall.

Neither Maftoon nor Mojedaji was pleased; both seemed to think Wahab had played a clever trick on them, and both agreed he wouldn't keep his position as Principal very long.

Listening to their bitter mutters, he made his aching face smile. He was sure now that while he did remain in command he would know what to do, and would not hesitate, through fear, to do it.

To Mojedaji he said, handing back the packet of notes: 'I have found I cannot be bribed. You are surprised? I am surprised myself. But it is true.'

'What do you propose, Wahab?' asked the mullah, with a grin. 'I do not think you are fit to accompany the boys to the airport.'

Maftoon murmured that it would be better for him to go home and rest.

'No, I shall go, otherwise what must only be an act of courtesy will be turned into a political demonstration. But first, there is a telephone call I must make.'

He could tell from their faces that they were wondering

whom he intended to telephone. Perhaps Mojedaji thought
it was Habbibullah and Maftoon thought it was Naim. If so,
they were both absurdly wrong; he was going to telephone
Laura. He had meant to do it first thing that morning, but
finding Mojedaji in his office had driven it out of his mind.

After giving orders to the teachers to distribute the little
paper flags and have the boys lined up ready to march off, he
hurried upstairs, or at least he tried to hurry, finding by the
second step that it was impossible, so excruciating and
crippling were the stabs of pain in his groin. Therefore
he had to creep up, supporting himself against the wall.
Some boys ran to offer their help, but he smilingly refused it.
When he reached his office he had to collapse into the very
chair Mojedaji had occupied. With trembling fingers he
undid his fly buttons and looked to see what damage had
been done. There was swelling all right, some laceration,
and a great purple bruising. Fear pierced him that he had
perhaps been emasculated, and in the midst of that terror a
fondness for Laura and an overwhelming need of her
brought tears again into his eyes. Getting up, he limped
to the telephone, and the difficulty of his every step made
him realize how inadequate had been his sympathy for her,
whose every step all the long way from childhood had been
difficult.

It was Mrs Moffatt who answered.

'Good morning, Mrs Moffatt,' he said. 'This is Abdul
Wahab.'

'Yes?'

He was surprised by her curtness. 'I wanted to ask how
Laura is this morning. I hope she is better.'

'She isn't.'

He felt panic. 'What do you mean? I know she was not
well last night, but it was only tiredness, I thought.'

'It was more than tiredness.'

'Is she really ill? Has she been poisoned? Did your servant

not boil the water? Have you sent for the doctor, the British Embassy doctor?'

'We are looking after her, Mr Wahab.'

'Is she too ill to speak to me now?'

'I'm afraid so.'

To hell with the procession, he thought. 'Tell her I shall come immediately.'

There was a pause. 'No, don't do that.'

'But why? I want to see her, and I'm sure she wants to see me.'

'No, she does not.'

'She does not?'

'That is so. Here is my husband to speak to you.'

'Hello,' said Moffatt, sounding much too cheerful.

'What is this your wife has just said?'

'That Miss Johnstone isn't feeling too well?'

'Yes, yes. But also that she does not want to see me.'

'I'm afraid it's true.'

'But why? What is the reason?'

Moffatt paused. 'I really don't know. I thought perhaps you might.'

'What do you mean? No, the truth is, you have all been poisoning her mind against me.' Even as he said it he knew it wasn't true.

'What happened yesterday?' asked Moffatt.

'What do you mean?'

'When you went to see your new house.'

'What has she said?'

'Nothing to me. But she's said something to my wife.'

'Your wife has not told you?'

'No. Apparently she promised not to. But I can guess. So I'm sorry, Wahab, but in the meantime there's no point in your coming here.'

'Not ever, I think.'

'Well, that may be so. What did happen?'

Now, needing to weep more than ever in his life before,

he found he could not. He looked at the cold black mouth of the telephone, and he had a vision of himself rotted in his grave. 'I made love to her,' he whispered.

Moffatt's voice was rough. Were there traces of sympathy and amusement in it? 'I know it's none of my business,' he said, 'but – was she willing? After all she couldn't have been more than six hours in Kabul. Wasn't it a bit hasty?'

'Yes, it was hasty, Mr Moffatt, though I've longed for her for months, no, years. It was filthy, too. It was unforgivable.' Yet afterwards had she not asked him to kiss her, and had she not said that he was worthy?

'I think she'll get over it, Wahab,' said Moffatt, 'but you'd better wait and see. Good-bye.'

Wahab's hand shook so much he could scarcely replace the telephone on its cradle. As he sat crouched over his desk, feeling again the agony in his groin, he thought, with an attempt at a smile, that the policeman who had struck him there had not been summoned by Maftoon at all, but rather by someone far mightier than Maftoon and far less scrupulous. No, he assured himself, as he pulled himself slowly to his feet, I still do not believe in God, but how am I to endure a life that contains neither God, nor self-respect, nor Laura?

At the door two teachers shyly met him.

'The boys are ready,' one said.

'They have their flags,' said the other.

'Good.'

'They want you to march at the front.'

The teachers looked at each other, but could find nothing to say.

Boldly, in spite of the pain, Wahab proceeded downstairs.

Behind him it occurred to Rahim, a small, timid, gray-haired man, to suggest humbly that the Principal ought to wash off the blood encrusted on his nostrils, but he decided not to, safer to keep silent and let some more daring colleague take the risk.

Twenty-Three

THE previous night, after Wahab had gone and Laura was at last asleep, the Moffatts had discussed their guest.

'She's like a spring that's been too tightly wound up for months,' said Harold, 'and it's suddenly snapped. What did happen between her and Wahab today?'

'No, I promised her I wouldn't say.'

'I think I can guess.'

'I prefer to see her simply as a woman who for months has placed far too many hopes on a man whom she now realizes isn't worthy of them.'

He noticed again that rather pedantic sharpness of judgment which Lan had lately developed, ever since, he supposed, his public humiliation of her. She had slipped off as neatly as a snake its skin her former imperturbable charitableness, and in its place had quickly grown this promptness to judge and lack of reluctance to condemn. She had gone further: toward people malicious towards her she was prepared to show in return a malice more intelligent and therefore more effective than theirs. She had decided to become like the people among whom she lived, and so, though she gained in companionableness, she had certainly lost in distinction. It seemed to him she was getting ready to protect the children to whom he at last had agreed. He even imagined that in so short a time she had grown a little stouter, a little thicker in the neck, outward physical signs of the deliberate coarsening of spirit. She laughed oftener and more loudly, but that secret smile which had seemed to him to have concentrated in it so much mystery, beauty, and compassion, was now seldom seen. Her friends, more at ease in her presence, liked her better, and he himself supposed that on balance it was preferable to have this shrewd, ready-witted, popular woman as his wife than the enigmatic priestess; but he would be haunted for the rest of his life by that lost serenity.

Now, discussing Laura and Wahab, she was as femininely commonplace as Paula Wint could have been.

'And she was actually weeping?' he asked.

'Like a child.'

Laura indeed had clung round Lan's neck as she sobbed out that incoherent, horror-stricken, yet fascinated account of what had happened at the house that afternoon. She had mentioned swans, and Lan had supposed she must have seen some in the fields by the river Kabul on the way to the house. Listening, Lan had recalled the evening when she had bathed Wahab's eyes, and had heard for the first time about Laura's lameness. She had been sure then that his protestation of love had been sincere, and she was still sure now: an outburst of impatient lust could not disprove nor even much dishonour love.

'It's easy enough to see what's happened,' said Harold. 'Judging from what we know of him, he'd no sooner get her into the house than he'd start tearing the clothes off her and flinging her on to the bed. Mind you, I think she would be ready for it, but no doubt he didn't use the patience and finesse that the books say are necessary in such cases. You know, of the two I'm more sorry for him. Laura doesn't strike me as ever having been an easy woman to love. After all, the Mancunians seem to have found her resistible enough.'

Lan smiled. 'Her nightdress,' she murmured, 'is transparent.'

He laughed. 'I'm not surprised. She's well up in the theory. Did you notice poor Wahab this evening? He reminded me of Manson Powrie the way his hands kept clasping and unclasping. In Powrie's case it's because he keeps remembering it's not quite the occasion for prayer; in Wahab's it was just sheer misery. If ever she's going to have a child, that's how his hands would go. It's a cliché at the birth, but rather novel at the conception.'

Again Lan smiled. Laura had asked if it was likely she would have a child.

'What do you think will happen?' she murmured. 'Will they still get married?'

'Why not? Don't you?'

'Yes, but it may depend on us.'

'Us?'

'Not only on you and me. All of us: Maud, Howard, Paula, Muriel, everyone who knows about her and Wahab. She's in a state to be influenced. She's already asked when the next plane out of Kabul is. So we've got to decide again what advice to give her.'

'I think you're wrong, you know. No one's going to influence Laura. She's come, she's seen, she's been deflowered, and in her own way she's thoroughly enjoying herself. All we'll be allowed to do is to stand by and watch her handle the situation. She'll tell us when to applaud.'

Lan smiled and nodded.

Looking at his wife's face, still beautiful but blemished by that knowing human grin, he could at last picture her kneeling by her dead sister's body, with her face transfigured by hatred of the murderers and desire for their punishment.

'Lan, darling,' he murmured, and took her in his arms, smiling, and realizing that from now on, if ever she had to be protected against the kind of crass persecution of the two men in the Singapore restaurant, she would be able to do it far more successfully than he. One of the gang now, she knew and applied its ways. For a moment his heart went cold.

In the morning when Lan went to see how Laura was, she found her awake, lying listening to some woodcutters chopping wood in a nearby garden. She asked what the sounds were.

'Yes, I thought so,' she murmured when Lan told her. 'Will they have beards?'

'No, as a matter of fact they won't. Woodcutters are always Hazaras, who never have beards: thin long mustaches sometimes, but not beards.'

'I notice your ceiling is plain wood. Some have carvings on them, haven't they?'

'Yes. Our sitting-room ceiling has.'

'I didn't notice. This whole country is full of men with faces like Christ.'

Lan sat down on the edge of the bed. 'Well,' she said, cheerfully, 'maybe as far as their beards are concerned.'

Laura closed her eyes, and looked sad. 'I have decided to go back.'

'Rome, you mean?'

'Yes.'

'Most Western women take months to get used to Afghanistan; some, I admit, never do.'

Laura's hand crept out and clutched Lan's. 'It isn't that,' she whispered. 'It wouldn't matter if I never got used to it. I could suffer that. What I could never suffer is the feeling that I was not worthy of him.'

Lan said nothing.

'For many reasons. Just look at me, and you will see the first. I am older than he is.'

'Is that important?'

'Not in England, maybe; but you know it is here. What age is the average Afghan woman when she gets married?'

'About eighteen.'

'Or even younger, sixteen. I am more than double that.'

'But Wahab knew that.'

'Yes, as a sum in arithmetic, but in another more important way, how could he? I didn't myself, until yesterday afternoon. It isn't just that I'm thirty-three with gray hairs and a sagging neck; it's something far more serious.' The fingers round Lan's wrist were now stroking it. 'When he was making love to me, I felt disgusted. I thought it was the vilest thing that had ever happened to me. Please don't tell me that that's a common reaction the first time. I am sure it wasn't with Mrs Mossaour, for instance. No wonder poor Dul was so bitterly disappointed. I knew it would happen. Oh, I've read books, I've even humiliated myself by writing to a magazine for advice. I know many married couples after a difficult start go on to do it thousands of times, as a habit, like washing their teeth. But a man must find pleasure and satisfaction, mustn't he? For him it's said to be the profoundest and happiest communication with the woman he loves. I've even read that he feels during it like a kind of god. That's rubbish no doubt, but still he oughtn't to be made to feel guilty and belittled.'

'He didn't show you much consideration, did he? Most women don't like being assaulted.'

But Laura in her mind had already changed the subject. 'He's on the threshold of a brilliant career. It's not out of the question for him to become Minister of Education one day. But if he marries me, all that's unlikely.'

'Did he say so?'

'If I were young and attractive, it might be different. But, as you know, I am not; and I have a limp. He is unwilling to let me meet his family. There is no doubt they will refuse to give their consent. Who could blame them? In what possible way could it be an advantage to him to marry me?'

Lan could not help thinking that though Laura might be

sincere enough in this self-depreciation, she was at the same time finding much peculiar enjoyment in it. Her intention appeared to be to pretend never to be going to see Wahab again, and indeed to carry the pretence to the point of refusing, for a few days at least, to let him come near her. But really it was all a kind of cruel game, and her true desire, which she would be as implacable as a tigress in achieving, was marriage to him and the opportunity at leisure to unravel this tight knot of sexual revulsion. Well, there were innumerable approaches to love and marriage, and this had as good a chance of success as many others.

'He will come to see you. What has he to be told?'

Laura smiled. 'Yes, he will come, won't he? Say I'm ill, and I never want to see him again. No, perhaps that would be going too far. After all, it isn't his fault. Poor Dul. He's so temperamental, up in the clouds one minute, down in the mud the next. I suppose all Afghans are a bit like that?'

'They are emotional.'

'Still, he's got to learn. Yes, say I'm ill, and I'd rather not see him, in the meantime. But let me know at once if he does call.'

'Of course.'

'It's very kind of you. I know I have no right to burden you with my troubles. But there is one thing more. I should like very much to have a talk with Mrs Mohebzada. Could it be arranged?'

'Yes.' But Lan was wondering if she should arrange it. It was one thing to let Wahab be the mouse to this strange cat; it was another thing altogether to expose Liz Mohebzada to these unscrupulous pounces and deadly claws.

'Ever since your husband and Mrs Mossaour pushed her forward as a dreadful example to me, I have felt I must meet her.'

Lan rose. 'I must see to breakfast. Do you want yours in here, or would you rather have it out on the terrace with us?'

Laura laughed. 'If I had it here, who would bring it? It's very strange having only men servants.'

'I should bring it myself.'

'Oh, I won't trouble you. I shall get up.'

'Very well.' Lan turned at the door. 'Mrs Mohebzada's very young. Perhaps she's not very intelligent, either; and it's true she came here expecting a life of luxury. But she's suffered a great deal.'

'I doubt it. I've had some experience of her type. As you say, unintelligent and self-seeking; but worse still, unimaginative. Can you suffer deeply without imagination?'

'Yes, I think you can.'

In the sitting room Harold saw at once how disturbed she was. 'What's the matter?' he asked. 'For God's sake, don't tell me she's really ill?'

'She's not ill at all. She's having breakfast out on the terrace with us, though she might have taken it in bed if either Sofi or Zahir had taken it to her.'

Harold laughed. 'And she still in her honeymoon nightie?'

'I can't laugh at her. She's decided Wahab's not to be allowed to see her for a day or two.'

'Letting him simmer in his remorse? She's taking a risk.'

'She's aware of that. I don't know what her cards are – she takes care to deal them herself; but I do know she'll play them very cleverly.'

'I'm sure of it. This Wahab's a reckless fellow. Does he think he can deflower a Bachelor of Economics from Manchester, and get away with it? But I hope she's taking into consideration the fact that, if the shaddry is abolished, the streets here will be full of Cleopatras.'

'I'm sure she's thought of everything.'

Then the telephone rang.

'It'll be Wahab,' said Lan. 'You answer it.'

'My dear, it would be kinder if you did.'

'Do you think so? I don't feel particularly kind towards him.'

They both went out to the telephone and spoke to Wahab. Then Harold strolling on to the terrace found Laura already there, wearing a white dress and with – to his astonishment – a white ribbon tied in a bow in her hair. It did make her look younger, in a crafty, precocious way.

She had started breakfast. 'Was that Dul?' she asked.

'It was Abdul Wahab, yes.'

'What was he saying?'

'That what he had done was unforgivable.'

She said nothing, but went on enjoying her cornflakes.

'As I don't know what he did, I can't of course tell whether he was indulging in the national habit of enthusiastic pessimism.'

'You don't like the Afghans, Mr Moffatt?'

'As a matter of fact, I do; but not them all.'

Lan joined them.

'It is beautiful here,' said Laura. Her face was already flushed with the sun. 'Your husband was telling me that was Dul who phoned.'

'Yes. I told him.'

'What?'

'What you asked me to tell him. That you were ill, and didn't want to see him.'

'Yes.' She paused in her spreading of marmalade on a piece of toast. 'Perhaps I should have spoken to him myself. Scotch marmalade? Can you buy that here?'

'Only at the Embassy commissariat.'

'Are all British subjects allowed to shop there?'

'I'm afraid not,' said Harold. 'You'll have to suck in with someone in the Embassy.'

'For the sake of Scotch marmalade?'

'And cornflakes. And English beer. And Scotch.'

'No, thank you. I read somewhere that women in purdah

often have bad complexions, owing to the lack of sunshine. Do you think that's true of Afghan women?'

It was, so that the Moffatts exchanged glances, like bridge partners surprised by consummate skill on the part of an opponent.

'Many of them do have poor complexions,' admitted Lan.

'And surely they must all lack – to use a good northern word – gumption? Otherwise surely they would have banded together to get rid of so ridiculous a convention. For of course that's all it is. There's nothing in the Koran which requires women's faces to be hidden. Mrs Mohebzada never wore a shaddry, did she?'

'No.'

'I'm surprised she stood out against it. I suppose hysteria would give her a kind of courage.'

Before Mrs Mohebzada arrived, Mrs Mossaour came, invited by Lan by telephone. As she walked towards the Moffatts' gate, she saw Paula Wint being set down outside it by Alan, dressed as a First Secretary, in a hurry to drive off to join the Ambassador at the airport in the diplomatic corps' reception of President Voroshilov.

A small, bare-bottomed, nomad boy with a skull cap of dusty faded gilt was tending three emaciated cows that grazed on the strips of grass along the ditch by the side of the road. Because of the way the warm breeze was blowing, a stench of human excrement came from the park, behind whose walls were the most public of lavatories. Paula, fresh from her husband's kiss, stood with her freckled nose wrinkled a little, as if entranced by the small shepherd's playing of his pipe. Under her wide straw hat adorned with red artificial flowers, and in a lavender-coloured dress, she looked beautifully at ease, as if this were an English lane in mid-summer, with cricket noises in the background. Yet, so voluptuous and pinkly plump, she did have too that nymphlike calmness and amplitude, which Harold Moffatt had once celebrated in a poem. But to Maud Mossaour she was always a brainless and conscienceless fool; purring like a served pet cat, yet with claws that could draw more bitter blood than Maud's own honester slashes.

Physically the two women were alike. To people who remarked on the resemblance, Paula might say, with a smile: 'Ah yes, but Maud's clever; she has had the sense to see that English looks like ours, so fair and pink, are insipid, unless set in contrast with the dark romantic handsomeness of the East, such as Pierre's.' Maud, on the other hand, would merely shrug her splendid shoulders, but inwardly she always made the same comment: 'The difference between me and Paula Wint is simple. Out of her white plump body have come two white plump children; out of mine two thin dark ones.'

Now, as they met outside the gate, Paula raised her hand languidly in greeting. It would not do, thought Maud, for the Head of Chancery's wife to have dark sweat patches under her arms. Hence in the heat of the sun this catlike economy of movement.

'Good morning, Maud,' she said. 'I often think how lucky you people are who live in town. Think of all the local colour we outcasts miss at the Embassy.'

Maud sniffed grimly.

'Yes, isn't it horrid? Alan's off to the airport to meet Voroshilov. So I thought I'd take the opportunity to come down and say hello to the famous Miss Johnstone. I believe she arrived yesterday.'

'Yes.'

'You were there to meet her?'

'Yes.'

Paula laughed. 'I know, Maud dear, you always contain your enthusiasm so admirably, but you're sounding positively discouraging.'

'I have made no comment.'

'Maud, you're absolutely in a cloud of comment. I can hardly see you for it. In what way has Laura fallen so far below your expectation?'

They watched an Afghan family go by, the husband in front holding his small son by the hand, the shaddried, red-bloomered wife a few paces behind, carrying a baby.

'You know,' said Paula, 'I've been here for two years and they're still as mysterious to me now as they were that first day I arrived. If you had judged me then, Maud, you would have found me, too, far below expectation. Of course, my dear, you have such frightfully high standards. What in Miss Johnstone has disappointed you so much? To tell you the truth, neither Alan nor I expected very much.'

No, hyenas never do, thought Maud; and then found herself feeding the female, which was the more gluttonous of the two.

'I did not expect her to have a limp,' she said. 'Apparently the Moffatts knew, but they did not tell me.'

'A limp? What do you mean? Has she hurt herself?'

'It's permanent, a legacy of poliomyelitis; but it's very slight. She's a good bit older than I expected. I saw a snapshot, but it must have been taken years ago. Her hair's gray.'

'Well, well. I am surprised.'

'And she has as much sexual attraction, I should say, as one of those cows.'

Paula turned and looked at the cows. 'Yes, I must say I am surprised. I mean, let's be frank about it, these Afghans are pretty sexy. It's not the first time I've had my behind pinched black and blue, not in the bazaar, mind you, but at some party given by the Prime Minister and attended by all their big men. It stands to reason, really. Aren't they shut off from women all their adolescent lives? And this fellow Wahab, from the little I've seen of him, struck me as true to type. You and I can tell, Maud, where women like little Lan, for instance, seem unable to: we have the right kind of apparatus for detecting repressed lusts. I felt when Wahab's nice brown eyes were on me that they were busy taking every stitch of clothing off.'

'Howard was at the airport, too.' Maud mentioned that, because she wondered if he had passed on to Paula that remark about Wahab.

'Yes, so he said. But he was maddeningly vague, and, now I come to think of it, rather gloomy. He said nothing about a limp. I believe Prince Naim was there too?'

'Yes, and rushed off in a great hurry as soon as he saw her.'

Paula laughed. 'Now I'm sure she's not as forbidding as all that, Maud dear. In any case, you know what they say about Naim. The most beautiful of us are of less interest to him than any chubby urchin in the bazaar.'

'According to Harold, Naim's been dreaming of her as some kind of goddess coming to give Afghanistan her blessing.'

This time Paula's laughter was hearty, showing her fine teeth and healthy gums. 'But Harold's a poet! Now when you have a conversation between a poet and a fairy, royal or not, you must look for goddesses. Between ourselves, though, I thought Harold was finding one goddess as much as he could cope with.'

She waited to see if Maud would offer anything about the Moffatts: a smirk, grunt, wink, or scrape of the broad sandal in the dust would have done. But Maud remained as inscrutable as the Sphinx in her husband's native land. No, of course that was wrong. Pierre was not a full-blooded wog; he was merely Lebanese. However, there was no need for Maud's or anyone else's confirmation as regarded the Moffatts; Paula's own verdict was so obviously true it needed no support. Lan, the fascinating little witch, was still beautiful, and as long as she was she would hold her fat poet; but God knew how many Helga Larsens he would be saving up, for the time when the lemon was wrinkled and sour and dry.

Maud at last rang the bell, and while they were waiting for it to be answered Moffatt's small green car turned into the road at the mosque end. They saw Mrs Mohebzada sitting beside him. When the car stopped it was only the latter who got out. Moffatt spoke to her, waved to the other two women, and at once drove off again.

Then Paula saw what always astonished and even worried her a little: Maud Mossaour's compassion for this small thin pale nail-biting whining red-haired ex-shopgirl. In Maud's place she herself would have been inclined to resent Mrs Mohebzada's letting the side down, the side being that rather large company of Western women married to Asiatics whose manners might be charming but whose seed was always dark or black. She had not yet seen Mrs Mohebzada's child and indeed wasn't sure whether it was male or female, but she did know it was particularly dark-skinned, like Maud's own. Therefore with such shared vulnerability Maud might have been expected to despise the creature for her whining advertisement of their common predicament, especially as it was by no means the headmistress's nature to be tolerant with fools. Besides, who would have looked for compassion in Maud, no matter to whom displayed? Yet here she was again, still being her own tall dignified self, and yet at the same time being friendly – no, that was too weak a word – loving almost to this silly common young creature so improbably and for that matter so improperly a mother.

It occurred to Paula that Maud had never tried to get Liz Mohebzada into the Sewing Circle at the Embassy, as she had done with Lan Moffatt several times. It hadn't been the inevitable refusal, either, that had held her back; no, it had evidently been the desire to protect the girl from what Paula now for an instant saw would have been stupid, ill-bred callousness.

She listened to Maud's inquiries about the baby, and to its mother's quiet happy replies; it was quite recovered now, thanks to the German doctor.

'I believe it was Prince Naim who sent him,' said Paula.

'Yes.'

And how in heaven's name had the King's son come to send the King's physician to the half-caste baby of an insignificant clerk? Again Paula had a feeling that life had left its confines and was ranging wildly and fiercely; but while she was as usual seeking some inanity with which to tame it again, she glanced up and saw on the terrace Lan Moffatt, serene as ever, and the new arrival Miss Johnstone, thin-ankled, and grotesque with a white ribbon tied in a bow in her graying hair.

'You must forgive me, Lan,' she called, as she went up the terrace steps. 'I'm afraid I'm butting in. You see, Alan had to go to the airport to help receive Voroshilov, so I thought I'd take the opportunity to come down and meet Miss Johnstone. If I'm in the way – I mean, if this was intended to be some kind of private conference – just say the word and I'll go off bazaaring.'

'Not at all, Paula. You are very welcome.'

With a skill and graciousness that any ambassador's wife would have envied, Lan made the introductions. Paula was introduced first, a stroke of courtesy she had not expected, and so her greeting of the schoolteacher from Manchester lacked the assurance of the latter's greeting of her. Later she had to admit to herself that she might well not have been able to match that brazen assurance, no matter how well-prepared she had been. In the first place, Miss Johnstone stood up and walked a step or two, just enough to show, with such brave pathos, her slight lameness, and so proudly forfeited her right to have remained seated; secondly, her small lean hand had a purposeful grip like a man's; and thirdly, she managed to convey in the few correct conventional words the impression of a sharp, vigilant intelligence.

Paula was certain she could never like her, but finding adequate reasons might be very fatiguing.

Toward Maud Mossaour Miss Johnstone was similarly brisk and capable, but when she turned to shake hands with Liz Mohebzada her smile grew visibly warmer and her handclasp was noticeably longer.

When she had them all seated Lan asked what they would like to drink. 'Tea? Coffee? Squash? Sherry? Beer?'

'Squash, please,' said Maud. 'Grapefruit, if you have it.'

'Squash, please,' whispered Mrs Mohebzada, shy as a child among grown-ups.

'Me too,' said Paula, 'with a dash of gin in it, if you don't mind, Lan, please.'

'Would it be too much trouble,' asked Laura, 'if I had tea? I understand it is the drink of the country.'

Somehow, thought Paula, no remark could have been more ominous.

'Not at all,' replied Lan. She gave the orders to her servant, who had been waiting for them with a great grin. It wasn't every day his terrace was filled with white women, two of them at least so well worth sleeping with.

'Did you have a pleasant journey, Miss Johnstone?' asked Paula.

'Yes, thank you. But I was glad to arrive.'

'Yes, travelling can be so beastly exhausting, can't it?'

'It wasn't that. You see, I felt I was coming home.'

Then, while Paula was flicking her nose in patrician surprise, Liz Mohebzada burst into tears. She turned her head away, she covered her face with her freckled hands, she tried to control herself; but the weeping went on, and the thin body in the faded green and white dress shook. She kept trying to say something in explanation and apology, but all

Paula could make out was the word home, embarrassingly reiterated. (She remembered then how Colonel Rodgers months ago used to go about the Embassy murmuring that someone ought to do something about getting up a subscription to pay Mrs Mohebzada's fare home. That had been before the baby's arrival; now of course it was too late. In any case no one had got up the subscription.)

Maud had arisen and stood by the girl, with a hand on her red hair.

Even Lan did not know what to do, but Paula had to concede her helplessness was patient and becoming.

Miss Johnstone, well aware of her responsibility, did not get up; she sat leaning forward a little, with an eager-stranger expression on her face; it did not lack sympathy, but neither did it avoid condemnation. Paula was reminded of a Russian film she had seen here, in Kabul. In it there had been a woman judge who had looked at the prisoner, a girl accused of strangling her own baby, with this very expression. Paula had been impressed then, against her will, and now she was reluctantly impressed again. It was doubtless true, as Maud had said, that Miss Johnstone was without sexual attraction, but she seemed quite capable of discovering and using efficiently some substitute for it. What such a substitute could possibly be Paula refused even to think about. But into her mind for a moment strayed a sympathy for Wahab; next moment of course she chased it out again, but its intrusion left its mark.

Mrs Mohebzada had recovered sufficiently to mumble apologies and turn sobs to long sighs.

'I'm sorry,' said Miss Johnstone, 'I used that word. In the circumstances it was inconsiderate of me. But, you know, Mrs Mohebzada, there is in England today such a materialism, selfishness, smug contentment, and disgusting disregard for the millions in the world not so fortunate, that it was for me personally no hardship to leave; on the contrary,

it was a relief. I think I have already got rid of a great deal of
my own share of the guilt. I realize I shall have to work hard
to get rid of the rest, but I mean to try.'

The effect of that brief speech, delivered so solemnly, was
so shattering that it hurled into Paula's heart a sister feeling
for Mrs Mohebzada. For it was the latter who, while Maud
sneered, screamed in the defence of her fellow countrymen.
Paula could hardly make out what she said – the vulgar
London accent being exaggerated by anger – but she was
obviously claiming that the English were in every way far
more humane than the Afghans. Paula cried: 'Hear, hear!' At
the end, perhaps out of breathlessness, perhaps from inspiration, Mrs Mohebzada achieved an extraordinary calmness and lucidity. 'I've been told, Miss Johnstone,' she said,
'that this man you're going to marry is a politician. In this
country politicians become rich, if they're not shot.'

Miss Johnstone smiled as one might to a distracted child.
'You are mistaken, my dear. Or you have been misinformed.
My fiancé is a schoolmaster.'

'He's been made principal of his school.'

'And why not? He has excellent qualifications.'

'Qualifications don't matter here. He's one of the Brotherhood. They have the support of the Russians. Everyone
says either they'll seize the country, or they'll all be shot.'

To Paula's amazement Miss Johnstone then reached
forward to try and take the younger woman's hand; that
it was snatched away did not discomfit or annoy her. 'You
ought not to listen to envious rumours, my dear,' she said. 'I
am sure I know Abdul Wahab better than anyone. Yes, he
has faults, as we all have. But he is as good a person as I have
ever met. He is utterly devoted to his country. If he does
enter politics and accepts a position of trust and authority, it
will be for the public good.'

'That's what they all say,' retorted Mrs Mohebzada. 'Did
you expect him to tell you he was in it for what he could get

out of it? You'll learn that Afghans only tell the truth when it
suits them.'

'I am sorry to find you so cynical, Mrs Mohebzada. I am
proud to say I trust Abdul Wahab, and I hope to be at his
side to support him.'

For about the third time Paula noticed an exchange of
glances between Lan and Miss Johnstone; Lan's was
amused and quizzical, Miss Johnstone's haughty and defiant. Was it possible that what the latter was now saying
so high-mindedly was a contradiction of what she had
been saying previously in private, before Paula and the
others had arrived? Had not Alan, usually so perspicacious, come to the conclusion that this Johnstone woman
must be a Communist of some kind? Otherwise why
should she be so discontented with her own country as
to leave a good position in it to come here to poverty-
stricken Afghanistan? There could be no doubt now that
he had been right.

Maud Mossaour, provoked by the distress of her proté-
gée, was openly antagonistic: 'I notice, Miss Johnstone, you
say you hope to be at his side.'

'That is so.'

'You are adhering to your original plan then, of regarding
your stay here as experimental, to begin with?'

'Yes. I take it you have some purpose in asking these
questions?'

'Yes, I have. As headmistress of the International School I
have put your name down as a possibility for next session's
staff. That, I take it, is your wish?'

'Yes. I wrote you to that effect.'

'Exactly. I make the appointments, but they have to be
confirmed by a Board of Advisers. I doubt if they would
confirm yours if you were married to an Afghan.'

'Indeed? Will someone tell me what the name of this
country is in which we are sitting at this moment?'

'I'll tell you its name,' cried Mrs Mohebzada. 'It's called Hell!' And she began to weep again.

'The point is this, Miss Johnstone,' went on Maud: 'If you marry Mr Wahab you will become an Afghan subject.'

'Proudly so, I assure you.'

'Surely you'll try to retain your British nationality too?' interposed Paula. 'I understand Mr Gillie, the consul, always advises that should be done.'

'What good did it do me?' sobbed Mrs Mohebzada.

'The Afghans demand that the wife of one of their nationals must make a declaration forfeiting her original nationality,' said Maud.

'There will be no need to demand in my case, if I do marry Abdul Wahab.'

'Miss Johnstone,' said Paula, 'I really must protest against these insinuations.'

'What insinuations, Mrs Wint? I am merely saying that if I marry Abdul Wahab I shall most willingly accept his nationality, just as I shall accept his country's poverty. By so doing I may, it appears, lose whatever opportunity I might otherwise have had of buying Scotch marmalade out of the Embassy shop; but this is a sacrifice I am quite prepared to make.'

While Paula gasped, Maud pressed on coolly with her point: 'What I am trying to make clear to you is that the Afghans will probably not allow one of their nationals to teach at our school. At present they allow no Afghan child to attend it.'

'If I become an Afghan, Mrs Mossaour, is it not more likely that I should wish to teach in an Afghan school?'

Maud smiled, astonishing Paula who had thought her worsted in this swordplay of wills. 'You are very wise, Miss Johnstone, to keep reminding us, and yourself, that it is all conditional.'

'I must suggest, Mrs Mossaour, that you are now trespassing on what is private between myself and my fiancé. However, let me add this. Mrs Moffatt, I believe, will confirm its truth. I keep saying if because I am not convinced that I am worthy to be Abdul Wahab's wife.'

Paula was startled by the adjective into remembering the Langfords. Not that either of them of course had ever admitted such unworthiness. But for some reason their predicament flashed into her mind: each in his or her own way so intelligent and charming, yet together creators of hell. She even felt sorry for Miss Johntone then, but it seemed so superfluous a pity that she almost apologized aloud for it.

'I hope none of you think,' said Liz Mohebzada then, 'that I hate my husband.'

God, cried Paula within, this must be the end. Even if I do get my behind pinched again, better walking about the bazaar then sitting here listening to this craziness.

She rose therefore, with the kind of gestures she made when practising in front of the mirror for the time when Alan would be an ambassador. She felt herself blushing as her composure fell to pieces like a blown rose.

'I must really be going,' she said. 'I was right at first, you know, Lan. This was intended to be a private conference. I'm sorry I butted in. Still, it has been very interesting. May I wish you success, Miss Johnstone, in whatever it is you wish to do. I must say, though, I'm not sure what it is! And I hope your dear little baby gets better soon, Mrs Mohebzada.'

'He is better, Mrs Wint.'

'Yes, of course. So you told me. I am so glad. Good morning, Maud. You and Pierre must come to visit us soon. No, Lan, really there is no need to see me to the gate.'

Nevertheless she hoped Lan would, not because there was anything to be said between them, but because she needed reassurance; any sympathetic human company would have done.

Lan, however, took her at her word. 'I am sorry you could not stay longer, Paula,' she said. 'Please give my regards to Alan.'

'Thank you, I will.'

At the gate, which the grinning servant held open for her, she turned anxiously to wave to the four women on the terrace. They had already, it seemed, forgotten her. She must have waved four times before one of them, Mrs Mohebzada it was, noticed her and waved back. The others turned too and waved, but briefly, impatiently almost, as if they wanted her to hurry away and let them concentrate on what mattered to them far more. She suspected she was being unfair to them and to herself, but she could not help it. Her loneliness then was so acute that even Alan's presence would scarcely have alleviated it. As for her own children, Annette and Paul, whom she loved as much as Mrs Mohebzada did her child, she found herself wondering if they really did exist, far away in England.

Outside the gate she felt as if she had stepped inside a great beast's hot stinking mouth. Behind her dark glasses she gasped for breath. Sweat poured down her face and body like shame; she was almost lame with its damp clinging indignities. She should have sent Lan's servant for a taxi; now she would have to walk along until she found one.

The little herd-boy, who had been dozing in the ditch, woke up, shouted to her, and waltzed beside her, playing his pipe merrily. When he shot out his small dusty paw for money, she had no will to order him away; instead she took a few coins out of her handbag and flung them behind her on the road, as one might buy off an importunate dog with a biscuit. Down on his haunches indeed he went and hopping in the dust picked up the money. She saw his little naked testicles, so like a dog's, and she felt sick. Who was it had said, that after all the poetry, all the religion, all the grand spouting about humanity, it came just to these?

Walking slowly with her thighs sticking together with sweat and the stench from the park almost noisy in her nostrils, she tried to remember who had said that. Not the Ambassador, fond though he was of such songs as 'The Ball of Kirriemuir'. Not Alan, for whom poetry, religion, and humanity were all concentrated in his love for her, so gloriously sexual. Not Bob Gillie, a prig who wore silk underwear, married to a prude who wore cotton. Not Howard, despite his liking for bizarre quotations from Ezra Pound. Not the Colonel, who, as Alan and she had agreed, probably approached the conjugal bed, like one of his own model guardsmen, with sterile rigidity. Not John Langford, who had slept apart from Helen for years and who surely, in his monk's bed, had learned there was more to life than the means of procreation. And none of the junior staff would have had the impudence to refer seriously to sex in her presence. Who then could it have been?

She wondered why she should be sweating so much. Had she contracted some horrible Asiatic fever? The heat was considerable, but not any more so than yesterday when she had spent a delightful day in her garden, sipping iced beer and reading an Agatha Christie. Those damned women must have done it; how, she did not know; but any one of them, and especially the Johnstone creature, could set up as a witch.

I'm being silly, she thought, as she stood opposite the mosque, waiting for a taxi. A ghoddy came along and she almost took it, although Alan, fearful for her precious bones, had forbidden her ever to travel on one. An aeroplane began to be heard, at first as a faint whirr, then in a minute or two as a hum, loudening suddenly to a roar. Glittering beautifully, it passed low overhead, gliding down toward the airport. It had four engines and its silvery wings bore red Russian emblems; it was the aeroplane from Russia, bringing Voroshilov.

As it disappeared beyond some trees she returned to wondering who it was that could have uttered that terrible yet pregnant remark. Could it have been a woman? She tried to think of any likely; there was none; no woman, not even a whore like Helga Larsen, would ever admit herself shrunk to a mere counter-contrivance. Had she read it in a book? That wasn't likely, either, as she seldom read anything but detective stories. Was it possible that no one had said it, and nowhere could it be read? That the thought had never occurred to anyone before until it had occurred to her, watching that little boy crawl about like a dog? Or was it a thought that ultimately came to everyone, but which no one divulged, out of horror and shame?

At that very moment Voroshilov was probably meeting the King and the other dignitaries, among whom was Alan. How impressive and dignified every one of them would be. Saner surely to think about them than about that obscene child with his begging fist and dreary pipe!

Twenty-Four

EVEN if there had been no regulation requiring the Principal's presence in the school for two or three hours per day during most holidays, Wahab would still have gone there, this Jeshan time, as the only place where he would be able to find peace and stimulus enough to enable him, amidst his many anxieties, to drive on with his translation of a physics textbook from English into Persian. His desk covered with scribbled papers, dictionaries, and science reference books, he worked steadily and quite happily, with now and then a sigh, manfully elevated to a rueful smile, or a glance out of the window at the empty playground. His groin was still so sore and tender that once or twice when he involuntarily jumped with pleasure at some felicitous piece of translation, he gasped too a little, with pain. Only Sadruddin the custodian, Nawaz the clerk, and the old bearded janitors, were in the college with him. Maftoon as deputy-principal ought to have been, but he had telephoned to say that he had other more important work to do. He did not say what it was, and from his mysterious tone it might have been simply to play at bears with his three infants, or again it might have been to assist the Brotherhood in its present desperate intrigues. Now that Voroshilov had arrived with promises of millions of rubles, those who believed that their country's only chance of quick economic salvation lay in absorption by Russia recognized that here, with Jeshan or Independence Day so close at hand, was an opportunity to win over a multitude of supporters. Maftoon indeed had sounded surprised that Wahab should choose to hide himself away in the college, at such an exciting moment in the history of their country.

So, convinced that he had deservedly lost Laura, and that his tenure of the Principalship would soon be ended, he found consolation and a little forgetfulness in struggling to give science an Afghan look. Sometimes, however, remembering, he would get up and slowly walk along the corridors. Without the boys' bright faces to light them up the rooms were dismal, with the mud floors worn away, the walls discoloured by winter damp that had seeped through the mud roof, the glass in most of the windows broken or missing, the desks and benches crude and ugly, the blackboards rough and spiky with nails, and the teachers' chairs with broken spars or loose legs or missing seats. In England and other enlightened countries, he knew, prisons were more comfortable; but as he moved among the desks, placing his hand on them as if on the heads of the pupils who in term-time sat there, he was far from feeling contempt or despondency; no, what he felt was love and hope. As a member of the Brotherhood, as a guest at the International Club, as a friend of Prince Naim's, or as a colleague of Dr Habbibullah's, he had been a ridiculous fraud. No wonder the boys had been provoked to laughter by his boasts. With the unclouded wisdom of the young they had seen through him. But then, had he not always seen through himself, obtuse with stupidity, self-deception, and conceit though he had been so often? As a humble teacher, though, he did not think he was ridiculous.

He was back in his office, working away, when a commotion at the gate attracted his attention. Really, boys had been gathering there for the past hour, but he had hardly noticed them. Now, however, they came surging through the gate, no doubt having bribed its keeper to unlock it for them, and across the playground, at least a hundred of them. Groaning, he thought that here was another rebellion. This time they had come to burn down the school or to drag him out and pelt him with soft plums which they had bought cheap in the bazaar. He noticed Rasouf in their midst, and other Twelfth-Class boys, including the cheerful Farouq, who liked to cycle into town with him. He could not believe they were his enemies. Then he saw that they were carrying an enormous bouquet of flowers.

As he sat wondering whether to wait modestly or go down boldly to find out what it was all about, the telephone rang. He had to clear papers and books to get at it. Hoping it might be Laura he picked it up; but his eager smile instantly changed to a timid frown when the voice of Dr Habbibullah crackled harshly in his ear.

'Good morning, Wahab.'

'Good morning, Excellency.'

It was right of course to show the man, or rather his position, proper respect, but surely this tremor of subservience was ignoble, especially as the boys were now tramping up the stairs, shouting his name triumphantly?

'Maftoon was telling me you had some trouble yesterday.'

'Did he say *I* had the trouble?'

'Yes.'

'Let me tell you then that what trouble there was he provoked it by sending for the police. However, the matter was settled intelligently.'

'By you?'

'Yes. Yes, I think I am entitled to say so; but I should add I had the support of the boys.'

Habbibullah grunted, in surprise as much as in anger. 'I want to have a talk with you, Wahab. I find I can spare a few minutes this afternoon, at four sharp. Here, at my office.'

'As you wish, Excellency.' Wahab's voice was a little hoarse with nervousness, but it was bold too, for outside the office the boys were calling on him to come out.

'What's that noise?' asked the Minister. 'I understood the boys were on holiday.'

'So they are. It seems they have come to offer me some flowers.'

'Flowers? What for?'

'I do not know yet, sir, but I think in appreciation, which is usually the reason why flowers are offered. Please listen.' He held out the telephone as far as the flex would reach, with the mouthpiece towards the door.

'How many are there?'

'Hundreds, as you can hear. I think, sir, it is the most hopeful sign of all that our youth is so ready to applaud honesty and fairness, and to condemn corruption and in-justice. Do you not agree?'

Habbibullah grunted. 'I shall expect you at four.'

'I shall be there, Excellency.'

A slight pause. 'Come alone, Wahab.'

'Of course.' Wahab smiled. The Minister was alarmed lest he should march to the meeting escorted by hundreds of singing boys.

Replacing the telephone, with a tiny spit of disdain at it, he rose, knocked some pencil shavings off his jacket, and limped boldly towards the door. The key wasn't in the padlock as it ought to have been. He looked on the floor below, where the hole in the carpet was like a nest of lost keys; but when he stooped stiffly to investigate he found only cigarette-ends, spent matches, and a toothpick. The boys were now banging on the door, assuring him they were there in friendliness, and urging him to come out and receive a surprise.

He shouted as gaily as he could that he had mislaid the key, but they were making such a din themselves they couldn't hear him. He searched his pockets; it wasn't there. Wildly, he thought of getting out by the window, but the drop was at least twenty feet and he would be sure to break a leg. Now the boys were attributing his non-appearance to modesty, and their acclamations grew even warmer but he knew that if he did not soon appear all this generous emotion in their hearts might be driven out by disappointment and exasperation. Smiling, but whimpering too a little, he rushed about, looking on chairs, sofa, and the table, where at last, under his papers he found it. By which time he was so nervous he could hardly insert it into the small hole.

Outside, the landing and stairs were crowded. What struck him first, even before the wonderful friendliness on their faces, was the fact that the air was richly fragrant. Yet so few of them had baths in their houses. It was the flowers, of course. Grown in Afghan soil, they sweetened not only the air here and now, but the whole future. It was an enormous bouquet, as he now saw. Rasouf was almost hidden behind it.

When they saw him they cheered, clapped, whistled, and laughed.

He held up his hands. 'Why is this?' he cried. 'Is it not a holiday? It is strange for boys to come to school during a holiday.'

He noticed some laughing involuntarily as they heard how cautious his voice had to be because of his sore lip, but it was the kind of laughter that did not detract from their homage, but rather made it more human and acceptable.

Rasouf was pushed forward with the flowers. His stern young face peeped out from among them.

'Sir,' he cried, 'we have heard that you are going to marry an Englishwoman, who has arrived in Kabul. Please give these flowers to her, with our best wishes.'

From the shrieks and whistles of approval that broke out then it was obvious that they looked upon his acquiring of an English wife as the culminating stroke in his courageous defiance of what in their country's laws enraged them most: this having to pay for a wife, exorbitantly for a pretty one, dearly for a passable one, and excessively even for one ugly and ill-tempered.

He could not help catching a glimpse of himself through their admiring eyes. Unhappily he knew what they did not; that having jumped on her like a jowey dog, with slavering lust instead of love, he had been justly punished by losing her.

Yet there was nothing he could do but take the flowers. They filled his arms and tickled his swollen nose. Treacherously, they reminded him, not of Laura, but of Mrs Wint, wife of the British Head of Chancery, who had smelled like them and had hair like these yellow ones.

'This is very kind of you, boys,' he cried, with tears in his eyes.

Rasouf's eyes were dry and stern. 'Sir, I have been asked on behalf of the whole school to assure you that if they try to dismiss you for what happened yesterday we will all go on strike.'

It was only then that Wahab realized Dr Habbibullah's purpose in sending for him must indeed be to warn him he was going to be dismissed. Prince Naim was still Minister of Education, but for days he had not been at his office; in any case even if he wished to take Wahab's part he would not dare oppose Habbibullah and the latter's friends, who were said to include more than half of the Cabinet.

About to appeal to the boys not even to think of striking, Wahab thought again; in the meantime he gagged himself, as it were, with the flowers. Why should they not strike in such a cause? Yesterday when he had endured the policemen's brutality, he had not merely been Abdul Wahab, their Principal. He had been the representative of decency and justice; these were qualities worth striking for. That they had been embodied in him was incidental.

'Thank you, boys,' he cried, and then let his enthusiasm run away with him again. 'You and I have given each other strength and courage. I am now engaged in translating into Persian an English textbook. It is the first, but in a year or two there will be many others; and in less than ten years you will see in our land the most up-to-date achievements of science, not for destructive purposes, but to create wealth and happiness for all.'

Though they remained cheerful and well-disposed, many were openly sceptical. Even as they pressed forward to shake his hand they were shaking their heads too, in amusement at what they evidently considered his ingenuousness.

What, he wondered, is going to happen to a country whose youth are merry and cynical?

Ten minutes later they had all gone from the landing. His hand was numbed with shaking theirs. He could hear them laughing below in the hall and out in the playground. Some let out occasional cries, as of agony. He thought he knew why; like his own, their ideals were starving.

He spent a few minutes in arranging the flowers in the water jar. Then, after further hesitation, he lifted the telephone and dialled Moffatt's number.

Luckily it was Moffatt himself who answered. Had it not been he had been going to pretend he was someone else, with the wrong number.

'Mr Moffatt, this is Abdul Wahab.'

'Oh, good morning.'

'Please do not let anyone know it is I.'

'I'll do my best, but you know what women are.'

Wahab smiled sadly. 'I have a favour to ask of you, Mr Moffatt.'

'If I can, I'll be pleased to oblige.'

'Some boys have just brought flowers for Laura. I do not know how they found out about her; certainly I did not tell them. The flowers are very beautiful.' As he glanced at them he had the feeling that Moffatt must be smelling their fragrance, too. 'But, of course, as you know, it is all ended

between Laura and me, owing to my bestiality.' He imagined he heard Moffatt chuckle, but decided he must have
been mistaken. 'Nevertheless, I would like to send her these
flowers. Because the boys gave them they represent something important to me. What I want you to tell me – please,
be frank – is whether in your opinion I ought to send them
to her. I do not with to make matters worse. Even flowers
cannot remedy insult.'

'Send them. She'll be delighted.'

'Ah, you are just saying so to cheer me up.'

This time Moffatt did laugh. 'No, I mean it. I don't think
she's as much insulted as you fear.'

'But she must be.' Wahab felt indignant. Surely any
respectable woman would have been grievously insulted
by what he had done to Laura. True enough, afterwards
she had asked him to kiss her, but that must have been
nervous reaction.

'As a matter of fact, Wahab, I've been going to ring you
and suggest that you pay us a surprise visit.'

'To your house, do you mean?'

'Yes.'

'Is Laura still with you?'

'Yes. She's out at the moment, visiting the bazaars with
Lan.'

'Is she well enough?'

'Very well. In fact, remarkably well.'

Wahab frowned, distrusting Moffatt's chuckle. 'But she
was ill yesterday.'

'She's quite recovered. Yes, come along, and bring the
flowers.'

'You guarantee it will be all right?'

'I can hardly do that. Would you expect me to where a
woman in love's concerned?'

'You think she is in love?'

'Formidably.'

'Formidably?'

Moffatt laughed. 'You know what I mean.'

'I'm afraid I do not. You meant she is in love with me?'

'Who else?'

Wahab was about to consider possible rivals, when he realized its folly. 'But I do not understand why you should say formidably.'

'Well, you know Laura.'

'Yes, I think I can say I do know her.'

'Well then!' Again Moffatt laughed. 'I'm sorry, Wahab. I'm joking. But be sure to come.'

'When?'

'As soon as you can. Today, sometime.'

'I have an appointment at four.'

'Come at five then.'

'It is with Dr Habbibullah, the Minister of Justice.'

'In that case you'd better come at three. I've heard that people sometimes disappear after interviews with that gentleman.'

'You must not believe all you hear, Mr Moffatt. We may not be advanced industrially, but we are not quite in the Dark Ages legally.'

'Sorry.'

'I shall be pleased to come at five o'clock. I shall bring the flowers.' He had been working it out: he could hire a taxi to take him to Habbibullah's office; it could wait for him there, and afterwards take him to Moffatt's house. 'You are quite sure Laura is willing to see me?'

'Much more than willing.'

'I do not understand.' Two things really he didn't understand: first, why Laura should be willing to see him, and secondly, why Moffatt should be so eager to bring them together again. Before her arrival had not the fat Englishman been bitterly determined to keep them apart? Could it be that, after meeting her, he had decided that that was all she was worth, to marry an Afghan? Wahab found his tongue stumbling as he said: 'I assure you, I deserve only her displeasure. How can she forgive me when I find it impossible to forgive myself?'

There was a pause. 'Apparently that's a trick that can be done,' said Moffatt, with the banter gone from his voice. Next moment it was back again, but not so lightheartedly. 'She's been telling everybody she's got only one doubt in her mind.'

Of course, Wahab remembered, he too insulted his wife. Is that why he now sounds so strangely like a man under sentence of forgiveness? He has hinted that my Laura is a strong-willed woman; so she is, but not any more so, I fancy, than his own sweetly smiling small-breasted wife.

'And what doubt is that, Mr Moffatt?' he asked.

'She feels she may not be worthy of you.'

Wahab's eyes, bright for a moment, suddenly clouded. It had occurred to him that Moffatt, with Laura its instigator, was taking part in a plot to entice him to the house, there to be submitted to a punishment considered appropriate. Other men of the British community, such as Howard Winfield and Gillie the Consul and Langford the gin-drinker would be there too, lying in wait. He recalled stories he had read of American Negroes being castrated for having had intercourse with white women. Well, painfully suscep-tible though he was at present, owing to his bruised and swollen groin, he would courageously walk into their trap.

'I shall bring the flowers,' he said.

'By all means.'

'And the card. The English on it is rather quaint.'

'The quainter the better.'

Yet would Laura in the present circumstances see the humour of a card on which Rasouf, or someone with as little English, had written: 'nice gretings to or principul's wiv toby'?

'I know over a telephone's a cowardly way of apologizing,' said Moffatt.

Wahab frowned. 'I may be a coward,' he said. 'But I am not apologizing at the moment.'

'No, I am. I don't think I've ever properly apologized for throwing the whisky at you.'

Wahab felt his eyes smart and water. But was not self-pity the Afghans' whisky, that rotted their self-respect?

'You did apologize,' he said stiffly.

'Yes, but it was a bloody insult, the way I did it.'

'I do not expect a man to drop on his knees before me, Mr Moffatt. If your previous apology was sincere, then let us hear no more about it.'

'But it wasn't. So I'm trying again. Other things happened that night that I'll never forgive myself for.'

Wahab's heart went warm. His suspicion of a plot to capture and castrate him was madness. Moffatt's invitation, like his present apology, was sincere. Human life was short, and so much in it was inadequate, why therefore belittle what was good, such as friendship? Besides, he and Moffatt were in a way the victims of women.

'Let us be friends,' he said.

'Why not?' replied the Englishman.

'Some day I shall tell you something,' said Wahab, with a chuckle. He meant his having had Moffatt's expulsion in his pocket.

'Fine. In the meantime I'll not tell Laura you're coming. We'll keep it as a surprise.'

Suspicion wriggled again. 'Is there any special reason why she should not be told?'

'None. I just thought she'd prefer it that way.'

'Ah, of course,' cried Wahab, with enthusiasm. 'By all means let us keep it as a surprise. There I shall be, with the flowers. What will she say? What will she do?' He could not speak for laughing.

At the other end Moffatt was laughing, too. 'Good. Till five then.'

'Good-bye, Mr Moffatt, and thank you very much.'

Still laughing Wahab put down the telephone. In front of him the mathematical symbols which he had written were beautiful, and when he turned his head there were the flowers, beautiful too. He remembered the afternoon in the Prince's garden when he had picked flowers for Laura and then had let them drop to the green grass because their very loveliness had convinced him that she was not as far away as England merely, but as death. Now she was not only in Kabul, but in life, waiting to be surprised by him.

He was interrupted by a knock on the door. In poked Sadruddin's shaven head and gray corpse-like face, looking as if he'd just come from a vigil without food and water in a holy man's tomb among the dusty mountains. Thus he had looked when protecting his microscopes and maps, or when some boy had lost a jotter.

'Abdul Wahab,' he croaked, scratching at his bony chest as if about to rip out his heart and throw it into the world's face.

'Yes, Sadruddin. What is it?'

'There is someone downstairs to see you.'

'A woman?' Wahab almost leaped to his feet. Had Laura come to surprise him?

'Worse than a woman. An American.'

'I don't know any Americans.' That was not quite true, but certainly he knew none likely to come visiting him here in the school.

'We should have dogs to drive off such people.'

'Don't be ridiculous, Sadruddin.'

'An American!' Into the word Sadruddin squeezed years of envy, wonder, suspicion, hate, and scorn. 'They come here and live like rich men, with large cars. It is our money they spend. They say here is help for Afghanistan, and put it back into their own pockets.'

'This is silly bazaar gossip, Sadruddin. The Americans are the most generous people in the world.'

'This one's in disguise, Abdul Wahab. Take care. He did not come in a large car; he came on a ghoddy. And he has not shaved for three days.'

'Please go down and tell the gentleman to come up.'

'I think he has a gun in his pocket. They are saying in the bazaar that the Americans are willing to pay a million afghanis to anyone who will shoot Voroshilov the Russian.'

'What nonsense!'

'They are saying too that at the Jeshan parade tomorrow there will be hundreds hoping to win the prize. I know a man with a gun; he says he may try.'

Then behind Sadruddin was heard a voice, apologetic and a little hoarse, but unmistakeably American: 'Sorry if I'm butting in, but I thought maybe I'd be forgotten again. That's been tried on me so often this past week I guess you'll overlook my suspiciousness.'

Sadruddin slunk quickly in and stood behind an armchair, to get away from this ogre about to enter. But in came wearily a small, thin, sad-faced man in grubby, pink shirt and filthy, light-green trousers. Wahab recognized him as Bolton the author who had been in Afghanistan for nearly two years writing a book about the country; he was a friend of Moffatt's. There were rumours his book was full of lies and misrepresentations, especially about the position of women.

'Name's Bolton, Josh Bolton,' said the visitor.

'Please sit down, Mr Bolton.'

'Don't mind if I do. I've been on my feet for days. The roads are packed with folk walking in for Jeshan. I was talking to a family from Sarobi; that's more than a hundred miles away. But I've been walking farther than that, Mr Wahab, in circles.'

As he sank with a sigh into an armchair he gave a glance

first at the flowers in the corner and then at the papers and books on the table.

'You writing a book?' he asked, with a grin more ghastly even than the one with which Sadruddin now crept out of the room. 'If you are, I suggest you turn the key in that padlock.'

'I am translating a physics book into Persian. There is no need for secrecy.'

Bolton tried to show interest, but it disintegrated on his face in the midst of a sudden yawn. 'I guess you're wondering why I'm here?' He picked up the brief case he had brought in with him; he used only his little finger crooked round the handle. 'I couldn't have done that four days ago.'

'Have you been ill, Mr Bolton?'

'Four days ago this bag was fat as a cow due to calve.' He smiled with wan pride at the sad felicity. 'It calved all right.'

Wahab wondered if his visitor was ill or wrong in the head. Or was his wife pregnant? No, he did not have a wife. Worse then, his mistress? Or had she died in childbirth? American women of course wouldn't send even their dogs into Kabul maternity hospital. But that was not snobbish so much as prudent. If Laura ever was going to have a child, she too would stay at home or else fly to Delhi; that was to say, if they could afford the doctor's fees or the fare.

Meantime his visitor had been resting, with eyes closed.

'I am afraid, Mr Bolton,' said Wahab, 'I do not understand. In the first place, I am not a veterinarian.'

Without opening his eyes Bolton touched his brow in flaccid salute at what he took to be a witticism. 'Maybe it'll take a veterinarian at that,' he said. 'Those, sir, are very fragrant flowers. An offering from your pupils?'

'Yes.'

Bolton with a struggle got his eyes open. 'Mr Wahab, sir, for eighteen months I've been in your hospitable country writing a book about it.'

Wahab frowned. 'Did you come here solely for that reason?'

'Why else? It's my profession. Last country I did was Thailand. Nepal was to be next on the list.'

'Is it possible to achieve the necessary sympathy by that method, Mr Bolton?'

'I got bags of sympathy. Too much. I like people. I'm prejudiced in their favour before I ever see them. To be frank, with one exception: if a man's a Commie, I know he's a bastard, and I'm prepared to treat him as such. But sympathy's easy for me. I've been run out of a town in my own United States for showing too much sympathy; to the blacks.'

'So in your book your portrayal of us is sympathetic?'

'You're using the wrong tense. It *was* sympathetic. It's a thing of the past. Book, notes, sympathy, the whole damned lot are gone.'

Again Wahab suspected weakmindedness. 'I don't understand.'

'That's right. I haven't explained it to you yet. I keep forgetting, because I guess you're practically the only English-speaking Afghan I haven't explained it to. And I've been given the order to go; quick and sudden. Tonight at midnight my permit expires. And tomorrow's the big day here. Maybe history will be made. Maybe some guy will take a shot at Voroshilov. Maybe Habbibullah and his Russian pals are going to jump. But I'll not be here to see it. If you take a peek out of that window you'll see a couple of buddies of mine.'

Wahab smiled uneasily, but did not turn and look.

'Sure, you know. It's not news to you. They've been on my tail for four days now. If you're wondering why my Embassy has done nothing to help me, then I'll let you into a secret: that bunch doesn't know their own asses from a monkey's elbow. When you go to talk to them you've got to dig their heads out of the sand first; and then you find their ears are still full of it. Trouble is, they've made up what they call their minds that your country, Mr Wahab, is already halfway down the bear's throat. All right, maybe so it is, but it's not too late to take a good firm grip of its tail and haul it up again. And that, sir, is precisely what my book was, a good tight grip of your tail.'

'Do you see us as a wolf?'

Bolton ignored that rather wistfully put question. He again yawned. 'So I've come to you, Mr Wahab. Hal Moffett mentioned you as one of the new men here, one of Habbibullah's bright boys. Apart from that, who should I bump into in the street this very morning but Lan Moffatt and the little lady who, I understand, has come out to be Mrs Wahab.'

'You met Laura?'

'In person. Did you know you talk alike? Lancashire, I believe. I like it; it sounds honest.'

Wahab should have been pleased, but wasn't. There had been others in Manchester with that same accent but with blacker skins. Remembering them, and their thick lips and moist hopeful eyes, Wahab felt a spasm of hatred for the colour of his own skin; everything else could change, this never; his children too would inevitably be victims.

'If you could help me get back my book, Mr Wahab, I would be in your debt for life.'

'Has someone borrowed it,' asked Wahab coldly, 'and forgotten to return it?'

Bolton laughed. 'Oh, sure. That's a laugh. I'm not a rich man, sir, as one glance should tell you. My books haven't been best sellers yet. I'll let you into another secret. I've been so poor my Embassy sent for me once and suggested I get the hell out of it; you see, I was letting the States down by not wearing a clean shirt every day, and not driving about town in a big new Chevy. I told them that my dirty shirt and my ass wriggling on an Afghan bus seat were doing more for the States here than the whole goddamned Embassy and U.S.I.S. rolled into one. They weren't pleased.'

Wahab decided this disagreement among Americans was distasteful, and in any case none of his business. 'What happened to your book, Mr Bolton?'

'As you said, it was borrowed. By the chief of police. Yeah, seems the fat bastard came in person, but not in uniform, with half a dozen official thugs. They burst into my room at the hotel and took every bloody scrap of paper with writing on it. Even letters my mom wrote me. Even my budget calculations.'

'This is a serious accusation. Do you have proof?'

'About a hundred people saw them break in, but I guess that is not proof. Not here, it isn't.'

Wahab clasped his hands to keep them from trembling. That rage which had astonished him before was working up in him again. He had thought it safely extinct. But really, how could any man proud of his country and anxious for its good name hear of such barbarities and not feel such anger? Nevertheless, he strove to control, even to disguise it.

'I do not wish to condone what has been done,' he said, 'but is it not the case that you have been very indiscreet in your investigations?'

'What d'you mean?'

'Putting aside the question as to whether the shaddry is an anachronism or not, would you not agree that a people which preserve it might feel insulted at inquiries as to their sexual habits? I understand one of the things which you have tried hard to find out is the amount of prostitution that goes on here.'

'Why not, sir? People like to know these things. It's legitimate human curiosity. In Bangkok they used to let me visit the brothels to see for myself.'

'I am sorry, Mr Bolton, I cannot help you. It so happens

that I have an appointment with Dr Habbibullah this afternoon, but I think we shall have more important matters to
discuss than your book.'

Bolton said nothing, but for almost a minute sat in the
chair, his eyes closed; his mouth seemed full of vomit. Then
slowly he rose, and, picking up his brief case shuffled to the
door. 'I didn't come here expecting anything,' he said. 'I just
came because you were a human being I could talk about my
troubles to.'

Wahab had to clasp his hands still more tightly, though he
could already hear the bones cracking. 'I shall say this, Mr
Bolton,' he whispered, 'I agree you have a grievance.'

'Will you tell your boss Habbibullah that? Why should
you? You don't want the fat slug visiting you. I guess you're
going to have plenty of troubles without that. With a white
woman as your wife you're going to find things pretty tough
here in Kabul. I can read the signs. Once the veil's torn off,
there'll be a crusade to prove your native women are the best
in the world after all. Your prize will turn out to be a dud.'

Those remarks, unnecessarily malicious, reminded Wahab of a consideration that had already worried him. As an
Englishwoman teaching in an Afghan girls' school Laura
would be paid at Western rates, about five thousand afghanis per month; as his wife, and so an Afghan herself, she
would be paid at local rates, and would be lucky to get seven
hundred. Moreover, with the emancipation of the Afghan
women, many would want to become schoolteachers; these,
speaking the language, would get preference over her, in
spite of her much superior qualifications. The American's
way of expressing it had of course been bitter and spiteful,
but all the same it was very likely that Laura's value from the
financial and prestige points of view would fall. No honourable man, and certainly no repentant violator such as he,
could ever let such considerations influence him, but it
would not be human not to regret it a little, especially if

he were to resign from the Principalship or was dismissed from it.

Bolton was gone. Looking out of the window, Wahab saw him, a minute or so later, cross the playground and climb on to the ghoddy that was waiting for him outside the gate. The two policemen were already mounted on theirs, about twenty yards along the road; indeed, the two horses were neighing to each other. Bolton's driver cracked his whip, and off the horse galloped, with its hoofs striking sparks from the road. Holding on grimly, and bumping up and down, Bolton was carried off on an escorted journey that would in a few hours take him out of Afghanistan.

You are lucky, Mr Bolton, thought Wahab, remembering Manchester, London, Paris, Rome; and then, aware of his treachery, he shook his head, renouncing tears, and set to work on his translation. But it was at least three minutes before he could see clearly enough to be able to write.

In the taxi, on his way to the interview with Dr Habbibullah, Wahab with face among the flowers decided to think of himself neither as scientist nor poet, but simply as a man. As such he might grovel to Habbibullah, but then again he might defy the dictatorial Minister and his many uniformed thugs. The one reaction would be as human as the other; and indeed most human of all was this uncertainty as to which his would be.

Into his mind and out again, too, wayward as a butterfly, came fluttering the elusive, frail-winged thought that his final decision as to Laura herself was still to be made.

All the way to the heart of the city these human contracts or contradictions rather kept leaping to his mind. For instance, the taxi driver had pasted up on the cracked windscreen the coloured picture of an Indian actress, with breasts like melons about to roll out of a purple bag; yet the driver himself was thin and quite ugly, with a half-healed boil on the back of his neck. Then there were two donkeys making their water copiously under one of the triumphal arches. Along the streets decorated to celebrate freedom, brutal-faced policemen scowled and strutted. A large pink Buick car, no doubt belonging to one of Mr Bolton's rich compatriots, crept behind a camel cart in which were crouched a nomad family with all their belongings; those, in terms of money, were worth less than the horn which kept sounding so peevishly.

Yet the strange thing was that as the taxi, after the driver had anxiously made sure it was there Wahab really wanted to go, crept through the large, thickly guarded gates of the Ministry of Justice, Wahab did not feel cowed or depressed; on the contrary, he was elated by a sense of illimitable possibilities. All his sentimental hopes were surely realizable in a world of such shocking variety; his tears in fact were pearls. With fingers that fairly vibrated with anticipation he plucked off a flower and thrust it into his buttonhole. Since it was intended, partly, to represent Laura during the coming interview, he chose, instead of the showy yellow ones so reminiscent of Mrs Wint's hair, a small dark-red rose with faint scent and tiny sharp thorns.

The taxi driver objected to being asked to look after the rest of the flowers. He pointed out that the courtyard, the entrance, and the vestibule, were swarming with tough brutal policemen, every one of whom no doubt liked having a flower to twiddle in his fingers and hold to his nose. If they came forward and demanded flowers, did Wahab think he, the taxi driver, was going to protect them at the cost of a kicked behind or even punctured tyres?

'This happens to be the Ministry of Justice,' replied Wahab coldly, 'and these men are policemen, upholders of the law.'

The taxi driver agreed, with a great shudder.

'But you need not be afraid,' went on Wahab. 'They will not interfere with my flowers.'

He marched, or rather swaggered, in spite of his sore crotch, up to the entrance. There with authoritative forefinger he stopped a sergeant.

'I have an appointment with his Excellency,' he said.

The sergeant saluted, with a respect that spread all round and even reached the taxi.

'I should be obliged,' added Wahab, smiling just at the right moment, with just the right degree of friendliness, 'if no harm came to the flowers in the taxi. They are for my mother.'

'Yes, sir. Is the lady ill?'

'Very ill.'

'I offer you sympathy, sir. With God's help she will soon be better.'

'We are all in God's hands, sergeant.'

Then through the throng of saluting policemen he pushed and flung open the first door he saw in the hall. Several clerks were seated at work. 'I am looking for his Excellency's secretary,' he cried.

Instantly one sprang up and conducted him to an office a few doors along. There the secretary, a small, sneering man with a blue bow tie, was ready to lead Wahab to the Minister.

'His Excellency is waiting, Mr Wahab,' he said, with a respect that Wahab noted with relief. The sneer had worried him a little. Now he saw it had to do with the secretary's own troubles.

The part of the building where the Minister's office was had carpets everywhere, even here and there on the walls, which were of green marble. The soldiers standing discreetly about the corridors wore new uniforms and their boots were polished; the bayonets on their rifles gleamed, as did their eyes with a kind of sinister intelligence. Nevertheless they gazed on Wahab with submissiveness.

Dr Habbibullah was seated at an enormous desk that

somehow reminded Wahab of a great brown beast crouching; perhaps it was the Minister's great tamer's fists laid lightly on its back that gave him that impression. The face too was powerful but relaxed; gleams of private savage joy kept lighting it up. In such a mood might a man be who had just witnessed the extinction of a dangerous enemy.

Yet Wahab's own mood, he now discovered, as they shook hands, was not of fear. Rather did he feel excitedly confident. At his command he knew he had an agility of conscience that would elude the grip of this ruthless conscience-tamer; its source no doubt lay in the instinct of self-preservation, but only partly so; a nobler and higher source was his remembrance of the boys' homage to him that morning.

'You will understand these are busy days, Mr Wahab,' said the Minister. 'Tell me briefly what happened at your school yesterday.'

'Certainly, Excellency. Some of the boys staged a patriotic demonstration in the playground. It culminated in a symbolic act: they all bent and rubbed their hands in the dust. Unfortunately, Mr Maftoon, who as you know is my deputy, misinterpreted this. He and two or three other teachers attacked the boys with sticks. The boys resented this. There was a disturbance. Mr Maftoon, again rather rashly, telephoned for the police. They came very quickly. Not surprisingly, they misread the situation. But I was able to set them right and convince them they weren't required. The matter had to be dealt with swiftly and decisively, and in a way that would not forfeit the confidence of the boys. In my opinion their support is indispensable.'

'Mojedaji was there. What part did he take in all this?'

'To be frank, Excellency, he was upstairs in my office; he had been trying to bribe me to prevent the boys from marching to the airport to greet President Voroshilov. He appeared after the police had gone.'

'All the boys were not at the airport.'

'No. I thought it prudent in the circumstances to leave the decision to them. The only persuasion I used was to let it be known I would be accompanying the procession. The result was that the boys who chose to go were the active ones, the leaders; those who went home were the sheep. We know at any time where to find them grazing. I think I can claim that our contingent may not have been the largest at the airport, but it was certainly the most enthusiastic.'

'That was noticed.'

'I am afraid, however, Mojedaji isn't pleased with me.'

'Nor with me. It has been considered expedient to have him placed under house arrest. A close watch is being kept on the rest of the family. As you know, tomorrow the veil is going to be removed.'

'That is still the intention, Excellency? I was afraid there might have been a change of heart.'

'The Prime Minister has signed the order; so has the King. Any prejudiced fool who opposes will be dealt with as he deserves. The police have been given their instructions: to arrest on sight any man, or woman, molesting a woman who is wearing no shaddry.'

But today, thought Wahab, and all days previously, the police had been instructed to arrest any woman daring to lift even a part of the veil. So, by signatures on paper, did a nation advance to enlightenment. After tomorrow then, the streets would be bright with the faces of laughing, beautiful Afghan girls. Among them he would walk with Laura. No need to panic, though. No need to think now about her limp or shrunken salary. The situation would be young and revolutionary. Opportunities and inspirations would bloom like flowers.

'What I'm going to say now, Wahab,' said the Minister, with a glance at his huge wrist watch, 'is merely preliminary. It's not just talk, however; it's been mentioned at the highest level. We've been looking at your record again. I didn't realize you had been such an outstanding scholar.'

'By our standards, sir,' murmured Wahab daringly.

'By English standards, too. At Manchester University you gained a degree of Bachelor of Science. According to the professor's report you would have made an excellent re-search scholar.'

Yes, and how he had frantically tried to get the professor and the University authorities to find some way of financing a prolongation of his stay in England. Another two years, a doctorate, and he would have been there for good. Who was it that had advised resolutely against his trying to stay? The Afghan Embassy, yes, but Laura too. He heard again her calm, clear, dutiful voice. 'Afghanistan is your country, Abdul; your duty is to it. In any case, here there are thousands of men with science degrees. How many are there in Afghanistan?'

Now, smiling at the Minister, he could have wept with pity at himself so falsely advised.

'I had no right,' he murmured, 'to expect more public money to be spent on me. Besides, I felt I had been away from home long enough.'

'And of course you now speak excellent English.'

'I may say I was top of the English class at the University. You see, Excellency, I had to learn the language because most of the science books were written in it.'

'You have brains and ambition, Wahab.'

'I want to be in a position where I can help to the best of my ability.'

The Minister grinned appreciatively. 'At the moment there are two possibilities being considered. For obvious reasons, Prince Naim is being urged to resume his duties as Minister of Education; for the time being. He will need an assistant, who will really be an adviser. The other possibility is that a college solely for the teaching of science is going to be set up. The Russians have promised to equip it. We shall recruit teachers from abroad, but the principal must be an Afghan.'

So, instead of being dismissed, I am being pushed up so fast I feel giddy and breathless. Or is it shame that's stuck in my throat? The trouble seems to be that I have in me too many different kinds of sincerity. In this am I unlike all other men, or is it not that I am too human, too clever first at seeing what's for my own good, and then at devising unassailable reasons for pursuing it?

Into his mind then flashed memories; some were expected, but others took him by surprise: himself approaching with such careful modesty and demeaning terrors the group of people waiting for him on the International School veranda; his father's bare feet; Laura's naked bosom; Mussein boasting about dancing in private with his wife; Moffatt's hand with the emptied whisky glass held up as if some kind of toast had just been drunk; the flowers in the taxi; Mrs Mossaour at the airport, with her sex purposely displayed like a peacock's tail; and Rasouf leading the boys in the silly act of rubbing their hands in the sterile dust.

I am not sure, he thought; no man can be sure; but what does appear to emerge is the necessity of looking after oneself; that assured, there may be opportunities for looking after others.

The Minister too had been remembering. 'What about that fellow, Moffatt?' he asked. 'What have you decided to do about him? By God, if he'd flung whisky in my face, I wouldn't rest till I'd seen him booted out of the country. There are some things that just can't be forgotten.'

'I have not forgotten, Excellency.' And when he touched that secret spot in his pride he found it as raw as ever. 'But if he is expelled, how can I watch his humiliation?'

'What humiliation?'

'His wife is Chinese.'

'I know that.'

'She is pregnant.' Had not Laura seen it, with envy's or intuition's eyes?

Dr Habbibullah laughed. 'What mystery is there in that? Aren't there six hundred million Chinese?'

'Yes.' For some reason that immensity depressed Wahab. Perhaps it was because this spite, selfishness, and treachery which he was displaying were bearable only if he felt that they were restricted to himself; to be reminded that they were probably in every man, and therefore were throughout the world in colossal abundance was terrifying and intolerable. Another memory came into his mind. Once, visiting a small town near Kabul, he had needed to relieve himself. There was no such place as a public lavatory. Asking a bus driver, he was directed to a gap in a wall, itself the colour of dried excrement. When he had hurried there he had halted in the gap, appalled. Within was an enclosure as big as a football field, but he had not seen it as such. It had looked to him like a battlefield; the dead men, thousands of them, in every part, were the individual heaps of shit, in various stages of desiccation in the hot sunshine. It had been like a vision of the end of the world. Shocked and nauseated, he had nevertheless to venture in and, holding his breath, add to the dead. Now his soul was like that place, only in it the sad filth was moral.

'Moffatt is a very proud man, Excellency,' he said, with a smile. 'All his friends know this. He is a poet and an idealist. He dreams of perfection. Therefore it is disgusting to him that his children should be impure.'

'Impure?'

'Half-caste.'

'His wife is a beautiful little woman.'

'So might his children be beautiful, Excellency, in your eyes and mine; but not in the eyes of his Western friends; therefore not in his.'

'I see.' The Minister grinned. 'And you think you should keep him here until the child's born?'

Though Wahab nodded and smiled, he not only hated but was afraid of himself. If he was capable of such evil, all those many millions were also.

'Did you know, Wahab, that some people have expressed the opinion that you are too squeamish, too afraid of hurting people?'

'They cannot know me, Excellency.' How could they, when he was just learning to know himself?

'No, they can't,' agreed the Minister, laughing. 'Very well. You can have Mr Moffatt. But here's something that's more important. I thought you'd raise objections about this, but now I'm not so sure. I'm referring to this Englishwoman you're supposed to be going to marry. I believe she's arrived in Kabul. Do you still intend to marry her?'

'Excellency, this is a sudden question after more than two years of promise.'

'Yes, yes. But we're Afghans, Wahab. We may love our wives as much as other men do, but we are a bit more realistic about marrying them.'

'Indeed.' Yet, as Wahab smiled he remembered what he had heard said several times, that Habbibullah's wife was much younger than he and very beautiful. The Minister was said to love her almost as much as he loved ambition.

'You're a young man, Wahab. After tomorrow, the situation here will become wonderfully exciting for a young single man with good prospects; such as yourself. What a choice before you! On the other hand, this Englishwoman's older than you, she's gray-haired, and she appears to be lame.'

So the dogs have been set after us. Were their filthy noses snuffling outside the bedroom window? Well, whose filthy nose had snuffled outside Moffatt's, that moonlit night?

'I'm offering no advice, Wahab; just making sure you

understand the situation. It's up to you. Probably this woman has remarkable qualities.'

'She is a Bachelor of Economics.'

The Minister seemed unable to keep from laughing. 'You're an extraordinary fellow, Wahab,' he said. 'I should have known this woman would turn out to be remarkably efficient.'

But not at making love. Then, as his soul was about to crawl toward that disappointment, as nervous as a homeless dog sniffing at some house's refuse, suddenly it was transfigured, became so grand and bright as to be almost terrifying, and everything seen in its light, even the gray hairs growing out of the Minister's ears, shared in the transfiguration. Then into the terror flowed a great tenderness. He knew what had happened, what was still happening, and what would keep happening for the rest of his life. His love for Laura had at last thrown off all its ignoble disguises, was no longer a cringing cur, a furtive monkey, a gluttonous wolf, a worm, a rabbit forever bolting into its hole, but was for the first time its own self, and he was astounded by its glory, especially as all its ingredients, recalled with miraculous simultaneity, were as ordinary and human as those hairs, and among them even were what others would call faults. No flower in the world, not even one held in his first child's hand, would be as beautiful as this small dark-red rose on his jacket. Its fragrance, faint but distinctive, would come about him and invade every cranny of his soul whenever he even thought of her.

The Minister was now on his feet. 'Well,' he was saying, 'efficiency's something we can certainly do with. Perhaps at our stage it's more important in a woman than all those other more conventional qualities.'

Such as loveliness of face and body, sweetness of nature, softness of voice and hand, loyalty to husband, and to her children a devotion that nothing under the sun, or beyond it, could diminish. But Laura possessed them all; others might not have noticed them, because she was not ostentatious in their display, as Mrs Wint and Mrs Mossaour were, for instance, or tantalizingly mysterious, like Mrs Moffatt; but he, who had been admitted into the intimacy of her soul, as no one else ever had, had seen them, not once or twice only, but as often as he had seen her. Yes, even during the fiasco of that first love making – but had it really been a fiasco? – had she not revealed by her patient endurance of his lust a loyalty greater than he deserved, and after it had she not flowered into a meekness with nothing ulterior in it, a surrender indeed, containing, he now saw, promises not of future submission but rather of an appreciation that, though she was in so many ways cleverer and stronger-willed than he, nevertheless as her husband he must be given his place as head of their family.

'Think it over,' the Minister advised, as he shook hands at the door. 'It's up to you, and her.'

The taxi was urgently fragrant with the flowers, and he found himself, greatly agitated, murmuring over and over again as if they were a prayer those last words of the Minister: 'It's up to her.' For of course it was, far more so than the Minister knew. In the next four or five minutes Laura would be given the chance either of transforming his love for her back to its previous slinking shapes, or of perpetuating it in its present astonishing glory.

Once, outside a pharmacy where he knew there was a telephone, he asked the driver to stop, and sat for a minute considering whether or not he ought to warn her not only that he was coming but also that so much depended on the way she received him. But to warn her would surely be to begin the retransformation. Therefore he asked the driver to drive on again, very slowly, so as to give him time to think. Yet was not thinking itself a sort of relapse?

He thought perhaps he should scribble a message and

throw it over the compound wall into the garden, or hand it to the servant at the gate to be delivered to her with the flowers. 'Darling Laura,' it would say, 'I am coming to you in a few minutes. You may not notice it in my eyes, and I do not believe I shall be able to say it in words, but the truth is my love for you has in the past half hour blossomed in my heart more gloriously than these flowers. It was always there, just as the beauty of the flowers was always present in the apparently barren soil of my country; but now, for reasons neither a poet nor a scientist could explain, it has blossomed into this magnificence. I am troubled at finding such a marvel in so ordinary a man as I. Laura my dear, this is the truth. As I have said, you may not believe me, for it will not be possible for me all at once to convince you. We are, after all, human beings like all the rest, and our powers of communication are so limited. But in the years to come there will be many opportunities for me to reveal this marvellous love, and for you to detect some at least of these revelations. Do not, my darling, especially if Moffatt and his wife are watching, or their servants, receive me with re-proaches, however much I deserve them, or with an attempt at retaliation, justified though it would certainly be. I cannot advise you how to receive me; that, my love, is up to you.'

But such a message would be a warning, and inexorably would start the degeneration. He would ring the bell, wait, not knowing what kind of smile to wear, the servant would open the gate, and in he would creep, carrying the flowers, to be met by her also seeking a suitable smile. Smiles, and the rest of the meeting, would be artificial. Even if they embraced amorously, what would that signify? Amorous embraces could be plotted beforehand. No, what he must do was simply carry the flowers and the glory to her as sur-prises; the rest must be up to her. This trepidation of his surely proved he was not confident she would rise to the occasion; ah, rise would hardly be enough, soar rather, taking him with her, like an eagle and its mate.

He remembered her saying once in Manchester: 'It's better to understand the kind of woman I am, Abdul. I'm just a typical, hard-headed, north-country woman, made a bit harder by my training and experience. Don't look for any romantic abandon from me. Distrust me if you ever catch me trying on that sort of thing. But I'll tell you this – women like me don't give their love cheaply. If I ever love a man it will be forever. It won't matter that appearances afterwards may indicate otherwise.'

Yes, indeed. But there had been times, even in Manchester in the murk and the rain, when he had felt that there might come occasions when forbearance and reticence, those proud guards, must give passionate devotion its freedom. Here now was such an occasion. She must not receive him in her role as Bachelor of Economics of Manchester University, representing the level-headedness and practicality which had been the female contribution to British greatness. No, just as he had too often been a self-conscious Afghan rather than a plain, happy man, so she too long had been stiff-lipped British. In most situations that was no doubt an honourable and profitable attitude, but not in the one about to be confronted.

There could have been no better way of banishing both his own and the taxi driver's Afghan self-consciousness, than by voluntarily giving the latter a tip of American generosity. About to lie, haggle, appeal, and sulk, the driver instead was stricken into a cheerful human grin; and Wahab, prepared to count out the afghanis with harsh exactitude, handed them over recklessly, dismissing for once the usual bourgeois excuse – well-founded, in most cases – that his own need of the three or four afghanis extra was proportionately greater than the driver's, who, being poor, could wear rags of any sort, eat nan, and sleep if need be in his taxi, whereas

Wahab had a standard of Western imitation to keep up. That tip for a minute or two freed them both, so that the driver drove off puffing kisses at his voluptuous actress, and Wahab, boldly grasping the flowers, strode across the bridge of dried mud to the gate.

Or at any rate made to stride across. Something in his path stopped him suddenly; for a few moments he did not know whether his mood of brave human confidence was strengthened or weakened by it. It was a scorpion. It had been asleep in the sunshine; but now, with his shadow over it, it awoke and brandished its sting like a little sword. His countrymen, seeing scorpions, shouted 'Death!' and looked for stones to crush them. As a scientist, he knew their stings, though painful, were not deadly, and that this hatred of them for doing what nature had ordained them to do kept the mind filled with harmful superstition. At the same time most Afghan children walked about with their feet bare, and a scorpion could not be expected to tell whether the foot trampling it was innocent or murderous.

The dilemma was about to weave him into his customary web of self-doubt when the insect scurried off into the grass of the ditch. Grateful to it, he stepped forward and rang the bell.

Little Sofi, who opened the gate, had his feet bare. When he saw who the visitor was, and what he carried, he stepped aside with a well-disposed if lubricious grin. Then he went outside into the road to have a look along it to see if any shaddried damsels were in sight. Afghans, as Wahab knew, acquired the ability to tell if the body under a shaddry was young and comely, or old and fat. Sometimes mistakes were made, and of course even the most perspicacious of lechers could not read the face. As Wahab stepped inside the gate and Sofi stepped outside it, in the former's mind these so essentially Afghan anxieties were beginning to skulk, like surprised scorpions.

He had not taken more than half a dozen shy steps along the path when a cry from the terrace made him halt. It was uttered by Laura, but whether in gladness or indignation he could not, in his confusion, tell. Even as she came hobbling down the steps, far faster than was safe, he was still not sure; but as she came running to meet him he knew that he had never before seen her so beautiful, although her face was still so intense that a stranger, or indeed anyone who did not know her so well as he, would not have been certain she was coming in love, not in anger.

Her embrace, of flowers as well as of him, was fierce but loving. He at any rate was convinced, and amazed too. Before his eyes age, harshness, suspicion, and doubt all dropped from her and lay like the petals of the flowers at their feet.

Beyond her Abdul, the other servant, watched from the guilty terrace, but visibly almost that guiltiness was vanishing. These kisses, so painful to his swollen lips and nose, absolved the whole world.

Then, with air as precious to her as a pearl diver, she drew back before again plunging into that depth of love. This time, though, she was not submerged so long; that brief sunlit scrutiny had revealed to her his hurts, and also the fact that he was not wearing his usual spectacles.

'You are hurt,' she cried, her fingers light as moths on his lips. 'What has happened? These are your old spectacles. Where are your other ones? Did someone strike you? Have you had an accident?'

As he took her hand and kissed it, he remembered the optician to whose shop she had taken him to have his spectacles renewed. He had been a small brisk man in a hard, white collar and a black, glistening waistcoat with gilt buttons, and he had spoken of how, as a solider in India, he had once visited the Taj Mahal. He hadn't liked it, because for all its magnificence it was a tomb for a dead wife, and his own wife, although alive, had been thousands of miles away.

'Who was it?' she cried fiercely, and half turned toward the house, as if blaming her host Moffatt.

'A policeman.' And then in a rhapsody of love and relief and pride he told her what had happened at the school yesterday, and that afternoon at the Minister's.

She listened, bright-eyed; and at the right moment, just before he burst uncontrollably into tears, stopped him; not this time sternly, as a mentor who knew his limits of folly and for her own pride's sake took care he did not exceed them; no, this time rather as lover, using her profound and intimate knowledge of him to give the guidance that not only he, but every man facing the temptations of the world, needed so often. These cries of joy and sympathy, and this loving tapping of her forefinger on his lips were her answers to the Minister's challenge. In them were foreshadowed the many subsequent answers she would also give, with the same delicate authority. If it was up to her, how capably they would succeed!

Moffatt and his wife had come out on to the terrace to greet them. Wahab, remembering his conversation with the Minister, realized he had really meant what he had said about wanting to keep Moffatt here to savour his humiliation. Now, remorseful, and apprehensive for his own happiness based on such evil expectation, he wished it was a simple thing such as his having in his pocket some paper incriminating Moffatt; all he would need to do then would be to take it out and destroy it. But what threatened Moffatt was lodged in his mind, and in Laura's too; there it might rest for ever, doing no harm, like a non-malignant tumour; but, on the other hand, it might become a monstrous growth, strangling even the youngest happy thoughts.

Thinking that in his guilt he was being morbid he turned towards Laura, and found her dangling the flowers in her arms, bending her mouth to them with the rapt possessiveness of a woman toward her baby.

Yet she whispered: 'Tell them nothing, Abdul. This is our business; it has nothing to do with them. If they ask, let me answer.'

'Yes, of course.' Perhaps, he thought, in the ruthless years to come, she would be the one to leave her mark on the development of her adopted country. She had the intelligence, the reticence, the devotion, and, yes, the ruthlessness.

Moffatt, he noticed, was grown so fat in the belly that his top fly button couldn't be fastened. Such grossness in so young a man was disgusting, but Wahab, who should have had hatred to reinforce his disgust, was not disgusted at all. On the contrary, he wanted to laugh and poke Moffatt in the belly and make jokes, like a friend.

Laura, however, was doing the talking. 'Aren't these flowers lovely, Mrs Moffatt? The boys of Abdul's school gave them to him for me.'

The card was in his pocket; he had been afraid she might not appreciate its assumption couched in such silly English.

Mrs Moffatt admired the flowers, holding her pale calm face close to them. 'What a thoughtful thing for them to do,' she murmured. 'But then, as I have said, Afghans are charming, especially the young.'

Moffatt had been as quick as Laura in noticing the swollen nose and different spectacles. 'I heard you had a little trouble at the school yesterday,' he said.

'There was no trouble,' said Laura sharply. 'Nothing that isn't over and done with.'

'You have very swift sources of information, Mr Moffatt,' said Wahab.

'It was Naim who told me. He telephoned. According to him you came out of it very well. He seemed most impressed.'

'And you seem most surprised,' said Laura, smiling.

Moffatt gazed at her and smiled too. 'Yes. It takes a lot of nerve here to stand up to the police.'

'It isn't only Englishmen who have courage, you know.'

Grinning, Moffatt scratched his belly.

Provoked, she cried: 'The Afghans have always been considered a very brave people.'

'In war, d'you mean?'

'Yes, but not only in war. I have been reading their history.'

'You'll have read then of Dr Bryden?'

'Dr Bryden?'

'Yes.'

'What does he matter now?' asked Wahab uneasily. 'It was more than a hundred years ago.'

'Yes, but my students often tease me about him.'

'Who was he?' demanded Laura.

'Abdul will tell you.'

'No, no. You will tell me. This Dr Bryden seems to have some special significance for you.'

'Not for me. For the Afghans, yes, I think so. At any rate they give him a gloating prominence in their history books. Every schoolboy will tell you, with pride, who he was.'

'Ah, not with pride, Mr Moffatt,' cried Wahab.

'Yes, with pride.'

'But it was such a long time ago; and there were faults on both sides.'

'That's true enough. You see, Miss Johnstone, a British army was occupying Kabul then.'

'By what right?'

'By the right of conquest. You and I might not accept such a right, but the Afghans of that day certainly did. They had to. Every chief held on to what he had by force.'

'We British have a great deal of experience of that sort of thing too.'

'Yes. Well, this army, consisting of about twelve thousand, mainly Indians, found itself surrounded here. The

Government at home couldn't make up its mind what orders to give.'

'How typical!'

'Ah, what nonsense all this is,' sighed Wahab.

'It is not,' said Laura sharply.

'Meanwhile the Afghan chiefs had got together an immense force. The British commander decided he should retreat; he asked for, and was given, solemn promises of safe passage. I don't suppose he, or anybody else, trusted those promises, but there was nothing else to do. The upshot was the Afghans ambushed and sniped at them all the way. It was a long way, too: a hundred miles. One survivor arrived in Jellallabad, one out of twelve thousand. He was Dr Bryden.'

Wahab saw the red blood glisten like flowers on the dry earth of those tragic hills. In anguish he pressed his fist against his cheek. Fist and cheek were as brown as those which had caressed the treacherous rifles. Was the blood that coursed in them the same too, embittered forever with useless spite and hateful longings for revenge?

Laura was smiling. 'What was his first name?' she asked.

'Bryden's, do you mean?' asked Moffatt.

'Yes.'

'Alexander, I think.'

'Well then, Abdul and I will call our first son Alexander Bryden Wahab.'

'No, no, Laura,' protested Wahab. 'The incident is forgotten. If not, it should be.'

'I don't agree. It should be remembered. We should not be afraid of history. We should profit from it.'

'But, my dear, a child with such a name might—'

'Might what?'

How could he explain to her who had been in Afghan only two days?

'We'll talk about it later,' she said.

'By the way,' remarked Moffatt, 'Gillie the Consul

phoned to say he'd be pleased to see you at his cocktail party this evening.'

'Me?' asked Wahab.

'Both of you.'

'Are you and Mrs Moffatt going?'

'I think so.'

Wahab was about to accept eagerly when Laura frowned him into silence.

'I take it,' she said to Moffatt, 'it isn't customary to invite people to these functions by telephone, particularly using go-betweens?'

Moffatt laughed. 'It's not unheard of.'

'But it isn't customary. There are usually printed invitation cards?'

'Yes.' Moffatt seemed amused.

'Delivered by post?'

'No. By runner. The postal services here aren't very efficient.'

'Mr Gillie knew yesterday I was here. Why didn't he send me the usual card?'

'But I must remind you, Laura,' said Wahab, 'that I have always found Mr Gillie friendly and helpful.'

'Besides,' murmured Moffatt, 'Bob didn't know yesterday how things stood between you. However, it's none of my business. I promised to pass on the invitation; that's all.'

'I think we should go, Laura,' whispered Wahab.

She ignored him. 'Who will be there?' she asked. 'I suppose the whole British community?'

'Most of them.'

'The Ambassador?'

'I expect he'll look in.'

'Will there be Afghans?'

'Yes. But only men, of course. Afghan women never go to such affairs.'

'After tomorrow they will,' cried Wahab.

Moffatt laughed. 'You still think so? I asked Naim. He was cagey.'

'Yes, Mr Moffatt, it is going to happen tomorrow.'

'If we do decide to go,' said Laura, 'is it necessary to inform Mr and Mrs Gillie?'

Moffatt noticed how pale she had turned. 'No, I don't think so.'

'Come with us in the car,' said Mrs Moffatt.

Wahab stood and bowed his gratitude.

Laura, nursing the flowers, looked up quickly from them, shook her head at his excessive courtesy, smiled, shuddered, tried to smile again, but instead, to everyone's astonishment, her own most of all, burst into tears. In an instant she had lowered her face to the flowers, but then, almost fiercely, she raised it again, to give them an opportunity to interpret that weeping as they wished. It was obvious she herself was mystified by it.

Twenty-Five

THE military parade was the highlight of Jeshan, the annual Independence celebrations. Military attachés, such as Colonel Rodgers, were convinced that the purpose of this display of tanks, guns, and aeroplanes, all of Russian make, was not to warn off neighbouring countries, one of which, indeed, was Russia herself, but rather to intimidate any potential usurper from the hills into giving up his ambition. Yet, as the same experts knew or pretended to know, those tanks, guns, and aeroplanes were not only built by Russians, but also serviced and even manned by them.

Left to the management of Afghans, Colonel Rodgers had reported, the jets would either never leave the ground or else would return to it like bombs; according to skilfully acquired information fifty-three Afghans had been killed in the past three years, during training as pilots. As for the tanks, whose serial numbers he made elaborate efforts to collect, it was obvious that these would be useless in any tribal uprising, if their crews were Afghans. They would get stuck in the steep, stony hills or would topple over and lie like dead rhinoceroses, while the battle was fought around them by bearded and turbaned horsemen with homemade rifles and curved, razor-sharp swords. Therefore, the Colonel had confidently written, these demonstrations of force at Jeshan were really in a military sense without purpose, except that they might perhaps give those Afghans who were advanced and alert enough to be patriotic some feelings of national pride.

It was no doubt noticed by the Colonel's superiors, to whom his highly confidential reports were sent, that he appeared to have a personal grudge against the parades, and, since some had been attachés in their day, they guessed the true reason. How unsporting of the Afghans, after a chap had spent months bumping about their difficult country, giving himself headaches by staring for hours through powerful binoculars, to go and put on public show what amounted to the total strength of their army and air force. You would almost think, as he put it to his wife Sarah, that the Afghans did it to thwart those attachés like himself who did their jobs conscientiously, and to benefit those others, such as Colonel Radford, his American counterpart, who did nothing but attend and give cocktail parties, and wait till Jeshan.

All the same, on this particular Jeshan, Colonel Rodgers made sure he was there early enough to get for himself and book for his British colleagues a front position in the diplomats' stand. This year, though, he had a new worry. Contingents of foreign troops had been invited to take part. Convinced that the Americans and the Russians would hardly condescend to enter into competition with each other in such an insignificant setting, he had advised the Ambassador to turn down the offer on behalf of Britain; but a contingent of crack U.S. Marines had been flown in from Berlin, and a squad of Red Guards from Moscow. Sir Gervase, reproached daily by the Afghan Foreign Ministry, had been furious with the Colonel. Therefore the latter's dress uniform for all its scarlet and gold, did not seem so brilliant this year, and his sabre kept getting between his legs more than usually.

Nevertheless, as he had said to Sarah a hundred times and said to her again as she sat by his side in the carpeted stand, his advice had been justified. The British position at these Jeshans was peculiar; after all, the independence celebrated was from them. What, dragged by mules, started off the procession? Yes, of course, those guns that the Afghans claimed to have captured from the British during the Afghan War of 1920. Well, for Christ's sake, really, would it not have been a farce having, say, the Coldstream Guards or the kilted Black Watch march past in splendour, after the ignominy of those guns? That the guns were, in his opinion, forgeries, made no difference. All these tens of thousands of Afghans, these ragged, stinking, turbaned chaps on the flat roofs and in the trees and along the walls, like starlings or monkeys, these others kicked and truncheoned into order along the street, and particularly the sleek-hatted bastards in the Ministers' box and even in the King's, where they would be hobnobbing with Voroshilov, every single one of them would have laughed his dusky head off and jeered like a baboon. Surely it was his duty to save our chaps from such humiliation? And, by George, there was a shower there, among fellow diplomats, such as Indians, Pakistanis, and Iraqis, who would pretend to be sympathetic, but would be hooting up their gold-linked cuffs with so-called anti-colonial derision.

Sarah, however, was much more interested in inspecting the dresses of the other women in the various stands and tents. There were of course no women in the Afghan stands or among the hordes of Afghan spectators. Tents striped like pyjamas had been set up along the route; in these were the foreign women without diplomatic status; among these would be Lan Moffatt, Maud Mossaour, and Jean Lawson. Among them too was a surprising number of pudgy-faced Russians. These, all the year round, were seldom seen; but on this particular day they always appeared in hundreds. But they were of little interest; none dressed stylishly.

She had to say something, for Bruce stiff by her side was waiting, like a clockwork toy that needed rewinding.

'But, dear,' she drawled, 'didn't you tell me their new band instruments were from London?'

Yes, he had told her that. It was a piece of information he had astutely obtained. The Afghan Army Band had been fitted out with new instruments, supplied by Boosey and Hawkes, London. In a way, as Sarah hinted, this might compensate to some degree for the disgrace of the guns, or it would if people knew about it. He had come determined to pass the word along as soon as the band appeared or was weirdly heard.

Then he realized that Sarah, and everyone else in the diplomats' stand, including his British colleagues had risen and were gazing down in astonishment at a couple who had just stepped out of a car. They were Afghan. The man was that sinister Russian-lover, Habbibullah, and the woman, in a shaddry of green silk, was his wife, said to be as haughty as he was ruthless, and as beautiful as he was brutal.

'That's jolly odd,' said the Colonel. 'I've never seen an Afghan woman here before.'

No one listened to him. All eyes were on Mrs Habbibullah as, cool and wonderfully graceful in that shroud of green, she went up the stairs into the Ministers' box and sat down, not in a discreet corner, but in the very front row, and in the centre of it. The high Afghan officials bowed as she passed them.

The diplomats resumed their seats and discussed it eagerly. Alan Wint presided over the British excitement.

'She's obviously here for a purpose,' he said, leaning across Paula so that they could all hear him. 'We can be sure of that.'

'We can,' grunted Bob Gillie, with a sneer that, thought Alan, nettled, hardly went with his morning coat, white rose, and subordinate position.

'Naming things that had no purpose,' added the Consul, 'used to be a game we played as kids. Earwigs was a favourite, but birds eat them, don't they? And boys poke them out of wooden fence-posts with bits of grass.'

It must be the heat, thought Alan; but he felt worried too. In this irrelevance of Bob's was always a hint of genius. Remember, for instance, that outburst on Moffatt at the policy meeting.

'I suppose,' said Muriel, 'it couldn't just be that she's nagged him into bringing her?'

'That's right,' agreed Paula. 'She's said to be an arrogant one. Why should the men get all the fun? Though God knows this isn't much fun, is it? By the time it's over we'll all be fried.'

Alan took command again. 'I meant an important, deliberate purpose,' he said.

'I think Muriel's hit the nail on the head,' said Muriel's husband. 'Haven't you noticed that behind all the official pomposities, all the pretentious façades, a very simple reason's to be found? Think of H.E.'s tantrums. Ninety-nine times out of a hundred they can be traced to some silly asperity of Lady B.'s.'

The Head of Chancery tried, but could not swallow that disloyalty to his chief; it stayed in his mouth, Howard Winfield noticed with a grin, like a beetle found in H.E.'s soup.

Suddenly Paula became excited, so much so that, though she thought her husband was building up a suspense, at the height of which he would disclose Mrs Habbibullah's important purpose, she could not resist interrupting, thus shattering the suspense, and, she saw with affection and annoyance, making his face ludicrous with the fragments.

'Look,' she said, 'for heaven's sake. Look who's being presented to her.'

They looked, even Alan, and they were all astounded. Being presented by Dr Habbibullah to his wife were Miss Laura Johnstone and the odd little Afghan, Wahab, whom she was going to marry. Last night at the Gillies' cocktail party she had amused some, insulted many, and saddened a few, by, in spite of her obviously plebeian origins, putting on what could only be called a queenlike air, because she had not yielded even to the Ambassador himself. He had spoken to her, nicely enough, and had been told, quite gratuitously, that after her marriage she would no longer regard herself as British and would work for her new country, not for the international community. She had spoken of her plans to him as if she expected him to be interested.

Now here she was again, queenlike, in wide-brimmed hat and long white gloves, being introduced to the mysterious woman at the centre of the scene. Wahab was there too, unlike her, uneasy in the limelight.

'I know he's said to be one of Habbibullah's boys,' said John Langford, 'but I must say I didn't think he was the type when I spoke to him last night.'

'Oh, John,' cried Paula, in surprise. 'He is the type, surely. Habbibullah would kick a rival out of the way without a flicker of compunction. Laura's little friend would find you any number of pious and moral reasons why it was necessary.'

'You're making him sound damn like a human being,' said Gillie.

'Among his reasons,' said Alan, 'foremost among them, would be patriotic necessity. I had quite a searching chat with him last night. I got the impression I wasn't speaking to a human being at all, but rather a lump of conceit, ambition, and hypocrisy.'

'To be a lump of conceit, ambition, and hypocrisy does not disqualify from being a human being,' said Gillie. 'On the contrary. Besides, he's got two ears, though they are somewhat darker in shade than ours.'

Alan frowned. He appealed to Winfield who grinned, to Langford who also grinned, and to Rodgers who didn't understand.

'And a nose,' added the Consul, 'and a heart, and a couple of legs.'

'I don't understand the point of this catalogue, Bob,' said Paula, roused to Alan's defence, 'and I'm sure no one else does, but while you're at it, please include that member for which, I'm told, there are more names than there are for God. To conceit, ambition, and hypocrisy, add lust.'

'I accept the addition,' said Gillie. 'Don't tell me, any of you, you are free from those: conceit, ambition, hypocrisy, lust. The trouble with Wahab is that he's too human. It's the trouble with Habbibullah, too. And with Voroshilov, for that matter. Bruce's toy soldiers aren't human, I'll grant you that.'

'What about my soldiers, Bold old man? I don't quite get your meaning.'

'I'm trying to say I like Wahab, that's all. I'm not so sure about her, but he's all right. He deserves success, but I can't say I'm confident he'll find it with her.'

'All the same, old man,' said the Colonel, 'I'm afraid I don't see what my soldiers have got to do with it. As for Wahab, well, I had a chat with him last night, too. Shifty, I thought; clever, one of these intellectual wrigglers; wouldn't trust him an inch. Still, he's an Afghan, impossible for us to fathom. Ask any Afghan general. Know what he will tell you? That treachery's as legitimate a tactic as surprise. They've always believed that, of course. In the past they've slaughtered thousands of our chaps on the strength of it. But to get back to the hooded lady. What is her purpose, Alan?'

But before Alan could answer the King and Voroshilov arrived together. Everybody stood and applauded. It was really impossible, though some Americans tried it, to indicate that their handclasps were for the King only. He saluted affably and the white-haired President waved his soft hat. They climbed side by side up the stairs into the King's box. Behind them came the Prime Minister, the King's sons, including Naim, and the Soviet Ambassador. The latter's wife, Sarah Rodgers noticed with amazement, was wearing a dress that looked as if it had come from Paris.

Howard Winfield found himself not interested in those potentates. He looked for Wahab and Laura Johnstone, and caught sight of them in a corner of the Ministers' box. She was the only woman there, but for Mrs Habbibullah. Her white-gloved hands were clapping far more enthusiastically than Wahab's. On her face, as far as Winfield could make out, was again that expression of aggressive dedication which had been her disguise last night and probably would be for the next year or two. He himself had spoken to her at Gillie's party, but his sympathetic curiosity had been rebuffed as coldly as H.E.'s condescension and Wint's dutiful jolliness. He felt sure that even if Mrs Habbibullah at the end of the parade was going to inaugurate the shaddry's removal, Laura Johnstone was bound to be as unhappy in Afghanistan as Mrs Mohebzada had been, but of course for different reasons. In that dusty suffocating atmosphere of corruption, inertia, and inefficiency, her idealism would turn even sourer than it was now, or would, as her husband's was sure to, degenerate pardonably into self-enhancement. But perhaps he was being too pessimistic; he hoped so, not only for their own sakes.

With the King's arrival the parade could begin. It was headed by a very tall, thin, white-bearded old man, wearing a red turban and a Western overcoat down to his naked ankles; he carried a banner with an inscription on it in Persian. Behind him came, or rather shuffled, for they were quite unmilitary in gait and appearance, about a dozen similar patriarchs. They looked, as Alan Wint murmured, like the inmates of a home for the aged poor. Yet they were greeted with howls of homage by the mob, salutes of deference from the policemen lining the road, frenzied clapping by Ministers and officials, and an ostentatious

salute of honour from the King. For these were the representatives of that barren, border area which, now included in
the territory of a neighbouring country, was claimed by
Afghans as rightly theirs. The ambassador of that neighbour, too dusky to blush, smiled politely, as if, Roger
remarked, he had just thrown his handful of silver down
among these decrepit paupers and was waiting until their
keepers saw them safely back into their dingy cubicles.

'How could it come to a war?' asked Colonel Rodgers,
scoffingly. 'The Afghans wouldn't last a week. They've got
seventeen jets, the other chaps have got over three hundred.'

'But what if the Russians helped them?' asked Sarah.

'Well, damn it, my dear, the Americans would help the
others.'

'With hydrogen bombs?' She mentioned them as if they
were too gaudy roses on some other Military Attaché's
wife's hat.

'If necessary. Why not?'

'So those old fools could cause the world to blow up?'

Again her interest was slight, but her husband was strick-
en by a feeling her words might hide an importance; often
for this reason he consulted her when writing his reports.
Now he peered into the sunshine to the spot where the old
men, having done their stint, were being led aside past the
flags of the nations on to a piece of grass where, he
supposed, someone would attend to them. Beyond, he
saw the great mountains where their miserable homes in
the disputed territory lay, and unawares a compassion for
them so cynically used invaded his mind. He had often said
to Sarah that the wars of Genghis Khan might have been
puny in scale, but a sabre in a warrior's fist was altogether
nobler than a scientist's thumb on a button.

'Here it comes, Bruce,' chuckled Howard Winfield. 'Your
fraudulent ironmongery.'

The Colonel had already heard it rumbling along the

tarmac, and the clattering of the hoofs of the mules pulling it. Howard called it his, because he had sent to the War Office a ten-thousand-word memorandum in which he had sought to prove that these guns were really of German origin. He had enclosed photographs which had required pluck and ingenuity to take. He had got a reply, very obscure, which had seemed to imply that in the war of 1920 it wasn't out of the question that the British might have been using German guns. That had suggested another field of research which, however, he had found too vague and vast.

Then he brightened, for after the guns came tribesmen on horses. They were to him the most handsome sight of the year. These were descendants of the great Khan's soldiers. Stern, aloof, black-bearded or thinly moustached, splendid in scarlet or golden or green or orange tunics, billowing silken trousers, and calf-length high-heeled boots, they had felt their enemies' blood spurting over their hands and faces, and, in tents of silk, on cushions of swans' down, had raped mysterious princesses.

He almost cried out, for one of those violated noble-women had, in his dream, produced a knife and thrust it between his ribs. It was Sarah, prodding him excitedly and pointing to a scene at which all the others were also looking.

'What is it?' he asked.

'Harold Moffatt. A policeman's taken his camera from him and ripped out the spool.'

'By Jove, that's a bit steep.'

Moffatt, in the tent reserved for such lowly officials as University teachers, had been taking photographs, as indeed were dozens of Europeans. The policeman had chosen him at random. Someone, who looked like Bill Lawson, was holding Moffatt back. Lan was there too, and Jean Lawson; the former especially, Mrs Rodgers noted, was beautifully dressed.

Alan Wint was worried. 'Of course it's damnable the police should be allowed to do such things, but what really is the use of protesting?'

John Langford grinned. He had come without Helen; at that moment, indeed, she was practising putting on a shady part of the lawn.

'Harold will insist on a protest being made,' he said.

'I know,' replied Alan. 'Yet he can't have it both ways. He professes we're useless, and yet when there's any trouble he looks to us to get him out of it.'

'I doubt,' interposed Gillie, 'if anything we can do will convince him he ought to change his opinion about our usefulness.'

Muriel nudged him, and whispered.

'Well, what will we do?' he asked, louder than ever. 'Send a polite snivelling little note to their Protocol Department, pointing out that, in the confusion, and so forth – And what will they do? Send back an equally polite sniggering little note, saying how regrettable it was that, in the confusion, and so forth – It's too bloody hot, though. I doubt if I'll be able to stand it.'

'That's hardly an excuse, Bob,' said Alan coldly, 'for being so damned surly.'

Paula laughed. 'I don't think he's worth quarrelling about. After all, to whom did he go when he was in that trouble over Lan? You remember, when he got drunk and insulted her so vilely? To whom did he go then for help?'

'Lan,' said Langford.

She glared at him; she too was feeling the heat. 'Eventually, no doubt. But at the time? Helga Larsen.'

'I fancy,' said Gillie, 'he'd find it just as profitable going to her this time, too.'

A company of tribesmen, rifles held above their heads, went past, doing a war dance that sent their long, black hair leaping.

'I'm afraid,' whispered Alan to Paula, forgetting that that front row of the diplomats' stand, with the Chinese behind them, was hardly their bed where confidences such as he was now about to utter were usually exchanged, 'something will have to be done about Bob.'

'Or about Muriel.'

'What d'you mean, dear?' For Muriel, amiable little woman, always gave the Head of Chancery the respect he deserved; indeed, an instant's reflection revealed she was the only one who did. 'Muriel's all right.'

'Darling, she's at a certain stage.'

'Eh?'

A dimpled elbow in his side replied.

'God, can that be it?'

'Darling, that is it.'

Of course; she was just at the age. A discreet glance at Bob's big red, sweating, scowling brow revealed so many repressions coiling there like snakes that Alan was amazed he hadn't noticed them before. His rather surprising reaction was to feel indignant: what a poor show for the Embassy really, the Commercial Attaché and the Consul both sexually ill-adjusted. It was just as well that he, Head of Chancery, and H.E., had sweet, willing, and able wives. In diplomacy a clear brain was necessary.

'Now this, I'm sure you'll all agree, is deucedly unsoldier-like.'

It was the Colonel, commenting on the performance of the first contingent of foreign troops. These were Turks, and though every man at rest would have looked bellicose enough, in motion he advanced with little gallous skips that gave to the whole troop, doing it in near unison, a look of jocular effeminacy.

'Yet, as you all know,' added the Colonel, 'it's the Turks who've been training the Afghans.'

That was so, and Wint, his brain clear, wondered if any

diplomatic secret was to be dug out of this odd situation where the Turks trained the Afghans in manoeuvres, and the Russians supplied them with weapons and uniforms. Was there possibly some secret agreement between the Turks and the Russians that N.A.T.O. did not know about? The supposition was not as risible as Bob Gillie, for one, would too readily conclude.

'What's odd about that?' asked Gillie, true enough. 'In every other way the Afghans are sitting on the fence. Why not in this way, too? And if you ask me that's a bloody sensible perch for them, receiving gifts from both sides. Good luck to Wahab, and the rest of them; that's what I say.'

For revenge Paula studied Muriel closely; she found it in the restless fingers, the twitching left nostril, the talcumed pouches under the eyes, and the mouth turned virginal again after thirty years of marriage. Her childlessness was in her eyes like a plea. Paula felt sorry for her.

Then from further along the route where the ordinary Afghans were came tremendous cheering and clapping.

'The Russians,' muttered the Colonel.

He was right. Along they strutted, massive in their gray-blue, red-braided uniforms.

'Our own Guards could put up as good a show,' he added. As good, yes; but not better. He had to admit that these huge fellows, chosen from a nation of over two hundred million, did everything, the salute especially as they passed the King and President, with an efficiency that surpassed the human element in men.

'I understand they and the Americans were to toss for priority. Too bad they seem to have won. I mean, it won't be easy beating that, especially for Americans. Their standards are different, you know.'

'The time's coming,' said Gillie sourly, 'when the fate of the world's going to depend on the toss of a coin.'

A man's crassness, reflected Alan Wint, is bound to

damage him, particularly in a service where subtlety is essential. Of course, if a man judiciously held his tongue, he could be damned near an ambassadorship before his stupidity was discovered. He remembered the curious episode of the cigarette pack, and others just as trivial; and tightened his own lips.

Indians marched past, Pakistanis, and Persians. Then, rousing only moderate cheers, and causing gapes of disappointment on faces from Salt Lake City and Boston, came the Americans, those picked Marines from Berlin. Some were chewing gum, some slouched, some grinned, and all went past, as Gillie said, like men.

'Mr Ambassador's furious,' reported Wint, after a long stare into the ambassadors' box.

'Why should he be?' demanded Gillie. 'He should be grateful like the rest of us.'

'Grateful, Bob?' The Colonel really did not understand.

'Yes. For reassuring us that soldiers are human beings.'

'Was there ever any doubt about that, old man?'

'When those Russians goose-stepped past, there certainly was.'

The trouble with Bob, thought the Colonel, was simply that, like Howard and Harold Moffatt, he was an intellectual. No doubt he didn't read poetry as they did, but still, all his life he'd worked at a desk.

'If I were giving a party tonight,' said the Consul, 'I wouldn't mind inviting those Americans; but I'm damned if I would the Russians.'

Curious, reflected Wint, how a stupid man like Bob, even when making so acceptable a remark as this, was capable of rousing strange suspicions of fundamental disloyalty.

Then, as Howard Winfield put it, everyone had to settle down to watch the whole Afghan army march past, like one long fashion parade of not quite up-to-date Russian guns, trucks, armoured cars, and tanks. These last worried Muriel

Gillie; their caterpillar treads tore up the soft tar of the road. She protested at least three times. Her husband patted her hand and told her not to worry, she wouldn't be asked to do the repairs. No one would do them, that was the trouble, she said. Nevertheless, not to worry, he repeated with a grin. Paula, who had recently been discussing Freudian ideas with Alan, knew there was a connection between this anxiety about the ravaged road and the onset of perpetual infertility.

Occasionally a jet aeroplane roared low overhead. There was speculation as to whether its pilot was Afghan or Russian.

'D'you think,' asked Gillie, 'the King and all these bigwigs would allow an Afghan to fly as low as that over them? No damned fear. And we should all be grateful.'

Yet you do not look like a man grateful for anything, thought Wint.

The Colonel had to agree Bob was probably right. It was his turn to worry; it seemed to him to savour of treachery to have to owe his life to the skill of a Russian.

For two hours the army marched and clanked past in the dust and heat. The King, President, Ministers, Ambassadors, and Diplomats had all to sit and at least appear attentive. It was not so easy for the last-named, as their grandstand had no awning to protect them from the sun. The groundlings, on the other hand, among whom were included the Moffatts, Lawsons, and Mossaours, were luckier. They were able, whenever they chose, to stop watching and go off for a stroll in the grassy park behind their tents. What they could not do, though, any more than their trapped superiors in the grandstands was relieve themselves. In what other country in the world, asked Maud Mossaour, did the authorities cause to congregate a crowd of at least fifty thousand without providing one single convenience? Did not this prove that their claim to be civilized was fatuous, in spite of their jets and tanks? When it was pointed out to her, quite unnecessarily, that the Afghans themselves all around her were showing the utmost promptness and nonchalance in pissing, she refused to withdraw her opinion, and rejected Harold Moffatt's suggestion that this disregard for absurd convention and idiotic modesty indicated that they were in advance of civilization rather than behind it. She would have asked Pierre to take her home but for two things: their car was at the heart of the crowded, chaotic parking space, and she wanted to be there at the finish to see what Dr Habbibullah's wife intended to do. She herself thought nothing out of the usual would be done, but the Moffatts thought otherwise.

Even Colonel Rodgers' interest was flagging when the last truck-load of soldiers trundled past. But not many people had sneaked away early; most shared Mrs Mossaour's curiosity, and so, when the King, exchanging politenesses with his guests, descended and was driven off, not many gave him their full attention. Nor was much interest taken in Voroshilov's departure. Everyone was watching Mrs Habbibullah. It was noticed the King himself had turned to gaze toward her before he left. The Prime Minister, the Princes, and the other Ministers remained in their places. Somewhere the army band kept playing, over and over again, the national anthem. The lady sat on, as if waiting for a sign.

Even if she does remove it, thought Alan Wint, well, what of it? It should have been done years ago. This atmosphere of suspense and expectancy, as if Christ were about to rise again, is ridiculous and unhealthy; it means that far too many hopes are being placed on what, after all, has been commonplace in more civilized countries for centuries, the sight of a woman's face in public. Yet, despite this smooth functioning of his intelligence, he found his heart hammering as loudly as anyone's; and as he gazed at Paula's face, now glistening with sweat and grim with curiosity, he felt, in an inspiration that lasted less than a second, what this seeing of his wife's face in the public street must mean to an Afghan. A second after, such was the incalculableness of the human mind, he found himself reflecting that perhaps there was something to be said for purdah; there ought surely to be some things a man should be allowed for his own secret pleasure, and one of those things could arguably be the beauty of his wife's face.

His introspections were ended by many gasps, cries, and even groans. Mrs Habbibullah had at last risen. As if she had rehearsed it well, she clutched her shaddry by the skirts and slipped it over her head so skilfully that her magnificent coiffure was not disturbed. The shaddry, of fine silk, could be held easily in one red-nailed hand. She did not, though, as many expected, toss it from her with a gesture of aversion; she merely dropped it at her feet. Then, head high, she faced the multitude.

Those who had wondered why the Minister of Justice's wife had been chosen now saw the many reasons. She was an excitingly beautiful, exquisitely groomed, superbly dignified woman. Turning from her to Paula, Alan Wint was for a moment dismayed; he had to recall his children and those thousands of loyal intimacies in order to restore her confidently to her supremacy in his mind. At the same time, he had to admit, as he was sure every married or affianced man there was admitting, Harold Moffatt included, that, granted this was truly an historic occasion for Aghanistan, then this black-haired woman, dark as Cleopatra, was more fitted to adorn it than his own wife or sweetheart. Paula – and he thanked God for it – was domestic in comparison; she was home to him, as a lush green field with cows in it, was home; her loveliness was as English as buttercups or honeysuckle. Mrs Habbibullah, on the other hand, was remote and predatory; but he would not, for the rest of his life, forget her as he now saw her, standing in the front of the stand, smiling and representing not only the dignity and courage, but also the mystery and menace of her sex.

Not far from her, a mouse to a tigress, stood little Miss
Johnstone, unconsciously or perhaps consciously, he could
not be sure, imitating the posture of defiance of the taller,
more beautiful woman; but in her, so puny, so ordinary, so
obviously transplanted, it was pathetic and ludicrous.

Yet as he turned to look down at the thousands of
turbaned Afghans below, and watched them becoming
agitatedly aware that this dark-skinned woman staring at
them was not an Indian or Pakistani but an Afghan like
themselves, he had again that same feeling which he once
before had felt as he had tried to imagine the destiny of
Harold and Lan Moffatt's children, that, for all the clarity
and smoothness of his brain, there were still in the world
many exciting, unexplored, sunlit roads leading to opportunities of fulfilment, which he himself could not even
imagine, far less journey along and reach. That the mob
below began to hoot rather than cheer, and policemen
gathered in strength, increased rather than diminished his
feeling. As he clapped and shouted, sharing in an abandon
that had seized everyone about him, especially Bob Gillie, he
noticed, among many other things, that Wahab had taken
Miss Johnstone's hand as if he was about then and there to
go running with her along, yes, along one of those perilous
sunlit roads.